THE THRILLING LIBRARY:

VOLUME 1

BY

NORMAN A. DANIELS

AND

FRANK JOHNSON

INTRODUCTION BY

TOM JOHNSON

THRILLING PUBLICATIONS

2017

TABLE OF

CONTENTS

TOM JOHNSON

THE CRIMSON MASK was another of those late creations from Ned Pines' Standard titles, appearing in *Detective Novels Magazine* (Better Publications) beginning in August 1940. Bylined Frank Johnson, the stories were initially written by pulp scribe Norman Daniels before being handed off to Leo Margulies' stable of writers.

Pre-dating the Purple Scar by a year, Doc Clarke would be something of a chalkboard for plastic surgeon, Doc Murdock, whose police officer brother was murdered by gangsters. When Murdock's brother washed ashore, his face was bloated and discolored. The plastic surgeon made a hideous mask that resembled his dead brother's face, which he wore to frighten criminals. Doc Clarke's father, also a police officer, had also been murdered; shot in the back of the head. The result caused a strange crimson discoloration around his eyes. A pharmacist by trade, Robert Clarke dons a black suit and crimson mask to battle gangsters. Another similarity in the Purple Scar and Crimson Mask, both had offices in a poor neighborhood, where they helped the down-trodden and were well thought of by the community. Doc Murdock was active with his plastic surgery clinic, while Doc Clarke was a pharmacist at the corner drugstore on Carmody Street.

There's little doubt that both series were created by Leo Margulies through editorial committee.

The novelettes were typical formula, and so too were the characters. Sandra Gray, a nurse at the local hospital was Doc Clarke's love interest. He was also aided by David Small, a friend and former classmate. And the ever-present police official, in this case former Police Commissioner, Theodore Warrick. Naturally, the Crimson Mask would step in when a case surfaced that was too baffling for the police.

Oddly, for a pharmacist, Doc Clarke is a scientific criminologist as well as a ballistic expert and make-up artist. He can crack a safe, use ventriloquism, and has knowledge of the nerve centers in the human body. No science escaped his study in the pursuit of criminals. I might add that these traits were part of the make up of all of the masked crime fighters. And there's also little doubt that the same authors who were churning out the Phantom Detective and Dan Fowler also were involved in the Crimson Mask's adventures, as well as Standard's other lead stories.

That the series lasted for 17 stories is proof that it was successful. The Purple Scar only made it for four adventures, and the Masked Detective ended after 13 stories. But this success might be attributed to the magazine title, *Detective Novels Magazine*, which was running numerous short story characters at the time, including a very popular Jerry Wade, the Candid Camera Kid.

Unfortunately, very few of the late pulp entries had a successful run beyond a few years. The war in Europe, coupled with the paper shortage in America, and many of Standard's stable of writers heading off to the war effort forced a shortage in the pulp industry. Not to mention the poor economy at the time. And with the price of the magazines jumping from a dime to fifteen cents by the mid 1940s, readers were undoubtedly being more selective with their change; Standard would end up dropping most of the late-comers, relying instead on the original titles that that had brought them this far. *The Phantom Detective* and Dan Fowler (from *G-Men Detective)* would continue until the end. Only one of the 1940s titles would make it, and that was the Black Bat in *Black Book Detective.*

All in all, it was a shame, though. Characters like the Crimson Mask were a lot of fun, and added much color to otherwise formulaic detective stories. They deserved to have their day. Too bad, it was so short lived.

Happy Reading.
Tom Johnson

I

ENTER THE CRIMSON MASK

CHAPTER I

THE LEMON DROP MAN

THE GROWN-UPS of the crowded downtown neighborhood called Robert Clarke "Doc," the youngsters called him "Bob," and the little ones knew him as "The Lemon Drop Man." He owned the drug store.

It was an old-fashioned drug store—one of the few left in Manhattan—with red and green vases of colored water in the windows. There was no soda fountain, no lunch counter, no circulating library, none of the things people are accustomed to find in drug stores today. Proprietary medicines, prescriptions, and sick-room supplies were the only things offered for sale, in addition to a service to physicians who cared to send in specimens of blood, sputum and the like to be analyzed.

The two jars on the marble-topped counter, one containing lemon drops, the other lime drops, were not for sale—they were free to the kids. The oranges in the bowl behind the two jars were also free to the kids, only under less pleasant circumstances—the taking of castor oil. A layer of orange juice on the bottom of the glass and a layer on top of the in-between castor oil, helped—a little.

People entering the old-fashioned, high-ceilinged shop for the first time, expected to find a proprietor to match—an irascible old codger who smelled of all the powders, unguents, capsules, infusions, and pills he had compounded in a long lifetime. They found instead a young man in an immaculate white coat, with a strong, kindly face, keen eyes, and an athlete's build. If they were merely transients, they wondered why this young and skilled apothecary should have chosen to bury himself in this poor section. If they settled in the neighborhood, they soon found themselves hoping that he would stay on forever.

The neighborhood folk swore by him. Nearly all of them had stories to tell about his helpfulness. Mrs. Murphy, for example, never tired of telling hers.

1

As the kidnapers reached the foot of the stairs, Doc's gun swung downward.

"In I goes that mornin'," she said, "an' I sez: 'Doc, 'tis the divvil's own tummy-ache my little Timmy's got, an' I'll be after givin' him some castor oil. Wrap me up a dime's worth.'

"'An' is the pain very bad, Mrs. Murphy?' sez Doc."

"'It is, indaid,' I sez, 'an' 'tis in a big hurry I am to git back with the oil, though 'twill take all my strength to make Timmy down it.'

"But nivver a move does Doc make to get me the castor oil. Instead he sez: 'Maybe, Mrs. Murphy, your Timmy felt a little sickish to his stomach after the pain? Tell me, now—didn't he?'

"'He did indaid,' sez I, gittin' impatient.

"'And maybe,' sez Doc, 'he gave up his breakfast too.'

"Well, that's exactly what little Timmy'd done, an' I was jist about to say so an' insist on gittin' my order for castor oil filled without no more gabbin', when Doc leaves me flat an' goes into the phone booth, where he dials a number.

"He leaves the door open, so's I can hear, an' who do you suppose he's callin' but Doctor Barnes. An' he tells the doctor to shoot over to my flat, where he's likely to find a case of appendicitis! Appendicitis, mind you! An' that's exactly what it was! An' if I'd a-givin' Timmy the physic, his appendix would have bust, an' I'd be weepin' instead o' laughin' now. Thank heaven for the day that sent that young feller into our midst to buy that old drug store from Old Man Rainey! He's a blessin' to our community!"

HOW AMAZED Mrs. Murphy and the other neighborhood folk would have been to learn that this young apothecary was a blessing not alone to their community but to every community in the city! How amazed they would have been to learn that this young pharmacist had still another name! This man who was "Doc" to the grown-ups, "Bob"

to the youngsters, "The Lemon Drop Man" to the little ones—was known to two other men, and to only two, as a personality other than Robert Clarke, Ph.G.—Graduate Pharmacist.

That personality was—*The Crimson Mask!*

The Crimson Mask—anonymous crime-fighter and servant of the law. The Crimson Mask—proprietor of an old-fashioned drug store, known as Doc, Bob, The Lemon Drop Man—

No wonder Doc's laboratory behind the store was always kept locked, its steel door successfully camouflaged to look like wood. Only Doc and his drug clerk, Dave Small, ever entered that laboratory. Only one other man knew how unusual that laboratory was—ex-Police Commissioner Theodore Warrick. These were the two who knew Doc Clarke's double identity, and that the drug store, while a genuine and serious occupation, was in addition a perfect front and base for the Crimson Mask's crime-fighting activities.

In that laboratory were ultra-microscopes, calibrators, calipers, fingerprinting equipment, moulage material, and a hundred and one other things more suited to the needs of a criminologist than a druggist. In it also was the telephone by which Theodore Warrick could reach the ear of Doc Clarke—and call upon the services of the Crimson Mask. Through Theodore Warrick, and through him alone, could the Crimson Mask be contacted.

That name—Crimson Mask—was no mere piece of bravado. It had a history. Doc Clarke's father, Tom Clarke, had been a police sergeant. He had died in action, when a gangster's bullet had plowed into the back of his head. Internal blood-seepage, which Bob Clarke later came to know by its medical term, *extravasation,* had resulted temporarily in a freakish manifestation on the dead man's face—across his eyes there seemed to rest a red mask.

The undertaker removed all traces of this, but not before it had been viewed by Tom Clarke's son, and by his personal friend, the then-Police Commissioner Warrick.

BOB CLARKE, pledging undying enmity against the underworld in that moment, remembered that mask when years later, back from his studies in the great police centers of the world, he prepared to make good that pledge. He had completed his pharmacy course on the money his father had left him. Theodore Warrick had financed the rest. He would be a druggist, so far as the world knew—but to the underworld, feeling his vengeance and justice, he would be the Crimson Mask! One other man besides Warrick would know—a class-mate at the College of Pharmacy, Dave Small. For he would need a trusted man to take care of the store when the Crimson Mask was called elsewhere.

And so it had turned out. The secret was well kept. The Crimson Mask remained a mystery to police and underworld alike. Who would have thought that he was the proprietor of an old-fashioned drug store in lower Manhattan, three blocks away from the East River? Certainly not Mrs. Murphy!

The two young men slept in rooms above the store. Dave Small came down to open for business at seven in the morning. Doc Clarke descended at ten, having usually been out late the night before. All phone calls to the store went to the booth. The calls to the Crimson Mask—and only one man could call him—came into the phone in the laboratory. Since the ringing of that phone could not he heard out in the store, Doc Clarke had rigged up a circuit that would flash a light on and off beneath the prescription counter whenever the laboratory phone rang. There was an extension upstairs.

Never did either of the two stand behind the prescription counter without wondering if the light would flash one time that day. Never did they retire at night without wondering if their sleep would be broken into by the telephone's ring, summoning the Crimson Mask to his anonymous work. Never did Doc Clarke dispense medicines, distribute lemon drops, or fill prescriptions, without thinking that perhaps some time, during that day or night, a call would come in, summoning him to fill another kind of prescription—a prescription for murder!

They were both behind the counter on this particular evening, when Dave Small, hearing the scarcely detectable premonitory buzz, glanced down and saw the white light flashing on and off. A customer was coming in. Dave nudged Doc.

"I'll take him," he said in a low voice. "You answer the phone. Good luck, Bob."

The Crimson Mask was being paged!

CHAPTER II

THE MYSTERY GUN

THE CHAIN of circumstances that led up to that flashing of a light in an old-fashioned drug store, began earlier in the week in a private office high up in one of the canyons of New York's financial district. It was the private office of Owen Martin, of Owen Martin & Company, Investments. Owen Martin himself, rugged of body, strong of face, sat behind his huge mahogany desk as a king upon his throne. And that was what he was—a king of finance.

Nearby sat a princeling—his nephew, David Martin, in charge of handling estates.

Ellery Duke, floor trader, third member of the firm, quick and nervous in all his movements, sat on the edge of his easy chair, like a man waiting for orders, which was exactly what he was doing.

The fourth man was one of the firm's clients—Drew Latham, white-haired but robust and ruddy-cheeked—a tempestuous personality who easily flew off the handle.

The voice of Owen Martin rang out with authority.

"Charley Henderson is playing ducks and drakes with us! Get down on that floor, Ellery, and *sell!* There's the list. Get going!"

Ellery Duke had his orders, and he went to carry them out. The exchange long remembered that day. Charley Henderson, big, bluff and hearty, jumped the price of his key stocks two points on his opening bids. Ellery Duke promptly offered ten thousand of each issue for sale at three points lower. Henderson merely smiled, raised his bids another point—and the battle was on.

Toward mid-morning, Charley Henderson saw that he was up against the full strength of Owen Martin & Company. He reversed his tactics, suddenly began to sell. The prices sank. Ellery Duke began to buy.

The falling issues began to climb. Charley Henderson still smiled, but it was a set smile, and great drops of sweat beaded his forehead.

Whispers rose: "Henderson is being taken to the cleaners… he can't go on like this… he's a fool to buck that crowd…"

"He didn't intend to," someone pointed out, "They started bucking him…"

Henderson heard some of the whispering, and experienced a hot flash of inward bitterness. He was going broke. Well, he'd been broke before. What rankled was that the fabulously wealthy House of Martin was apparently doing this to him without cause.

Once, in the crush of the trading, Henderson was pushed squarely against Duke. The Martin trader jumped and glared at him.

"Don't be childish!" he snapped. "It won't do you any good to stick pins into me!"

Henderson gaped. "Pins? Are you crazy, Duke? Isn't it enough that you're cleaning me without trying to make a fool of me too? Out of my way, you're cramping my style!"

Ten minutes later, Ellery Duke suddenly turned purple. His face grew congested, darkened. He tried to speak but he could not. His eyes rolled wildly, he collapsed to the floor.

The Exchange doctor pronounced him dead of heart failure.

THREE NIGHTS following the sudden death of Ellery Duke on the Stock Exchange floor, Drew Latham was closeted with Owen Martin in the private study of Latham's elaborate home.

Latham was bristling, his eyes glittering angrily.

"Owen," he said abruptly, "you know now why I asked you to come here tonight. What have you got to say? You know the conditions under which you handle my affairs—absolute secrecy."

"I know," Martin said quietly, his face as impassive as a poker player's.

"Then why are my deals becoming common knowledge?" demanded Latham. "When I gave orders to sell my Telephonic Incorporated, the stock was raided before unloading, and by the time your brokers got through with it, I was out nearly a quarter of a million."

"I can't control the whole stock market, Drew," Martin said dryly.

"But that isn't the only time it's happened," snapped Latham. "What about that United Granaries deal? The stock skyrocketed for no reason, just as I ordered you to buy—and cost me a cool hundred thousand. And it's happened to others, to my knowledge. It can't be coincidence."

"There's something wrong," Martin agreed, shrugging wearily. "But what it is, is beyond me. And I wish you'd drop your accusing tone. I'm doing all I can! I've begun an investigation—"

In the heat of their argument both men had risen. They faced each other. But what Latham was about to say, whether his words would have been apologetic or accusing, Owen Martin was never to know.

A gunshot rang out, and Latham, his eyes glazing, his white shirt-front stained with red, slumped to the floor, turning half on his side.

Robert Clarke, Ph.G.

Blood dripped, drop by drop, onto the hardwood floor, and the ticking of the great clock seemed to keep time with the drip-drip-drip of the blood. Drip, drip, drip—tick, tock, tick, tock...

And Owen Martin, looking dazedly down, beheld a gun in his own hand! A little smoke still curled ceilingward out of its muzzle. Drip, drip—tick, tock...

Martin stared stupidly at the gun. The whole room seemed to be enveloped in a haze of unreality. But there was nothing unreal about the body. It was Latham—and Latham was dead. Yet Martin stared down at it with unbelieving eyes. He—No, he couldn't have!

"Can I help you, sir?"

Martin wheeled around, terribly startled. Latham's butler stood in the doorway, wide-eyed.

"I thought I heard a shot, sir—" Fuller stopped short, gulped, eyes on the body.

OWEN MARTIN'S mind struggled to bring order out of its fevered chaos. "I didn't do it," he told himself wildly. "I don't remember a gun in my hand, pulling the trigger. Something very strange has happened. I don't understand it. What shall I do?"

"Mr. Latham has been shot—killed, Fuller," he said quietly. He was getting a grip on himself.

Fuller, mouth open, eyed the gun in Owen Martin's hand.

"You, sir," he chattered. "You didn't—"

"No," Martin said dully. "Listen carefully, Fuller. You've known me a good many years, haven't you? You knew me in my own home long before I gave in to Drew's insistence that I let you come to him—you know how he always had to have his own way. And I believe you know I'm telling you the truth when I say I did not kill him.

"It's essential that this be kept from public knowledge. If it is necessary—later—I'll give myself up to the police, but for the present no one must even know I've been here. This must be an accident, when you call the police after I'm gone. I'm taking this gun with me to get rid of it. You get another of Drew's own—careful, not to get your own fingerprints on it. Lay some cleaning materials on the floor beside it.

"I'm trusting you with more than my life, Fuller, in the name of old friendship. You'll hear from me—soon. Will you do as I say, Fuller?"

"Of course, sir," said Fuller. "Your word is good enough for me."

Fifteen minutes later, Owen Martin walked into the living room of Theodore Warrick's New York apartment. It was natural that Owen Martin should go to the experienced former commissioner for advice in his serious predicament, the more so since the two were old friends.

"Glad you dropped in on an old bachelor, Owen," Warrick greeted. "Join me in a highball? Or perhaps some brandy. You look as if you could use it."

Owen Martin sank into a chair. "Brandy," he said thankfully. He received his glass in silence, and then drained it at a gulp.

Warrick's keen eyes missed nothing.

"What's on your mind, Owen?" he asked.

"I just saw Drew Latham shot," Martin said abruptly.

"What!"

"I want your advice and your help, Ted. I want it badly. I'll tell you all I know about it—though it seems too fantastic for belief. Latham sent for me to come to his house tonight. When I got there, he accused me of mishandling his funds. He implied that I was a crook. We got into a heated argument. The next thing I knew, he was dead—and I—I had a smoking gun in my hand!"

"Good Lord!" exclaimed Warrick. "Did you call the police?"

"No. That's why I wanted to talk to you. I—I… Well, I've always laughed at people who declare everything went blank at a crucial moment, but—" He paused briefly and wiped his mouth. "But this is God's truth, Ted! I never saw that gun before in my life! And I didn't shoot Latham!"

"Extraordinary," murmured Warrick. "Who did, then—and how?"

"The only thing I can think of is difficult for even me to believe. The killer could have been hidden behind a pair of drapes in back of me, and I could have been so dazed by the suddenness of the tragedy that he could have shoved the gun into my hand without my knowing it, then escaped."

WARRICK LAID a comforting hand on the banker's shoulder.

"Owen," he said, "I believe you. I've known you too long to believe you'd ever commit a murder, even in hot blood."

"Ted," Martin said gravely, "Latham was right. There *has* been serious tampering in my firm. I only become aware of it in the last week. John du Bois, the best private detective in the city, is conducting an undercover investigation for me. But so far, he's found out nothing. That's why I'm here, Ted. You are the only man—"

"Who can contact a certain other man for you," Warrick finished for him. "Is that what you mean?"

"Yes," Martin answered, his voice involuntarily sinking to a whisper.

"He'd do it, even if only for me," Warrick murmured, "and the issues seem bigger than that. Yes, I'll call the Crimson Mask for you..."

A minute later, a light flashed on and off in a certain old-fashioned drug store...

CHAPTER III

MIDNIGHT VISIT

WARRICK WAS alone in his apartment when the bell rang in the series of tinkles that heralded for his ears alone the coming of the Crimson Mask. When he opened the door, a stranger stood outside it.

The stranger chuckled softly. Warrick closed and locked the door behind them.

"The expression on your face, whenever you see me in a new disguise," the Crimson Mask said, "always seems to indicate some doubts about my genuineness. Shake."

They shook hands, and the secret grip assured Warrick that no one else had intercepted the call and come here in the role of the Crimson Mask.

"You look like a playboy ready for a tour of all the night spots," Warrick said admiringly. "You certainly can work miracles with makeup. The folks down in your neighborhood would never recognize their favorite storekeeper."

"I had a good teacher—the best actor in the *Comedie Francaise,*" Doc said. "Thanks to you. He certainly charged plently. Now tell me—what's behind this call? Is it worth losing a night's sleep over?"

"I believe it is."

Briefly, Warrick told him Owen Martin's story.

When he had finished, Doc sat thinking for a few minutes. At last he spoke.

"Either Martin killed Latham or he didn't. He says he didn't, and you believe him. For the time being, I'll believe him too. Which means that we'll have to accept as a mystery Martin's suddenly finding himself with a smoking gun in his hand, a dead man on the floor, and not even the ghost of a recollection of how the gun came to be in his hand. That's pretty hard to take, but we'll take it—for the time being. Where's Martin now?"

"I sent him to my place in Tuxedo. He'll lie low until he hears from you or me."

"That's good, if he's not guilty. If he's guilty, it's bad—he might run out. Well, we'll take that chance. What about the shenanigans Martin called in du Bois to investigate?"

"Owen had nothing to tell me on that."

"I'll question du Bois. He's a good detective. Maybe he's made some progress since he last reported to Martin. By the way, didn't a member of Owen Martin & Company pass out suddenly the other day?"

"Yes, Ellery Duke," Warrick answered. "Heart failure, as a result of over-excitement on the Stock Exchange floor."

"I read about it," Doc said. "There were big doings on the floor that day. Charley Henderson, Broadway's answer to a gold-digger's prayer, was cleaned out—yet that hasn't stopped him from hitting all the night spots since then."

"How do you know? What are you getting at?" Warrick demanded.

"I read the gossip columns," said Doc with a grin. "Henderson still seems to have plenty of money to spend. At present, from all reports, he's spending it on the beautiful and expensive stage celebrity, Renee Lawrence. Let's see—what have we got so far?"

HE ENUMERATED on his fingers:

"Ellery Duke of Martin & Company, dies suddenly on Stock Exchange floor—presumably from the excitement of a financial duel with Charley Henderson. Owen Martin, aware of shady doings in his firm, hires a private detective to investigate. Owen Martin, three days later, finds himself with a freshly fired gun in his hand, and one of his firm's best clients dead at his feet. Charley Henderson, presumably cleaned out

Theodore Warrick

three days ago, still hits the night spots with Renee Lawrence. What does all this add up to? For the present, nothing. I'll call du Bois."

Quickly Doc riffled through the telephone book, found his number and dialed it.

A voice on the other end said, "Hello."

Doc promptly but quietly hung up.

"He's home," he said. "That's all I wanted to know."

"How do you know du Bois himself answered the phone?"

"Recognized his voice. Heard it a couple of times before. I'll shoot over there now. The Crimson Mask usually gets more information when he appears suddenly than when his arrival is expected. Du Bois, conducting a confidential investigation, might not think it proper to reveal anything even to me, without authorization from Martin. So I'll descend on him suddenly, and maybe he'll talk before he has time to remember his detective etiquette. So long, Ted."

That was why, a half hour later, John du Bois, alone in his living room, and, for all he knew, alone in his apartment, had the startling experience of knowing suddenly that he was not alone at all! There, coming out of his bedroom into the living room, was the Crimson Mask!

"The Crimson Mask calling," said Doc softly. "I hope you'll pardon my making use of the fire-escape instead of the front door. My mask is rather conspicuous."

Du Bois' hand came out of the pocket of his heavily quilted, satin dressing gown, into which it had instinctively gone to grasp the pistol that wasn't there. In a time-tick, he had recovered his poise.

"Gives a man quite a turn," he said. "A sudden visitation like that."

In a way, it was a meeting between equals. Du Bois, too, pursued detective work, and had achieved an enviable reputation. Du Bois, too, was backed by money, only in his case it was his own, whereas Theodore Warrick had financed the training of the Crimson Mask.

Du Bois' deep blue eyes betrayed a keen intelligence, which was borne out by his reputation both as a man of independent wealth and as an efficient and discreet private investigator.

"What brings you here, Crimson Mask?" he asked. "What can I do for you?"

"You can give me the results so far of your investigation into the affairs of the House of Martin," the Crimson Mask said bluntly. "I assure you that that will be in accord with Owen Martin's wishes."

DU BOIS chuckled. "The joke seems to be on me," he said. "Apparently you already know more about the case than I do—you know at least where Owen Martin is. I've been trying to locate him. As for the affairs of the House of Martin, I have not thus far given them my personal attention. One of my men, Parks Benton, a pretty smart operative, is doing the spade-work. I expect his report in the morning. But I gather, from this midnight visit, and from the fact that Owen Martin has seen fit to call in the Crimson Mask—incidentally you can't blame me for feeling a little hurt in my professional vanity on that score—well, anyway, the matter seems to be urgent. I'd suggest, therefore, that you call on Parks Benton yourself. Here's his address. You won't need to use the phone—he'll be at home."

"The phone? Oh, I see." The Crimson Mask grinned. "So you cottoned to that, did you?"

"Two and two together," du Bois said. "That dead phone call didn't mean anything a half hour ago, but now, seeing you here—well, I'm glad to be working with you, Mr.—by the way, what *does* one call you? It wouldn't be Mr. Crimson, would it?"

"I've often wondered about that myself," said Doc. "Maybe just plain 'Mask' would be simplest. Good night. You won't mind if I go out the way I came in?"

"Not at all. Good night... Mask."

The abode of Parks Benton was in sharp contrast to that of his wealthy employer—a shabby furnished apartment in the West Seventies.

Benton, a short, powerfully-built man, with ferret's eyes, opened the door.

"Who're you?" he asked. Doc wasn't wearing the mask.

"Du Bois sent me."

"Okay. Come in. The Chief phoned to say you were coming. I was goin' to bed, but I'll fix us both up a snort. So you're the Crimson Mask, eh? Pretty important stuff we're both workin' on, eh, Mask? Okay. There she lies. Them papers on the desk. Maybe they'll mean something to you. They don't to me."

CHAPTER IV

HAMMERING FISTS

DOC'S RAPID examination of the papers showed him that they were little more than routine reports of ordinary Stock Exchange deals. In fact, it looked very much as though Parks Benton had been soldiering on the job. Perhaps Benton guessed what he was thinking, for he now said:

"It's like this, Mask. Maybe there was funny business going on in the Martin Company, but it stopped short when du Bois was called in. When the du Bois Agency gets on the job, crooks pull in their horns."

"Okay, Benton. I've seen enough. Good night."

It had been a fruitless visit. That was Doc's conclusion as he descended the stairs. Yet there might be something significant about this very lack of material to work on. Parks Benton, on the surface, did not seem to be much of a detective. Yet a rough exterior like his often concealed considerable finesse. Otherwise du Bois would not have put him to work on a case as delicate as this one.

On the other hand—the thought struck Doc as he reached the bottom step—Benton might very well be holding out on his employer for purposes of his own. He might be making use of information he was not showing either to the Crimson Mask or to du Bois. Why? Blackmail? Doc Clarke, skilled in judging character, concluded that Benton would not be above a little blackmail.

The hallway was dimly lit. Doc headed for the door, wondering what his next step ought to be. His hand was on the knob when the sound of a soft step behind him warned him of possible danger. He whirled— but too late. Something came crashing down upon his head. The dim light in the hallway kept burning, but for Doc Clarke it was out, and the light of consciousness had gone out with it...

HE CAME slowly back to consciousness—how much later, he could not tell. The first thing he saw was a ceiling. He was lying on his back, his head felt as big as a house, and throbbed painfully.

He tried to lift a hand to his aching brow, and found that his wrists were tightly bound. So were his ankles.

"Nice going," he thought. "The Crimson Mask walks into a case with his eyes open and gets slugged and trussed up at the first bell."

But he had learned one thing—somebody had shown that he didn't want the Crimson Mask snooping around. Who—and why? Benton? Yes, it was logical to suppose that Benton had had him slugged. Why? Had Benton acted for himself or for somebody else?

Doc rolled his eyes. He was in a cheap bedroom. The walls were cracked and spotted, and one wooden chair and a table on which stood a battered desk lamp were the only furniture except the rusted brass bed on which he was lying. The door was open, and from beyond it he could hear voices.

Grimly he began working on his bonds. His initial efforts merely succeeded in tightening them. Yet he did not give up. He had for too long practised various escape-techniques not to know that the human body, however trussed up, could be made to do remarkable things in the attempt to free itself. As a matter of fact, Dave Small was finding it harder and harder to think up new ways of tying him up for experimental purposes.

His captors had been smart enough to tie his wrists behind him. Well, there was a way of meeting that problem. He swung his forelegs back, got onto his knees, bent his torso back in an inverse arc—back, back, back.

It was torture. Sweat bathed him, and every muscle and tendon cried out in protest. His body formed a broken circle whose ends were slowly moving to meet each other. And at last the circle was full, wrists met toes—then, with a sudden, sharp, agonizing snap, his wrists, though still tied, were in front of him!

That was the first battle, fought and won! Now he forced his bound hands into a special pocket concealed in the shoulder of his coat. The pocket was fastened with a thumbnail zipper, and it contained a curved combination knife and file.

It made short work of his wrist bonds. He rubbed his hands to restore circulation, cut the ropes around his ankles. His body was free. Yes, his body was free, but he was not. He had to get out of this flat. His gun was gone. He was in an inside, windowless room. That meant only one thing—he had to go through the flat.

He was moving quietly, panther-like, toward the door, when he heard voices again, and this time the words were distinguishable.

"I'm going to take a look at him, Butch. The guy's been out a long time."

"Don't be so jumpy, Happy," growled another voice. "He'll come out of it soon enough."

BUT FOOTSTEPS came toward the door.

Doc moved softly over to the table, switched off the dim light. Then he crouched at the foot of the bed as the door opened a crack. There was a cry of alarm!

"Hey, Butch! Something's screwy. The light's off!"

The door swung open wide. Two men stood silhouetted in an oblong of yellow light. One was short and dumpy, the other tall and thin. Doc leaped.

He was almost on the two before they saw him. Happy, the tall one, cried out, but Butch fired instantly at the leaping shadow.

The bullet zipped by Doc's head. He hurled himself at his captors in a football block, kicking high at Butch's face as his shoulder struck Happy. His arm encircled the tall crook's knees to throw him to the floor. The two went crashing down.

Butch was already on the floor, out, blood spurting from his mouth and nose. Happy, who proved lithe as an eel, pulled away before Doc could get set properly. Both leaped to their feet. The tall man reached for his armpit.

Doc shot for the chin—left, right. A punch to the wrist with the heel of his hand sent Happy's gun flying through the air.

But the hood backed away skillfully before Doc's charge, his shoulder high, his chin in, his feet dancing lightly over the floor. The man knew a thing or two about fighting.

Doc flashed a wicked straight left at his head, but the tall hood was under it, bobbing and weaving, and smashed a brace of punches to Doc's ribs. Doc momentarily and strategically gave ground.

Dodging a hard slashing right, Doc sent in a sharpshooter to the Adam's apple. It prepared the thug's downfall. Doc followed up with a tremendous punch to the kidney. Happy grunted in anguish, his knees buckled. A solid right to the jaw finished him.

With both his captors unconscious on the floor, Doc straightened. The way was clear now. He could get out. He—

He stopped short on his way to the door. Parks Benton was standing there.

"Nice punch, Mr. Crimson Mask—very nice."

CHAPTER V

THE DEADLY SHAVE

THINGS HAPPENED very quickly then. Butch, coming to, got up dazedly.

"What happened?" he mumbled.

"Looks like little brother here kicked you in the face," said the operative. "Nice couple of mugs you are. The Boss wouldn't have liked it if he got away. I told you the Crimson Mask plays rough."

"Well, so do I," snarled Butch. "I'm going to pull him apart, startin' gradual an' workin' up to a roarin' finish."

He walked over to Doc and slapped him back-hand across the face. Doc acted. He was of no mind to be beaten to a pulp by this thug, despite the gun in Benton's hand. He caught the wrist of the mayhem specialist, and transformed what was intended to be a nose-crushing punch into a wrestler's trick. With a quick twist, he gave Butch a full flying mare.

The crook's short, stubby body sailed through the air, smashed against the wall, and was once again unconscious. But there was still the menace of Benton's gun. Speed was the only answer to that problem.

Even as he tossed Butch through the air, he leaped to one side, coming down on one knee beside the wall, a spin perfectly timed and executed.

Benton fired, but Doc was too swift for him, and the next instant his crouched body streaked through the air toward the renegade operative. Benton fired again, but Doc's shoulder struck his gun arm upward with such terrific force that Parks Benton crashed into the door jamb. His head cracked against the hard jamb as Doc's right found his jaw. He went limp, sliding down to the floor.

Doc's keen eyes had not missed the coil of rope in one corner. He used it now to hobble his three unconscious victims together expertly, so that if one tried to struggle free, all three would only be entangled the more.

Going through their pockets he found only the usual indiscriminate assortment—handkerchiefs, cigarettes, cartridges, keys,

Charley Henderson

money; mostly small change. Parks Benton carried a gold watch, and from Butch's pockets came a tattered newspaper clipping.

Doc found his own gun in the next room. None of the junk from the pockets of his recent captors interested him except one item—Butch's clipping. It did more than interest him, it excited him. It related to the recent dramatic death of Ellery Duke on the Stock Exchange floor! Carefully, Doc Clarke read the item.

A CERTAIN Doctor Clement Leeds, it appeared, had emphatically declared that the death of Ellery Duke had *not* been caused by heart failure. Doctor Leeds said that he had examined Duke, who was an old patient of his, a week before his death, and had found Duke hale and hearty. The medical examiner, Doctor Leeds averred, had made a mistake.

This was important stuff, Doc realized. It was important for very definite reasons. It was an intimation that Ellery Duke had been murdered! And, with nothing more to go on than he now had, Doc was prepared to believe just that.

He was prepared to believe it solely on the basis of that clipping being in the pocket of Butch, who worked for Benton, who worked for du Bois, who worked for Owen Martin, in whose firm Ellery Duke had been a partner!

The next step, of course, would be to check with Doctor Leeds. But before that, even, he wanted to see du Bois about his precious operative, Benton.

There were several things that Doc wanted to find out about Benton. And du Bois, after all, was his employer. His *legitimate* employer, Doc quickly amended, as he thought about the matter. For he felt convinced that the operative was serving two masters.

The quick mind of the man who had become the Crimson Mask had not missed a small detail which might have escaped the ordinary man. When Benton had spoken to Butch, he had referred to "the Boss," but when he had been talking to the Crimson Mask in his apartment, he had called du Bois "the Chief!"

A small enough distinction, but significant, psychologically. A man like Benton, dividing his allegiance, would instinctively make such a distinction.

It was three in the morning when he let himself in through the back door of his drug store and went upstairs. Dave Small, who slept like a cat, heard him undressing.

"How was the fishing?" he called out sleepily.

"Got a couple of minnows which I threw back in. I can always get them again, and if left free to swim they may lead me to the sharks. Go back to sleep, Dave. You'll be running the store alone for a few days, I think. Good night."

The sun was high in the heavens when Doc awoke the next day. A shower, a shave and breakfast were followed by a quick session in the laboratory. His former disguise was no longer serviceable—three enemies had seen it—Benton, Butch and Happy. His fingers played swiftly over his face, enlarging his nostrils, changing the contour of his eyes, altering the jaw-line. He walked out of the store as a customer. A neighbor entered, but there was not a flicker of recognition in her eyes.

DOC SPED uptown in a cab to the du Bois Detective Agency. He told the girl in the richly furnished waiting room that he had to see the private investigator on an urgent matter.

"Tell him it's about the Martin case," he added.

In a few seconds, he was ushered into the luxurious private office of the head of the agency. Du Bois looked up from some papers on his massive mahogany desk, his blue eyes puzzled.

"I don't expect you to recognize me," Doc said, smiling. "I'm the Crimson Mask."

Du Bois' eyes cleared.

"Oh!" he said, relaxing. He chuckled. "Getting to be a habit, your dropping around. But I'm glad to see that you're being a little more—er—conventional. What's on your mind?"

"First, let me ask you something. Does Benton ever call you 'Boss'?"

Du Bois blinked at the apparently irrelevant question and his eyebrows lifted quizzically.

"Why, no," he answered. "Most of my men call me 'Chief.' I rather like the name." He smiled. "I'm afraid I'd quickly discourage 'Boss.' It's too vulgar. But why—"

"It doesn't matter," Doc said. "I was just checking on something. Now, tell me, have you heard from Benton yet?"

"No," the private detective said. "I expect him in this morning with his report. Why? I must confess you've got me totally in the dark."

"I doubt if you'll get your report," the Crimson Mask said. "Benton seems to be playing a little game of his own."

He gave a brief account of what had occurred the previous night, enough only to indicate Benton's duplicity in the affair.

All the good humor disappeared from the well-groomed face of the agency head. His jaws set, and his fingers drummed a deliberate beat on the polished desk. He reached out for the phone on his desk.

"What are you going to do?" Doc asked quickly.

"See if Benton is at his apartment," du Bois said briefly.

"I don't want him warned," Doc said. "I want to give him rope."

Du Bois nodded, waited awhile as the phone on the other end kept ringing and then hung up.

"No answer," he said. "Did you find anything in his reports at all?"

The Crimson Mask shook his head. "Nothing but routine stuff."

Du Bois' blue eyes looked grim. He leaned forward and flipped a switch on the inter-office communicator in front of him.

"Get me Mac," he snapped into the box. To the Crimson Mask he added: "We're not fools up here, you know. Even if he had reported with the kind of papers you tell me he had, we'd have suspected something.

A deep voice interrupted from the communicator.

"Yes, Chief?"

"Listen, Mac," du Bois said curtly. "I want a double-check on Benton. Funny stuff on the Martin case. Put a man on Benton's apartment, and get somebody to work immediately on his previous connections according to our files. Tell them to watch their step—but I want action."

HE FLIPPED the switch back and turned to the Crimson Mask.

"So Parks Benton thinks he can double-cross the du Bois agency, eh?" he said, leaning back in his swivel chair. "We're pretty careful in choosing our operatives, you know—but sometimes we slip. That's why

I've got a separate department of trusted, proved men whose work it is to check on our field operatives whenever I think it necessary. Benton won't get away with this!"

"Unless he's not just playing a game by himself," Doc said softly. "I think he's working for a mighty shrewd man—somebody who's supplying the brains Benton lacks."

Du Bois smiled, and it was not a pleasant smile.

"He's got some brains opposing him, too," he said quietly. "Yours—and if I may boast a bit, my own. I didn't build up this agency to the eminence it enjoys by being exactly stupid." His resonant voice deepened. "And, Mask, I pride myself on the agency I own. I don't need the money, but it's been my life work, and I don't intend to see a double-crossing rat like Benton mar its name!"

Doc Clarke nodded sympathetically. "Fine," he said, getting up to leave. "I'll get in touch with you soon—maybe tonight. You might find out something that will be of help to me. If Benton should report— which I doubt—don't tip your hand. We might get more that way."

One of the hoodlums clipped the bodyguard on the head.

Du Bois rose and shook hands. "Don't worry, Mask. I'm with you, and if I can be of any help, I'll feel myself honored by the association."

Downstairs, Doc got into a cab and gave the driver the address of Dr. Leeds' office.

The doctor was not there. "He's at his home, ill," a white-uniformed nurse informed him. "Doctor Benton is temporarily handling his practice. Would you care to go to him instead?"

"No thank you," Doc said crisply. "It is of the utmost importance that I see Doctor Leeds himself. I'm not exaggerating when I say that it's a matter of life and death."

"Doctor Leeds is quite sick," the nurse said worriedly, "but I'll give you his address. There you are, sir."

"Thanks."

Some premonition made Doc take a cab—he wanted to get to the doctor's house in a hurry.

HIS PREMONITION was all too justified. No sooner had he crossed the threshold of the Leeds' front door when he knew he was standing in a house of death. A grave-faced man, evidently a doctor, came downstairs to see him. Doctor Leeds, he said, was dead. "How did he die?" Doc asked very abruptly.

"May I ask the reason for your interest? Are you a physician, or perhaps a relative?"

Doc bent close, whispered.

"Oh," the doctor said in a small voice, then: "My name is Jameson. You will understand my being somewhat shocked at the advent of death to my friend, Leeds, and the entrance so soon after of such a personage as you. The cause of Doctor Leeds' death was tetanus—lockjaw. A most sudden and virulent case."

"Any idea of how Leeds picked up the infection?" Doc asked.

"Who knows? Anything that opened the skin could have caused it—one of his own hypo needles, a tack on the bathroom floor, any one of such little things."

"Doctor Jameson," said Doc Clarke abruptly, "I'm going to ask you to allow me to make a little investigation here—and to keep it strictly to yourself. I've good reasons for this strange request. Don't disturb Mrs. Leeds. Your permission is sufficient."

"You have it," said Dr. Jameson.

Doc's desire to investigate this third death rested upon his suspicions about the first—that of Ellery Duke. Ellery Duke had died, supposedly, of heart failure. One man, however, had believed otherwise and had said so. That man was Clement Leeds. Now Leeds was dead. Was he dead because of his belief and the expression of it?

Assuming that Duke had been murdered and that his death had been cleverly arranged to simulate heart failure, would not the murderer be struck with consternation upon learning that another doctor was questioning the heart failure diagnosis? He most certainly would, and it would be in his interest to silence that doctor.

A criminal smart enough to make a killing look like heart failure—it could be done with an insulin or nitroglycerin injection—would be smart enough to handle tetanus germs too—and tetanus was certainly a perfect way of keeping a man quiet until he died. Besides, there were a thousand apparently innocent ways to inject the germs.

Nor did Doc forget that the clipping about Doctor Leeds' skepticism concerning the cause of Ellery Duke's death, had been found in the pocket of Butch. Hence, not only was there a connection between the death of Ellery Duke and the death of Leeds—there was a possible connection, also, between those two deaths and the death in between—the death of Drew Latham. The *murder* of Drew Latham.

The Crimson Mask went up to the death chamber alone.

The Victorian bedroom was that of a conservative, quietly successful man. The man who had occupied that room was distinctly not the type to stoop to squabbling in the public prints over a matter of diagnosis unless he'd had the strongest sense of his own correctness.

Doc found a few hairpins, and in a tray on the bureau were a number of pins, and a curved pair of manicure scissors. They were sharp instruments, but none of them interested him.

The bathroom further emphasized the fact that Doctor Leeds had been a strictly conservative man who clung to old-fashioned habits and things. He even used an old-fashioned long bladed razor. It lay beside the shaving mug. Doc held it up to the light, was about to put it down when he looked at it again. Several minute notches broke the smoothness of the edge.

He went back to the bedroom and lifted the sheet from the corpse. By careful scrutiny of the twisted, bearded face, the Crimson Mask discovered the little abrasions he had felt sure would be there. Returning to the bathroom, he wrapped razor, strop, brush, tube of shaving soap, and lather mug in a towel.

Doctor Jameson was waiting for him when he went downstairs.

"I'm convinced that Doctor Leeds was murdered," Doc Clarke told him quietly. "A tetanus culture was introduced to the blade of his razor, which had been finely notched so as to abraid the skin when used. It came either from the tube of cream, from the brush, the bowl, or the strop, and was virulent enough to fog the blade since it was last used. I'm sure a bacteriologist's report will bear me out."

"But why should anyone want to murder Leeds—one of the finest men who ever drew breath?" Jameson asked helplessly.

"He was murdered because, unwittingly, he was threatening to expose another murder," Doc said soberly. "And I imagine that whoever left a tetanus culture for Doctor Leeds must have broken into the house. That would be—safer."

With his bundle, the Crimson Mask made his way home in a round-about way. He had spoken to Doctor Jameson of a bacteriologist, but he himself was that bacteriologist.

An hour later he had finished with his analysis. The shaving cream held the tetanus germs.

CHAPTER VI

GAY PARTY

FOR THE first time in his life, probably, Doc Clarke was interested in what was going on in Wall Street. He turned first to the stock market reports when Dave Small brought in the afternoon paper.

The death of Drew Latham had brought on no calamity as yet. Thanks to the quick work of former Commissioner Warrick and to the Crimson Mask the facts of that death were not in the news so far. And only the Crimson Mask had any inkling that other deaths probably were connected with that of the wealthy Latham. For he was sure that eventually the deaths of Ellery Duke, Latham, and now of Doctor Leeds would be found to be traceable to the same source.

Doc turned back to page one to look again at a certain picture on it. It was of two people—lovely Renee Lawrence and bluff Charley Henderson. The headline of the accompanying story read:

STAR ELOPES WITH WALL STREET MAN

Doc Clarke wondered. For all her beauty, it was well known that Renee Lawrence had a shrewd ability for taking care of Number One. Why, then, had she suddenly married Henderson, who was reputed to have gone broke?

Henderson fitted into this murder mystery somehow, Doc was sure, even if only for the fact that his financial difficulties had been most recently engineered by Owen Martin & Company. That reminded Doc—a talk with Owen Martin had been too long delayed.

He called Theodore Warrick's Tuxedo residence. There was no answer.

Doc set the phone down on its cradle grimly. Owen Martin, who was supposed to lay low in the Tuxedo place, was not there. Had he run away? Was he guilty, then, after all?

Or—and at the thought Doc shivered—had the murderer got to Martin? Had Martin been kidnaped perhaps?

Doc lit a cigarette and sat down to review the few facts he had in his possession. Latham had been murdered as had Leeds. Duke also. Each murder implied the other, reasoning both forward and backward. And the Crimson Mask, in an attempt to discover the killer, had escaped with his own life only through sheer luck. Through that experience he had discovered his only absolute fact—that the private operative, Parks Benton, was in this thing up to his neck.

But poison by tetanus and sudden death on the Stock Exchange floor were not Benton's methods. His would be the brutal direct attacks of the professional gangster.

Thinking of the Stock Exchange brought Doc's thoughts back to Henderson. If he could not talk to Owen Martin, he could at least do a little investigating of Charley Henderson. Obviously, however, the Crimson Mask could not approach Henderson and ask the speculator pointed questions. The man would shut up like a clam. But someone whom Henderson knew...

DOC CLARKE grinned. He had it! He would appear before Henderson as Owen Martin! His guess was that he might find the newlyweds just now at the most hilarious of the currently popular clubs—the Baghdad, where movie stars, actors, society favorites and the cream of the sporting set gathered to call one another by affectionate nicknames and to exchange gossip behind each other's backs.

There was need for haste, though. From a book shelf Doc took a volume recently published on the lives of prominent Wall Street men, and studied the half tone photograph of the head of the House of Martin minutely. Then, closing his eyes, he called on his photographic memory to visualize Owen Martin, his proud walk, and deep voice. Martin was big. He was lean enough, however, so that a loosely tailored suit would give the Crimson Mask the proper proportions.

Quickly changing his clothes Doc sat down at his make-up table. With Owen Martin's likeness propped up before him he started to reproduce it, superimposing it over the countenance of Bob Clarke. When he had finished it was the heavy-jowled, strong-chinned face of white-haired Owen Martin, even to the bushy eyebrows, and trim, full mustache that looked back at Doc from his make-up mirror.

When Doc entered the Baghdad, he made his way quietly to the bar where he ordered a cocktail. A group clustered around a corner table shifted and Doc saw that he had guessed right. The newlyweds were there all right, holding court.

But it was with a slight shock that the Crimson Mask noted Renee Lawrence Henderson's appearance. She was as poised and smiling as usual, but the dark circles under her eyes, her strained expression, were not the result of one night of revelry and emotional excitement. No, something had happened to Renee—something frightening.

Then Charley Henderson spotted "Owen Martin" and came toward the bar, grinning cheerfully. He clapped the Crimson Mask on the shoulder.

"How are you, Martin?" he greeted. "Just to show that there's no hard feelings, come over and have a drink with my charming new wife!"

"Delighted," said Doc, in astonishing mimicry of Owen Martin's deep basso. "I'm sorry about the other day. Fortunes of war, I suppose. Nothing personal."

"You're a plain pirate, Martin, but that's okay with me," said the speculator, laughing. "We're sailing for Bermuda on the *Queen* at three-thirty."

Then Doc Clarke was smiling and bowing as he was introduced to the bride.

RENEE LAWRENCE was tense and restless, and her long-lashed eyes looked haunted. Yes, some secret worry—or fear—was taking its toll.

Henderson's blitheness was equally inexplicable. For a man as financially embarrassed as he was to have married the star was insane enough, but it seemed sheer madness for him to be boasting of this contemplated wedding trip and a return by plane in a month or so, whenever the spirit moved them. He seemed to be in no need of a new fortune, judging by the way he bought champagne.

All at once Doc Clarke became aware that Renee had slid over close beside the man she believed to be Owen Martin. And as she looked up at him there was desperation—or terror—in her dark eyes.

"Mr. Martin," she said, low and urgently, as one hand with coral-tipped fingers rested on his arm, "tell me the truth-how did Drew die?"

Doc was startled by the unexpectedness of the question, amazed by its implications. What was this girl's interest in Drew Latham? What did she know that had made her suspect that the stories given out concerning Latham's death were not true? And what could any secret knowledge she possessed have to do with her obvious terror?

"All I know is that Latham was accidentally shot while examining a gun," he murmured. "That was all in the papers."

"Oh!" she said nervously. "I was afraid—"

She shrugged and moved away a trifle as a tall, broad-shouldered young man approached—a man who did not seem to belong in this environment, in spite of his smartly-tailored apparel. It was rather hard to tell, though. The young fellow gave the impression of being a rough-neck under his English-tailored tweeds, but appearances were deceptive.

The newcomer was an outdoor man, obviously, as attested by his ruddy, wind-burned skin accentuated by the shock of deep red hair and dark brown eyes. He was striking enough for the Crimson Mask to note him in passing, vaguely wondering which one of Renee's many admirers this one was. He held no interest for her, though, for as he bent deeply over her slender hand a moment offering his congratulations, she gave him a wan, frightened smile, then turned away.

Moved by what Renee had said, Doc instantly made up his mind to stick with the party until the bridal couple were at sea. He had to talk with Renee alone. Could it be that she suspected her new husband of being responsible for Latham's death?

HENDERSON, HOWEVER, seemed unaware of the strain under which his bride was laboring. He continued to pour drinks into himself. To Doc, though, his joviality seemed forced-as if he were covering up something. What? At last, however, Henderson got to his feet, resting his knuckles on the edge of the table to keep his equilibrium.

"Come on, everybody!" he invited hilariously. "Let's go down to the boat and finish the party up right!"

Doc got his chance to speak to Renee alone when, by the simple expedient of helping the speculator to keep his feet, he got himself into the same taxicab with the bridal pair. As soon as the taxi started, Charley Henderson promptly went to sleep. His bride sat stiffly erect, staring straight ahead.

"Look here, Mrs. Henderson," said Doc, "you look awfully tired. And, if I may say so, a trifle frightened."

She looked at him as though it were difficult for his words to sink in.

"I'm not frightened," she said in a monotone. "I'm terrified."

"But surely you have nothing to fear," insisted Doc, with the voice inflections Owen Martin would have used, an almost fatherly tone. "You have married a pleasant fellow, and should be happy."

She bit her lip and stole an enigmatic glance at her sleeping husband.

"If I only were certain that—"

She broke off abruptly and again stared into the distance. Several times Doc tried to draw her out, but got no response.

"Good Lord!" he thought. "She's in love with him and afraid of him!" But his hoped-for talk with her was a flat failure.

It took a bottle of smelling salts from Renee's handbag to rouse Henderson when the procession of taxis reached the pier. Then the newlyweds were being swept up the gangplank by their celebrating well-wishers, who all trooped across the deck with them to their cabin.

CHAPTER VII

DEATH AT THE FEAST

AS OWEN MARTIN, Doc was permitted the luxury of a chair to himself while the rest sat on beds, tables or floors indiscriminately. He recognized a few celebrities in the sailing party, and other familiar night spot habitues, including the husky young roughneck wearing the incongruously smart clothing—the fellow Doc had noticed in the Baghdad.

The speculator had come to life amazingly well. Renee was trying desperately to be gay, but every so often her eyes would stray to her husband's massive figure, and again the Crimson Mask would see that look of horror in her eyes. Merriment went on unabated, though, as more and more champagne was opened and passed around in paper cups, tumblers, or whatever came handy. An exuberant guest leaped up on a chair, lifting his glass high.

"To the bride!" he shouted. "May her trip on the ocean of matrimony be as pleasant as the journey on which she is about to embark!"

Bumpers were drunk and glasses refilled as rousing cheers went up.

"To good old Charley!" cried the self-appointed toastmaster. "His gambling bad luck has been more than atoned for. In fact, he owes the Exchange money for the good fortune that has come his way."

Again there was a loud cheer. But this time it did not subside normally, but rose to an appalling crescendo as Renee, her face a ghastly gray, shrieked piercingly.

Her glass fell to the floor and shattered. Her eyes grew oddly glazed, and her face was contorted with agony. Her lips were blue and parted slackly.

Again she screamed—a scream that ended in a choking, gurgling gasp as with an instinctive gesture of agony, her fingernails tore at the flimsy material of her dress over her abdomen. Her eyes rolled upward and she toppled forward just as the Crimson Mask, Henderson, and the husky redhead leaped through the screaming, terrified crush to catch her.

Together they lifted Renee's writhe body and laid her on one of the beds. Her face was turning blue, and her breath was coming in weak little gasps.

"Get a doctor—quick!" Doc Clarke shouted to the redhead, for Henderson was standing by helplessly, white and shaking.

The Crimson Mask started to work feverishly, giving the feebly moaning Renee artificial respiration. To an alarmed ship's officer who appeared in the doorway he shouted:

"Get a stomach pump! This woman's dying!"

But even as the officer disappeared, Renee's slender body arched in another convulsion, and then she was gone.

"My God!" moaned the white-faced Henderson.

"Your wife has been poisoned, Henderson," Doc said grimly. "How, why, or by whom you probably will not know until an autopsy is performed."

The Crimson Mask's opinion was confirmed when the ship's physician came on the run moments too late. The poison that had killed Renee Lawrence Henderson was a mystery to him also, he admitted.

The Crimson Mask's mind was racing as he listened to the doctor and stared at Henderson through narrowed eyes. The poison could not have been in the champagne, or everybody in the cabin would be dead by now. Then how had it been administered to Renee? It might, of course, have been some rather slow-working poison that could have been surreptitiously dropped into her food and drink while at the Baghdad. But who could have done that?

DOC'S LIPS tightened grimly as across his memory screen flashed a picture of the husky redhead he had been hearing called Gerald Smith, bending over Renee to congratulate her. The crudest sleight of hand artist could have dropped something into her plate.

And where was Smith now? Apparently he had vanished as swiftly as all the other Henderson "friends," even before the ship's doctor left to report to the captain and call the police. They would all have to appear for examination, of course, when the police took over, but now they had all disappeared like rats deserting a sinking ship. The room was suddenly empty save for the Crimson Mask and Charley Henderson, on his knees beside his dead wife, his bowed shoulders heaving.

The Crimson Mask stood regarding Henderson with calculating eyes. Was this grief real? Renee unquestionably had been afraid of her husband, who *might* have been responsible for other deaths that interested the Crimson Mask. Could Henderson have…

He spun around as an imperative knock came on the door. Quickly he answered it and stepped into the corridor, closing the door behind him. Gerald Smith stood there, apparently laboring under great excitement, for his eyes were narrowed, and he was breathing hard.

"I've got to see Henderson," Smith demanded sharply.

"Not now," said Doc.

Smith smiled crookedly.

"No?" he drawled. "Then in that case, I want to see you, Owen Martin."

Doc felt a pistol suddenly shoved into his ribs.

"Don't try to make any funny moves, Martin," Smith said tightly. "I'd as soon shoot as look at you."

There was no arguing with a gun. Doc went along with Smith, aware that a new angle had entered the case, and prepared to profit even through peril.

The two were moving casually down the gangplank, with Gerald Smith's gun gripped firmly in his pocket when an ambulance shrilled its warning along the dock.

As they left the pier and stopped beside a waiting limousine in West Street, Doc Clarke recognized an acquaintance. It was the thug, Happy. Happy sat at the wheel and his face showed plenty of proof that he had come off second best in his more recent encounter with the Crimson Mask—though he could never guess that this dignified "Owen Martin" was his late sparring partner.

"Get in, Martin," Smith ordered.

They proceeded uptown as fast as traffic permitted, but Doc noticed now that they were heading for the east, instead of the west side. But naturally it had been the part of wisdom to abandon the west side hangout as soon as their previous prisoner had escaped and the bound thugs had been found. Doc wondered if it was Gerald Smith who had found them.

AT LAST they stopped in another tumble-down warehouse section— far over in the east Bronx—before a rickety frame dwelling jammed between two old storage warehouses.

Parks Benton and Butch were awaiting them inside, a sorry-looking pair of vicious thugs. The damage suffered by Happy was nothing compared to the destruction Doc Clarke's heel had wrought on the countenance of his squat comrade. After a few brief instructions to Benton, which Doc could not overhear, Smith left the place.

Benton's swollen jaw made speech difficult, and a big lump on the back of his head was another souvenir of the previous night's battle. He was still furiously angry, and snarled at Doc when Smith had gone.

"So, Mr. Martin," he spat out insolently, "we meet again. Only this time it's not in your office."

"So I see," boomed Doc in the financier's deep voice. "Well, Benton, what is the meaning of this?"

The detective laughed mockingly, then stopped short and clapped a hand to his painful jaw. He glared at the supposed banker.

"You may be hot stuff downtown," he mumbled, "but you can't go round murdering people and get away with it. Maybe you can buy your way out with servants, but some of us have a sense of justice."

"Rot!" barked Doc. "Who's paying you for this outrage?"

"Santa Claus!" said Benton. Then turning to his battered henchman: "Take him upstairs and lock him up. We'll have to hold him until word comes from the Boss."

"You'll pay for this, you—" declared Doc with all the outraged dignity he could muster.

Benton shrugged again.

"Go over him, boys," he ordered. "See if he's got a gun. He's pretty handy with them, as we've heard."

Practised hands found quickly the holster in Doc's belt and removed his gun. Benton eyed it curiously.

"We had one of that make in our hands last night," he observed. "Must be good, if experts like 'em. Run him along, boys!"

Doc was prodded up the rickety stairs and shoved roughly into a bare, unfurnished room, thick with dust. But this room was a first-class prison, for the door, outside, was reinforced with sheet steel and had two strong bolts.

There were two windows, but all the light they gave might as well have come from a glowworm, for the warehouse next door shut the light off completely. And the windows were fitted with iron bars.

Doc leaned against a wall, and considered his situation. Here he was Benton's prisoner again, and with far less chance of escape than before.

Was Owen Martin actually the murderer of Drew Latham, a fact which this gang knew, and were using as a lever for blackmail? If so, *why* had Martin killed Latham? Or was Martin's story true, and somebody else intended to make Martin the scapegoat? That also brought up other questions. *Why* should the unknown have desired the death of Latham? What was to be gained by it, and by the death of Ellery Duke? And now, how did killing Renee Lawrence on her wedding day figure? The reason for Doctor Leeds' death, of course, was fairly plain.

IN FIRST tackling the murder of Drew Latham, Doc had considered the possibility that Owen Martin was the killer. Latham had accused Martin of defalcations—perhaps reason enough in Martin's mind to kill a man.

The first contradiction Doc had encountered was when Benton had kidnaped the man he knew to be the Crimson Mask. Martin would hardly hire the private detective agency of du Bois to look for irregularities in his firm, then hire du Bois' own men to do away with the Crimson Mask—the very man whom Martin depended upon to prove him guiltless of murder. And now, with Benton kidnaping the Crimson Mask again, believing him to be the financier, all suspicion that Owen Martin was the killer vanished.

Charley Henderson seemed to be a far better possibility. Henderson had every reason to hate the House of Martin. And the man's bluff, good-humored exterior could be assumed. Henderson had seemed to know Gerald Smith who had had an opportunity to poison Renee. Of course, it would not have been difficult for Gerald Smith to pretend to know Renee and Henderson, and so insinuated himself into their party. Both Renee and Henderson had met so many people in their rounds that they probably did not even remember half of them.

But was Henderson ruthless enough to have removed Doctor Leeds from his path? If so, he would not have hesitated to remove his own wife, should he have discovered that she knew too much.

As his thoughts sped with kaleidoscopic swiftness, Doc's eyes became accustomed to the dim light. A closet across the room interested him, and he went over to examine it.

It appeared to be empty. Then he saw something black stuck away in a high corner of the broad shelf. Standing on tiptoe, he dragged it down. It was a telephone, from which a short end of wire dangled. That was an odd find, but the Crimson Mask quickly decided that Benton must have taken this swift and sure way to see that the phone in this room was out of commission when he turned the place into a prison.

There was no phone box in the room, but the Crimson Mask's keen eyes quickly found the other end of the cut wire, near the baseboard— only a few inches of insulated wire, sticking out from a tiny hole.

CHAPTER VII

CEMENT CURE

ELECTRIC WIRE splicing was one thing for which the Crimson Mask was not equipped. But from his small hidden case of varied little tools he selected a small hooked device that would have to do, though usually he used it for manipulating locks.

The splicing was a tedious job, one that brought an ache to his arm muscles.

And then, when he was almost finished, he heard footsteps outside the door! Quickly he tiptoed across the room, lit a cigarette, and leaned against the wall. The doorbolts slid back, and the leering Benton entered carrying Doc's own gun in his hand.

"I thought you might like to know what's going to happen to you, Martin," he drawled, grinning like a battered gargoyle. "This is your gun, see?"

"Yes," Doc said quietly. "I see."

Benton's grin was spine-chilling as he said casually: "When night comes that last slug in this gat is going into your head. And then it's going to be found in your hand—not here, though. Get, it? Thought I'd give you time to think about your sins, Martin. Good-by, big shot."

Benton slammed the door shut and shoved the bolts home. As Doc went back to work on the extension telephone, his lips were grim and tight. He understood to the full the devilish ingenuity of the plan of these thugs. If Owen Martin were found a suicide, probably with a note beside him, confessing to all the connected murders, the real murderer could go blithely on his way. Everyone who had reason to suspect him would be out of the way.

"Very neat," he told himself grimly as he completed his task.

He picked up the receiver and held it to his ear. Benton was on the wire downstairs.

"Woods?" he was saying. "This is Benton. We've got Owen Martin locked in upstairs, and as soon as it gets dark, we're going to carry on according to the instructions Smith left with me. I just want to check."

So the mystery man's name was Woods. The name meant nothing to the Crimson Mask. But the voice might mean a great deal.

There was a dry chuckle from the other end of the line.

"You've done magnificently, Benton," said Woods. "There seems to be just one little hitch, which I'll tell you about in a minute. But before I forget, Latham left some papers which have not been found. Did you take care of that?"

"I can't do everything, Boss," said Benton. "Remember, I've got to lay low. I didn't report to the Chief because you said it might be too dangerous. The Mask could have got to me through the agency. The Chief has a tail on my apartment, I found out. I've got to watch my step, Boss. But we can handle that Latham business later."

"Never mind now," the mysterious speaker said. "I'll see that it's attended to." Suavity dropped from his voice. "As for Martin, it happens that I just received word where Owen Martin is—and he's not in your place! I'll give you one guess as to who's locked in your room upstairs."

"The Crimson Mask!" snarled Benton as Doc hastily and silently replaced the telephone in its cradle.

THE CRIMSON MASK had barely time to cross the room before the bolts were shot, the door flung open, and Benton and Happy stood there, both with black-muzzled guns in their hands.

"Come on downstairs, Martin," snapped the private detective. "We've changed our plans."

Again prodded with guns, Doc was marched downstairs into the rundown kitchen. Butch was emptying what looked like grayish sand into a wooden box. A fiendish grin spread over his damaged face as he looked up at Doc.

"Well, *Martin*," growled Benton, "we've decided not to let you be found a suicide. Know what that stuff is that Butch is mixing?"

Doc knew well enough what it was—and what it was used for. The "cement cure!" The most diabolical method ever devised by warped criminal brains for eliminating rivals. They would pour that stuff around his ankles. When it grew solid, he would be heaved into one of the rivers. And bodies so disposed of were seldom seen again.

Somehow Doc managed to keep his composure, even with such horrible death staring him in the face. There was even a smile of mockery on his disguised countenance as Butch and Happy moved toward him, snarling. But Benton ordered them to stand back.

"Hell!" pleaded Happy. "Let me go over him just a little, Benton! I got it coming to me."

"Get back, damn it!" shouted Benton. "We want the Crimson Mask to *enjoy* his last hours in full possession of his senses. How will he know what's coming to him if you knock him stiff? Come on! Truss him up, Happy. That ought to give you some satisfaction."

If he had expected to startle Doc by abruptly announcing that he knew he was the Crimson Mask, he was disappointed. Happy moved forward with a set of ropes rigged like a harness. It fitted over the Crimson Mask's chest, holding his arms against his sides. Another loop was slipped taut around his wrists, and his legs were tied together at the knees.

Not until he saw the pulley in the ceiling, though, did Doc realize the full horror of what he was up against. One rope, from which his wrists were fastened, was tossed through the opening in the block. If he tried to move in any way while the cement was hardening about his feet someone would pull on the other end of the rope, applying unbearable pressure on his torso. He would be under a relentless double hammerlock caused by his own weight, which would eventually break his arms. In any case to remain in this harness long would numb him until physical action would be impossible, even if by some miracle he got a chance.

HIS SHOES and socks were yanked off, the box was shoved under his bare feet, and he was lifted until his toes just touched the wooden bottom. The strain was agonizing as the cold cement, gritty, slimy, was poured over his feet. For the first time in all his career of daring, the Crimson Mask, gray-faced and agonized, felt utterly helpless and hopeless in this room where three armed men were lusting to kill him, and where he was so tied that not even a Houdini could make an escape without loss of limb.

"How do you like it, Mask?" gloated Butch as he gave the rope a yank until Doc could not think for pain.

When Butch lowered him, the cement actually felt good in comparison to the other pain.

"Come on, Happy," said Benton. "We've got work to do. Butch, you can keep our friend, the Crimson Mask, company."

"It's a pleasure," said the grinning gangster.

He saluted happily as the other two left the room, then lit a cigarette and threw the match in Doc's face.

Doc waited until he heard the slam of the front door. Then alone with Butch, he went into the only action possible. With herculean effort he lifted his knees to get leverage for his feet. The cement dragged heavily, but he managed one hard shove that knocked the box over, spilling the cement on the floor. Butch sprang at him with a howl of fury. It was what Doc wanted.

"You damn red devil!" Butch shouted. "Now you will get it!"

Doc took the chance of breaking his arms. He heaved himself up with all the strength latent in his brawny forearms, shot out his legs, and then caught Butch's neck in an unbreakable scissors-grip. With on mighty twist, he broke Butch's neck. Then, panting, he stood once more on the overturned box.

He shivered. It had been a terrible way to kill a man, but necessity had compelled it. Now, free of interference, he made short work of the harness, retrieved his shoes and socks and put them on.

He found the telephone in the next room and called Police Headquarters, telling them to pick up the body of Butch. He was gone before the police cars arrived.

There was much to be done. First, who was "Woods?" Was it Henderson? If it were, Doc had not recognized his somewhat blurred voice. It could have been Henderson, though he was supposed to be home by now under police surveillance, grieving over his wife's death.

Second, Latham had left papers that Woods and Benton had not yet located, and wanted badly. So did the Crimson Mask. For he knew that nothing of importance had turned up in Latham's various deposit boxes. That probably meant a secret safe—in Latham's home.

Yes, the Crimson Mask decided, he was going to be busy after dark. Woods would not dare make a move before then.

In his bedroom in the small apartment over his apothecary shop he set his alarm for ten o'clock, and lay down for the few hours needed for recuperation…

IT WAS not the alarm that wakened Bob Clarke, however, when darkness had fallen over Manhattan, but the shrilling of the telephone. He sat up with a jerk, feeling surprisingly rested and refreshed.

It was Theodore Warrick on the wire. His voice was taut with worry.

"Bob!" he said excitedly. "What do you think of this! Owen Martin has been kidnaped!"

"How do you know?" Doc inquired, though he was already certain of that from what he had overheard in Benton's hideout.

"He called me this morning and wanted to come back to town to talk with me. Said that after thinking it over he believed he could clear up some of the mess. He never arrived—and Thompson, the bodyguard I'd insisted on sending with him, was picked up on a country road, slugged. When he came to, and hurried up here, all he could tell me was that their car had been side-swiped off the road on the way into town. Thompson says he got out and started to raise his automatic rifle when one of the young hoodlums attacking them came up behind him and clipped him on the head. That's all he remembers."

Doc whistled. This was bad. Now the mysterious Woods had a real chance to put through the suicide frameup. He must have had some other men on the hunt for Martin when Smith had captured Doc.

The Crimson Mask had to get Latham's papers now, for they seemed his only possible lead. If they worried the gangsters, they must contain information the Crimson Mask wanted.

"I've got a job to do," he told Warrick. "Something that may help. Then I'll come directly to your house."

As soon as he had hung up, Doc donned his loose gray flannels. For disguise, he made a change in his nose, and generally lightened his dark pigmentation. Then, checking his pockets, he set out for the home of Drew Latham.

CHAPTER IX

A DISPATCH BOX

LEAVING THE subway, Doc walked two blocks and past the Latham home in the smart East Side section. It was a typical city house of the wealthy, the white stone of its narrow facade gleaming dully under the street lights. Beside the great front door was a smaller entrance, evidently for tradesmen and servants.

Doc stopped a few doors away when he was sure no one was on guard in front of the house, and drew a little leather key container from his pocket. Slipping back to the servants' entrance, he made use of one of the odd-looking keys. In three minutes the lock clicked, and he slipped silently inside.

In the long hall in which Doc found himself, enough illumination seeped through the glass of the door for him to make out the stairs. He climbed them noiselessly. When he had reached the main floor he went right on up to where he believed Latham's study would be located.

He could now hear the murmur of voices. Servants, probably, since Latham had had no family.

Doc knew the general architectural details of such houses as this, which usually conformed to a set plan. That gave him the idea he would find Latham's study on the second floor, convenient to his sleeping chamber.

Cautiously he opened a door in the front of the second floor corridor when he silently reached it. There was a dim light in the hall, but no sign of anyone. Satisfied he pushed the door wider and slipped inside. He had guessed right. He was in Drew Latham's study, a handsomely furnished octagonal room with windows on three sides, a fireplace, and walls lined from floor to ceiling with bookcases.

That presented a poser. If a safe were hidden behind those rows of morocco-bound volumes, it would take all night to locate it. He crossed the room on tiptoe and glanced out of the side window. To his left, riveted to the side of the house, was an iron ladder. Below was a small garden with a wall that could be scaled, if necessary.

Turning back, he sat down at the desk. Concentrating deeply, he attempted to reconstruct the mind processes of the man, now dead, who had so often sat there, and to recall all he had gleaned of Latham's personality.

Latham's disposition had been fiery, and unpredictable. At one moment he would be irascible, a man who would not part with a dime; the next he would be willing to make a five-figure loan—if there was something that he wanted. He would go to any lengths to get what he wanted. Once the possessor, however—and he had to get it at the *moment* he wanted it—it no longer had any value for him.

It was this peculiarity of Latham's of "wanting what he wanted when he wanted it" that most interested the Crimson Mask. If the man had hidden something valuable in this room where he could put his hands on it the instant he wanted it, where would he have put it? Not behind the books, for he would have been too impatient to remove the volumes and replace them. Latham, too, had been too subtle to select a hiding place in the desk or under the floor.

WHERE THEN? Doc's keen eyes searched the room again—and suddenly he grinned. The fireplace! Logs lay on the andirons, with ashes heaped beneath them. But the red brick showed not the slightest trace of soot or smoke.

Leaping to his feet he hurried to the fireplace and began to examine each brick. Methodically his long, sensitive fingers tapped every one on the hearth, up the sides, and across the reredos—a tedious job. Brick after brick.

He had reached the last row just under the mantel, with hope fading when suddenly, as he touched the second brick, his heart leaped. The brick was a false front that drew out and slid neatly over its neighbor. And a flashlight beam showed the dial of a safe.

But Doc's real task had only fairly begun, for it was a modern and difficult type of lock. Rubbing the fingers of both hands against the bases of his thumbs to sharpen his sense of touch, he took gentle hold of the dial, as he crouched with his ear close to the opening. It was delicate work, but Doc Clarke was skilled, and at last the tumblers fell, one by one, and the safe door swung open.

His groping hand discovered that the depository contained only a padlocked steel dispatch box. Doc drew it out. This was going to be more difficult to open than the safe itself. He would have to take it home with him.

He was just straightening up with the bulky dispatch box in his hands, when suddenly he stiffened. Someone outside was coming softly toward the study! Doc had taken only two steps toward the open window, though, when the door opened, and a man's figure was silhouetted there. Instantly Doc dropped behind the desk, but the steel dispatch box, striking the chair, rang out like a Chinese gong.

"Come out—I have you covered," ordered a dry, determined voice, and Doc recognized the heavy voice of Gerald Smith, as well as the man's now familiar bulky outlines.

So Woods had sent his suave henchman on this mission instead of the blundering Benton! That was showing pretty keen intelligence.

Like a menacing shadow, with his gun glinting in the dim light, Smith started to move toward the desk. But he did not move far. Doc, crouched, was in a perfect position to spring. As he launched his attack, his shoulder struck the man's knees, just as the fellow hurled himself forward with his gun upraised—not to shoot, as he had threatened, but to crash it down on the Crimson Mask's head.

Smith was crushed back against the book-shelves now, too close to shoot if he had wanted to, but still he fought to club the Crimson Mask with the butt of his weapon. Doc's own weapon was the steel dispatch case, and as he swung it he caught the fellow square above the eye. Smith grunted and fell forward full length.

POUNDING FOOTSTEPS were coming toward the study. Men were on the run to investigate the sounds of the rough-and-tumble. Doc sped to the door and locked it before he raced for the open window and scrambled down the iron ladder to the garden. He could hear the servants battering at the study door as he reached the ground, and from the front door a police whistle shrilled.

Hanging on to his precious booty, he climbed over the wall. A bullet whined past him as he dropped over, to find himself in a narrow alley. He shot a glance upward, and saw that the bullet had come from Smith's gun. The man had come out of it quickly, and was making his getaway also. Angered at being forestalled, he had stopped on the iron ladder long enough to take a potshot at the escaping Crimson Mask. A futile shot. And Doc knew that Gerald Smith could never overtake him now...

At home safely, taking care not to disturb Dave Small's needed sleep, Doc immediately set about opening the strongbox, which proved to be a long and tricky process, as he had guessed. But he was rewarded when finally he swung back the lid of the dispatch box.

On top of the box were packages of bonds, and a folder of currency containing twenty thousand dollars in cash. The value of the securities amounted to almost half a million dollars, and were gilt-edged.

Doc shook his head. A lot of money to be concealed in a man's study, even in the study of such a wealthy eccentric man as Drew Latham. But when he opened and read a legal document lying beneath the bonds—Drew Latham's properly attested last will and testament—he knew the answer.

The most interesting part of the surprising revelation read:

> ...as already adjudicated in previous testaments drawn up by me to which this testament is a legalized appendage, I have put away certain properties, said properties consisting of cash and bonds, in a strongbox whose hiding place is known to but one other person. To this person, Renee Lawrence, whose kindness and discretion in easing the declining years of an elderly man are fully appreciated, I bequeath the contents of the aforesaid strongbox. It shall be hers to claim at any time after my death that she sees fit. The legatee is in full knowledge of this bequest.

NOW DOC CLARKE knew why Renee had been so worried about Latham's death. But how on earth could she have suspected murder? And she had certainly hinted as much to Doc himself.

Then Doc's lips tightened. Charley Henderson! Renee had been in love with him. What more natural than for her to tell the man she loved of the legacy she would receive at Latham's death?

At last Doc had enough circumstantial evidence to demand the speculator's arrest! For here was a made-to-order motive for the slaying of Latham. Why Ellery Duke had been killed was still a mystery, though Doc had seen why Doctor Leeds had been a victim. Now he believed he also saw the reason for the slaying of Renee.

As Doc put the papers in the strongbox, a small sheet of stationery drifted onto the desk from between two of the packs of securities. It was a portion of a letter addressed to Owen Martin.

> Dear Owen:
> I am writing this to call to your attention a condition of which you should be informed. I am convinced that my accounts with the House of Martin have been seriously mismanaged. As you know, they are in David's hands, and I should hate to cause the young man any inconvenience, but—

The letter ended abruptly. Doc laid it down, and stared into the distance. At last he was beginning to see something of the pattern that lay behind the crimes, though he still had to get at the root of the motive. But with Owen Martin in such peril of death, Henderson must be arrested at once.

Before he left for Theodore Warrick's house Doc called Police Headquarters. He told the commissioner briefly of his reasons, and asked for Henderson's arrest. He also suggested that all police be on the lookout to pick up Benton and his two remaining aides.

The thought of Benton recalled du Bois to his mind, and he snapped his fingers. The agency head might have learned something during the day in his check-up. He dialed the private investigator's apartment.

"I'm sorry to trouble you at this hour," he apologized when du Bois answered and he'd identified himself. "But it's urgent. Did you find out anything about Benton's connections?"

"Yes and no," du Bois answered. "Mac gave me a list of names he'd been checking on to trace any relations between Benton and somebody possibly connected with the House of Martin. There's only one that might have some bearing on crooked work in the Martin case, from what I know of it—Charley Henderson. Benton worked for him on some matter before he came to work for me. Does that help you any?"

"It certainly does!" Doc said grimly. "Thanks a million, du Bois."

So Benton had worked for Henderson! Well, that fit right into the pattern that had been forming in Doc's mind!

Warrick was pacing the floor when Doc arrived, his face furrowed with strain and worry.

"I can't hold out much longer, Bob," he said. "I feel responsible for Owen Martin, and now—"

"I think we're getting places, Ted," Doc said. "Here's what I know. You can carry on, if anything happens to me."

Swiftly he told all that had happened during the last twenty-four hours. Ted Warrick shook his head gravely.

"Suppose you're wrong on Henderson?" he asked.

"I might be, but we'll decide on that bridge when we cross it," said Bob Clarke. "Right now, I'm going after him. The police should have him by this time."

But the police did not have Charley Henderson, as Doc quickly discovered when he called Police Headquarters. The man had gone home when his wife had been taken away for an autopsy, but as quickly had disappeared.

"He even slipped the tail we had on him," Doc was told ruefully. "We haven't been able to pick him up—but we'll get him."

Doc's lips were tight as he hung up. Every moment Owen Martin was in greater peril—and the Crimson Mask's hands seemed tied! Well, one thing at least he could do—make a hurried visit to the speculator's East End Avenue apartment to see if he could find anything there to give him a clue to where Henderson had gone. Or where Owen Martin might have been taken.

CHAPTER X

SURPRISE ATTACK

WHEN THE Crimson Mask arrived at the apartment house he found a policeman in the lobby and identified himself.

"I'd like to look over Henderson's apartment," Doc told the bluecoat. "Come along with me if you want to."

Together they went up to the speculator's apartment where the Crimson Mask made a rapid and thorough search. He found only a few inconsequential business papers in the desk in the study, but in a bureau drawer of the bedroom he found a stack of love letters from Renee

Lawrence. He would have been somewhat ashamed of reading such intimate notes, except that in them one name was rather enigmatically mentioned. And that name was Woods!

"Nothing here for me," he told the officer. "I'm on my way."

Outside the apartment house he grabbed a taxi, giving Renee Lawrence's address.

In the lobby of her hotel, he learned the number of her suite but was told that she had just been married, and had sailed for Bermuda. So the hotel people did not know what had happened—which meant that the police had not yet taken over. That was a break! But he would have to work fast. They were likely to be here any minute.

As soon as he reached the doorway of Renee's apartment, however, he made a disappointing discovery. The keyhole had been plugged by the management, probably at the tenant's orders, since she had intended to be gone for some time. But somehow he must get into that apartment at once. He might find something there that was vital for him to know.

The servants' entrance must have been treated in the same way by the management, so there was no chance of getting in there, short of breaking the door down. Doc moved swiftly to the window at the end of the corridor, and looked out.

The headlights of cars far below were a blur of light making a luminous ribbon of the streets. But of immediate interest was the narrow ledge, about a foot and a half wide that ran from this window to the windows of Renee's apartment to his left. It was a dangerous chance to take, to try to gain entry by that means, but he had to take it. Throwing up the sash, Doc clambered through. His hands found a fingergrip in the granite blocks of the facade, but immediately a gust of wind smote him with such force that he was almost torn loose from his precarious hold.

But he set his jaw and went on grimly, step by step. The Crimson Mask's fingers, strong though they were, were tiring from the strain before he reached the window on which he kept his eyes. Holding on with one hand then, he reached for the little case in his pocket and pulled out a bit of metal with a round, spur-like diamond point.

Dexterously he cut a piece of glass, big enough for his hand to reach through to the lock. A moment later, he had shoved up the sash and was climbing into the dark, silent room.

"I've been waiting for you," said a rough voice. "Get your hands up!"

IT WAS the part of wisdom to obey, so the Crimson Mask raised his hands. A light switch clicked, and he saw Charley Henderson, with a gun held steadily on him. Henderson's face was sunken, and his eyes were deep-set—glittering, dangerous.

"I only wanted to get one look at you before I blast you to hell!" he snarled, and his knuckles whitened as he pressed the trigger.

Doc dropped to the floor as the gun roared, and a bullet whined over his head. He made another desperate sideward leap as the gun spurted fire again, and a bullet ploughed into the wall. Then Doc charged. To wait an instant longer would only be to be shot down before he could get out his own weapon.

His shoulder hit Henderson, driving the enraged speculator into the wall. He saw the flailing gun barrel, and with both hands made a lightning grab for Henderson's wrists, caught them, and spun around in the same hold which he once used on Butch. Henderson's big body flew across the room, landing with stunning impact against the baseboard. The next instant Doc had him covered with his own gun.

"Come on, Henderson," he said grimly, "the police want to have a little talk with you—but I want one now. You've a lot to answer for, Henderson, but first of all—why did you kill your wife?"

The speculator's mouth fell open. His shoulders shook, and he buried his face in his hands, his whole heavy body racked with sobs.

Watching a strong man break down is never pleasant, but Doc had no time to waste on sentimentality.

"Get up!" he snapped. "Answer my questions! Then tell me why you were fool enough to try to hide out here."

Henderson got slowly to his feet. He gulped as he sat heavily down in a chair.

"Why did you kill your wife?" Doc repeated grimly.

"My God, I didn't kill her!" Henderson shouted. "I didn't!" He stared hard at the Crimson Mask. "Who the hell are you?"

"I'm the Crimson Mask," Doc told him.

Henderson's mouth fell open again. "Lord!" he chattered. "I wouldn't have shot if I'd known. The one man in the world I wanted to see, but thought I couldn't get to. Get my wife's murderer! You can! You've got to!"

"All right," Doc said coolly. "Then you start out by helping me. Who is Woods?"

The speculator's face became hard as granite. Deadly hatred was in his eyes—not for the Crimson Mask.

"I wish to God I knew! I thought you were Woods when you came in here. He's after me—but I'm going to get him first! He thinks I do know who he is—thinks my wife told me, which she didn't. He wants to shut my mouth. Good God, if I only did know who he is, so I could go after him!"

"Why was Renee afraid of you?" the Crimson Mask demanded.

HENDERSON SIGHED heavily.

"She thought I was a murderer," he said bitterly. "Thought I'd killed Drew Latham. Listen here, Crimson Mask, I'd like to make a clean breast of everything. I've nothing to live for now, except to find my wife's killer, and maybe I can tell you something that will help you to find him.

"I'm broke—flat broke. Last night, while I was out with Renee, I called up a financial writer I know to find out something for me, and he told me, casualy, that Latham was dead—'accidentally' shot. I didn't tell Renee at once, but I did do something pretty rotten to the girl I loved more than my life-and who loved me. I knew all about her friendship with Latham—a pretty idyllic friendship it was, too—and of the money she was to inherit from him. Something like half a million.

"I don't need more than a fraction of that to run it up to seven figures, in a week, so I thought I was justified in what I did, in a way. It was for her. And God, I wanted to marry her—and I was broke! I persuaded her to elope to Armonk with me. But when she heard this morning about Latham, she got it into her head somehow that I had killed him, and—"

He dropped his head in his hands and groaned, but lifted it to look at the Crimson Mask and add forlornly:

"I can't understand it. She always trusted me so. Why, only a week ago she borrowed a hundred thousand dollars for me."

"Wait a minute!" Doc said quickly. "Where did she get that much money? That's a lot to get together in cash."

"I know it," Henderson said wearily. "That's why I kept at her until she told me. It was this fellow Woods—and I don't even know who he is. All I know is that he's some fellow who was after Renee to marry him. She wouldn't have anything to do with him, though, because she knew he was mixed up in something pretty off color. What, she wouldn't tell me."

"But she went to him for money?" Doc prodded.

"Yes, damn it!" growled Henderson. "She didn't tell me till early today. Then we had a row. On our wedding day." His lips curled in a bitter smile. "If I hadn't married her, she'd be alive now. Woods killed her—I know it!

"I had her key and came up here to be alone with her things. I heard them put the plug in the door. Nobody knew I was here. I was going to commit suicide. But when I heard you fussing with the plug in the door, and then later at the window, I thought you were Woods. So I shot at you. Thank God I missed! I've botched things up enough as it is."

"You heard me fussing with the plug in the door?" asked Doc, tautly. "I didn't touch the plug."

Doc handed the speculator his gun.

"There should still be a few bullets in it," he said quietly. "I think we're going to need all we've got." He drew his own gun from his shoulder holster.

"You mean—" Henderson asked.

"That it's a safe bet that Woods or his men will shortly pay us a call. One of his gang was around here and found the doors plugged, evidently. They'll probably make their try to break in through the servants' entrance. Less noise breaking the door down there than from the main corridor."

All signs of weakness brought on by grief vanished from Henderson. His eyes gleamed with the madness of anticipated vengeance. And it was at that instant that a crash came from the direction of the serving pantry.

"Get under cover!" Doc whispered quickly. "When they come in here, we'll take them."

Doc ducked behind an armchair where he was in line with the pantry door. Henderson had just squatted behind a big couch when, with a rending crash, the back door gave way, and running footsteps were pounding toward them. Parks Benton, gun in hand, burst through the door, with Happy behind him.

"Hands up!" Doc said quietly, covering them from around the chair.

His answer was a shot that doused the ceiling light. Henderson's gun spat fire, and there was a responding burst of flame from the doorway. Henderson grunted, but his gun blazed again. Doc saw a movement across the room and fired. A man's howl of agony died away in a choking gurgle, as a body thudded on the floor.

Running footsteps sounded again, but receding. Before Doc could start in pursuit the door of the service elevator clanged shut.

"All right, Henderson?" Doc cried.

"Creased." growled the speculator. "Right across my damn potbelly."

When Doc switched on a floor lamp he saw Happy lying on his face near a wall, with two bullets in him, either of which would have finished him.

"Nice teamwork," said Henderson. "Now, if we'd only got the others—Woods—"

"We're going after them—at least I am," said the Crimson Mask. "The trail's still hot."

INTERRUPTED KIDNAPING

TO DOC'S surprise, when he and Henderson reached the lobby, there was no commotion. Apparently the disturbance, high in the tower as they had been, had not been heard.

"I've changed my mind, Henderson," Doc said when they stepped into the street. "I want you to do what I say, for your own protection. You've got to stay alive for a few hours, at least."

"Your show, Mask," said Henderson. "I'll take orders."

"Oh, one more thing, Henderson—I forgot to ask you," Doc said casually. "Did you recognize one of the men who attacked us?"

Henderson looked at him sharply. "No, they shot the lights out before I could see them clearly."

"Well, did a man named Parks Benton ever work for you?"

Henderson's brow creased. "Benton? Why, no—oh, yes! A private detective, isn't he? Yeah, a couple of years ago I hired him to follow somebody around." He rubbed his jowls ruefully. "You know, a speculator in stocks like me has to be careful sometimes. I was in on a big stock deal, and I was kind of suspicious of one of the men in the deal with me. So I hired this Benton fellow to find out all about the man. Nothing ever came of it, though."

Doc nodded, flagged a taxi and then drove with Henderson to the home of Theodore Warrick to whom he made a hurried explanation.

"Stay here until you hear from me," was his parting injunction to the speculator. "I may have some interesting news for you."

He was thinking of Henderson's story about Benton as he drove off to make one more necessary call. It might be true, although it sounded a little lame. Du Bois, after all, in checking on his operative, couldn't have gone into the details of any of Benton's previous jobs. All he was doing was searching for significant highlights which might bear on the Martin case. And he didn't know too much about the affair. Well, when Doc got around to it he'd go into that Benton connection with Henderson a little more carefully.

His taxi pulled up in front of the handsome bachelor quarters where David Martin lived, just as the silence of the early morning was shattered by shots from the house. Hastily thrusting a bill at the frightened driver, he leaped from the cab and up the front steps into the dark entranceway, pulling his gun from his holster with one hand, and jerking out his key holder with the other in anticipation.

But no key was needed. The door gave beneath the pressure of his hand. He stepped quickly inside, adjusted his crimson mask, and flattened himself against the wall. He could hear sibilant whispers from the landing above, and bumping, dragging sounds. Darting across the hall in the semi-darkness he ran head-on into a silently advancing man—a lookout, apparently, whose attention must have been distracted elsewhere when Doc had burst in.

The fellow grunted with surprise, but the only sound after that was the crunch of the Crimson Masks' gun on the man's skull. Doc eased him to the floor silently.

The wail of a police siren came from the distance. Doc's taxi driver evidently had wasted no time finding a police car.

Then Doc could see the dark silhouettes of two men at the head of the stairs, carrying a limp form. He tensed himself for action. He had run head-on into another kidnaping!

"All clear, Gerry?" came a husky whisper from above.

"Okay," he whispered back.

Gerald Smith again, eh? And once more the Crimson Mask had knocked Smith galley-west. From the way he had just crowned the man with his gun, though, the fellow wouldn't get away so easily this time.

The men with their burden were halfway down the stairs, hurrying. The wail of the siren was coming nearer.

"Lend a hand, Gerry!" one of the men on the stairs panted. "We've got to get out of here!"

Doc lent a hand, but there was metal in it. As the kidnapers reached the foot of the stairs, Doc's gun landed on the jaw of the foremost man, and he went down like a felled steer. The other man and his unconscious victim tumbled on him in a heap. Doc's gun butt swung again, and there was another sickening crunch, then silence.

The police car roared up outside a moment later. The Crimson Mask pulled his special police card from his pocket, felt for a light switch on the wall, and pressed the button. In the sudden blaze of light the hallway looked like a battleground. Three unconscious men were stretched on the floor near the foot of the stairs, two of them unquestionably members of Benton's crew. And Young David Martin, unconscious, was the victim the thugs had been carrying.

DOC LOOKED around for Gerald Smith—and he was gone! The man must have had a head of concrete, for again he had survived an almost murderous head blow, had come out of his fog, and somehow managed to get away before the police arrived!

Two policemen, armed with automatic rifles burst through the door. They looked around at the shambles, then at Doc, nodding as they saw the card he held.

"Mackerel!" cried one of them. "What is this—a waxworks?"

"It's a pretty fair haul for you," Doc said sharply. "One of these men is young David Martin, of the House of Martin, and these other lugs were kidnaping him."

The bluecoat whistled. "They sure were after a big shot!"

Other police cars arrived, and the hall was quickly filled with uniformed men. Doc quickly explained what was necessary. The police took charge of the unconscious criminals and spread through the house to search for the missing redhead, Gerald Smith.

Doc went into a huddle with the lieutenant in charge, and twenty minutes after the arrival of the ambulance the still unconscious scion of the House of Martin lay stretched on a couch in Theodore Warrick's study, as a doctor hovered over him.

There was still hope that the elder Martin was alive, since he had not been discovered a suicide, leaving a confession of the crimes. The real killer might now have other plans, with the failure of Benton's gang to kidnap and do away with David Martin.

Still, there was no time to lose. So while the Crimson Mask waited for David to regain consciousness there was an experiment it was necessary for him to try.

"Will you please have your dictaphone brought out here, Mr. Warrick?" he asked.

"What are you going to do?" Warrick wanted to know.

"I hope," Doc said grimly, "that I'm going to discover the identity of our elusive Mr. Woods."

Warrick had the machine wheeled in, while Doc jotted down a list of names—the names of every person to whom he had talked, even remotely connected with this case.

With the machine before him, he leaned close and uttered a few words without warning. Henderson almost jumped from his chair, and stared. For it was Henderson's own voice saying: "You've done magnificently, Benton. There seems to be just one little hitch, which I'll tell you about in a minute…"

Every inflection of Henderson's voice was there. That may have astounded the Wall Street man, but it was no mystery to the proudly smiling former police commissioner who well knew that Bob Clarke had trained himself in ventriloquism and phonetics until he could reproduce perfectly any voice he had ever heard.

FOR THE next ten minutes the Crimson Mask was busy repeating into the dictaphone, in the voice of every man whose name he had jotted down on paper, those same words that he had heard spoken by the mysterious Woods over the telephone in Benton's hideout.

"Now," he said to Henderson and his sponsor, "you're going to hear the voice of our friend, Mr. Woods."

He spoke the words once more, this time in the sinister, well enunciated tones he so well remembered. With that done, he played the record through from start to finish, catching every inflection of every voice, comparing it with the voice that came last. Finally he sat back, satisfied. There was an odd gleam in his eyes—for now he knew the identity of the man who called himself Woods!

"Now," he said, as he turned off the machine, "I can do nothing more until David Martin recovers consciousness. I must talk to him before I start out on the final lap."

"That won't be long," assured the doctor. "He's coming around nicely." He glanced at his patient. "Wait! A little brandy, please. He's coming out of it now!"

At the first gulp of brandy David Martin choked, coughed, and opened his eyes.

"Look out!" he mumbled. "I'll shoot!" Then he stared about, bewildered. "Where am I?"

He tried to sit up, but the doctor forced him back. Young Martin's eyes were filled with horror.

"They came to kill me," he muttered.

Doc stepped forward. "You're all right, Mr. Martin," he said. "They only got you through the thigh. Flesh wound. You lost a lot of blood.

Now pull yourself together and answer some questions. Your uncle's life depends on it."

"Who are you?" young Martin demanded.

"Some people call me the Crimson Mask," said Doc.

David Martin nodded weakly. "All right," he said. "But you're too late about Uncle Owen. They've already got him."

"I'm not too late," said Doc. "Mr. Woods doesn't care for electric chairs. That's why he came after you—to keep you from answering questions that would point to him."

David Martin grasped the Crimson Mask's wrists desperately. His eyes were burning.

"Where did you find out about him?"

"Never mind," said Doc. "I even think I can tell you why you got mixed up with him in the first place."

Martin's eyes fell. "I suppose I may as well tell you everything," he muttered. "For I want your help, Crimson Mask. First of all, I've got to admit that I used some of the depositors' money to cover my personal losses in the market. I thought, being inside the firm, I could clean up. But I had some tough luck and kept losing. So—"

"So you got help from Woods," said Doc. "You gave him confidential information about your clients, as in Latham's case, and Woods used it unscrupulously in playing the market for the two of you. But that wasn't all that Woods was interested in. He was playing a bigger game, wasn't he? What else did he want you to tell him?"

DAVID MARTIN was slow in answering. But when the truth did come from his pallid lips, it was almost too difficult to believe.

"He wanted me to tell him about the dispositions of the major estates we handled," said Martin. "And then, every time, the person died a natural death within a month! It was uncanny! And I never laid eyes on the man in my life! I know Woods is not his real name, but I've no idea who he is!

"I first heard of him through a club acquaintance, who was killed in an automobile accident shortly afterward, so I couldn't even question him about Woods. I was into Woods so deep by that time, though, that I couldn't do anything but what he demanded—he had so much on me. He wouldn't even let me talk to him face to face."

Doc Clarke nodded grimly. A suspicion of this gigantic plot had been growing in his mind, and now it was confirmed. The listening men were horrified. This was no attack on the House of Martin, to ruin them, but plain out and out murder business!

Woods had been getting some hold on the heirs of wealthy men, then killing the man who would leave each one a fortune, knowing the heirs could be forced to pay through the nose.

Had Dr. Leeds not become suspicious about Duke's death, this might have kept on indefinitely. For that the killer was a master of obscure poisons that would make death seem natural was proved by the deaths of Duke and Dr. Leeds. It was also doubtful if it would ever become known just what poison had killed Renee Lawrence.

"Did Woods make you tell him about Drew Latham's estate, too?" Doc asked.

Henderson drew a sharp breath as David nodded.

"And was your uncle beginning to ask you awkward questions?"

"Yes," David said slowly. "Just a day or two before he disappeared."

"You let Woods know about that?"

With David's nod the final pieces in this puzzling jig-saw of murder fell into place, and Doc had a clear picture in front of him.

The whole case had been confused by the coincidental relations of the murdered men to the House of Martin. Ellery Duke was killed, not because he was a partner of the investment house, but because he was a wealthy man—with an heir who could be controlled! Drew Latham had been murdered for a similar reason. There was a fortune that the mysterious Woods thought he could get his hands on through the bequest to Renee Lawrence.

And here the cunning murderer intended to kill two birds with one stone. Latham's death would be blamed on Martin, he had figured—and he had intended to get rid of Martin by having him found a suicide. Thus, Martin himself would be one of the victims of the gigantic murder scheme. For young David Martin was already under Woods' control!

The entrance of the Crimson Mask into the case had spoiled Woods' plans. He had been forced to change them, accordingly. Martin had suddenly become unavailable—had disappeared, so the suicide planned had been delayed. The death of David Martin had become imperative now, because things were getting too hot. Woods had to cover up. And Renee Lawrence was killed because she had unexpectedly married Henderson. The fortune she was heir to could not be secured—through her. But by killing her, Woods would prevent her from getting the fortune, and he could search for the secret strongbox he knew existed to get the bonds for himself.

"Just one more thing, young fellow," he said quickly, for young Martin was fast dropping back into his coma. "What was Woods' phone number you called?"

Martin weakly passed his hand over his forehead. "Let me think…" His brows wrinkled in concentration. "It was—oh, I know it as well as I know my own name! It was—Beacon Hill—two—ten—eight—seven." His eyes closed as he sank into unconsciousness, exhausted.

"I'd like to make a couple of calls on your private wire in your bedroom, Mr. Warrick," Doc said crisply.

WARRICK NODDED. He knew that Doc wanted to give some instructions to Dave Small, whom he often called when he wanted to learn something in a hurry.

In a few moments Doc was back, but he was restless, anxious until the telephone finally rang. He grabbed up the receiver and listened tensely.

"Good!" was the single word he said, then hung up.

The next moment he was dialing Police Headquarters, asking for the commissioner, to whom he gave the private password that would identify him as the Crimson Mask.

"I've got something for you to go to town on at last, Commissioner," he barked. "Yes—on the House of Martin-Wall Street case… The mysterious Mr. Woods… Surround the Beaufort Building—yes—yes… Riot guns, gas, everything. I'll meet the boys there to give them the lowdown."

He hung up again and whirled to Henderson.

"Let's go, Henderson, if you're coming along for the show," he said grimly. "And you'd better grab plenty of cartridges to be all set for a dogfight. You'll likely have a chance to settle your score soon now."

Doc pressed Warrick's hand and raced out of the house, with Henderson at his heels.

CHAPTER XII

TOOTH AND NAIL

S QUAD CARS were pouring into the block, their sirens silent, as Doc and Henderson alighted from their taxi before the sixty-eight-story Beaufort Building. The net was being tightly drawn around the mass murderer the Crimson Mask had tracked to his lair. He was up in that tower, high above the streets, secure in the belief that no one who had felt his slimy clutch would dare betray him.

Lieutenant O'Brien, from Headquarters, in charge of the raiding squad, stepped up to the Crimson Mask the instant he spotted the distinctive identification card in Doc's hat. His instructions from his superior had been to look for that card.

"What do we do now, sir?" he asked.

"We go in and get Owen Martin, who is being held in the tower on sixty-eight. And we take the men who are holding him."

The officer gave a signal to his men and with them followed the Crimson Mask to the great bronze doors as solid as Mount Everest. There was the dull clangor of a deep-toned bell from somewhere in the building as the Crimson Mask pressed the button at one side of the doors. Then slow footsteps sounded hollowly as the night watchman approached.

The watchman fell back as he saw the uniformed men outside when he opened the door on the heavy chain.

"Open up!" ordered Doc. "Make it snappy, and keep still."

The moment the doors swung open the police, with riot guns held at ready, rushed inside. They piled into the elevators waiting on the ground floor, with two policemen operating two of them, and the jittery frightened watchman at the other.

The raiding party shot up to the sixty-eighth floor to the tower with its one suite that was the private office of the chief stockholder of the building. The elevators stopped silently, and the heavily armed police trooped out into a small corridor with two more heavy bronze doors opposite the elevators. The Crimson Mask well knew that the only answer he would get for a demand to be admitted would be a blast of gunfire, for already he had spotted the small peephole at one side of the doors that would give anyone inside a view of who wanted admittance.

"Break in!" he told Officer O'Brien crisply.

The officer barked orders. Two uniformed men pushed through the raiders with a blowtorch. Quickly the hiss of the torch accompanied the flame as it bit through the valuable doors.

And then, from inside the doors, came the muffled roar of two quick shots. The Crimson Mask groaned. Was he too late, after all?

"Hell!" shouted O'Brien. "They're shooting it out amongst themselves! Snap it up, men!"

At last a piece of the door, wide enough to permit a man to reach through for the lock, fell out. Slowly the massive doors swung back, and armed police, with riot and gas guns, entered with the Crimson Mask leading.

The huge room was filled with acrid, thinning smoke. And in the middle of the floor, lying flat on his face, was a man. No one else was in sight.

"GOOD LORD!" shouted O'Brien, as he sprang to the prone man. "There wasn't but one of 'em and he's done a Dutch!" He lifted the man whose head lolled. "Why—why, it-it's Owen Martin! And he wasn't kidnaped! He croaked himself! See, here's a note in his hand—"

"I thought there would be," Doc said dryly. "And he's not dead, O'Brien, and didn't shoot himself. Somebody tried to kill him, but was in such a hurry he only creased Martin's skull. Call an ambulance—quick! Have some men look out for Martin. You and I and the rest have got to get after the man who shot him!"

O'Brien looked at him stupidly.

"But there ain't anybody here. There ain't even a closet in this or the other room. The boys haven't missed anything. That door's the only way out, and I'm damned sure nobody got past that."

"But somebody has been here and got away," Doc said hurriedly. "And we've got to find him—or them!"

His eyes were darting all about the huge, luxuriously furnished place. It did seem impossible for anyone to have escaped from this tower, sixty-eight stories in the air.

A swift survey of floors and ceilings showed no trap-doors. But the Crimson Mask was stubbornly sure he was right.

"Get busy tapping these walls," he ordered.

For ten tense minutes the only sound in that place so high above the ordinary street sounds was the tap-tapping of gun butts. Then a policeman working in the smaller room let out a yell.

"It's hollow back of this! Say—"

Doc leaped to his side and quickly verified that. His eyes gleamed.

"Break through!" he commanded. "But stand back! Don't go too near!"

An ax in the hands of a brawny bluecoat swung and crashed through a thin partition.

"Wait!" shouted Doc. "Keep away from there!"

O'Brien followed him as he rushed to the hole that had been made in the wall, swung his flashlight into it.

"Good grief!" yelled O'Brien. "A private elevator shaft! Right alongside the regular elevator block! But whoever went down that way is already caught by the boys in the lobby. Nobody could get out that way!"

"If you'll remember, O'Brien," Doc snapped tautly, "there were no other elevator doors in the lobby except the main ones… Come on, all of you! He mustn't get away now!"

One of the elevators shot them down to the lobby. There it was proved that Doc had been right. There was no sign of any other elevator entrance except the main ones.

"How many stories underground in this building?" Doc shot at the watchman.

"Five," the man said. "But I ain't ever seen no elevator in this here buildin' except these, honest."

"You will if you stick around," Doc said shortly. "Take us down. I want a look at each of the basement floors."

WHEN THEY had reached the lowest, five stories underground, there still was no sign of any private elevator entrance.

"O'Brien," Doc ordered, "send men to cover every manhole in this neighborhood for three blocks in every direction. Bring on those blow-torch men. We're breaking through this main elevator wall."

Hastily the puzzled O'Brien barked orders, and the men with the blowtorch came on the double quick.

It was a less difficult task for the torch to eat its way through the metal elevator wall than it had been to conquer the bronze doors, but every man was on tenterhooks before a passageway was cleared into the shaft that the Crimson Mask had known would be there.

It was into the private elevator car itself that they finally broke, and Doc, Henderson, and the armed police squeezed their way through. The private elevator door, on the opposite side from the regular elevator doors was open, leading to a narrow, dark, dirt-walled underground corridor.

"You wait here with your men, O'Brien," the Crimson Mask said. "No sense of all of you running into an ambush, should there be one— and this is my job. Keep your riot and gas guns ready to make a rush if you hear a ruckus. Henderson, I promised you first crack at this man, Woods. Want to come along?"

"Lead on," Henderson said grimly.

In the darkness they groped their way along the corridor that wound and twisted beneath the huge building and the streets—a private way of escape that could only have been built by the man who had had a free hand in the erection of the building.

"This leads to a manhole somewhere, unless I miss my guess," the Crimson Mask whispered. And then, as a door suddenly loomed up ahead, its white oblong showing dimly against the blackness: "And there's where our quarry is holed up—if O'Brien's men have covered all those manholes and driven them back."

The Crimson Mask stopped before the door and listened. The door was thin, but his phenomenally keen ears could hear no sound from inside. Cautiously, fraction of an inch by fraction, he tried the knob. The door was not locked. Probably it had no lock. Only the man who had had this hideout built knew of its existence.

"You stay here, Henderson," he said, his lips barely moving. "I'm going in."

Henderson's expression was stubborn for a moment, then he shrugged, resignedly.

"Okay," he moved his own lips to whisper. "Here stays nothing."

Doc opened the door and stepped across the threshold, his gun held loosely in his hand. He had taken but one step when abruptly two men rose up from behind a couch, with the black muzzles of their guns dead center on his heart, before he could swing up his gun. Scowling Parks Benton, and the man who called himself Gerald Smith.

"COME IN, Crimson Mask, and drop that gun," Smith said suavely, and, taken more by surprise than he had expected, Doc's gun clattered to the floor. "We've been waiting for you—ever since we discovered someone had been smart enough to figure out our manhole getaway. Nice of you to come without your bluecoat boy friends. But then I understand you always were a little too bravo for your own good—foolishly brave and egotistical, eh?"

"You can't get away, Mr. Gerald Smith, as you call yourself when you're not calling yourself Woods," Doc said coolly.

Benton looked at Smith, then at the Mask, and Doc could see he was puzzled. Smith's eyebrows lifted. "As I call myself?" he repeated jibingly. "Dear me, what else would you call me?

A cold, merciless glitter was in his cruel eyes. He was enjoying this—baiting the man who had tracked him down, knowing that he had no possible chance of escape himself, for one gas gun would finish him, but determined to make the Crimson Mask pay in full before he went to his own death.

"You know that I know who you are!" snapped Doc. "Which is more than your rat lieutenant, Benton, knows!"

Benton went wild, forgetting his orders.

"Rat, eh?" he yelled, and fired.

Doc had been playing for that move, and ducked. His hand jerked his hideout gun from his shoulder holster. Benton's shot grazed his shoulder, but his own gun spat fire three times in rapid succession. Benton toppled forward, blood pouring from his chest, and lay still on the floor. Doc's gun had already swung to Smith—or Woods. But oddly, neither of them fired.

"Now I'll have to soil my hands by taking care of you myself," Woods said. "A pleasure, since you've so nicely spoiled all my well-laid plans, Crimson Mask" He grinned mockingly. "Shall we make our duel at three paces?"

"Just a second," Doc said coolly. "We may not be able to resume this pleasant acquaintance in—an afterworld. There are two things I would like to check on first. How did you manage to get that gun into Owen Martin's hand after you'd murdered Latham? You dazed him with some chemical vapor, didn't you?"

Woods laughed harshly. "You're quite clever, Mask. Yes, just the right amount of dilute amyl nitrite, sprayed at Martin with an atomizer, gave me the twenty seconds or so I needed in which to frame Martin."

"All right," said Doc calmly, as if he were on a lecture platform instead of on the fatal spot. "That satisfies me. Now, one final detail. You killed Renee Lawrence because she married another man. Was it simply jealousy alone or also because you no longer could gain Latham's fortune through her?"

"That's one question he'll never answer!" shouted Henderson, as he catapulted into the room, straight at the throat of the man he hated, in the face of the gun.

Smith-Woods fired, but he had been taken too much by surprise to aim. He had counted on what he considered the Crimson Mask's vanity, and that Doc would be alone, wanting to take him single-handed.

He stumbled backward under Henderson's onslaught, his gun knocked from his hand. He fought—desperately—but every cunning trick that he knew was useless against the white rage of Henderson. Again and again Henderson's fists smashed into his enemy's treacherous face, beating it to a bloody pulp. Woods staggered backward before the attack, and suddenly as the speculator flung himself furiously at his wife's killer, Woods was knocked off balance. He fell with a crash, his head striking sickeningly against the stones that formed the walls of the cell-like room.

Henderson was still gripping the killer's throat when Doc pulled him off.

"That's all, Henderson," he said soberly. "He's done for. You've avenged Renee—with your bare fists."

A MOMENT later the police were bursting into the room. Lieutenant O'Brien looked from the Crimson Mask and the panting Henderson to the two dead men on the floor.

"I thought we were after big shots," he said. "I know this Benton louse, but I've never seen this other bozo before."

"Suppose you pull that red wig from his head, O'Brien," Doc suggested, "and remove the wax moulages from his nose and cheeks, and those dark shells from his eyes. Then see what you think."

O'Brien hastily obeyed.

Mr. Gerald Smith, alias Woods," Doc said, "is John du Bois!"

"Good Lord!" ejaculated O'Brien, the red wig dangling in his hand as he stared at the distinctive black and white hair of the well-known private detective.

DOC NODDED grimly. "Mr. John Ferdinand du Bois, who will never step into the shoes of Burns or Pinkerton now. O'Brien, I wish you would tell your commissioner that the Crimson Mask confesses to having made one bad mistake in this case, or it would have been solved sooner. I couldn't conceive of a man such as I believed du Bois to be, running a blackmail and murder racket. I didn't even believe he knew Benton was a rat. I thought Benton must be doublecrossing du Bois and working for someone else. Even Benton thought he was working for somebody else!

"Now that I know where du Bois' money came from, even enough for him under the name of Woods to be the largest stockholder in this great building and have a free hand here, I am no longer surprised. I should not have been fooled, even from the start. Du Bois was not subtle in selecting one of his aliases. The French name, du Bois, means Woods. I was getting on the right track, I think, but had no firm footing until tonight when I made an experiment—"

He went on briefly to tell how he had tested voices, while the police listened, awed.

"When I realized that Smith-Woods' and du Bois' voices were the same, it was all over but the rounding up."

"Good Lord!" muttered O'Brien. He was speechless, save for his favorite ejaculation.

"Come on, Henderson," the Crimson Mask said briskly. "Let's go!"

Not until he was outside, after giving final explanations to the police, did he add to Henderson:

"We've got to get back to Mr. Warrick. There are a lot of things he will want to be knowing."

"And I'm thinking there'll be an end to any feuding between Owen Martin and me from now on," Henderson announced. "Seeing that I was a witness to what du Bois said about killing Latham, I'll testify to that—gladly."

The Crimson Mask smiled. But he was thinking of his friend, the former commissioner. There always were a lot of things Theodore Warrick wanted to know when Bob Clarke completed each dangerous case. And he was thinking of Dave Small too—Dave would want to hear all about it. Yes, Doc thought, he'd be glad to be back in the store again, filling prescriptions, handing out lemon drops to the kids—until the next case for the Crimson Mask came along.

II

THE CRIMSON MASK'S MURDER TRAIL

CHAPTER I

MURDER OR ACCIDENT?

THEODORE WARRICK, gray-haired, trim of figure and as agile as he had been in the days when he was police commissioner of one of the nation's largest cities, craned his neck upward to follow the lines of the twin skyscraper apartment houses that were being erected. The orange-painted girders gave the steel skeleton a carnival air and the shouts of the riggers and ironworkers augmented this suggestion.

The Sheridan Apartments, when completed, would be a small city. Fifty-five stories of steel and concrete to house hundreds of families. The two buildings were separated by a wide space which eventually would be a court. Tenants who lived in these swanky apartments were entitled to see a bit of green grass now and then, for the prices they would pay.

Warrick saw a slender dapper man standing beside a huge steel girder to which workmen were affixing the thick chains by which it would be carried aloft. Warrick made his way gingerly over the littered ground, avoiding puddles and mud, and stepped up to the man beside the girder with outstretched hand.

"What do you think of our new project here, Ted?" the man asked, as he shook hands.

"Magnificent!" Warrick smiled. "But you asked me to come here about something, Sellmer."

George Sellmer's eyes quickly signaled for caution, as he spoke in a low voice.

"Yes—and it's extremely important. About poor Whither. Remember? He was one of the five men who financed this building. Day before yesterday he slipped off a girder and was killed. I've been quietly investigating and I don't like the looks of things. There's more to that death than meets the eye. In fact, Ted, I called you here to see if you'd contact the Crimson Mask for me. I need his help desperately."

The CRIMSON MASK'S

The Mask seized the skinny man's wrists, shoved him against the window.

Warrick nodded. "If it's as important as you make it sound, Sellmer, he'll help. I—"

"Quiet," Sellmer cautioned.

Two men were walking toward them, well dressed, middle-aged men who were surveying the construction work with the possessive air of landlords. Warrick knew Jim Stark and Matt Karling, knew them as among the most ambitious real estate developers in the East. He shook hands with them. Sellmer climbed onto the girder.

"I'm going up," he said, and when Warrick looked worried, be smiled. "Don't be alarmed, Ted," he assured. "You've forgotten that I used to be a riveter and practically lived on girders. Stick around until I come down."

Sellmer raised his right hand in a signal.

The giant crane, perched some fifty stories above the ground, went into smooth action. The girder lifted as neatly as a passenger elevator. Jim Stark, a portly man, but still exuding quiet strength, lit a cigar.

"I hope Sellmer is luckier than Whitner," he remarked. "Which brings something to mind, Mr. Warrick. We ought to have a man of your ability and experience around here. Police experience, I mean. For the last week we've had a number of bad accidents on this job, and finally came

MURDER TRAIL

Whitner's death. That's not all either. Somebody—for a reason none of us can figure out—is sabotaging the building. Poor cement, weak girders, cracked rivets. There've been several instances of this. In fact, Sellmer is going up now to examine a whole section of girder just riveted into place. A workman reports that it looks weak to him. Flaw in the steel or something."

WARRICK LOOKED up at the girder now far above their heads.

"And you'd like me to investigate? I'm sorry, Mr. Stark, but when I severed my connections with the police department, I ceased all that kind of work. Anyway, if there is sabotage, that's a matter for the present police commissioner—not for a has-been like me."

Karling gave a good natured snort of derision. Like Sellmer, he had been a hard working iron man in his day and it showed in his powerful shoulders and slender waist. Advancing years had not softened Karling.

"'Has-been'?" he scoffed. "When you were police commissioner, Warrick, we had the best police force in the world. You could go in there today and improve on it even now, good as it happens to be."

"Thanks," Warrick answered, and kept staring at Sellmer.

The girder was some twenty stories above the ground and Sellmer looked like a tiny doll perched high in the air.

He was standing on the girder, one arm wrapped around the steel guide chain. For some reason Warrick found that he was sweating and that an agonizing worry tore at his heart.

Sellmer had been ready to talk about something vitally important. What? He certainly had hinted that Whither's death may have been something other than an accident.

Thirty-five stories above the ground—then it happened. Warrick could see Sellmer plainly. Suddenly, even though the girder was going up slowly and on an even keel. Sellmer seemed to lose his balance. The arm, wound around the guide chain, relaxed its grip.

For an instant George Sellmer stood on the narrow piece of steel that separated him from eternity. Then death claimed its own.

Sellmer seemed simply to sag outward, and then plunge off the girder. His body made a strange whistling noise on its way down. Screams of horror were stilled abruptly. When Sellmer's body hit the ground, there was a deathly silence from fear-tightened throats. The ground shook under Warrick's feet as the body landed.

Warrick was the first to regain his wits. He vaulted a pile of girders and raced to where Sellmer's corpse lay sprawled out, with every bone smashed. Automatically, Warrick knelt beside the body and picked up a wrist that felt like soft putty. The gesture was purely from habit developed over his years as police commissioner.

He knew, before the body hit, that there would be no pulse.

WARRICK AROSE slowly, eyeing the ring of men who hemmed in the grisly scene.

"No one is to leave the premises," he said curtly. "No one is to touch this corpse. Stark, get to the nearest phone and notify the police."

Karling raised his bowed head. He looked heart-broken. There were unrestrained tears in his eyes.

"Sellmer was one of my closest friends," Karling said in a broken voice. "We grew up together—companions as boys and then as iron workers and contractors. But—but you speak as though you think he was *murdered*, Mr. Warrick!"

"Perhaps he was," Warrick retorted grimly.

"But how? You saw him! We all saw him! Sellmer hadn't been aloft on a girder in months. He forgot that when you lay off that long, you may get dizzy up there. That's what happened to him. I know just how it feels. Everything becomes black. You forget to hang on. Murder? Impossible! He was ten feet away from the building. Nobody was on the girder with him, and unless he was shot, certainly no one on the ground could have killed him. Warrick—you didn't see any evidences of a bullet wound?"

"I did not," Warrick answered curtly. "Still it may have been murder. Stranger things than that have happened. But this matter is out of my hands. I'm simply holding the fort until the police arrive."

They came, soon afterward. An ambulance surgeon made a swift examination of the body.

"No wounds of any kind," he announced. "Except the natural one from dropping off the girder; death was, of course, caused by the fall."

Warrick took a detective-lieutenant aside.

"Just to be sure," he advised, "have an autopsy performed. This man may have been fed some drug that made him dizzy or dopey. It's just a hunch, but sometimes they're worth playing."

"Yes, sir," the lieutenant agreed. He had served under Warrick and respected his abilities. "I'll have it attended to at once, sir."

Morgue attendants rolled the horribly limp form onto a stretcher and the grim truck rolled away. Detectives were questioning the workers, photographers were closing up their camera cases.

Warrick knew what the verdict would be—accidental death. And perhaps that verdict would be in order. Certainly there was nothing to indicate that this could be murder, except the fact that Sellmer wanted to tell Warrick something about the first accidental death that had occurred.

Deep in his mind Warrick was thinking that one man could solve this riddle—the Crimson Mask! It would require a man who could work unhampered by the red tape which impeded regular detectives. Nothing impeded the Crimson Mask—at least not for long.

In the annals of crime history, he knew that the Crimson Mask would go down as one of the most feared men who ever fought crime—fought it with its own methods of ruthlessness, slyness, trickery, or open gun warfare. Whatever the occasion demanded, the Crimson Mask guided his efforts accordingly.

He had been born under a sign of vengeance. When he had been only a boy, his father, a sergeant of police, and Theodore Warrick's closest friend, had been shot and killed by cowardly gangsters. As young Bob Clarke had stood beside Warrick, looking down on his father in death, they had both noted the crimson band of blood which had suffused the upper part of the dead man's face—from internal blood seepage—until it seemed that he wore a crimson mask.

FROM THIS, Bob Clarke, grown to manhood, had taken the name—the Crimson Mask. It was no mere bravado to frighten criminals, though he had dedicated his life to eradicating them.

He wore a mask of crimson when such protection was needed, or when he wanted to work openly as the Mask. For the most part, he assumed a disguise. For during those grim moments when, with his small hand gripped in Theodore Warrick's, he had looked at his dead father, the boy, Bob Clarke, had resolved to fight crime unrelentingly—to prevent more of such brutal murders.

Robert Clarke had gone through college with his own money, and had emerged a pharmacist. Theodore Warrick had financed the rest. As with everything also, young Clarke had gone at his new work thoroughly, studying every phase of criminology and the fighting of crooks. He had mastered their own arts, too, and if the Crimson Mask had ever become a crook, he would have been among the greatest. His features were especially adapted to disguise which had become one of his greatest assets.

"Ted" Warrick, ex-police commissioner, was thinking of all this as he was driven home. He was proud of his own small part in the Crimson Mask's success as a crime fighter, since he had been too old to undertake any of the physical work that Bob Clarke could accomplish. And he was proud that he was the Crimson Mask's only contact, that only through him could the Mask be approached.

Here was work for the Crimson Mask now, he thought. For more and more Warrick sniffed murder, with the true instincts of a trained manhunter. Why hadn't Sellmer screamed as he toppled over the edge of the girder? Why hadn't he waved his arms or tried to find some grip on the narrow platform from which he had catapulted? The bravest men, facing certain death as Sellmer had faced it, will automatically scream. Yet not a sound had come from his lips. Men working on floors almost parallel with the girder had testified to that. It was not unusual.

Warrick entered his home, closed the door of his study and opened a drawer. He took out a telephone, always locked in that drawer. It was a direct wire to the Crimson Mask's headquarters.

CHAPTER II

THE MASK INTERVENES

THE DRUGSTORE on a corner of two none too prosperous-looking streets, was a staid, old-fashioned place. Its windows were decorated with the old-time crystal jars filled with colored water. The sign indicated that Robert Clarke, Ph.G., was the owner. The grown-ups of the crowded neighborhood called him "Doc," the youngsters called him "Bob," and the little ones knew him as "The Lemon Drop Man." The two jars on a counter, one containing lemon drops, the other containing lime drops, were not for sale—they were free to the kids.

Inside the store there was no soda fountain, no racks of neckties and other haberdashery, no magnificent display of candies or perfumes. At the back of the store was a spacious room where prescriptions were filled. There was a white-tiled laboratory, too, where Bob Clarke did analytical work for physicians. He had the equipment needed to analyze blood or sputum, to count bacteria in milk or to quickly discover the nature of poisons which patients might have taken by accident or otherwise.

However, only two other people knew that this laboratory was also used in helping to solve many of the bigger crimes. The same instruments necessary in routine analytical work could be used to examine clues, but here also were ultra-microscopes, calibrators, calipers, finger-printing equipment, moulage material, and a hundred and one other things more suited to the needs of a criminologist than a druggist. But only two people knew of that, for the laboratory was a *sanctum sanctorium.* The two who did know, were Theodore Warrick and Dave Small, a classmate of Bob Clarke's. Bob had needed a man to take care of the store when the Crimson Mask was on a hunt for criminals, and his close friend, altruistic-minded Dave Small filled the bill.

The young man behind the counter now was good-looking in a rugged sort of way. He had a pleasant face and clear, laughing eyes—but they could become as icy as Arctic wastes when occasion demanded.

A short, rather pudgy man, with fair hair and healthy pink cheeks came from the back room. Dave Small, Bob Clarke's assistant pharmacist and the Crimson Mask's aide looked little like a man who held such a secret as that this drugstore was the Crimson Mask's headquarters and the quiet young man who compounded prescriptions was the Mask.

"Quiet, eh, Bob?" Dave Small asked, with a sigh.

Bob Clarke grinned. "Do you mean the drugstore business or the other? Well, in either case, don't plan on retiring just yet. Every minute of the day and night, somewhere warped minds are concocting new angles on how to make money without labor. There's always something in the wind." He sighed. "Well, while we wait, let's pretend to be busy. Suppose we change the stock from that third shelf to a show case. Maybe if we display those vitamin capsules, somebody around here will buy them for their kids. Heaven knows there are too many pale faces and thin bodies in this neighborhood."

Dave Small grunted. "Buy 'em, did you say? If the mother of some brood of kids so much as glances at those vitamin capsules, you'll make her a present of a month's supply."

They went to work on the show case first and were half through when Dave Small gave a low, excited ejaculation. Beneath the counter a small red bulb was winking. That meant a call on the private line that Warrick used. Bob Clarke walked quickly to the back room, climbed a flight of stairs and closed a door behind him. That door looked as if it were fashioned of oak panels, but in reality it was created of strong steel.

HE ANSWERED the phone and listened without interrupting as Warrick appraised him of what had happened at the construction job.

"Looks interesting," Bob Clarke commented then. "First of all we must check with the morgue. Suppose you be there in say, an hour, to meet the estimable Dr. Hugo Danton whom you have asked to examine the corpse."

Clarke returned to the drugstore and chuckled softly when he saw Dave Small wrapping two boxes of vitamin capsules for a woman who had two undernourished children tugging at her skirts. Dave coughed as he handed over the package.

"Those pills are just samples, Mrs. O'Morrissy," he murmured. "They don't cost us a cent. You try 'em and let's see how they work. If those good-looking kids of yours get pink cheeks like mine, I'll see if we can't find some more samples. The cod-liver oil? Oh—fifteen cents will cover it."

Dave gravely rang up the sum which represented about one fifth the actual wholesale price of the bottle of cod-liver oil. He opened the door for the woman and bowed her out with as courtly a gesture as if a limousine had been waiting at the curb for her.

"Samples, eh?" Bob Clarke derided.

"Well, I—" Dave looked flustered. "Oh, damn it, you'd have done the same thing yourself… Bob, what was the call? Action?"

Bob nodded. "I'm not sure. It's about the death of George Sellmer this afternoon. You heard the news flash—he fell off a girder. Warrick seems to think something lies behind it, and that Sellmer was murdered. Stick with the store, Dave. I'm going to fix myself up to look like an eminent doctor and visit the morgue. When I'm ready to pass inspection, I'll buzz you."

Twenty minutes later Dave slowly shook his head in admiration.

"Bob," he declared, "you're getting better all the time—and I thought you'd already reached the peak of perfection."

For Bob Clarke had become middle-aged, sedate looking, with black hair, striped trousers, and a well fitted black coat and pince-nez. A physician's thermometer was clipped to his vest pocket. A small Vandyke beard gave him a quietly important appearance.

He drew on a pair of kidskin gloves, nodded to Dave, and preceded him into the store. When he emerged to the street, several pedestrians who knew Bob Clarke well gave not the slightest sign of recognition…

Ex-Police Commissioner Warrick, impatiently striding up and down a short beat in front of the morgue, saw a man alight from a taxi, but paid no attention to him. The stranger halted and waited until Warrick passed near him. Then he stuck out a gloved hand.

"Can it be that you have forgotten Dr. Danton, Mr. Warrick?" he asked, smiling.

Warrick gulped in admiration and shook hands.

"Some day," he said in an undertone, "I'll see a milk wagon horse acting strangely familiar and I'll think it's you. You amaze me—Dr. Danton."

Warrick had already made the arrangements necessary to inspect the corpse. The coroner's report was given to them when they entered the morgue, and the Crimson Mask studied it.

"Nothing here," he told Warrick. "No traces of any drug. Suppose we have look at the shoes Sellmer was wearing."

They were brought out. The Crimson Mask turned them over and indicated the thick gobs of dried mud adhering to the instep.

"See that? Suppose you were standing on a girder high up in the air. Suppose you slipped and felt yourself falling. You'd automatically try to brace yourself. You'd try to dig into the steel with your feet and they'd only slide off with all your weight and strength against them. Any mud on your shoes would be knocked away. The soles would show streaks of oxidized orange paint used on the girders. Somehow, Mr. Warrick, Sellmer was rendered incapable of saving himself. I don't know how, but we have eliminated the use of stupefying drugs. Suppose we look at the corpse?"

The Mask and Warrick followed an attendant into the storage room. Sellmer lay on a slab with an identifying tag around one ankle. The Mask bent over the corpse and made a thorough examination of the flesh, especially that around the dead man's right arm and hand. He shook his head slowly and sighed.

"It's a complete puzzle," he admitted. "I believe, with you, that Sellmer was murdered—and cleverly, too. This is one of the few instances where the killer left no clue. You were saying they've discovered sabotage on the building. Perhaps Sellmer discovered who was responsible and was killed before he could talk. That's only a theory. It seems to me that if Sellmer had found anything definite, he would have gone to the police at once and not asked to have the Crimson Mask investigate. I'm going over to that building, Mr. Warrick. I want to look around. It's almost time for the men to quit work and I'll have a free hand."

Warrick stroked his chin. "I think it's murder," he said. "Also I haven't been idle since Sellmer died. Here are the facts. Sellmer and Whitner, both dead, were members of a five-man partnership organized to construct this building. The surviving members are Oliver Durthen, Jim Stark and Matt Karling. The last two gentlemen were by my side when Sellmer plunged to his death. So—you still have to watch over three persons, because my idea is that the murderer is intent on wiping out the men who control that building."

The Mask fell into step with Warrick as they headed toward the exit.

"Then it appears that someone wants full possession of the building," he mused. "Why? There can be only one reason—greed. The share which Sellmer and Whitner owned will probably pass into the keeping of the three survivors—one of whom *might* be our man. Suppose you check that angle, find out who really profits financially from the two deaths. Let me know later tonight."

The two men parted outside the morgue. The Mask took a taxi which deposited him not far away from the skyscraping towers of the Sheridan Apartments. He sauntered onto the grounds and while he seemed to be just another kibitzer, his eyes and ears were wide open. Three workers were pulling off their overalls and talking in low voices. The Mask drifted closer to them.

"I don't like it," one was saying. "If anything else happens, I quit. This job is jinxed, that's what. First Whitner falls off the girder, then Sellmer. Them two guys knew how to handle themselves on jobs like this. They were iron workers just like us. Then, about an hour after Sellmer is dead, some nit-wit drops a hammer and busts poor old Bill Bagley's shoulder. If he'd got that hammer on the noggin', he'd be as dead as Sellmer right now."

"Yeah," another offered morosely. "When a job gets jinxed, it's no place for healthy guys. Me—I'm takin' a rivetin' job at the shipyards if anybody else gets hurt."

THE MASK wandered away with a fresh idea. If the murderer were intent on slowing up or even completely stopping all work on the building, then his efforts were fast becoming successful. Iron workers, men who risk their lives high above the ground on precarious footholds, are almost all superstitious. Every one of them would quit if another death or accident occurred.

By casual questioning that aroused no suspicion, the Mask found the girder upon which Sellmer had ridden to his death. Making sure he was unobserved, the Mask examined the surface intently. He saw no scratches or marks indicating that Sellmer had tried to save himself. Apparently, the man had simply collapsed and had offered no resistance to his horrible fate. More than ever, the Mask was positive that this had been murder, accomplished by someone highly skillful in hiding clues.

Gradually, the workers left the premises. The Mask slipped into a tool shed to wait until all except the two or three watchmen were gone. He wanted a look at the derrick which had lifted the girder. Unless he found something there—and he had no idea what to look for—he was completely stumped.

The lower part of the huge building was already walled in and he could easily climb the stairs until he reached the open construction work. From there on the going would be more difficult, but the Mask gave that no thought.

It was growing dark when he finally emerged from the tool house, slipped into the building and started up the stairs. So far he had seen no signs of any watchmen, but he was careful not to expose himself. Watchmen frequently are armed and the men on this particular job would be jittery from the events that had so far happened. The Mask had no desire to be a target for their bullets.

When he reached the fifth floor, he hesitated a moment. He was almost certain that he had heard the sound of shoes scuffling along the rough flooring. His hand darted toward a hip pocket and the gun that nestled there. He drew it, pushed down the safety and headed in the direction of that sound. The various apartments had already been cemented into shape and there were scores of doors along the corridor.

Something scraped behind him. He started to turn, but at that instant a thick wooden club whizzed through the air and collided with his skull. The Mask clawed at air. His gun dropped to the cement floor, and he followed it a second later.

The attacker was obscured by shadows, but he seemed to be slender. He stepped over the Mask, grinned viciously and used the club again. Satisfied that his victim was completely unconscious, the man hastily turned the Mask over and studied his features. He grunted in dismay at sight of a man of such professional appearance.

Then he shrugged, seized the Mask's ankles and dragged him into one of the rooms. Making certain, again, that his victim was unconscious, he hurried away, climbing to the top of the great building with the dexterity of an ape.

When he reached the derrick controls, he sent the great chain down to the ground. There was a small platform elevator used in conveying heavy materials to the upper stories. He used this to reach the ground where he hastily affixed the steel chain to that same girder from which Sellmer had fallen.

The elevator whisked him back to the floor where the Mask lay sprawled out. A glance told him there was plenty of time, but still he worked hurriedly. Soon the great girder was slowly moving up until it was level with the window beneath which the Mask lay. Outside, it had grown so dark that the movements of the killer were well veiled.

CHAPTER III

A MATTER
OF BUSINESS

MOMENTS LATER, the Mask recovered consciousness, with a feeling of buoyancy, as though he were floating through thin air. He opened his eyes and saw nothing but darkness. His stomach felt as though it was being pressed by something hard, and head and legs were certainly on anything but an even keel with his torso.

Gingerly, he extended one hand, found nothing but empty space. He turned his head—and gasped. He was lying across a girder and being hoisted high above the ground. From the position of the street lights he figured he was probably near the fifteenth story of the building and still going up. He reached back, got a grip on the girder and gradually drew himself up until he straddled the long steel platform.

The Mask was no iron worker, and dizzying heights had the same weakening effect on his nerves that they would have on anyone not connected with this kind of work. It took all his will power and stamina to clear his brain.

The stories of the building slid by silently. Only one thing was in his favor. The killer, wherever and whoever he was, could not see that he had recovered consciousness.

The Mask saw the heavy chains linked around the ends of the girder. If he could reach one of them and cling to it, he still might save himself, unless the killer planned to drop the cable and girder both. Soon now, the height would correspond with the open steel work of the higher parts of the building.

The dangling girder was ten feet from the wall, but the Mask had already determined to risk a leap across that quick path to eternity. If he could reach the solid girders of the building, he might be able to negotiate a dangerous path to some safer spot. It was his only hope.

Then, as he inched his way toward the steel cables, a new motion sent his wits rocking. The girder was beginning to swing. Each arc took him closer and closer to the brick sides of the building. The killer was trying to smash him against the bricks before he sent him crashing to the ground!

The Mask's fingers bled as he clung to the girder. He had been in tight spots before, but always where he raced something vulnerable. There was no fear in the Mask's heart—only grim despair. A man cannot fight thin air, a strip of steel or a solid brick wall.

One end of the girder struck the wall. The Mask looked up. He was within three stories of the uncompleted sections where he might have a chance. He held on doggedly, praying that the girder would not hit the wall with such jarring effect that he would be thrown off.

But those prayers were not answered. A moment later the whole side of the girder hit. The Mask slipped, and only the mighty strength of trained muscles kept him from falling. Then the girder was swinging out again. The next blow against the wall was bound to dislodge him.

He wound his legs around the girder, gripped its edges with all the power he could muster.

The girder was swinging back now, but the crane was lifting it at the same time. The end of the wall construction passed by. The Mask loosened his grasp and prepared for the one long chance that spelled the difference between life and death. Clinging to his narrow support with his hands, he drew himself up until he was kneeling. There was no time to worm his way to the thick chains and the probable support they might render. Instead he had to perch where he was and take his chances.

THE STEEL supports of the building came at him with lightning-like speed. He drew a sharp breath and leaped. He aimed for an upright pillar and reached it. Arms and legs wrapped themselves around it with the grim tautness of despair. Sweat poured down his face. He clung there until his heart stopped pounding and a quick look over his shoulder told him that he was comparatively safe. The girder, during its outward swing, had climbed another half story.

Working carefully, he wormed his way around until his feet hit a solid girder. He felt like dropping onto it and sprawling out to rest, but there was no rest until he was safe. Balancing himself on the narrow support, he gauged the distance to the next upright and put all thoughts of the height out of his mind.

Like a tightrope walker, he reached the next upright. It took minutes before he saw a ladder which led down into the building and the solid floors not far below. There was just one more balancing act to do—one more girder to cross. Midway of it he was suddenly aware that the hum of the crane motors had stopped. Then he heard a single shot and a bullet hit an upright behind him, ricocheted and whizzed by his head.

The killer had seen that his plans had gone awry, and was trying to make sure his victim would never reach the ground alive. The Mask realized the precariousness of his position. He was completely exposed to the gunfire of the murderer somewhere above him.

He began running across the girder. Once he slipped but some miracle saved him, for he recovered his balance quickly. Then he was sliding down the ladder, not bothering with rungs. Another shot rang out and the bullet screeched about a foot away from him.

His feet hit the solid cement of the highest completed floor. A wave of weakness swept over him which he put out of his mind only by the most intense concentration.

His own gun was missing—stolen by the killer who had slugged him. Defenseless, the Mask sought safety in retreat. He went down the partially completed stairways as fast as he could travel. Once he stopped to listen intently, but no sound of pursuit reached his ears.

When he finally reached the ground he saw that the elevator hooked up to the outside of the building, was down. The killer had ridden it to safety. He might be lurking anywhere in the darkness; still primed to kill. The Mask raced across a cleared portion of ground and ducked behind a stack of kegs filled with rivets. There he recovered his breath and steadied outraged nerves.

Five minutes later he climbed into a taxi, fumbled in his pockets and found a cigarette. Lighting it, he leaned back and relaxed for the first time in what had seemed to be a decade.

Now he no longer had any doubts but that Sellmer and Whitner had been murdered. Not in the way an attempt had been made on his own life, but in a more subtle manner. One thing the Mask knew now—that a man atop a girder high above the ground will dig his heels and fingers against the steel with all the strength it is possible to muster. Neither of the two previous victims had done that, which meant they had somehow been made incapable of trying to save themselves.

The Mask dismissed his cab in a well-lighted business area. He went into a tobacco store, made a small purchase and killed a few moments there. When he emerged, he walked rapidly north. It was possible that the killer might have trailed him and the Mask wanted to know before he went into action.

WHEN HE was absolutely certain that no one followed him, he turned into a drugstore, entered a phone booth and dialed Theodore Warrick's private number.

"This is Dr. Danton," he said. "The patient displays plenty of life yet. In fact he nearly turned the tables on me. I'm positive of my diagnosis now. Have you learned anything?"

"Can I talk freely?" Warrick asked and when he received an affirmative reply he went on. "There is something odd about all this. I told you the names of the first partners in the Sheridan Apartments enterprise. Well, that job runs way up into the millions, and one man is financing those five. His name is Jay Jens—you've heard of him. He loaned money to the partners individually. Wouldn't handle it by any other method. Each loan was for a million dollars, and—listen to this—Jay Jens insisted that each partner be insured for that amount with himself named as beneficiary. So you see he gets his money back at their death. It's just an ordinary business transaction, but on the heels of murder it looks suspicious."

The Mask glanced out of the window of his telephone booth. The store was empty except for a fountain clerk who dozed over a magazine.

"I think I'm safe here," he said. "But, listen—how could Jay Jens profit? Upon the deaths of Sellmer and Whitner he got back only the amount he had loaned. He can't get his principal back also. Under the provisions of business insurance, if the insured dies, the lender simply gets back the exact amount he has invested. The surplus goes to the estate of the dead man. However, Jay Jens may know something, and if there was ever a hard-headed, cement-hearted business man, he's it. I'll have a talk with him immediately. In fact, I think I'll look him and his methods over before I reveal myself. Thanks for the information."

When the Mask reached the home of Jay Jens he found it to be a huge house, surrounded by tall trees and carefully trimmed hedges. The Mask quietly leaped over a hedge, dropped to the ground and sought the protection of a big bush. Removing the Vandyke beard, he scraped a hole in the soft ground and buried it. Then he took a crimson mask from an especially created pocket of his coat. The killer had apparently searched him, but the Mask would have defied anyone to find this piece of crimson-colored silk.

He affixed the mask and crawled toward the house. There might be guards posted outside, or watchdogs. He did not want to tangle with either, for his nerves were still shaky from that horrible few moments on top of the girder.

No one challenged him and he reached the side of the house beneath a window that was open about two inches. He risked a quick look inside, saw that the room was empty and then straightened up. Sliding the window wide open, he hoisted himself over the sill and quietly closed the window again.

There was a big desk in one corner of the room and he moved toward it as silently as a cat. Briefly he examined papers strewn on the desk, found nothing of interest, and tackled the drawers. In a lower one he found a file labeled "Sheridan Apartments."

He drew out the papers and studied them intently—and emitted a gasp when the full significance of his find became clear. Jay Jens had loaned five million dollars to the five partners engaged in the construction of the vast buildings. He had carefully crossed out two names—those of the dead men—and credited the amounts loaned them as being paid in full. Apparently the insurance company had already indicated they were ready to pay. But what interested the Mask even more was the fact that Jay Jens had scribbled a few notes pertaining to the finances of the remaining three partners. There was one sum under the heading of

The Mask risked a leap across to the ironwork.

deficit. The Crimson Mask knew then that the work on the buildings had eaten away all the money loaned by Jens.

Why was he interested in figuring this out? Did he intend to take control of the building, forcing the other three partners out of it, possibly using the two million he would receive from the insurance company as necessary cash?

It seemed so, and under the crimson silk, the Mask's forehead was wrinkled in deep lines of thought as he stowed the papers back into the file and carefully replaced it in the drawer. At least here was something to work on—a logical suspect either to eliminate or crush under a mantle of facts. Even though Jay Jens should prove to be wholly innocent, through him the Mask might obtain a lead.

He opened the big center drawer next and his eyes fell upon a sheaf of correspondence from several banks. He read these letters, all of which had note notices attached. The Mask's eyes narrowed. Jens was not quite the wealthy man that he seemed. Some of his investments had gone sour and he was desperately in need of cash.

How could he obtain such sums as were indicated on these bank notices that he needed? There was one way—by cashing in on the insurance policies covering his loans to the men engaged in building the Sheridan Apartments. He could not demand payment of these loans, for they were not yet due—but if those men died he would derive a quick million dollars from the death of each one.

The Mask put the papers back in the place he had found them.

CHAPTER IV

LADY OF MYSTERY

AS THE MASK closed the drawer softly he suddenly jerked erect. He had heard no sound in the house, but he had been concentrating on those papers and someone might have slipped into the room. At least the gun now pressing against the back of his neck had no ghostly qualities.

The Mask raised both hands shoulder high and slowly arose. He turned, tense and ready to leap straight into the face of that gun if he saw the slightest chance of surprising the person who menaced him.

Then the Crimson Mask's consternation grew even greater. It was a girl who kept the gun trained on him. An exceptional girl too. Ordinary girls did not have such a smooth, creamy complexion, nor such full, beautifully curved lips and cool, gray eyes. She was neatly dressed too—not expensively, but she certainly possessed both a knack for wearing clothes well and recognizing those which looked best on her.

"Good evening," the Mask said calmly.

Her eyes seemed riveted on that crimson mask. She backed away a few steps.

"Don't move!" she warned in a whisper. "You're a thief or you wouldn't be wearing a mask. I'm going to call the police."

"I hardly blame you," the Mask agreed. "However, I am not a burglar, although I confess to making my entry to this house by a means any crook might have taken. Perhaps you have heard of me. I'm the Crimson Mask."

Her eyes flicked over him from head to foot. The gun in her hand never wobbled a hair's breadth.

"Perhaps you are—perhaps you are not," she countered. She cocked her head suddenly, then gestured with the gun. "I'm not sure what I'll do, but someone is coming. Get behind that big drape and stay there. Hurry!"

The Mask did not wait to argue. Heavy footsteps were approaching. He ducked behind the curtain and cursed himself for allowing a slip of a girl to force him to jump through a hoop of her own making. How much better off was he now? The girl still had her gun and she looked as though she would shoot if he gave her much provocation.

He parted the drapes a fraction of an inch and peered out into the room. The girl was hastily stuffing the gun into her purse. A man was striding across the floor with outstretched hand and a specious smile on his face—Jay Jens, the financier who was wealthy enough to hand out five millions of dollars in a lump sum.

Jens had been good-looking in his youth and was still a striking personality. Good will was in his smiling face, but his narrow, crafty eyes belied the expression on his lips. Jay Jens had accumulated his fortune by shrewdness. Never quite dishonest, some of his deals carried with them a slight odor.

"So sorry to keep you waiting," Jens boomed. "We'll get right down to business. Your work is quite satisfactory—what I've seen of it, at least. All we have to do is agree on compensation for your services."

The girl's eyes flashed toward the curtain behind which the Mask was hidden.

"Yes, of course, Mr. Jens."

She started to walk toward a chair facing the big desk. Somehow one of her high heels seemed to catch in the rug and she fell forward, flat on her face. Jens rushed to her and raised her.

"I—I tripped," she apologized. "I'm quite all right. Just feel a little woozy. Must have hit my head."

"I'll get you some water!" Jens exclaimed. "Be right back."

AS HE disappeared through the door, the girl raised her head quickly. She faced the drapes and spoke in a low voice.

"Now is your chance. Run, you fool!"

The Mask came from behind the drapes, bowed slightly and hurried to the window. He opened it, leaped out and closed it again. He saw Jens hurrying back into the room with a decanter and glass in his hand. He saw the girl drink the water gratefully. She was a good actress. Every motion she made carried with it the illusion that she had been hurt. The falling act had been skillfully done, too. Even the Mask had thought it genuine.

He made his way back toward the hedges near the street, wondering just who this girl could be, why she carried a gun and did not seem a stranger to the art of handling it. What was she doing in Jay Jens' home? What did all that talk about her satisfactory services and her pay mean?

Bob Clarke, the Crimson Mask, had found little time to devote to girls. His police sergeant father had left him only enough to help with his education, and Bob had worked all the time he had been in college. The drugstore with all its responsibilities had come after that. To top all that off, he had become the Crimson Mask and as such, his mind was eternally on the problems of fighting crime.

Yet if he could have selected any girl in the world for his own, this one with the creamy skin and gray eyes would have been his choice. And here she was—quite evidently in the pay of a man whom the Crimson Mask suspected of being, at the least, a profiteer from murder.

She might even furnish an important lead. The Mask determined to find out just who she was, and how she came to be involved with Jay Jens.

He knew that she had looked him over carefully, and had probably pigeonholed his height, weight and general contours with her cool, clear-seeing eyes. She would recognize his "doctor's" clothing, too, so if he followed her now, she might recognize him. Therefore, this became a job for Dave Small.

It was almost time for the drugstore to close anyway, so the Mask hurried to a phone and called Dave. He gave him explicit orders, then returned to take up a vigil outside Jay Jens' house.

Twenty minutes later Dave Small sauntered by, paying no attention to the Mask. He stopped beside a big oak tree, leaned against it and lit a cigarette. The Mask walked rapidly away in another direction, secure in the knowledge that Dave would handle things from this end while he obtained a little much needed rest.

Dave Small was a patient individual. Although almost an hour passed, he never moved from his post. Then he saw the girl emerge, recognized her instantly from the Mask's description, and whistled softly in admiration. He crunched out a half-consumed cigarette, watched her hurry up the street, and started a careful job of shadowing.

When the girl turned a corner abruptly, Dave kept right on going and turned the same corner. He swallowed hard when he saw her looking into a store window. He kept on walking, but he felt a little silly. Perhaps something in that window had really attracted her attention, or perhaps she had simply stalled there to see if she was being followed. If so, she certainly had spotted Dave.

HOWEVER, SHE resumed her brisk pace a moment later and Dave emerged from a doorway where he had sought shelter. This time he was more careful. She walked directly across town to a less inviting section of town than that in which Jay Jens had his home.

When her pace slowed, Dave held back. She passed by a cheap-looking brownstone-front house, turned back abruptly, and Dave barely got out of sight in time to avoid being seen. She climbed the steps to the front door, took a key from her pocket, opened the door and disappeared.

Dave made a mental note of the address, but he wasn't satisfied yet. When he reported to the Crimson Mask, he wanted to tell whether this was the girl's home, or whether she was merely visiting someone.

To do this, he had to gain admittance to the place. Dave shrugged. Why not? He doubted that she would recognize him, even if they met face to face, for she had had only a fleeting glimpse of him as he rounded the corner.

Dave looked around, saw that he was unobserved, and ran up the steps to the door. Did he dare risk pushing the bell? On impulse, he grasped the door knob and it turned easily. The door was open. Something warned Dave that this might be a trap, but his instincts were not as keen as those of the Mask. He decided to take a chance.

He stepped into a dismally-lighted hallway, saw stairs leading to the floor above and after he had gently closed the door, he made his way up them. Nothing stirred. He heard no voices, no footsteps—not even the swish of a skirt to indicate that the girl was in this house.

Dave had a mild case of jitters when he reached the second floor landing. He suddenly realized that his impetuousness might have placed him in a bad spot. The utter silence of the place was almost uncanny. If someone had screamed in his ear, Dave felt as though he might actually have enjoyed it.

"I'm a fool," he told himself. "I shouldn't have come in here. Even the Mask doesn't know much about this girl. Maybe she's right in with the killers and if I'm found here—what will happen to me won't be funny."

Impulse told him to beat a hasty retreat but a certain doggedness kept him going just a little longer. As long as he was this far, he might as well go on. He passed two closed doors and saw that no light streamed from beneath them. But as he looked at another door at the end of the corridor, lights were turned on inside.

Dave crept a little closer, and placed an ear against the panels.

"Go on in," a voice growled from behind him. "The lady knows you're comin'."

Dave gulped, straightened up and looked into the uncompromising muzzle of a gun. To his eyes it looked bigger than the entrance of the Lincoln Tunnel. Behind the gun was a scowling man with all the earmarks of a thug.

The door opened, and the girl stood there, in full view. She was smiling, but there was cold fury in her eyes.

"You heard what Mickey said. Come on in and tell me just why you followed me here."

The gun prodded Dave's spine.

"Yeah," the thug called Mickey rasped. "Speak up! Then I can put a slug through your dumb skull that much quicker. You walked in here, pal, but they'll carry you out."

CHAPTER V

LURE TO DEATH

WHEN ONE-THIRTY in the morning had arrived, Bob Clarke looked worried. Dave's assignment had been simple. Trailing a girl was not difficult, and she must have gone somewhere by now.

Why hadn't Dave called? Had he walked into a trap? Was the girl associated with the killers responsible for sabotage and murder on the Sheridan Apartments job?

Another half an hour passed and still no word. Bob Clarke waited no longer. Dave must be in trouble. Nothing except physical restraint would have kept him from calling by now.

Clarke sat down before a mirror and applied a make-up which he used when it became necessary to work freely without a mask. It changed his appearance radically, but the disguise was so devised that if anyone tried to remove it, that would have been impossible.

There were no false whiskers nor aluminum cups to enlarge the nostrils or the cheeks. Only a clever skin dye, a coloring to change the hue of his naturally brown hair, bits of putty securely fastened between cheek and gums, and a radical reshaping of his eyebrows did the job. Even Warrick or Dave Small would not have recognized this man for Bob Clarke.

He slid a gun into a hip holster, placed his crimson mask in a well concealed pocket and left the premises by a route that took him through alleys and courtyards. The Mask had but one way to solve this problem of Dave's disappearance. He had to find that girl! The sole method lay in making Jay Jens reveal her identity.

The Mask wondered if those cool gray eyes set in that lovely face were just a blind for a crafty crooked nature. He prided himself on being a fairly good judge of character, but even experts missed their shots at times.

The Mask boldly entered Jay Jens' estate once more. He knew the layout from his previous experience. The same window was still open. Jay Jens was seated behind his desk, studying sheafs of papers and making notes occasionally. Deep in his work, he heard no sound.

In fact, it would have required some exceptionally good hearing to have detected the Mask's stealthy movements. Jay Jens felt, rather than heard, the presence of an intruder. He looked up, gave vent to a startled oath and dug into a top desk drawer for a gun.

"I wouldn't," the Mask said calmly. "You're covered, or does this thing in my hand look like a water pistol?

"What do you want?" Jens barked.

"Information. I'm the Crimson Mask. Whether or not I may be able to help you depends wholly upon your own attitude, Mr. Jens. You've heard of me. You know I'm not a crook, despite the mask that covers my face. You know the police trust me and that I have never knowingly harmed anyone who is innocent."

"Yes, I know that about the Crimson Mask," Jens admitted. "But how do I know you really are the Mask? Anyone could put on one of those masks and claim to be the Crimson Mask. But suppose I grant that I am satisfied with your identity. What do you want with me? How can I help you?"

THE MASK leaned against the corner of Jens' desk.

"By being perfectly honest with me," he said. "The information I need is simple. Who was that girl you interviewed tonight?"

Jens gasped. "How in the world did you know she was here? I didn't even know she was coming myself. But if that's all you are after, I don't think I'll violate any confidences by talking. First, however, I'll exact a promise from you to tell me whether or not that girl is honest. If she has aroused the interest of the Crimson Mask, there must be something wrong with her. Is it a deal?"

The Mask nodded.

"Good," Jens said. "Her name is—"

He opened his desk drawer carefully and lifted out a blue notebook with two fingers. Above all, he did, not want this crimson-masked gunman to think he was reaching for the weapon in the drawer.

"Ah, yes—here it is. Name—Gloria Sanders. Address—Fifty-five Western Avenue, a lodging house, I believe. She came here to get a job as my secretary. I've been practically retired for some time, but recently I've thought of getting back into business. A big real estate deal. Now—I've told you all I know. Is it safe to employ that girl?"

"I don't know," the Mask replied. "There is some reason to believe that she may be connected with crooks. If I verify that, you most certainly will know about it. Now, if you don't mind, just lift that gun out of your desk and place it before me."

Jens automatically started to obey the orders. "Well, it won't be necessary to let me know. If you even suspect her, she's out so far as I'm concerned. I... Say, what's the idea of asking me for the gun?"

The Mask's weapon gestured impatiently. Jens produced his revolver. The Mask extracted the bullets and threw them out of the window. Then he laid the weapon down on the desk.

"In my business," he said softly, "you learn that it is dangerous to trust anyone—even those who seem to be above reproach. Good night, Mr. Jens, and thank you for the information."

The Mask backed toward the window, and a moment later was racing toward the sidewalk. He had what he wanted, but other thoughts were humming through his mind, too. Jens had been amiable enough, but that matter-of-fact statement concerning his entering the real estate business had struck home.

Was he preparing to profit by the deaths of Sellmer and Whitner? Had he devised some sly method of wrestling control of that giant enterprise from the other three surviving members of the original partnership of five?

The Mask was in a hurry. Without question, Dave was in some serious trouble and with only the girl's address to go on, precious time might be used up. The Mask soared over the hedge, landed lightly and drew back into the shadows. A car was pulling up in front of Jens' home. One man got out, looked around slowly and then entered the gate. The Mask knew him. It was Oliver Durthen, one of the men involved in the Sheridan Apartments project.

IT FLASHED across the Mask then, that Durthen had not been at the scene when Sellmer had plunged to his death. The only two members of the partnership with cast iron alibis were Stark and Karling.

When an opportunity presented itself, the Mask determined to check on Durthen's whereabouts at the time of the killing. It might be desirable to examine any alibi which Jens might offer as well.

But now Dave Small occupied the Mask's mind. Removing his crimson domino mask, he hailed a taxi and went straight to the girl's address. It was an ungodly hour to call on a girl who lived in a rooming house, but the Mask put aside such inconsequentialities.

He rang the bell. After several minutes a woman of about sixty admitted him.

"I'm looking for Gloria Sanders," he told her. "I know it's an odd time to be calling, but this happens to be most important. It's about a job she was seeking."

"But she isn't home," the landlady explained. "I don't understand why she is out so late. Usually she's in bed by midnight. If you wish to wait, the parlor is on your right."

"Thanks." The Mask removed his hat and sat down in a comfortable chair. "I'll stick around for awhile. Please don't stay up on my account. If Miss Sanders arrives, we'll discuss this matter here. Thanks again."

He waited about ten minutes before he softly climbed the stairs. He listened outside several doors, heard the sound of rhythmic breathing, and passed on to one room after another until he found one that was unoccupied. He opened the door, using a small piece of metal for a key, closed it behind him and turned on the lights.

It was a neat room, smelling faintly of good perfume. On a dresser he saw a picture. It was a likeness of the girl he knew as Gloria Sanders. He walked over to it, studied the features and sighed faintly. If she was an active participant in this whirligig of murder, he would never judge people by appearances again. Then his eyes fell on a comb, brush and mirror, engraved with initials. He grunted in surprise for the initials were S. G.—Gloria Sanders in reverse. Was she living under an assumed name?

The Mask heard a phone bell jangle in the distance. He darted out of the room, ran down the stairs lightly and was seated in the parlor when the landlady entered the hall to answer the phone. From her conversation the Mask knew that the caller must be Gloria Sanders. The landlady hung up, walked into the parlor and nodded to the Mask.

"Miss Sanders just called. She's staying with a sick friend, but she said that if you're here about the job with Mr. Jay Jens, she'd like to have you go and see her. She says it won't bother her girl friend any—I guess she ain't that sick. Will you go? She needs a job very bad. In fact, she owes me two weeks' rent now, but I haven't the heart to make any trouble for her."

The Mask arose. "Of course I'll go. And if things work out satisfactorily, I'll see that she is advanced money enough to settle your account. Now—the address."

"Oh, yes! It's a house on the corner of Thorpe and Reveler Streets. She'll leave the porch light burning so you can't miss it. She's a good girl, Mister. There ain't nothing phony about her."

THE MASK went out into the night. He knew the approximate location of the address, and didn't like it much. The place was no more than a dozen blocks from his drugstore and the section, was filled with cheap joints which crooks occupied when they were on the lam. He shrugged and had himself driven there.

The porch light was on, revealing the place as a brownstone front which in its day had probably been considered quite smart. Now it was rundown and dirty-looking. The Mask climbed the steps, pushed the bell button and waited. The door opened as his hand covertly sought the reassuring feel of his gun. He relaxed, for Gloria Sanders stood in the doorway smiling at him.

"You must be from Mr. Jens," she said. "Please come in."

The Mask stepped into the hallway. She closed the door, walked past him and turned around to face him. The smile died away and her eyes narrowed in hatred.

"Welcome—Mr. Crimson Mask! How does it feel to meet people who can think faster than you?"

Two guns were jammed against the Mask's ribs. He raised his hands promptly, felt himself relieved of his gun, and then two leering thugs lined themselves on either side of the angry-eyed girl.

"We'll take you upstairs to see a certain fog-headed person," the girl said blandly, "had an idea he might work for you."

"And after that?" the Mask asked coldly.

Her lips curled in contempt. "What do you think?"

She preceded him up the stairs and the two gunmen followed, their weapons at a ready angle. Both knew just how wily the Crimson Mask could be, and they were ready to send a hail of lead into his hide at the slightest suggestion of trickery.

With each step, the Mask's mind registered disappointment. The girl was in league with a gang. Moreover, she had called the landlady of her boarding house and deliberately lured the Mask into this trap. Yet how could she have known that the Crimson Mask was on her trail? Only

Jay Jens knew that he had her address. Jay Jens—and possibly Oliver Durthen. Jens might have boasted of the Crimson Mask's visit and told Durthen what he had come for.

Truly those two men now rated a thorough investigation if—the Mask thought grimly—he was ever in a position to investigate anyone again.

The girl unlocked a door. The Mask was suddenly seized by the two thugs and thrown bodily through the doorway. He tripped and fell heavily. The girl's laugh grated in his ears. Then he looked up and groaned.

Dave Small was there. He stood against a heavy, old-fashioned drain pipe about six inches from the wail. He had been cruelly strapped to the pipe and there were ugly bruises across his face.

CHAPTER VI

DANGEROUS ESCAPE

DAVE FINALLY raised his sagging head and looked at the Mask. But no recognition dawned, for the Mask was disguised in a manner which Dave had not seen before. Instantly the Mask determined to fool even Dave. The girl had admitted that she and the crooks believed Dave worked for the Mask.

If that idea were carried through, they might force Dave to talk, or one of their number might recognize him as the assistant pharmacist at Bob Clarke's drugstore. Either way would mean the end of the Crimson Mask's anonymity. Above all, this must not happen. Dave must in no way be associated with the Crimson Mask.

The Mask got to his feet and brushed off his clothes.

"Looks like we're in the same boat," he said to Dave. "What they got against you?"

Dave groaned. "I don't even know what this is all about. A friend of mine gave me the address of this house—or anyway I thought he did. I was going to call on him tonight. The door was open. Nobody answered my ring, so I just walked in. Then they grabbed me."

"Must be a kidnaping," the Mask said vehemently. "The same thing happened to me. Maybe I can get you loose. Funny those mugs didn't tie me up.

The Mask walked over to Dave and fumbled with his bonds. Dave's face was bland and innocent, but deep in his eyes lurked suspicion. This man was just a spy, sent to make Dave talk and reveal his connection with the Crimson Mask. That explained why they had not tied him up, too, or handled him more roughly than they had.

Suddenly the door was flung open. The girl and three men came in. Two of the men were the thugs who had captured Dave and the Mask. The third was old, stooped, and almost thin enough to be transparent. He had yellow teeth, stained from years of tobacco chewing. His head was bald except for a fringe of gray hair, but his eyes made the Mask wince, They were cold and venomous-like those of a startled and angry serpent. His face was as pale as a ghost's and his lips kept moving, as though talking to himself had been a habit too long to be broken.

"You feel like singin' yet, rat?" he said as he stepped up to Dave. "Or would you like some more of the same treatment the boys handed out? They'll bust your jaw this time."

"I tell you I don't know who the Crimson Mask is," Dave protested. "You can beat my head off, and I couldn't tell you."

The old man snarled something under his breath, stepped up to the Mask and grabbed his wrist. He had skinny, but strong fingers. They bit into the Mask's flesh. He yanked himself free, but those talons clung like steel hooks. Instantly both of the thugs rushed over to the Mask and kept their guns trained on him.

"Then take a good look at this man," the skinny crook yelped. "Take a good look at him. He is the Crimson Mask!"

For a fleeting instant Dave's eyes almost gave away his alarm and surprise. Then he shrugged his shoulders.

"Maybe he is. How would I know? Look—tell me what you want. If it's money, I can raise a couple of hundred dollars…"

"Quiet," the skinny man snapped.

He let go of the Mask's arm, took the girl aside and they talked hurriedly. They made no pretense of secrecy.

"Fat Face," the girl said, "is on the level. I must have made a mistake. Now that I have a good look at him again, I don't think he is the man who trailed me from Jay Jens' house."

THE SKINNY man rubbed his chin with the back of his thumb.

"Yeah, I guess you're right. We know this other guy is the Crimson Mask, though. No mistake there. If the other sap knew him, they'd have started to talk fast when we left them alone. They didn't, because I listened at the door. Yeah, it's tough on Fat Face, but we better get rid of him."

"Why do that?" the girl asked. "Let him remain tied up. We'll take care of the Crimson Mask and blow out of here. This place is too dangerous now. Suppose we make some plans—downstairs where we can talk."

The Mask, standing against the wall between his two guards, tensed for action. Both thugs had put their guns away and relied on their brute strength to overpower the Mask if he attempted an escape. The girl and the skinny man headed toward the door.

Suddenly the Mask's right fist sailed upward and he pivoted on his heel at the same instant. The fist cracked against the jaw of the thug on his right. The man's head bobbed back, hit the wall hard, and he slid to the floor as ungracefully as a falling sack of potatoes.

The second thug danced back a few steps and went for his gun. The Mask gave a long leap that carried him halfway across the floor. He swept the girl aside, wound a brawny arm around the skinny man's neck and pulled him toward the one window in the room.

The skinny man possessed abnormal strength for one so scrawny. He battled every inch of the way, but the Mask was younger and more powerful. The second thug was closing in, gun raised. It came down, but the Mask avoided the blow by giving the skinny man a hard shove and ducking under the gun. Once he had a glimpse of the girl, standing near the doorway, one hand near her throat and horror in her eyes.

This could not last. No one realized this more than the Mask. The thug he had knocked down was slowly getting to his feet. A thick skull had softened the jar of the blow and enabled him to recover conscious-ness quickly. The second crook was hovering nearby, still trying to get in a bone-smashing blow.

The Mask suddenly seized the skinny man by both wrists, forced his hands up and shoved him back against the window. For a fraction of a second he held him there and then he saw that the game was lost. Both thugs were closing in. The Mask gave his victim a hard push, sent him reeling into the middle of the room and then raised his hands high.

"I know when I'm licked," he said coolly. "You can't blame a man for trying."

The skinny crook yowled a string of curses and flung himself at the Mask. His fists beat a savage tattoo against the Mask's face, cracking his lip, reddening the flesh and drawing blood from his nostrils. The girl ran forward, seized the skinny man and pulled him away.

"What's the use wearing yourself out like that?" she demanded. "Lock the Crimson Mask in here until we decide what to do with him. Come on downstairs. The window is barred. He can't get away."

"I don't have to figure out what I'll do to him," the skinny man rasped. "I got that all figured out already. But we'll go downstairs. I got things to do. Important things."

BY THE way he glared at the Mask it seemed that these important duties concerned him entirely. One of the burly thugs sauntered closer to the Mask, raised his inverted gun suddenly and sent it sweeping toward the Mask's skull. The Mask saw the gun coming and rolled back with it so that the full effects of the vicious blow was lost. Still there was sufficient power behind it to send him slumping to the floor. The skinny man administered a cowardly kick, gestured, and was the last to leave the room. A key turned in the lock outside.

The Mask sat up and gently massaged his head. He looked at Dave and a slow grin made his lips part slightly.

"Well," he said, "you don't show much surprise to find yourself in the presence of the Crimson Mask."

"Why should I?" Dave retorted angrily. "I don't even believe you are the Mask."

"If I called you Dave Small, told you that giving away vitamin pills to poor people is expensive, then would you believe it? Dave, you old horse's neck."

Dave's jaw dropped, his eyes grew wide.

"I—I thought at first that you were a plant—to make me admit I know the Mask. Get me loose, will you? My arms are numb."

The Mask fell to work on the ropes and soon had them off.

"I didn't reveal myself at once," he explained, in a low tone, "because I thought you might unconsciously give away the fact that you do know the Mask, and I wanted to see the doubt in your eyes when they accused me of being—myself. It convinced them that you are innocent all right, but that isn't getting us out of here."

Dave rubbed his wrists to restore circulation.

"There isn't a possible chance," he groaned. "I've been here for hours, and I know. Say, I don't approve of your ideas concerning women. She's nice-looking all right, but boy, she's one top hand at double-crossing. Smart, too. She lured me into this mess. How'd you get here?"

The Mask was trying to raise the window, but it had been nailed down. He seemed particularly careful about the way he touched the glass.

"Tricked—by Gloria Sanders alias something else," he admitted. "She fooled me too, Dave. But what's even more important is this. I'm telling you just in case both of us can't get away. I visited Jay Jens tonight and got Gloria's address from him. On my way out I saw Oliver Durthen going in to see Jens. Durthen is the fifth partner in the Sheridan Apartments enterprise. One of those two men phoned the girl—told her the Crimson Mask was on her trail and to get ready for him. She did—well too. I... Quiet! They're coming back. Be ready to give them a run for their bullets."

But only the girl and one thug entered the room. She carried her purse under one arm, approached a small table in the middle of the room and laid the purse down on it. She faced the Mask.

"You know what's coming to you, sooner or later," she said coldly, "but I've convinced my thin friend that this doesn't happen to be the right time. You may go free, Mask—mostly because our work is about finished and you can't stop us. I'm smart enough to realize that if we kill the Crimson Mask, every police officer in the country will be ready to track us down.

"They'll be able to trace you here, tie me up in the case through outside sources, and—well, I'd rather go to prison for a few years than be led to the electric chair to feel that horrible shock running through my system. The wires—filled with juice, ready to kill."

The girl stood slightly in front of the tough thug with her. The Mask's face remained impassive, but through his brain whirled an eddy of astounding thoughts. This girl—talking of electricity and the electric chair like a half-mad woman, saying that the Mask could go free—that she had convinced the skinny crook that he should be allowed to live. The Mask well knew that no one nor anything would be strong enough to erase the urge to murder in that man's cunning mind.

"Thanks," he said stonily. "What happens? Do we just walk out?"

"You will wait exactly five minutes, and then the way will be clear for you. It's quite dark, but just follow the corridor outside this room. And don't forget—there are people with better brains than yours. Next time we meet you may not be so fortunate."

She backed out of the room and the door closed. Dave sprinted toward it, but the Mask called him to a halt.

"We'll wait the allotted time." he said. "And Dave, take a look at the table. That girl left her purse on it. The last time I saw that handbag she was stuffing a gun inside it. Let's see."

He opened a purse and drew out a twenty-five caliber automatic, its magazine completely full of small but deadly cartridges. His face wore a puzzled look as he slid a bullet into the firing chamber, moved the safety off and started for the door.

"Did she do that on purpose?" Dave wanted to know.

"I'm not sure," the Mask answered. "But I can't imagine her being so careless—not after the cleverness she has displayed so far. And the way she spoke about electrocution! I wonder what she meant? Well—let's go! Be ready for plenty of trouble. This won't be any picnic."

CHAPTER VII

BUILDING OF SUDDEN DEATH

PICKING UP a chair, Dave broke it with one mighty tug. He separated a thick leg from the wreckage, hefted the cudgel and indicated he was ready. The Mask opened the door a crack, saw only darkness outside and at that instant the lights in the room winked out.

Deathly silence hung over the old house, a silence pregnant with grim horror. The Mask bit his lower lip, and at that moment he would have sold his drugstore for one sixty-cent flashlight.

He still clutched the girl's handbag under one arm and ten feet down the corridor he stopped so short that Dave bumped into him and grunted in alarm.

"Stay exactly where you are," the Mask warned. "I'm going to try a little experiment."

He opened the purse again, fumbled inside and located a metal vanity case. He palmed this and suddenly threw it, just above the floor. A bolt of blue flame illuminated the corridor and in one brief instant showed up several strands of wire strung across the hall, about ankle high. One of them was no more than two feet in front of the Mask.

As the crackling of the flash died away, the skinny man's voice rose shrilly.

"Get them. Riddle them with bullets! They spotted my little surprise!"

The two thugs came lumbering down the corridor. The Mask could not see them, but he knew they were advancing with the certain knowledge that only two unarmed men opposed them. Apparently the juice had been turned off because he heard one of the men curse as he stumbled against a wire.

Then the first of them loomed up. The small gun in the Mask's hand jolted flame. The thug gave a sharp scream, reeled aside and fell over against the wall. At the instant that he yanked the trigger, the Mask gave Dave a hard shove floorward and ducked down himself.

The second thug opened up, but he aimed chest high—in the direction of the flash from the small automatic. But his own gun made a marked man of him. The Mask fired twice—fast. A groan attested to his marksmanship. Then he heard feet racing down the stairs. A door slammed and a moment later a car motor roared, and tires screeched as the gas was fed too fast.

By the time that Dave Small and the Mask reached the front door, the skinny man and the girl had vanished. The Mask found a light switch, snapped it, and rushed back to the second floor. Both thugs were badly wounded and unconscious. In another room he found a skillfully-made electrical apparatus. There was a phone in one of the downstairs rooms. The Mask dialed Police Headquarters.

"Listen carefully," he told the bluecoat operator who answered. "In a house at the corner of Thorpe and Reveler Streets you will find two wounded men. I shot them in self-defense. They may know something vitally important and they are to be held under guard at the hospital. This is the Crimson Mask."

He lung up and with Dave Small at his heels, raced out the door. They were three blocks away before the first radio car's siren whined notice that the alarm had been sent over the air. Small and the Mask fell into step and walked briskly back in the direction of the drugstore.

"WELL," THE MASK said, smiling, "what do you think of that girl now, Dave?"

Dave Small sighed. "I don't get it, Bob. First she deliberately traps both of us. Then she hands over a gun and practically tells you that her skinny pal had a trap set to electrocute us. What's her angle?"

"I wish I knew," the Mask said. "We'll just walk around for an hour or so. I want to go back to that house. Forgot something."

"Forgot something?" Dave frowned. "What the dickens did you leave?"

"Remember how I sailed into that skinny crook? It seemed foolish, didn't it, for me to think I could polish him off before his two pals could knock me stiff? I had no hopes of getting away, but when I pushed that anemic rat to the window, I pressed both of his hands against the glass. We've got a set of ten beautiful fingerprints—I hope."

Dave whistled softly. "So that was it. But suppose his prints aren't on file."

"They'll be filed," the Mask said. "Did you notice how he kept talking under his breath, telling himself audibly just what his brain was thinking? Actually speaking his thoughts before he put them into action? After a man has been in prison a long time, he develops that habit. Also that skinny man was a little too pale. I'll lay you five to one he has spent more than ten years in prison, and that he hasn't been out more than three or four weeks…"

At eight o'clock the following morning work was just beginning on the huge construction job that would finally result in the completion of the Sheridan Apartments. A queue of about ten men was lined up in front of the employment agent's office. Several men had quit the day before, unwilling to return to a job so filled with disaster. Men were needed—badly.

The fourth man in line entered the employment shack, removed his cap and displayed bronzed hands and calloused palms.

"Name of Walt Freeman," he told the employment agent. "Unskilled. Was a sailor until the war busted up schedules. I'll do any kind of work. I can swing a pick and shovel, and I ain't scared of high places."

The man in charge glanced at him quickly, and nodded.

"You'll do. Report to the gang foreman."

The man who called himself Walt Freeman mumbled his thanks and walked with short, brisk steps across the muddy ground between the two skyscrapers. He looked exactly like a man who must rely on his muscles to gain a living. His calloused palms displayed mute evidence that he had done this type of hard work all his life.

Those callouses were a work of art. Bob Clarke had labored a full hour fashioning them to look real. This laborer was Bob Clarke in one of the neatest disguises of his career.

He had slept only a short time the night before, but he was as fresh and alert as if he had spent eight full hours in bed. He realized that if he wanted to get a real slant on the sabotage which threatened to wreck the enterprise that he would have to be on the grounds. The best way to do this was by working there.

He was given a shovel and put to work digging a staked-out ditch that ran from one building to the other, directly across the middle of the bare ground that would become the courtyard.

"THERE ARE two buildings, understand?" the foreman told him. "Only one of 'em will have a power plant and a heating unit. Steam and juice will be piped underground to the other building and you start digging so the pipes can be laid. Knock off at noon for thirty minutes and then work until five forty-five. There's extra dough for overtime, so make that shovel talk."

The Mask bobbed his head, shouldered the shovel and walked over beside one building. He began to dig, working steadily, but not too fast. Every ten minutes he would pause, rub his hands and then wipe them across his thighs. He stared up at the two buildings, apparently awed by their height.

At eleven o'clock he heard excited voices. Ten minutes later an ambulance came to a howling stop, backed across the court, and a man was carried from the back of one building and placed on the stretcher. One arm dangled limply from beneath the blanket and a trickle of blood ran down off the fingertips.

"What's happened?" the Mask asked one of the steel workers who came striding by.

"What's happened? Listen, mucker, if you want to keep your health, throw your shovel down and quit. This damn job is jinxed. That was Pete Vicchio, one of the best rivet men in the business. Some lunkhead dropped a sledge-hammer from way up high. It hit Pete on the head. His own wife and kids won't recognize what's left of him. Yes, I'm drawing my time. To hell with working on this job! I'd rather go hungry."

Half a dozen other men quit within the next half hour. The Mask ate a quick, cheap lunch down the street and returned in time to make a short tour of the entire premises before he had to go back to work.

He noticed that four men kept to themselves, avoiding the other ironworkers. This quartet talked in whispers and kept eyeing every new man on the job. The Mask was examined critically, too, but he had no worries. This disguise could fool anyone.

And also he found an opportunity to watch the men. They certainly were not real riveters or ironworkers. Their eyes were too shifty, their manners too sly. The Mask had an idea that if any more sledge-hammers were dropped during the course of the afternoon that one of these men would be responsible.

He worked steadily until three o'clock, and now found that he could keep two of those suspicious men under observation while he worked. They were busy installing window frames twelve stories above the ground. Below, laborers wheeled their barrows, mixed cement and helped to unload the big trucks that pulled up.

Suddenly the Mask let out a yell. Almost a dozen loose cement blocks came hurtling down on top of the hapless laborers. Two of them dropped in their tracks, another let out a screech of pain, and clutched a broken shoulder. Instantly confusion reigned. The foreman's voice was drowned out in the angry shouts of other workers. Steelworkers came down from their high perches.

The Mask looked up. He caught sight of a grinning face watching the scene from the twelfth floor. The Mask laid down his shovel, took a hitch in his pants and went over to the building. He entered, climbed the stairs rapidly, and slowed up on his way along the corridor to the room from which those bricks had fallen.

HE LOOKED inside. Two of the suspicious-appearing men were leaning out the window. The Mask stepped into the room, advanced without being heard, and both hands suddenly darted down to fasten on the collars of the murderous pair. He jerked them erect and before they could recover from their astonishment, he sent one of them crashing to the floor. He stepped back, doubled his fists and came at the other with the speed and fury of a tornado.

The fight was short, the Mask's heart was filled with rage. Innocent men were being killed and maimed just so some crook could accomplish his desires. These hired killers did the strong-arm work and now they were getting a taste of their own medicine.

The first man crumpled up half a minute after the Mask moved against him. The second was broader of shoulder, and four inches taller than the Mask. Furthermore, he knew all the angles of dirty fighting, and began to display them. His first act was to kick out. His foot did not go back as he intended it to. Instead the Mask gripped him by the ankle, pulled him off his feet and let him drive against the wall. He stood waiting until the man arose again.

This time the thug scowled blackly, reached under his overalls and drew a clasp knife. He grinned evilly as he touched a spring and a fat, dangerous-looking blade shot out. With a yell of triumph he made a lunge for the Mask.

The Mask stepped back, giving ground rapidly. The killer came on, murder in his piggish eyes. The blade rose, fell swiftly—and cut thin air. Then a fist that felt as if it were molded of concrete hit him squarely between the eyes. He reeled back, made an ineffectual attempt to use the knife again, and took a wide swinging right that landed on his nose, flattening it. He rubbed blood from his face, tried to locate this dancing demon who never stood still long enough to sink a knife into.

He saw him just too late. The Mask brought up a fist from near the floor. It raised the killer completely off his feet, cracked his jaw-bone, and plastered him against the wall.

The Mask brushed his knuckles as though they were tainted. Then he strode out into the corridor, looking for a piece of rope. He glanced out of a window. Along with two ambulances, a big car pulled up. Four men climbed out—Jay Jens, Jim Stark, Matt Karling and Oliver Durthen.

Jay Jens seemed to take immediate command of the situation, getting facts from the foreman listening to the ambulance surgeons' reports.

CHAPTER VIII

THE "SQUEEZE"

BUSINESS ON the ground for the Mask now was more important than tying up that pair of killers. They wouldn't go far for some time anyway. The Mask hurried down the steps, emerged from the building through a rear entrance and stepped behind a supply shed.

The four men under observation went into a huddle. Jay Jens summoned the foreman and he led them toward the shack behind which the Mask was hidden. The four men entered and the Mask peered around to be sure no one observed him. Then he listened intently.

Jay Jens spoke first. "Well, there you have it, gentlemen. Each man working on this building is convinced that his life is in danger every moment he is here. The only way to finish this job is to transfer all rights and title to someone else. I happen to know that you three do not possess capital enough to finish the work. You are completely broke, gentlemen. No bank will advance any money on a building which shows no promise of ever being completed."

Jim Stark spoke in a bitter voice "That's where you come in, Jens. I wouldn't be surprised if we finally discovered you were behind this sabotage. Well, we're waiting for your offer. We're entirely at your mercy, and you know it."

Jens rubbed his hands and beamed. "Spoken like a wise man. Now, you men are all indebted to me for a million dollars apiece. Of course I'll have to take over because it's impossible for any of you to pay me back. That is—unless you die." Jens chuckled in good humor and went on. "My offer is final. I will give each of you three quarters of a million dollars for your interest in the building."

Stark gave a growl of anger. "What kind of a racket is that? We owe you a million. You give us three quarters of a million. We lose the building and still owe you two hundred and fifty thousand dollars. Besides that, our own money—more than a million—is invested in the building. Are you crazy, Jens? Or do you think we're weak-minded?"

"Come now, gentlemen, I'm not as crude as that," Jens said. "I'll go this far. I'll advance each of you a hundred thousand in cash. Whatever you put into the building was a gamble, and you lost. That's my one offer. Take it—or go bankrupt. As far as the debt you owe me, I can still collect when you die. And to put it frankly, none of you are young men."

Karling's voice rose in an accusing shriek.

"Murderer! You're a killer, Jens! Sellmer and Whitner never died by accident. You killed them! Then you got us in a corner. I'd rather go to prison than turn this building over to you. This is just another example of the crooked business methods that made you a rich man!"

Jens raised both hands in a gesture of protest.

"Now listen to me. I know nothing about the murders you accuse me of. I have no reason for killing anyone. Business is business, and I have violated no laws in making this offer to you. But murder! Be a little more careful in your accusations."

"What Karling said goes for me too!" Stark shouted. "I think you are a murderer, besides being a business pirate."

Oliver Durthen was calmer.

"Come now, this is no time for cheap theatricals," he soothed. "I suggest that we talk the matter over and give Jens our answer tonight. We're licked. Jens can legally take action against us on the loans he made. Any court would give him a judgment. I think we should seriously consider his offer, and do it quietly."

THEN THE door of the shack opened and all four men came out. The Mask pretended to putter around. He was facing the shack, and a fairly large window in it. The reflection of one side of a skyscraper was plainly visible in it.

He saw something move, and glanced over his shoulder. A man was standing in the window of the third floor, waving a cap frantically. He was trying to attract the attention of one of the four men who were walking away. That, in itself, was not particularly important, but what was important was that the man in the window was the bald-headed, skinny crook who had tried to murder the Mask!

Suddenly Durthen took a long lingering look at the building, as though it were his last. He saw the skinny man in the window and seemed to become excited. He darted away from the rest of his party and the skinny man vanished from sight at almost that same instant. When Durthen rushed into the building the Mask followed, slowly, so that no suspicion would be aroused.

All work had ceased. Not a man remained on any of the floors. Until the stigma of hard luck was removed, this whole gigantic enterprise would be at a standstill.

The Mask had a glimpse of Durthen as he turned through a door that led into the cellar of the east building. The Mask went after him, transferring a gun from hip holster to a more convenient place just under the bib of his overalls.

The basement was practically completed. There were huge boiler and power rooms, a laundry of spacious size, and various supply rooms. Durthen was going into the laundry, and he seemed to be pursuing someone. The Mask broke into a run, but before he could reach the entrance, the door slammed shut and a bolt shot into place on the other side.

The door was made of wood, and not particularly thick, but as the Mask drew back in an attempt to smash it down, he heard the sound of angry voices. Then several blows were struck. Someone moaned and fell heavily.

The Mask made a lunge at the door. The panel cracked under this first attempt, but he spent five full minutes before the door finally crashed open. He rushed in, gun ready. There were no windows in this room and no other doors. The walls were of stucco and had been in place for weeks. Yet there was no one in the room! No one, that is, unless a skeleton could be called a person.

The Mask's shoulders drooped and a cry of mingled horror and amazement came from his lips. The skeleton lay in the middle of the floor. Beside it rested Durthen's gray fedora and on one outflung, bony hand was a wrist-watch. A watch that still ticked.

The Mask recovered his wits with an effort. The noise of breaking down the door had not been heard outside. He was quite alone and able to make a thorough investigation. But of what? A skeleton that had been a living, fighting man not more than five minutes ago?

Kneeling beside the grisly thing, the Mask removed the wrist-watch. He turned it over and saw Oliver Durthen's initials engraved on the back. With a grunt of exasperation he picked up one brittle bone. Whoever this man had been, he had been dead for years. This could not be Durthen's skeleton. Where then, was Durthen?

Then an idea struck him. What if Durthen had met the skinny killer in this room, faked a fight with plenty of noise, placed the wrist-watch on the bony hand of the skeleton and somehow both he and the skinny crook had made their escape from the room.

HOW? THE Mask could not figure that out. He knew that when the door had crashed in and the skeleton had been revealed that he had rushed into the room instantly. By moving quietly and fast, Durthen and the skinny crook might have slipped out and not been seen or heard. The whole thing was screwy.

Something gleamed dully, just under one shoulder bone of the skeleton. Somehow that object had been crushed against the bone and had adhered to it. The Mask pulled it free and saw that he held a cheap, badly corroded brass button in the palm of his hand...

Only a few minutes later, there was another upset to his plans. When he returned to pick up the two thugs, he had knocked out, they were gone.

An hour later, still in his disguise of a working man, the Mask sat in Theodore Warrick's home. The brass button lay on the corner of the desk in front of him.

"It's impossible to denude a body of all flesh and organs so quickly," he told Warrick. "Furthermore, I examined a section of the skeleton in my lab. The bones are dry. The body had been buried for years. Some dirt still clung to a few rough places."

Warrick leaned across his desk.

"The skeleton doesn't interest me half as much as the story you told about Jay Jens," he said. "He's our man. He must be. Can't you see how he sabotaged the building until the owners were in a financial stew and unable to get out of it? Then he comes along and magnanimously offers to take it off their hands at a tremendous loss—but not to himself. Jens never loses. I tell you, Bob, the police should handle this affair from now on."

Bob Clarke shook his head.

"We have no evidence," he said reluctantly. "I think I know how Sellmer and Whitner were murdered, though. You are having the prints of that skinny crook checked right now. Perhaps through him we can learn the real truth about this. I have an idea that there's more than those twin apartment buildings involved. There are too many out-and-out crooks mixed up in this. Jens would use more finesse, and Mr. Warrick—too many crooks make a very suspicious broth."

The door-bell buzzed. Warrick arose and Bob Clarke stepped into an ante-room, but left the door open a crack. Warrick returned, preceded by—Gloria Sanders! Bob Clarke almost let out an audible cry of pleasure. He found that he actually had been longing to see this girl again, and obtain a full explanation from her.

"I came to you, Mr. Warrick," Gloria said, "because you are the only person who can contact the Crimson Mask. I did him an injustice. I tried to make it up to him, and I think I did, but please ask him to meet me. Anywhere you say. I must talk to him."

Warrick nodded. "I think that might be arranged. If you will call me in about an hour, I shall have the arrangements made."

Warrick picked up a pipe and stuffed tobacco in it. His eyes were not watching the girl, but the Mask's were. To the Mask's amazement he saw the girl look down at the brass button and give a visible start. Then her hand flicked out and the brass button vanished.

Why in the world had she filched a corroded, worthless piece of brass? Of what possible interest could it be to her? The Mask did nothing. Warrick escorted the girl to the front door, let her out and at the same time admitted another caller. The new arrival was Jim Stark. He and Gloria looked at one another without recognition.

THE MASK remained hidden and listened to Stark's bitter condemnation of Jay Jens.

"I know the Crimson Mask is at work on this case," Stark said. "I want to help him. There is no question in my mind but that Jens is behind it all. Perhaps I could get real evidence against him—enough to convince any jury of his guilt. But I'm an amateur in these things, and I don't know how to go about it. I thought you or the Mask might have some suggestion."

Warrick sat down slowly, puffing on his pipe.

"You are in a good position to help," he admitted. "Suppose you pretend to agree with Jay Jens' offer, gain his confidence, offer to cooperate in every way. Jens might slip and reveal something significant. I'm sure the Mask would make that same suggestion. You and I know that Jens has no good alibi for the time when both Sellmer and Whitner were killed. Neither has Durthen, for that matter, but he can't be involved, because he stands to lose everything."

Stark brought his right fist smacking into the palm of his left hand.

"I'll do it! I'll tell Jens I'm ready to play ball and, for a consideration, make my partners capitulate. I'll worm evidence out of him. Thanks for the idea, Mr. Warrick. You'll hear from me as soon as I get the lowdown."

CHAPTER IX

TWENTY-YEAR-OLD CRIME

S TARK HURRIED away and the Mask came out of the ante-room. Warrick grinned.

"Looks like Bank Night," he observed. "Two visitors in as many minutes, and both interested in meeting the Crimson Mask. So that was the girl who trapped you, and then saved your life! Shall I make arrangements for a meeting?"

"Yes. When she calls, tell her to meet me in the basement of the north apartment building of the Sheridan Apartments at exactly nine o'clock tonight. I'll be busy until then. And Mr. Warrick, if things work out, I'll show you a murderer by midnight."

The Mask returned to his drugstore and changed his disguise to the simple one he had elected to use when he worked more or less openly. Warrick phoned before he left.

"Those fingerprints are filed all right," he said. "They belong to an old-time burglar named Novak. He was sent away in 1920 and served twenty years. Released a month ago. And listen to this—his parole record indicates that he is working on the Sheridan Apartments job as a crane operator."

"Does his prison record show that he knows anything about electricity?" the Mask asked.

"Does he? For fifteen years he worked in the power plant at the prison. Shall I have him picked up?"

"No. He'll be more useful to me free. I want to find out how he and Durthen could vanish through a cement wall. Thanks, Mr. Warrick."

For more than three hours the Mask worked busily. He visited several newspaper offices and read mountains of old files. What he learned from them made his eyes glisten. He knew what lay behind this murder and violence now. Next, armed with a picture of Novak, the skinny ex-convict killer, he visited the homes and offices of Sellmer, Whitner, Durthen, Stark and Karling. At each place he asked questions, showed the picture, and received answers that made his brain reel.

At eight-thirty he was finished. He took a cab and went back to the vicinity of the Sheridan Apartments. For hours he had looked forward to his meeting with Gloria. He did not doubt now but that she was on the side of the law. Such a girl would be of great value to the Crimson Mask.

He approached the north building, crossing the court to reach it. Once he tripped and almost fell across a thin wire lying on the ground. He kept on going, entered the building and made his way into the basement.

He heard a glad cry of welcome as he passed beneath a small light suspended from the ceiling of the corridor. A moment later Gloria was at his side. She recognized him because he wore the same disguise which he had assumed when she saw him last.

"I was afraid you wouldn't come—after what I did to you," she said eagerly. "Believe me, Crimson Mask, I couldn't help it. I placed two lives in jeopardy that night. The man who escaped with you seemed to be following me, and I thought he might be—someone connected with the director of a murder ring. I had to know if I was under observation, so I had him captured. However, he had nothing to do with all this. Then Novak—he was the pale, skinny man you saw-received information that you were on my trail. Novak made me phone my lodging house. When I learned someone was there, Novak told me to lure you to that old house. I did, but I made up my mind that I'd save you even if I died for it."

"You did even things up," the Mask told her, with a smile. "But what is your interest in this? I know your name isn't Gloria Sanders, and I'll give you odds that it is really Sandra Grey. Right?"

"How did you ever find that out?" the girl asked, with wide eyes. "I—I thought no one knew."

THE MASK took her arm and piloted her to a small room just off the laundry.

"I saw you pick up that brass button from Warrick's desk," he told her. "It was a button from a uniform. Your father's uniform. Twenty years ago he was a guard in the Apex Jewelry Company—one of the most famous jewelry houses in the world. One night a gang of thieves gained admittance to the store. The police could see only that this had been done with inside help, and your father was the only man who could have accomplished it.

"The safe was blown open, three million dollars worth of gems were taken. Since that night nothing has ever been heard of your father, the crooks or the jewels. They never turned up in any domestic or foreign markets. Police records indicate that your father took his share and disappeared. Now—you go on from there."

Sandra Grey talked in a low voice, broken now and then with a dry sob.

"You seem to know everything. But you don't know what it is to live under a stigma of dishonesty, even if you had nothing to do with it. I was pointed out in school, at work—everywhere—as the daughter of a man who had turned traitor. It killed my mother, finally, and then I went away. But I promised myself that some day I'd return and find out what really did happen that night of the robbery and my father's disappearance.

"I worked my way into a minor mob of slick crooks, and then graduated into the bigger lines. When Novak was released from prison, I knew he would join the gang I had associated myself with. You see, Novak was the only clue I had. The morning after the robbery he was picked up on an old charge of burglary.

"They found a partly filled bottle of nitroglycerin on him. The only robbery within any reasonable distance, in which nitro had been used, was the break in which Dad vanished. A man like Novak wouldn't be running around with a bottle of nitro. It's too dangerous. He just didn't have a chance to get rid of it."

"Logical reasoning," the Mask declared. "It so happens that your ideas and mine agree. I'm afraid that when we've run down this thing to the bitter end, your personal interest won't have happy results."

"You mean about my father?" she asked quickly. "I know he's dead. He never lived through that awful night. But if I can clear his name, then I will have accomplished something to which I have devoted my whole life. I have never expected to find him—alive."

"Then we'll get on with it," the Mask said. "Next door to this room is the laundry. I have an idea that the secret of what happened twenty years ago lies there. Are you up to facing some rather gruesome things?"

"I'm ready," she said, "And I'm not afraid."

They entered the laundry and the Mask was glad that he had arranged with the police to remove the grisly skeleton which he had found there that afternoon. The Mask picked up a short piece of iron pipe, warned the girl to listen closely and watch for signs of trouble. Then he began tapping the stucco walls, inch by inch. He used a flashlight, too, studying the rough wall intently. Almost an hour passed before the Mask gave a grunt and summoned the girl.

"See there? Tiny cracks and a faintly hollow sound when I tap the wall indicates that there is a hidden door here. It's been cleverly fashioned. Wait right here while I go outside and find a pick."

RETURNING IN a few minutes, the Mask used the pick effectively. He cut a deep gouge in the wall near the hidden door and finally he was able to pull it away. The well-hidden spring, by which the door could be opened, was revealed only then.

Behind that small door, through which the Mask could go only by crawling, was a narrow, low tunnel. It had been recently dug, because the earth smelled fresh and was moist. He sent the ray of his flashlight ahead and started crawling forward. Sandra Grey came directly behind him. They had negotiated a distance of about fifteen feet when the Mask stopped, looked back at the girl, and spoke softly.

"It's clear enough what happened. Twenty years ago, the crooks tunneled along this same course and reached the floor under the jewelry store. They entered, attacked your father. Then they blew the safe door open, looted the place and returned to the tunnel. They carefully replaced the section of floor they had dug out and no one ever suspected that there was a tunnel. The police simply leaped at the easiest conclusion—that your father had admitted the crooks and had made a get-away with them."

"But what did happen?" Sandra asked.

"They crawled back into the tunnel, taking your father with them. But in blowing open the safe, so much nitro was used that the shock weakened the roof of the tunnel. When they were crawling back, it caved in. Everyone was killed except Novak. He got clear somehow, but he was picked up on another charge.

"He kept his mouth shut, took the sentence handed out to him and planned to get at the loot some day. When he discovered that the jewelry store had been torn down and that a building project threatened to reveal the secret only he knew, he got busy at once. First of all, work had to be stopped on the building because they were ready to start digging across the site of the jewelry store. That's why the workers were intimidated by a number of accidents."

"Then they have the loot already?" Sandra asked. "They dug this tunnel secretly to reach the spot where the cave-in took place twenty years ago?"

"I'm not sure," the Mask said. "They may have recovered the loot. I do know they reached the vicinity of the cave-in. That's how the button from your father's uniform was located. We'll keep on going a few more yards anyhow. Grab my ankle and hang onto it. I won't use the flash unless necessary. If this tunnel should go all the way through we might run into some of the mugs hired to do the strong-arm work."

The Mask crawled forward again. Something warned him that danger threatened. He snapped on his light for an instant. A foot away from his head he saw a thin copper wire. With horror he remembered the other wire which he had tripped over on the ground above this very spot.

Three minutes later there was a dull roar in the tunnel. The whole roof came down, but on the surface of the ground there was no indication of what had happened. The tunnel had been dug too far below. From the opening in the laundry room, a wave of dirt came flying out and then silence, grim and final, held sway.

In one of the shacks above ground, the killer, Novak smiled grimly and removed evidences of the electrical apparatus which set off the explosion...

THEODORE WARRICK sat in his study, nervously drawing on his extinguished pipe. Hours had passed since he heard from the Crimson Mask. Dave Small, at the drugstore, had received no word either, and it was after midnight. The Mask had promised results by then. What had happened to him? Was he dead—a victim of the murderous gang he fought?

The jangle of his phone made Warrick jump in excitement. This must be the Mask. He put the receiver to his ear and emitted a groan. It was Jim Stark—not the Mask.

"I've done it!" Stark cried eagerly. "I had a long talk with Jens. I pretended to fall in with his scheme and promised to make Durthen and Karling agree to his terms. I insisted on knowing everything that went on, and Jens has promised to give me the complete low-down, within the next thirty minutes. I'm to go to his home and I want you to be there.

"Here is my plan. I'll go in, but I'll arrange so that the front door won't close tightly. I'll keep Jens occupied so you can slip into the house and hide in a convenient spot. You'll hear him make his offer again, and outline his plans to me. Both of us can swear in court as to what we hear. Warrick, we've got him cold! Will you help me?"

"I'll be there," Warrick said. "At exactly one-ten I'll enter the house and slip into a hiding place. Then you draw Jens out, make him reveal everything. I'll be armed, in case he makes trouble."

Warrick hung up and leaned back in his chair. It looked as though the case would be broken wide open without the presence of the Crimson Mask.

The ex-police commissioner grew more nervous by the minute. Something must have happened to the Mask, but Warrick knew that he could not wait here any longer. It was his duty to expose Jens as the master crook. Once that was done, he could make Jens talk and tell what had happened to the Mask—if he were in peril.

Warrick slid a gun into his hip pocket and drove over to Jens' big house.

CHAPTER X

DOUBLE FOR A CORPSE

REACHING THE Jens' home, Warrick parked around the corner, skirted the hedges around the estate, and took refuge in a dark spot. He waited until he saw Jim Stark drive up, get out of his car and enter the house.

Warrick glanced at his watch, saw the second hand move with incredible slowness to the appointed time, then he crept toward the front porch. Jens and Stark would be in the big study at the rear of the house. He tried the door and it opened. Stark had followed the prearranged plans well by covertly pressing the lock button so that the outside knob would turn the latch.

He stepped into the reception hall and heard voices from the back of the house. Warrick drew his gun and moved forward. He reached the door of the study and saw Jens and Stark, each with a glass of whiskey and soda before him, seated opposite one another. They were talking about finances, with Jens holding the floor most of the time.

Then Stark looked at has watch, saw that it was one-ten, and suddenly leaped to his feet.

"Jens," he shouted, "you're finished! Don't talk, or I'll be compelled to use force on you. I've listened to your proposition—a plan meant to ruin me and my colleagues. You're a crook! You always were, but this time you've met your match. You organized a gang of hoodlums to sabotage the apartment building. You wanted work stopped on it so we'd never be able to get a loan and finish the job.

"Then you stepped in, like a vulture waiting for its prey to die. You made us an offer, one so stupid that we saw through it immediately. You wanted to buy in—take over the project. You murdered Sellmer and Whitner to get the million dollars worth of insurance on their lives! That would give you active capital to carry out your plans."

Jens' face grew alternately white and crimson. He shot out of his chair and grabbed Stark's shoulder.

"You're out of your head!" he yelled. "Why, you little pipsqueak, of course I wanted that building and I'll get it. But I don't have to commit murder to get what I want. I've got brains! I'll shove you and those halfwit friends of yours out on their necks. I'll—"

Stark suddenly lunged for Jens with a short jab toward the face. Jens let go of him, moved—backward suddenly—and then every light in the house went out. At the same moment a floor lamp crashed, Jens had tripped over it and somehow the whole system had been shorted.

Warrick, gun in hand, rushed into the room. Some one came toward him. Warrick raised the gun, but in the inky darkness he had no target and he did not want to shoot Stark. A hard pain glanced off his cheek and sent him careening to one side. Feet pounded up the staircase.

Warrick knew that only one man had left this room. It must be Jens, for he alone had the more logical reason for getting clear.

Warrick wheeled and took up the chase. He was badly encumbered by the darkness and an utter unfamiliarity with the layout of Jens' big mansion, but he reached the staircase and started up it. A jet of flame lanced out from the landing above and a bullet whined past his head. Warrick ducked to one side, raised his gun and fired point-blank at the spot from which the jet of flame had emanated.

He heard a yell of pain, and then a body crashed to the floor. But Warrick did not rush up. Jens must be tied in with the gang of thugs who had been so prominent in this case. They might be upstairs, and disposing of one of them was nothing when the others might be waiting.

WARRICK CREPT up the stairs as softly as possible, gun extended, finger tensed against the trigger. He reached the landing and stumbled over a form lying on the floor. Warrick squatted beside the form and listened. No sound reached him. This man must be Jens. He had opened fire in a desperate attempt to get clear—and had lost.

Fumbling in his pocket, Warrick found a match and struck it. But before he looked down at the victim of his gunfire, he peered down the long corridor. A hunch caused him to do that. One of the doors opened and a scowling, emaciated-looking man leaped into the hallway. Novak! Warrick recognized him instantly.

The gun in Novak's hand jolted. Warrick tried to drop flat, but he was close to the edge of the staircase and in his hurry, he lost his balance.

His gun fell from his hand and he rolled down half a dozen steps before he seized the bannister supports and stopped the descent.

But then a flashlight's beam cut the darkness. It centered on him. Novak was bringing his gun down. All that was clearly evident in the glare of the flash. Warrick knew that he had but a few seconds to live. Unarmed, he was at the mercy of this killer.

A shot rang out. The flashlight in Novak's hand dropped, hit the floor and rolled crazily. Warrick wondered why he didn't feel the impact of the bullet. Certainly Novak could not have missed at that close range. Then he saw a shape slowly collapsing. The flashlight, still lit, sent its ray against the further wall of the corridor and there was light enough so that Warrick could see dimly.

The shape seemed to double up and then it came rolling down the steps like a sack of potatoes. Warrick drew back against the bannister, gaping in awe. This was Novak, who had been ready to kill him! Someone else had fired that shot and the gunman had been struck.

Limp and weak, Warrick summoned his wits and energy, crawled back up the stairs and picked up the flashlight. The man he had shot was sprawled out on the floor. Warrick wrested the gun out of his limp hand. Then he turned the ray of the flash on his face and uttered a deep sigh.

Jay Jens was dead! A bullet had smashed through his chest!

Warrick felt vainly for a pulse. Then he stood erect and started a search of the rooms on the second floor. He invaded two of them cautiously, but when he came out of the second a groan from the first floor brought him to a halt. He raced down the steps, vaulted over the body of Novak who lay in a heap at the landing.

Flashlight in hand, the ex-police commissioner rushed into the study, Jim Stark was lying on the floor. There was a bloody welt on his forehead. Warrick helped him up, placed the flash on the edge of a table, and cleansed the wound on Stark's head.

"Did—he get away?" Stark asked weakly.

"Jens is dead," Warrick said. "Now, if you feel well enough, I'll leave you until I can get the lights working again."

Warrick found a fuse blown, replaced it and the house was flooded with light. Stark accompanied Warrick to the second floor and stood looking down at Jay Jens' body.

"He got what was coming to him," Stark said. "I'll tell you everything now. Jay Jens admitted to me that he hired a bunch of killers to sabotage the building. He killed Sellmer and Whitner to get the insurance on their lives. What's more—and this will hurt, Warrick—he also killed the Crimson Mask and secreted his body somewhere.

"I first suspected Jens a couple of nights ago when I visited this house. Durthen was here—he'd just arrived—and Jens tried to get us to sign over our rights then. Durthen flew off the handle—and Durthen is now dead. Anyone who opposed Jens was murdered. He boasted of that to me. Well, we'd better call the police."

WARRICK WAS leaning against the balustrade. His eyes were closed tightly and deep lines in his face showed the agony that coursed through his brain. The Mask was dead! Of course such a thing might happen. Warrick knew this very well, but now that it had actually occurred, the force of the blow seemed unbearable.

He opened his eyes wearily.

"All right, Stark," he said dully. "Let's get on with it."

They started toward the steps. Behind them the floor creaked. Warrick spun around. So did Stark. Both of them emitted gasps of astonishment. In the doorway of a room stood a man with a crimson mask over his eyes—and a gun in his hand.

"Thank you, Mr. Stark," he said grimly, "for convicting yourself. I wondered just how you knew I'd visited Jens and obtained from him an address which you turned into a death trap for me. I suspected Jens and Durthen, but I was wrong. You're the killer, and your motives have little to do with the apartment building. You wanted the jewels buried under the courtyard.

"Novak, whom I killed a few moments ago to save my good friend, Mr. Warrick, visited Sellmer and Whitner. He propositioned them about digging up the loot secretly. They thought he was crazy. He visited Durthen, too, and got the same reaction. But when he visited you—that was another story. You remembered that robbery, and believed him.

"But you had to kill Sellmer, Whitner and Durthen so they wouldn't get wise. You did this by cleverly framing Jay Jens. Don't argue—don't open your mouth. I've got the evidence. I can prove Novak visited the two men who fell off the girder. I know how their deaths were brought about. Novak was given work on the job by you. He operated a crane, the one which lifted the girder. He was clever with electricity, and he rigged up a coil that sent enough volts down the guide chain to knock out the victims. They fell off and were killed. There wasn't a single clue that it was murder."

"Wait a moment," Warrick exclaimed. "How do I know you're the Crimson Mask? He's dead!"

"He is supposed to be dead." The Mask laughed softly. "A tunnel was wired and blown up, but I managed to get out just in time, because Novak, who arranged the trap, grew careless and left wires exposed. Stark here saw a certain girl leave your home, Warrick. He knew she was an accredited member of the gang he hired. He had her trailed, saw her go to the rendezvous, and he had Novak set his death trap. She and I crawled out just in time.

"Let me get on. This afternoon Durthen spotted Novak trying to arouse your attention, Stark. Durthen's mind must have clicked. He chased Novak and met—death. Novak killed him, hauled his body and himself into the tunnel, but he didn't have time to dispose of a skeleton he had fished out of the tunnel. So he clumsily tried to throw me off by arranging things to make it seem that the skeleton was that of Durthen."

Stark made a wry face.

"Of all the silly stories! Warrick, this man can't be the Crimson Mask. Jens told me he was dead. Durthen is dead, too. So is this man called Novak—and Jens. I've had nothing to do with it."

"But if Jens were alive to repudiate all your statements you'd be in a bad position!" the Mask barked. "If he hadn't told you some of those things you have just told Mr. Warrick, your own knowledge of them would convict you. That's true, isn't it? You could have deliberately hit yourself on the head just a few minutes ago, for an alibi."

STARK LOOKED down at the still face of Jay Jens and shrugged.

"Why, yes, I suppose so. But there is Jens, and he certainly looks dead to me."

"Your error, Stark," a familiar voice said.

Stark turned his head. Jay Jens was coming down the corridor. Stark looked back at the corpse, at Jens again, and then gave a wild scream. He whirled and headed down the steps.

The Crimson Mask went down also, but he didn't touch any of the stairs. He launched himself through space, hit Stark and sent him crashing to the floor beside Novak. The Mask poised one fist and sent it home. Stark dropped flat.

The Mask arose and grinned at Warrick. "That man upstairs is one of Stark's crooks who tried to stop me when I slipped into the estate. I killed him in self-defense, and carried the body into the house. I suspected what was going to happen and I made up the features of the dead crook to resemble Jens.

"When the real Jens ran up the stairs I grabbed him. I fired a shot to draw your fire, Warrick, so you'd actually believe you had killed Jens.

Then Stark, thinking that Jens was dead, according to the plans he had concocted, talked—plenty. His own statements, heard by you two men, will convict him.

"I have the jewels that were stolen twenty years ago. They were in Stark's safe. I opened it just as easily as Novak could have done. Those jewels will help to convict Stark. There's nothing else to do now except call the police, while I fade out of the picture."

There was a car waiting around the corner. The Mask got in beside Sandra Grey.

"It's finished," he said quietly. "Novak is dead. Stark talked out of turn. Now I want to talk. You worked with me on this case—so cleverly and bravely that I can't forget it. I need you, Sandra. The Crimson Mask can't always work alone. If you say the word, I'll reveal my identity, enlist you in this fight against crime, and perhaps we can prevent such things as happened to your father."

She placed one soft hand over his. "I've been praying for hours that you'd ask me that," she whispered. "I'm ready, for any orders you may give, Mask—after you give me a better name to call you by, you might call me Sandy. I rather like it."

The Mask laughed. "So do I—Sandy. Now let's go home!"

III

THE CRIMSON MASK'S DEATH GAMBLE

CHAPTER I

PAY—AND BE MURDERED

THE JOB came as a godsend to Joe Hooper. Out of high school two years, without regular work, even the stiff fee exacted by the employment agency didn't seem to matter. He had a steady job! True, it paid only twenty-one dollars a week and the agency fee was fifty dollars, but jobs were scarce. Agencies, according to the manager of this one, had to work pretty hard in order to locate jobs.

The plant was a one-story affair. A huge foundry sprawling over three quarters of a mile of ground and well fenced in. There was a guard at the gate, a man who kept a .45 Army Pistol strapped to one hip. Jim Hooper thought nothing of this. With all the subversive elements raging and ranting about the country, such steps had been taken by almost every large plant.

Thirty minutes later he was at work. Stripped to the waist, with sweat oozing from every pore in his body, Joe Hooper followed the huge crucibles of molten metal, shifting weights from one mold to another. They were weights that reached as high as sixty pounds in some cases, and they had to be changed fast, before the crucible was ready to drop part of its intensely hot load into the next mold.

By noon, Hooper was staggering, and his back felt as though he could never straighten his spine again. His eyes and nose were filled with the residue of spelter that was used to clear the molten metal. Once, when he stopped to seize a dipper of water, a burly foreman yelled a string of curses at him. Hooper went back to work.

When noon arrived at last the cool air out in the yard felt good. He dropped weakly to the ground, supporting himself against the side of a small shack. Another man, armed with a lunch pail, sat down beside him.

"Hi, buddy," he greeted. "Working in the foundry, huh? Shifting weights. I know what that is. I did it too—for six months. Then they gave me a promotion."

"Six months?" Hooper asked in amazement. "Did you stand that work for six months? Why I—I thought it would only be for a week or so. The work I asked for was in the drafting department. I took up drafting in high school. I thought they were going to work me in a lot of different divisions until I knew the whole plant. I don't mind the foundry—not for a few days. But six months! And the way they push you around."

HIS COMPANION bit into a cold egg sandwich and munched it for a moment.

"Take my advice, pal, and quit," he said then. "I seen guys go nuts in there—crazy from the heat and that back-busting work. Me—I'd rather loaf the rest of my life than put in another five days in there. Your name is Hooper, ain't it? Seen them putting your new time card in the rack. I'm Max Lieber. Believe me, pal, you can't last. You're not strong enough."

"But I can't quit," Hooper protested. "It's the first job I've had in years and—well I borrowed fifty bucks from my mother to pay the agency fee. Just about the last of her savings."

Lieber shrugged.

"So it's your funeral, pal… Well, let's get back. They'll sound the gong in a couple of minutes and if you're late in this dump, they dock you—plenty. Sometimes I wonder what kind of a sap I am for working here. Say, why don't you join the army? They're looking for guys like you."

Hooper's eyes glowed.

"Gee, there's nothing I'd rather do." Then his face became glum. "But I can't. I've got to support my mother who has spent her last cent, seeing I got an education, and it couldn't be done on twenty-one bucks a month. She won't take charity, y'see. Maybe, if she could get something to do, I can join up."

Hooper slaved all afternoon, from one until six, because there were some late pouring offs. The last weight he shifted felt like a ten-ton trailer. He staggered to the wash rooms, cleaned up and went home. He ate, but he was too tired to enjoy his food. At seven-thirty he was in bed.

His legs were still shaky the next day, but he plunged into the heart-breaking job vigorously. The foreman, for some reason, seemed to enjoy driving him. Hooper wondered when the noon gong sounded, if he could last out the rest of the day.

Also Joe Hooper wasn't entirely a fool. All morning his brain was busy with a strange idea. This was not normal work. He was doing four men's weight-shifting and there was absolutely no reason why the foreman should be watching him so closely—unless they *wanted* him to quit.

What if there was a tie-up between that employment agency and the foreman of this factory, perhaps? Then that fifty-dollar fee could be shared, because while the contract which Hooper had in his pocket right now said that if he lost his job through no fault of his own, it also stipulated, in precise terms, that the employment agency would not be required to get him another job if he quit or was discharged for incompetence.

More and more this thought became stronger and stronger. On each of the tremendously heavy weights, Hooper could see the sly, greasy face of the employment manager. Bancroft, the man had signed himself, as manager of the Atlas Employment, Agency. Hooper forced a weak grin to his lips at the memory of the name. The work to which they assigned their clients was certainly work for Atlas.

At noon he met Lieber again and the short, dark-featured man was laughing at him.

"Boy, they sure wore you down in a day and a half. How much longer do you think you can last, buddy?"

"I'll last," Hooper said grimly. "I'll last or I'll find out what's going on. The foreman stood over me all morning. There were two other weight lifters who did just one-third the work he made me handle. Most of the time they were standing around. One of them even offered to help me, but the foreman swore at him.

"Look, Lieber! I think there's something wrong. I think they want me to quit—that they're driving me until I'll break. I don't know what the routine has been before, but I'll bet my morning's pay the other suckers who paid a fifty-dollar agency fee were men who couldn't figure things out. But I can—and believe me, something is going to bust wide open, and it won't be me."

LIEBER THREW an orange at Hooper.

"Stuff yourself with that. The acid is good for a guy who sweats like you do. Now I'm going to tell you something, pal. If I were you, I'd just draw my pay and walk out. It's healthier. Reminds me of one poor dumb ox who had your job a month ago. He wanted his fifty bucks back. Naturally they wouldn't give it to him, so he threatened to go to the cops. You know what happened? He quit work one night and as he crossed the street, a truck ran him down. Maybe the poor chump was so busy thinking about going to the cops that he didn't notice it. They took him away in an ambulance."

Hooper whistled softly.

"But look—there is confirmation of my story. If that guy will back me up…"

"You'll have to see him in hell or heaven, buddy. He was dead when they got to the hospital. No, sir, if I was in your shoes, I'd just scram."

Hooper got up, threw away the orange peel and wiped his lips with a blue-checkered handkerchief.

"Yeah—yeah, I'll scram. To the cops if that agency doesn't listen to reason. I think this is a racket."

As Hooper walked away, Lieber's face grew dark. There was a chunk of pig iron on the ground near him. He picked it up and then, as several workers strolled in his direction, he let it drop again. He closed his lunch bucket and made tracks for a telephone booth.

That night Hooper, much too tired to be abroad, marched into the Atlas Employment Agency. Bancroft, the manager, with his feet on the desk while he studied a batch of applications, looked up and smiled.

"Well—I've forgotten your name, but you're the man I sent to the Flanders Foundry. How is the job? I hope it was worth the fee I had to charge."

"It's killing me," Hooper blurted. "I'm going to quit and I want my money back. I'll give you every cent I've earned the last two days. It's not much, when the pay is only twenty-one dollars a week, but you can have it."

"Now, now." Bancroft got up and pushed a chair toward Hopper. "Sit down and cool off. These days, my friend, you've really got to work for a living. There are fifty men for each job. As for returning the fee, of course that's impossible. Legally you haven't a leg to stand on. If they laid you off because work got slow we'd have to get you another job, but if you're fired or you quit, there isn't a thing I can do."

"But there's something I can do," Hooper retorted. "I can go to the police and have them check to see whether or not you and certain people in that factory are running a racket. You could make a lot of money by taking stiff fees, especially when you knew the worker would either have to quit or go to pieces before a week was up. They've driven me like a work horse. I don't happen to be a complete fool, Mr. Bancroft. A man has a few rights in this country. We're not living under a dictatorship. I can quit my job and I can make you return most of my fee. What's more, I'm going to see about it."

Bancroft got up quickly and put a hand on Hooper's shoulder. His voice was oily and suave.

"Now, I can see they haven't treated you very well. Supposing I contact certain people at that factory and have a talk about you. Why, I wouldn't be at all surprised that when you reported for work in the morning you'd be transferred to a different department where you won't suffer that ghastly heat and that back-breaking work. Shall we let it go at that? You do want a job, don't you?"

HOOPER NODDED, half satisfied, but not completely trusting this too smooth article of an employment agency manager. He shook Bancroft's hand and agreed to give it another try. Bancroft went to the door with him, murmuring promises about influence and quick promotion with bigger pay, and all for the measly little fee of fifty dollars.

But when Bancroft closed the door, he also slipped the bolt, wheeled and, his face dark with rage, picked up the phone and dialed a number.

"This is Bancroft," he said, and his voice became fawning. "We've got another of those pig-headed fools to deal with. Threatens to go to the police and the D. A. Perhaps, if he had a small fatal accident—"

"Bancroft"—the tone of the voice at the other end of the wire was as though the man talked of the weather—"you're getting old. Don't you know better than to send out a man with an education? Now we're in another spot. You know we can't risk an investigation—now. Arrange that—accident. And be sure it looks like an accident, too. One more slip like this and you'll find yourself in a cold spot, Bancroft. They call it the morgue."

Bancroft shivered and hung up Then he dialed another number, and made cautious arrangements about the permanent silencing of Joe Hooper. It was done callously and cleverly. Joe Hooper would not have the ghost of a chance.

CHAPTER II

DEATH IS MERCIFUL

IT CAME at ten o'clock the next morning. Hooper was delighted to find that he was assigned to a mill room where huge castings were lifted by cranes that ran along tracks set high up near the roof. Lieber was employed in that same division and he welcomed Hooper with some degree of awe.

"Say, you didn't do so bad, kid. It took me a year to get up here. Well—we can't stall around or they'll shoot both of us back to the foundry. We hook these castings to the crane, see? We follow it along and unhook them at the other end of the room. Careful now—these babies weigh plenty."

This work kept on for half an hour. Hooper was actually enjoying it. The air was clean and cool. There were no searing crucibles of molten metal to scorch his skin and bring the sweat out in buckets. Hooper helped to wrap the chains around one giant casting. The crane picked it up fast and started moving at the same time.

Hooper, watching the procedure, saw the vast chunk of metal swinging in his direction. He paled, started to back up out of range, and then someone gave him a hard shove forward. He was catapulted straight into line with that swinging casting. It struck him on the head, threw him a dozen feet.

Lieber set up a clamor. First aid units rushed to the scene. Hooper, alive and half conscious, kept babbling something, but no one paid much attention. He was lifted onto a stretcher, carried to an ambulance and taken home.

His injuries, according to the factory doctor, were not necessarily dangerous. The doctor made a natural mistake. On the surface, Hooper's head seemed to have been gouged open, but his reflexes were good, his heart strong, and it was better that he recover at home than in the ward of a hospital.

Hooper's mother was old before her time. Her life had been anything but easy. Even the death of her invalid husband had not relieved the economic pressure much. And now this—her Joe all bloody and not able to talk right. Mrs. Hooper sped to a neighbor's house and called her own doctor, old Dr. Cassidy who had taken care of her husband so many years.

Cassidy was an ancient so far as usual medical practitioners were concerned, but there was a vast amount of knowledge tucked away in his brain. He took five minutes to make an examination. Then he scribbled on a prescription pad.

"Joe isn't very good, Mrs. Hooper," he said hesitantly. "He'll have to be taken to the hospital, but not right away. Too dangerous to move him. If he can get a little sleep, he'll be in much better condition by morning. Don't worry about expenses. And tell me—what's he muttering? Something about a racket and an employment agency?"

Mrs. Hooper was much too excited to answer the question. She took the prescription.

"I'll get it filled at Clarke's drug store and come right back," she said hastily.

The doctor replaced his stethoscope in his bag.

"Now don't worry," he soothed. "Joe is young and strong. He's been badly hurt, but he'll come out of it. Just have Clarke give you those pills. They'll make Joe sleep. That's what he needs, mostly."

And Mrs. Hooper, a shawl around her head, hurried two blocks east where the old-fashioned drug store of Robert Clarke occupied a corner. Mrs. Hooper had no idea that death hovered above her home and her son. Nor that by visiting Doc Clarke she was putting into operation a chain of events that would ultimately spell catastrophe for certain people who well deserved it.

ROBERT CLARKE, PH.G., was busy in the back room of his drug store, going over a thick wad of accounts, long past due. He made a stack of about thirty bills and with a grin at his assistant, Dave Small, he tore these into shreds.

"You can't get money where there isn't any, Dave," he said. "The people who ran up these bills did so through necessity. When someone is sick and needs medicine, a drug store must furnish it, whether it gets paid or not."

Dave whistled softly and went about dusting a row of reagent bottles. This was old stuff to him. If everybody who bought medicines at Bob Clarke's store paid up he might be able to get that Greenough Super-microscope he had wanted so long. Bob Clarke had a use for this instrument, too, because it was one of the most efficient devices made for the detection of clues.

Bob Clarke was no ordinary druggist. On the surface, yes. His store was an old-fashioned place which sold nothing but medicines. It contained none of the piled-up counters of coffee pots and women's hosiery so ordinarily found in more modern "emporiums," nor were there any elaborate soda fountains and luncheonette bars. His only concession to these types of drug stores was a large crystal container filled with lemon drops. They were for the neighborhood kids.

Clarke's store was located in the poorest section of the city, where people needed medicines badly when they need them at all. In this neighborhood, Bob was known as "Doc" to the adults and the "Lemon Drop Man" by the kids.

But Bob Clarke was someone else besides a supposedly conservative druggist. The underworld would have wrecked this store and its owner instantly had they the slightest suspicion of his other identity, or that here was the headquarters of the crime avenger known as the Crimson Mask.

The creation of this crime fighter had not come about by accident. Bob Clarke had deliberately gone into this dangerous work, knowing that the slightest slip would cost him his life. It had been planned for ever since the day when young Clarke's father, a Police sergeant, had been shot in the back by crooks. He had died, soon after, and in death some freak of nature had caused blood to well to the surface of his face until he had seemed to be wearing a crimson mask. From that phenomena, Bob had taken his name and his trademark—a mask made of crimson silk.

Dave Small knew his dual identity, of course. Bob Clarke needed someone to keep the drug store open while he prowled the underworld in search of crime and criminals. Dave also acted as an excellent liaison officer to be contacted easily, and often to take an active part in the Crimson Mask's fight.

Then there was Theodore Warrick, ex-police commissioner who had found retirement boring. A good friend of young Clarke's murdered father, he had also been instrumental in the creation of the Crimson Mask. Now, Warrick formed the only contact between the world and the Crimson Mask.

Not many weeks before, a girl had come into the small, compact group. Sandra Grey had proven her ability and courage in a close encounter with death. Of medium height and with a trim figure always neatly clad, Sandra had become one of the Crimson Mask's aides.

Clarke, who had found no time for girls during his busy college year and in the subsequent development of the Crimson Mask, found her not only an asset in his battles against crime, but had fallen in love with the girl. He had never spoken of this, however, for so long as the Crimson Mask existed and carried on his perilous work, Clarke felt that he had no right to discuss or even think about marriage. Yet he enjoyed being with Sandra, enjoyed her wit and her blond beauty.

THOSE THREE, then, were the Crimson Mask's assistants. They alone knew that he was Bob Clarke, and the grim secret was safe in their possession. Each would have died rather than admit what they knew. Like Bob Clarke, they considered themselves crusaders, a small group intent on combating crime in a way which the police could never have done.

Unhampered by red tape, the Crimson Mask battled the underworld with its own weapons. He used slyness against treachery. Bullet for bullet. He answered violence with his own brand of the same stuff.

Part of his assets consisted of being a master at disguise. He had studied this, and had perfected it only after months of constant work. The laboratory in back of his store, presumably used to analyze blood, sputum—even food suspected of being contaminated—also served as the Crimson Mask's scientific approach to crime. Here he could study clues, whether dust taken from a dead man's clothing, or poisons used by murderers.

Mrs. Hooper came into the store in a great rush, waving the prescription. Bob Clarke soothed her, glanced at the drug called for and frowned.

"Something happened to Joe? What was it?"

"Oh, he is so sick! So badly hurt, Doc. It was in the factory. He just got his job. This morning he was hit—on the head."

"Too bad," Clarke said sympathetically. "Factory accidents are never mild…Just a minute. This won't take long."

"But, Doc," Mrs. Hooper said, "my Joe, he keeps talking like some people do in their sleep. He keeps saying something about the crane coming toward him and somebody giving him a push. It's like it really happened and he can't help telling me about it."

Bob Clarke said nothing. He went back to his prescription counter, transferred a dozen quarter-grain morphine sulphate tablets to another bottle, registered the prescription for the Narcotic Office, and then he picked up his hat.

"Watch the store, Dave," he told his assistant. "Mrs. Hooper seems to be in some difficulty. Her son was hurt."

He took Mrs. Hooper's arm and piloted her toward the door.

"I'll run over with you," he told her. "This medicine has to be given quickly and I can do it better than you."

"Oh, thank you." Mrs. Hooper's eyes were moist. "I—I'll pay your fee. How much is it?"

"Why should you pay me?" said Clarke, as he led her around the corner. "You're not taking the medicine. Wait until Joe is better, then he can pay up. Did Dr. Cassidy say he'd be all right?"

"Yes—but he must go to the hospital after he rests. It's so expensive, but the doctor is a good man. He says everything will be taken care of."

Clarke preceded her up the dark staircase of the four-floor walk-up. He was glad that he had a few moments later.

His first inkling of trouble came when he saw the door of the apartment open. His eyes narrowed slightly, but he walked in. A low moan came from one of the rear rooms. He dashed in that direction, rushed into the room and quickly closed the door as he heard Mrs. Hooper entering the flat.

JOE HOOPER lay across the bed. Blood welled from a horrible gash in the back of his head. His face was already becoming pale with the ghastly color of death. One arm moved slightly. Clarke raised him, eased him into a more comfortable position. He bent over the dying boy.

"Joe—Joe, it's Doc! You've got to talk to me. Open your eyes. Concentrate—please, Joe. Somebody came here and hit you on the head. Who was it? Why did they try to kill you?"

"Atlas—Agency—racket—sure it's racket. Took my—money. Job—no good. Killed me. I wanted to go—to—police. Lieber—pushed me—in front of crane. Lieber hit me—on head. I—I—"

Death was merciful this particular time. Had Joe lived longer, it would have been in the most extreme agony. Bob Clarke saw that, for he knew almost as much about medicine as a doctor. Joe, first struck by a crane, as he had said, was later ruthlessly killed by another severe blow that finished what the crane had started.

Clarke's face was drawn and grim as be straightened up. He pulled a sheet over the dead boy's face.

"Lieber, eh?" he muttered. "Atlas Agency! I don't know what this is in about, Joe, but I'll get the men who did it. I'll get than and put them where they belong—in a death cell."

CHAPTER III

THE CRIMSON MASK MOVES IN

BOB CLARKE walked quietly out of the room, helped Mrs. Hooper into a chair and asked questions. From her he drew the information that Joe had secured a job by paying a fifty-dollar fee to the Atlas Employment Agency, but that the job he got was so hard that it had made a physical wreck out of him in two days.

Lieber, it appeared, was a man who had been friendly to Joe. He worked at the same plant—the Flanders Foundry.

As gently as he could, Clarke broke the news to Mrs. Hooper. Then he called Dr. Cassidy—and the police.

When the police arrived, Clarke casually drew certain information from one of the detectives. A burly man named Brady, with a sergeant's rating.

"He was murdered all right," Brady said. "His mother can't seem to understand why. The kid didn't have any enemies. How about it, Doc? You've been in this neighborhood a long time. Know anything?"

Clarke shook his head slowly.

"I'm afraid not. We don't have the elite down here, Sergeant, but most of the people who live in this neighborhood are good. They would not harm anybody—least of all, Joe Hooper. I'm afraid I can't help you. Tough—the boy just got himself a job. Through the Atlas Employment Agency. Know that outfit, Sergeant?"

"Umm, yeah, I heard of them. Rotten bunch, too. The D.A. has been watching a lot of those places lately. Seems they've turned into a racket… Well, I guess we start from scratch here. Thanks, anyway, Doc, for trying to help."

Bob Clarke walked back to his store—walked slowly while his brain tried to straighten matters out. Somehow Joe Hooper had become involved in this employment racket. He paid fifty dollars—an exorbitant fee—to get a man-killing job. Was that part of the nefarious game? To collect a fee and then have the job vacated soon so that another sucker could be taken in?

First of all, Bob Clarke wanted to see this man called Lieber. Then the Atlas Employment Agency could bear a going-over, and finally the factory wherein Joe had been so badly injured. Clarke realized that there must have been a pressing reason for the murder. The first attempt had failed and then, while the flat was empty, the killers had slipped in to make sure Joe would never expose what he had in his mind.

Lieber was first. He would have an unexpected visitor soon. A man who wore a Crimson Mask!

At the end of the work day, Max Lieber swaggered out of the factory gate and headed straight for a tavern. His swagger was adopted to hide the eerie feeling in his heart. Murder was one thing to talk about— something else actually to commit. Lieber could still see Joe Hooper's face, agony-lined and turning pallid.

He called for rye and downed two quick drinks. Then he got a stein of beer, walked over to a corner table and sat down, with only a casual glance at the other men in the place. Lieber did not know it, but that sallow-faced man with the light, bushy hair who lounged carelessly behind one table across the room, was his Nemesis. The lounging man certainly did not look like an avenging angel of doom—any more than he looked like Bob Clarke, Ph.G. Once again, the Crimson Mask's mastery of disguise served him well. And once again he was prepared in advance, because he had already obtained a description of Lieber, and had recognized him the instant he had entered the tavern.

TEN MINUTES later two men entered the café, looked around and then walked briskly over to Lieber's table. They were uncouth-looking, badly dressed, even though their suits apparently had cost a great deal. "Gangster" was stamped on their features. Here were two men who would kill quickly, and yet yell for help if they, in turn, were cornered.

"You put it over, okay," one of them said to Lieber, and grinned coldly. "The cops ain't got no idea who done it. The boss says we was to hand you this. It's five hundred smackers. Not bad for two minutes work, huh?"

"Five hundred?" Lieber said, then dropped his voice hurriedly. "I thought I'd get a thousand. He said I'd get a thousand. Listen—I'm not flirting with the chair for no five hundred bucks."

"No?" One of the men leaned closer. "Then how'd you like to get nothin' and still flirt with the chair, huh? All we got to do is tip the cops and you're cooked, pal. Now get some sense. This is just the beginnin'. Go back to the job. You'll find another sap there to take the last one's place. Only this time Bancroft got a dumbbell and you won't have no trouble. He'll last a day or two.

"Now get this—keep your lip buttoned. If anythin' happens, call Bancroft and stop shakin' like you see the chair. Listen—this outfit ain't run by no nit-wit. We got a real bigshot boss who knows more than the cops all put together. And just in case you get jittery—maybe we'll turn you over to the cops, and maybe not. If we don't, they'll find you—drilled."

Both men arose and walked out. Lieber raised his stein of beer and spilled half of it on his shirt. He swore, jumped to his feet and streaked for the exit. He turned left, walking fast.

Then he was aware that someone paced just beside him. Lieber's heart jumped and he stopped.

"What's the idea?" he snarled, as he turned. "I don't know you."

"You will," the sallow-faced, bushy-haired man said quietly. "You will know me, Max Lieber, and wish to heaven you hadn't. Keep right on walking. There is a cab just around the corner. We're going to use it, and should any silly idea of running away happen to develop in that, twisted brain of yours, the object you feel sticking into your ribs is a gun."

Lieber voiced his greatest fear. "You're a copper! I ain't done nothing. I am innocent, I tell you."

A hard poke with the gun sent, Lieber walking rapidly toward the cab. He got in and gave a sobbing gasp as the stranger sat down beside him. The driver apparently had his orders already for the cab swung right and started across town.

"Where are you taking me?" Lieber blubbered. "You can't do this! It's against the law!"

"So is murder," came the grim reply. "You're going to a funeral home, Lieber... Oh, stop shivering. You're worse than when your two friends spoke to you. How much did they pay off?"

"I don't know what you're talking about!" Lieber protested shrilly. "You must be nuts! I'm going to yell for a cop. You can't get away with this!"

Lieber's captor calmly rolled down the window of the cab.

"You can yell now," he said. "We're getting into traffic. I think there's a patrolman on duty at the next corner. Shall I have the driver stop?"

"N-no," Lieber gasped. "No! I—I don't like cops. Just tell me what this is all about. Why are you taking me to a funeral home? Are—are you going to—to kill me?"

"You deserve it," the Crimson Mask said. "However, I don't kill mice when there are rats much more dangerous loose. I let the mice lead me to their masters. First of all I want you to look at a corpse. Someone you knew, Lieber. His name was Joe—Joe Hooper. Remember?"

LIEBER SLUMPED down in his seat. Suddenly he gave a bleat and tried a grab for the door handle. An arm shot just across his face and he felt his wrist grasped in fingers that seemed like iron. Lieber moaned and relaxed.

The cab stopped finally and Lieber got out, always feeling that gun pressed against his side. He and the Mask walked down the street for half a block, then they turned into an alley. At the

The quarter-ton bucket was about to crash down upon them.

back of this was a loading platform and a sign indicating that deliveries to the funeral home were to be made here.

"But it's closed," Lieber, whined. "You can't go in there. I—I don't want to anyway. Sure I knew Joe. He worked with me. Nice kid, too. But why should I look at his corpse?"

"Artists and composers always admire their work," the Mask said. "Why shouldn't you? Stop blubbering. I know the truth." You murdered Joe Hooper and you're going to see exactly what you did. It isn't nice to look upon the body of a man you killed, is it? You'll see his face as long as you live. It will never leave you—not until the moment when the dynamos pulsate and send out the juice that will put you face to face with Joe Hooper's after-death presence. Step up in front of that door and keep very quiet or I'll slug you."

Lieber held back. A near insane terror shone in his eyes. He wanted to run, to get away from this place as fast as his legs could travel. If he looked at Joe Hooper's dead face, he would be haunted forever. His legs were tensed for a quick dash, but his brain warned him that he would take no more than half a dozen steps. No man can outrace a bullet.

"Who are you?" Lieber asked. "How—how did you know I—killed—"

"They call me the Crimson Mask," Lieber was told. "My work is to make criminals pay for their misdeeds. You're small fry, even though you did the actual murder. I'll make a deal with you. Tell me why Joe was killed and who paid you off. In return I promise that you won't have to look at your victim and that you'll be given every break when you go to trial."

"Trial?" Lieber blubbered. "You can't do that to me. They'll make it the chair. I'll burn! I don't want to die! I don't want to stay in prison the rest of my life either!"

The Crimson Mask's grip on Lieber's arm tightened.

"Then we'll go inside. You're a yellow little rat, Lieber. Too yellow, I think, to look on the face of a man you just murdered. Move along— before I forget that you might be useful to me and use this gun on your rotten hide."

LIEBER LOOKED at the, closed door of the funeral parlors and in his mind's eye he could see through it, see the casket and the death pallor on the face of a man he had killed. Lieber shuddered. Even the chair was better than that agony.

"I—I'll talk," he quavered. "I'll tell you all I know. It ain't much, and you got to believe me."

"Talk then—and fast."

Lieber did. "I got a job in the foundry, see? That was to give me a chance to size up the suckers and hand them some baloney about how the work will kill them. The idea was to make 'em quit, and then they couldn't get their fees back. The foundry foreman was in on it for a five-buck split. There was a job open nearly all the time, and nobody stayed more than a day or two.

"Most of the suckers were dumb dodos, but this guy Hooper—he was different. When he said he'd go to the cops, they fixed things to have him knocked off, like it was accidental. Yes, I shoved him in front of the crane, but he was off balance when it hit him and he wasn't killed. So they told me to bust his head and do a good job.

"I didn't want to do it. Hooper was a nice kid. I had nothing against him. But if I didn't go through with the job, they'd have knocked me off. You can see what a spot I was in."

"Yes, a very serious one," the Mask said sarcastically. "It never occurred to you that a visit to the police might have saved Hooper's life and prevented the stigma of murderer from being pinned on you. But because you knew they'd put you away for a couple of years, you stayed away. Very well—so far. A foundry foreman was cut in. The manager of the employment agency had a share. But who got most of it, Lieber? Who is the real big shot?"

"I don't know," Lieber half sobbed. "Honest I don't. Nobody ever mentioned his name. I think maybe he owns that employment agency, but I ain't sure. All I know is he gives the orders and anybody who lays down on the job gets filled full of lead. Once you get into that outfit the only way out is like—like Hooper. Dead. I'm scared. I'm more scared of the big shot and his strong-arm boys than I am of the cops. Turn me in! Only hurry! Them guys know everything that goes on. They even might—"

"Yeah," a harsh voice came out of the darkness. "We might even know you're here, huh, Max? And shootin' off your mouth too. Don't move— either of you guys. I ain't alone, and four roscoes are pointin' right at your hearts. Lift 'em—snap it up!"

CHAPTER IV

HOT SPOT

THE MASK groaned. He could see shadowy forms slowly closing in. Lieber would not be able to hold back the information that the man with him was the Crimson Mask and the moment that name was mentioned, it would mean sudden, ruthless death.

Yet there was nothing he could do except surrender. The Mask was no superman. His hide was as vulnerable to bullets as the next man's.

The quartette of thugs closed in until they formed a tight little ring around the two prisoners. Lieber was quaking worse than before. His lips moved, but no sound came from his throat for several seconds. Then the words did come, in a torrent.

"I trapped him, boys! It's the Crimson Mask and I got him for you. I knew you were tailing me so I kept on talking while you got closer in the dark. It's the Crimson Mask, I tell you! It's him!"

Instantly three of the guns were pressed against the Mask's ribs. The four killers were on their toes, ready for almost anything. The burly man who seemed to be in charge of them gave Lieber a shove that sent him reeling backward. He faced the Mask, scraped a match and held it close to the prisoner's eyes.

"You don't look like so much," he ground out. "I don't think you are the Crimson Mask. But we'll soon find out. Hold him like that, boys, while I frisk the sap."

The crook extracted the Mask's gun, grunted in admiration at the weapon and shoved it into his own pocket. He had thick hands, but the fingers were nimble. They went through the Mask's possessions expertly, but did not find the piece of crimson velvet, cut like a mask that was secreted in the lining of the Mask's coat.

The thug gave the Mask a hard back-hand slap across the mouth. Then he removed the captured man's tie, walked behind the Mask and used it as a rope to fasten his wrists so tightly that circulation stopped within a minute after the knots were made firm.

Lieber, slinking back like a whipped dog, still muttered that the prisoner was the Crimson Mask. He was led behind the Mask and the procession crossed a courtyard and reached the street where a sedan was parked.

One of the thugs went ahead to see that everything was clear. At his signal, the Mask was hurried to the car and shoved inside. Lieber came in next, wiping a bleeding lip. If ever there was a man between two fires, Lieber was that man. On one side sat the Crimson Mask, most feared of all crime investigators. On the other, were hired thugs. Lieber could see nothing but death in store for him—a horrible death too, if the stories he had heard about these strong-arm artists were correct.

The burly leader shoved his hat to the back of his head and glared at the prisoners.

"So you say this bozo is the Crimson Mask, huh? Okay, Lieber. Maybe he is and maybe he ain't, but you told him plenty. We figured you for a canary, so I had one of the boys tail you after you left the café. He phoned for help after you came here. That brought us, and it looks like we were just in time. How much did you tell?"

"I didn't say anything but a lot of lies," Lieber whined. "He was going to bump me off. And he knows I killed that Hooper kid. I don't know how he got wise, but he's got enough on us to ship us to the chair."

A thick hand slammed against Lieber's face.

"What do you mean—us? You knocked the kid off, didn't you? Listen, dope, the only way to square yourself is by knocking off this guy too. Only first we got to call the boss, and we also got to fix things so the cops won't have any evidence. How do you rub a guy out and leave nothin' behind?"

THE MASK, closely watching Lieber's face, saw that the double-crosser was thinking, and the light in his eyes indicated that he knew the answer. The Mask knew beforehand what Lieber would suggest and the thought of it sent shivers of horror through his body.

"I got it!" Lieber exclaimed triumphantly. "You can kill him and never leave a trace. Have the driver go to the foundry. There ain't nobody in the place this time of night. Only a couple of watchmen who hang around the office. I know how to get in—I got a key to the gates. We take him to the furnaces. There's always a big crucible of brass melting down for the next morning. By now it's nice and hot. There's room enough for this guy in that crucible and there won't be much left."

The burly thug slapped his thigh in admiration of the idea.

"You really got a brain, huh, Lieber? That's a good stunt."

He shouted to the driver and the car changed its course, heading toward the big factory. The Mask said nothing. He had given up any attempts to loosen the knots near his wrists. Cutting off the blood from his fingers had paralyzed them long since. Even if by some miracle he managed to get loose, his hands would be useless.

There was no possibility of help coming from anywhere. Dave did not know where he was, nor did Sandra nor ex-Police Commissioner Warrick. His only hope lay in the time element during which the unknown boss of this racket would be contacted and come down to have a look at the Crimson Mask. During those moments he had to be on the alert for the slightest loophole.

Yet how could one materialize with four armed and ready-to-kill gunmen always at his side?

The car slowed up at the factory gates. Lieber, accompanied by the driver, made a brief prowl around the fence to make sure the watchmen were nowhere in sight. Then Lieber opened the gate with a key. The car drove through, stopped, and Lieber came aboard once more. He seemed sure of himself now, as though he had been redeemed in the eyes of these murderers and that his reward would be the right to go on living.

"Get out—slow," the burly thug told the Mask in a hoarse whisper. "You make a noise and we'll smash your skull in. Lieber, you show us the way to the foundry. I'll grab a phone some place and make a call. None of you other mugs are to be near, understand?"

Lieber indicated phone booths placed in one of the corridors just inside the factory door. The burly crook entered one and stayed there for about five minutes. When he emerged, he rubbed his hands in glee.

"The big shot is coming down to have a look at this guy. He don't think he's the Crimson Mask either, but it don't make much difference, because he gets what's coming to him anyway. Okay, Lieber, show us the way to the furnaces and that melted brass."

Lieber was more than eager to obey. He trotted ahead, leading the way through heaps of molding sand, piled-up mold frames and the weights Hooper had all but broken his back on. The only light came from the dull glow of the huge fire pits at the far end of the big room. Even twenty feet away the heat was intense.

The Mask was shoved back against the wall. All four thugs planted themselves in a line not more than three feet in front. The Mask studied their harsh features in the light of the fire pits. If he ever got out of this he would know these men again, especially the burly one who seemed so high up that he knew how to contact the big shot.

SO LONG as he still breathed, the Mask never lost hope. He had experienced close escapes from death many times—probably none as certain as this one—but he kept nerves and muscles alert. If there seemed no other way out, he might be able to take at least one of these murderers to death with him.

The minutes crawled by. Lieber was posted to listen for watchmen and to give the signal when the leader of these men put in his appearance. One thing—the Mask would have a look at the brains behind the mob.

Then Lieber gave a hissed warning. A shadowy figure walked slowly down the path between the molder's benches. For a moment the Mask believed this man to be without a face. Then, as he neared the light from the fire pits, the Mask saw that his features were hidden behind a welder's metal hood. The voice, when the leader finally spoke, was obviously disguised.

"So you claim to be the Crimson Mask, do you? I hardly believe it, but I rather think you will tell us the truth very soon. Tyko, you mentioned something about me melting this man down with a lot of brass. It's a good idea. How did you come to think of it?"

Lieber came bouncing forward.

"I thought of it, Boss! I used to work in here, see? I got the suckers primed to quit. So I know about the big crucibles of brass. I can work the crane that lifts it out too."

"Then do it," the muffled voice ordered. "I want to find out if this man is the Crimson Mask—because if he is, then one of the biggest worries I have will be off my mind. Get that crucible down here, Lieber. Hurry!"

Lieber sped away. He operated the derrick with the expertness of experience. Soon the huge, glowing cauldron came down the derrick track, held high above the waiting men by thick tongs. Then Lieber lowered it gently. The heat became intense. The burly crook who had been called Tyko by this mysterious leader, covered his eyes and backed away.

The Mask suddenly lowered his head and started a run straight toward the settling crucible. He hoped that by exposing himself to the in tense heat he might slow up pursuit. But the leader, protected by the metal welder's shield, sprang into action. The Mask encumbered by his bound hands, skirted the crucible as close as he dared, wincing at the terrific heat.

Then the metal-hooded mystery, man was upon him. A powerful arm was wrapped about the Mask's head, pulling him back. A knee pressed painfully against his spine. The choking grasp cut off all air from his lungs. He felt his senses reel from the combination of the heat and the lack of oxygen.

Then the Mask was dragged back. Tyko grabbed him and began slamming hard blows into his midriff, and then as the Mask doubled up in pain, slugged him mercilessly on the face. The Mask dropped to his knees, and Tyko used his feet to continue the cowardly punishment.

"That's enough," the metal-hooded leader's voice snapped. He stepped closer to the Mask. "I want to know one thing. Are you the Crimson Mask? I don't care how you got onto Lieber's trail. You'll never tell anyone, but you can save yourself some intense agony by talking."

THE MASK'S lips were compressed. He gave no signs of weakening. Tyko stepped forward.

"Lemme go to work on him some more, Boss. I'll make him talk, or bust his neck."

"No. Two of you men carry over a pair of the heaviest weights you can find. Get some rope too. We'll tie our uncommunicative friend to the weights and have Lieber shift the crucible closer and closer. If he does not talk, he'll be seared to a crisp. You can put a gag between his lips, Tyko. He may not talk, but he'll scream all right."

Tyko drew out a dirty handkerchief, wadded it into the Mask's mouth and then removed the bonds about his wrists. He used the Mask's tie to fasten the gag in place. The Mask's hands, swollen and helpless, gradually began to acquire a certain amount of feeling again and he could flex the fingers slowly, even if that slight motion made him sweat in pain.

By the time Tyko's pair of hoodlums returned, almost all the pain had left his hands. But Tyko and his third hood stood close by with drawn guns.

Two heavy weights were dropped to the dirt floor beside a neatly stacked pile of silvery metal bars. The Mask was forced to the floor by the simple expedient of kicking his legs from under him. His arms were seized and his wrists tied to the heavy weights.

CHAPTER V

A LESSON IN METALLURGY

N OT MORE than a foot away from those light-colored bars of metal, the Mask was hardly aware of what went on. For an idea had swiftly come to him.

As a pharmacist he had studied chemistry in all its phases, even to metallurgy. He knew exactly how molten brass was prepared for the molds and in those silvery bars lay his one means of escape—his one hope for life.

As the others stepped back, he moved to the left slightly. The weights were of rough iron which had never seen a rolling barrel. Their purpose was simply to hold the two parts of the mold tightly together by sheer weight. The rope with which the Mask was tied to them was cheap hemp and badly frayed. In a hurry to obey orders the two thugs had not taken time to find a stouter rope with which to secure their victim.

The Mask maneuvered the rope around the two-inch hole through which it passed until he got it into the roughest possible spot. He was aware that the crucible moved slightly, scraping across the dirt floor, gradually drawing closer and closer.

The heat grew in intensity until his flesh almost withered under it. He smelled his hair singeing and his face felt like a piece of parchment. Another foot and he would suffer bad burns. Yet he kept sawing away at the rough edge of the iron casting and gradually the rope became more and more frayed.

Yet that crucible came closer, too, every second. The Mask had to close his eyes tightly to protect them, for the moisture was dried up in a flash. Then, when he thought he could stand the heat no longer, the crucible slowly moved away and the metal-hooded leader swaggered closer. The Mask fell limply against one weight to cover up his furious work of trying to part the rope.

"You can't last much longer," the leader said from beneath the hood. "Are you ready to answer my question yet? Are you the Crimson Mask? Nod if you want to answer."

The Mask shook his head stubbornly. The leader growled a curse.

"All right. You've asked for this. I'll have the crucible moved so close you'll yell for mercy. If you happen to be stubborn enough to withstand pain—then I'll see that you are thrown into the molten metal. Talk, and we'll use a bullet first."

The Mask made assenting reply with his head. He seemed on the verge of unconsciousness. The hooded man leaned down, set the heel of his palm against the Crimson Mask's chin and shoved his face around. Then he grunted, for there was dark challenge in the Mask's eyes.

The crucible scraped across the floor again. At the crane controls, Lieber seemed to be enjoying himself. He was showing that he could dish it out with the best of them. And hadn't he also captured the

Crimson Mask? Hadn't he accomplished what ten thousand of the most vicious gangsters in the nation would have given their right arms to do?

The Mask got to his knees and began sawing again. His body hid the motion from the view of his captors. Then he felt the rope weaken considerably. He tugged at it. In his weakened condition he was unable to budge the weight, but he did manage to break the rope. The supreme moment was at hand. He was gambling with life and death now—and all the odds were against him.

The crucible moved so close that the heat was excruciating pain. The Mask opened his eyes for a bare instant. His freed hand darted out and lifted one of the three-inch-thick bars of silvers' metal from the neat stack. Oddly enough, this seemed to require little effort. The metal was pure aluminum.

THE MASK turned his head and his eyes seemed to be imploring for mercy. He nodded frantically. Quickly the crucible was moved about two feet away and the hooded man strode forward. On his heels came Tyko, his three hoods and Lieber, fawning and smirking. The gag was removed from the Mask's mouth.

"Yes—yes, I'm the Crimson Mask," he choked. "I admit it. I can't stand this agony much longer."

Lieber gave a yelp of glee.

"See? I fixed him, didn't I? I made him talk!"

The metal-hooded man turned around slowly. He gestured to Tyko and the burly thug moved close to his side. There were whispered instructions and Lieber turned deathly pale. He began backing away slowly.

"Wait, Lieber," the hooded man checked him. "I am grateful to you. I ordered that you be given five hundred dollars for putting Hooper out of the way. I'll pay you another five hundred for your work with the Crimson Mask. Here it is."

Lieber, thinking of nothing but the sheaf of bills which the hooded man held out, approached in a hurry. He passed by Tyko. Suddenly Lieber felt something jab his side. He half turned. There was a muffled explosion. A gun doesn't make much noise—not the automatic type— when pressed hard against the body of its victim.

Lieber was hurled two feet away by the force of the slug. He doubled up in pain, and in the weird light of the molten metal his face contorted until it wore the eeriest lines of his death agony.

Tyko, the hooded leader, and the three thugs were intent on watching Lieber die. The sadism that coursed through their veins spelled disaster although none of them realized it. After all, the only other enemy in the place was the Crimson Mask, already half dead from the heat, and tied to the weights.

Therefore none of them noticed the Mask hastily remove the rope from his other wrist, crouch and throw the bar of silvery metal straight into the maw of that giant crucible.

A sudden flash of blinding light illuminated the foundry. The contents of the crucible seemed to be actually boiling, and huge, foaming bubbles of slag ran over the top. Then, not more than three or four seconds later, thick white fumes dimmed the intense light. It poured out of the crucible, creating a dense fog no eye could penetrate.

"The Crimson Mask!" Tyko yelled. "He did that! He's getting away!"

The hooded man gave sharp orders. Tyko and his men spread out to search, but all of them were coughing from the fumes and they plunged around aimlessly, unable, to see more than a few inches in any direction.

Meanwhile the Mask, as that intense light flared up, darted to the left. He vaulted a stack of mold frames, crouched behind a barrier of sand and stayed there until the white fumes, which he knew would emanate from the crucible, shielded his movements. He knew exactly in which direction to retreat and he reached the door long before Tyko or his men were even in action.

Clear, cold air cleared his lungs and eased the burning sensation in his eyes. He was tempted to hide and watch the departure of the quintette, but that was dangerous. There would not be much chance of the leader removing that welder's hood in front of Tyko's thugs.

THE MASK was unarmed, badly weakened by his ordeal, and he knew that if he wanted to avoid telltale blisters, he must treat his seared flesh promptly. Neither was there any hope of capturing these men single-handed.

The Crimson Mask was not given to rash action. He had little evidence as yet anyway. It was better to take care of his own seared body.

He had escaped only by using his head. He knew that aluminum is thrown into crucibles of molten brass to clear it of slag. The reaction is violent, providing a great deal of intense light, and the thick white fumes which in this case had so effectively masked his getaway. He hurried to the street, ran up it, and found a taxi.

Thirty minutes later he reached the rear entrance of his drug store and went up to his quarters.

Sandra Grey met him as he entered the door. Her usually smiling lips grew tight as she looked at Bob Clarke's red inflamed skin. He managed a grin and told her to call Dave. Moments later soothing applications were applied to Bob's flesh.

"I ran into a bit of trouble," he explained. "Incidentally I met the devil who controls this racket. I also know it is a racket. They get jobs for fat fees and then other members of the mob overwork the men who pay to get a job. They are forced to quit. At fifty dollars a head that can run into money. If they handle only ten a day that's five hundred dollars and I'm sure the number of victims runs into the hundreds. The mob is too well organized to exist on chicken feed."

"But if you saw the big-shot," Dave put in quickly, "you've got the mess cleaned up."

Bob Clarke groaned. "It's not as easy as that. In the first place I didn't see the leader's face. He wore a welder's hood that he got somewhere in the factory. I do know there is a tie-up between factory foremen and employment agencies though, and we may be able to develop something out of that. Dave—Sandy—we're not fooling with a bunch of ignorant gangsters led by a man of their own caliber. This leader probably moves around in society, possibly makes speeches in defense of the working man, puts on an eternal act to disguise his own rotten motives... Sandy, will you hand me the phone? I'm going to call Warrick."

Sandra pushed the telephone table closer. Bob Clarke had a secret, direct wire to ex-Police Commissioner Warrick's home and in a moment he had Warrick on the wire.

"Mr. Warrick, I need your help," he said at once. "A group of racketeers are preying on working men who need jobs. I'll explain the whole affair later on. Right now I want you to get the owner of the Flanders Foundry and whoever operates the Atlas Employment Agency string of offices to your home. Never mind how you accomplish it, but get them there. I'll show up later on."

"They'll be here," Warrick vowed. "If I have to pull strings with the Police Department."

CHAPTER VI

SEALED LIPS

WARRICK DECIDED to make certain the men would appear, so contacted Inspector Byrne of the Detective Division. Although retired, Warrick still found that his connection with the

Crimson Mask enabled him to exert a certain measure of authority. The men arrived, in the unofficial custody of Inspector Byrne, about forty minutes later.

Lawrence Carter, who owned the Atlas Employment Agencies, was a dour, none too healthy-looking individual, and the moment that he entered the room, Warrick's suspicions grew. Carter had served a one-year term in prison, despite his wealth. His methods in the brokerage business had been on the shady side, but with his license revoked, he had gone into the employment agency business, and had done well.

Carter was accompanied by a tall, strapping man dressed in a chauffeur's uniform. Warrick did not know him.

William Mitchell, who operated the Flanders Foundry, was short, obese, and inclined toward the greasy side. He, too, was accompanied—by a dapper, lithe, middle-aged man who carried a briefcase under one arm. Mitchell was properly indignant at the idea of being routed out of his home in the middle of the night by a detective.

"I fail to understand why a law-abiding citizen should be subjected to such measures," he complained. "I was in the middle of a big deal with Cullen, my business agent."

Cullen, the dapper man, moved forward with short steps.

"You may add my protests to Mr. Mitchell's. I insisted on accompanying him here to protect his interests."

"Gentlemen," Warrick said in a soothing voice, "you are not suspected of any crime. All of you know that I work with the Crimson Mask, so—"

"The Crimson Mask!" Mitchell, the foundry owner, blurted. "Is he coming here?"

"I hope so," Warrick answered. "It was at his request that I summoned both of you here. Mr. Cullen is also welcome—and your chauffeur, too, Mr. Carter."

Carter shrugged. "If I can help the Crimson Mask, I'm very willing to oblige. But before he appears I want to explain about Frenchy—he's my chauffeur. His full name is Frenchy Flavin, and I met him while I served time in prison. Frenchy also served a long stretch, but like me, he has completely reformed. I simply wish this to be understood when the Crimson Mask arrives because he will probably recognize Frenchy."

There was a movement behind the group and they all turned. A man dressed in dark clothing and with a crimson mask over his eyes, stood just inside the French windows. Mitchell, the foundry owner, gasped and moved back a step or two as though he feared this red-masked crime fighter.

WARRICK MOTIONED the men to chairs placed in a row. They sat down and the Mask approached slowly.

"Today," he said, "a young man was murdered because what he knew might have backfired on certain criminal elements. He was a victim of an employment agency racket. He paid an exorbitant fee to one of your officers, Mr. Carter. Then he was given a man-killing job, driven like a slave, and quickly forced to a point where he would quit. Thus his fee would be lost and the job open again for another unwary victim."

"But if Carter's agency is responsible, what was I brought here for?" Mitchell demanded.

"Because the young man was assigned to work in your foundry, Mr. Mitchell. I can assume there is a tie-up between some of your employees and this vicious racket. They provide the impossible work for victims sent over by the agency. I have made a cursory investigation during the last hour or so and I find that this racket is being conducted on a big scale for tremendous profits. I also know that someone with organizing ability heads the hoodlums who do the strong-arm work I want to know where both of you men were tonight—at nine-fifteen."

Mitchell spoke up first.

"I was at home, going over certain plans with Mr. Cullen here. He can vouch for me. As for this business being conducted in my factory, you have simply to name the men tied up with it and I'll see that they are discharged in the morning."

The Mask looked over Carter. The loan agency owner was fidgeting.

"I—I'm not certain just where I was," he admitted. "Do you remember, Frenchy?"

The ex-convict rubbed his chin.

"Yeah, sure I remember. You said you were goin' out for a walk and you left about eight-thirty. I wanted to pick you up some place, but you said 'no.' It was after ten when you got back. I dunno where you went, though."

"Neither do I," Carter groaned. "I take long walks—solitary walks. It helps me to think and plan my next day's work. Ever since I was in prison, I discovered just how sweet fresh, free air is. I haven't got an alibi, but I know absolutely nothing about this racket of which you've informed me.

"I—I can't possibly see how you could suspect me. Why, after I got out of prison, I devoted a lot of my time and money in reforming criminals. Most of them were friends I had made in prison. I discovered that a man with a criminal record is just as good as those he may rub shoulders with on the outside. Those men only need a helping hand."

"Yeah," Frenchy Flavin appended. "I did a five-year stretch for puttin' the heat on a bank. The boss—Mr. Carter—we met in the prison library where I worked all them years. He says when I get out to come and see him. So I did, and he made me his chauffeur. Now I'm on the level. Why, he even sends me to the bank with lots of cash and I always come back."

Frenchy grinned sheepishly as he finished, as though the admission he made seemed odd, even to his own ears. The Mask backed toward the window.

"I shall be gone a few minutes. You gentlemen will wait here until I return or phone. If you are not involved in this racket—and I doubt it myself—you have nothing to fear. The agency which sent this young man to the Flanders Foundry is managed by a man named Bancroft. You might compile a record on him, Mr. Carter, by telling Warrick all you know about him."

THE CURTAINS in front of the French door parted and, like some ghost walking noiselessly on air, the Crimson Mask vanished. Mitchell wiped a glistening brow and then shoved a cigar between his teeth. He forgot to light it. Carter relaxed, while Cullen, Mitchell's business agent, and the ex-convict Frenchy, showed neither alarm nor relief.

"Bancroft," Carter grumbled. "I never did trust him. He came with recommendations from a Mid-western employment agency and I took him on. His office showed the average amount of profit and I received no complaints about the way he handled the business. Personally, I know very little about him."

Warrick tried questioning the man, but Carter was either a brilliant liar, or he spoke the truth. Mitchell began fretting at the delay and his business manager kept whispering in his ear. Warrick found that he liked Mitchell much less than he liked Carter, even though the employment agency owner had a criminal record.

Thirty minutes after the Mask disappeared, Warrick's phone rang. He answered, listened a moment and then hung up.

"You may go now," he told the four men. "The Crimson Mask asks that you say nothing about this meeting, nor that you give away what you know by discharging the men he named as agents of the racket. That means your foundry foremen, Mitchell, and your agency manager, Mr. Carter."

Mitchell and Cullen left first. They climbed into an expensive sedan and vanished before Carter and Frenchy emerged from the house. Carter's car was a five-year-old sedan. Frenchy opened the door, helped

The Mask saw a knife protruding from the man's back.

his employer in, and then ran around the car to climb behind the wheel. They started away and a moment later another car pulled out of a side street and took up the chase.

This car was driven by the Mask. Carter, an ex-convict and, presumably, the helping hand to dozens of men with criminal records, was the most logical man to suspect. Tyko and the hoodlums he had assembled might all have been "helped" by Carter. It was a simple and effective way of creating a gang.

The Mask held well to the rear, and he was certain that at no time did Carter or his chauffeur realize they were being trailed. Then suddenly the Mask stepped on the brake and pulled over quickly. The car he followed had stopped. Carter climbed out, said something to Frenchy, and walked rapidly away.

The Mask also got out, left his car there, and followed on foot. He realized that they were close to the vicinity of the Atlas Employment Agency office, where young Hooper had first stepped into a death-trap.

Ten minutes later the Mask blessed the hunch that had urged him to follow Carter. The self-styled reformer was heading straight for that office. The Mask noticed that it was lighted. Probably Bancroft was there, expecting his employer.

He saw Carter look around nervously, open the lobby door with a key and close it behind him. The Mask broke into a run, fumbling in his pocket for a bunch of keys that would open almost any lock. Making sure he was unobserved, he stepped up to the door, examined the lock, and tried several keys before he found the right one. The delay had been no more than two or three minutes.

HE STEPPED into the lobby warily, his right hand closed around the butt of his holstered pistol. This was progressing almost too easily and the Mask wanted no part of another trap. Beneath the disguise which he had assumed, his flesh still burned from the effects of his exposure to the terrific heat of the crucible.

He went up the stairs quickly, reached the third floor and saw a gleam of yellow light down the long corridor. The door to the Atlas Employment Agency was ajar. He drew his gun, moved silently toward the door and paused outside to listen. Not a sound reached his ears.

Slowly he pushed the door wide, elevated the muzzle of his gun for a quick aim, and lunged into the outer office. He stopped short. It was empty. He opened a gate, passed by a receptionist's desk and reached the door of the private office. He found this unlocked. The room was dark.

Then the Mask's eyes made out the form of a man slumped on top of the desk. He found the light switch, turned it on and whistled in surprise. Bancroft was still there—but he would never talk. A knife had been driven to the hilt in his back. There were absolutely no signs of Carter.

CHAPTER VII

THE CRIMSON MASK'S SPY

REMOVING HIS disguise at home a little later, Bob Clarke explained all this to Sandra and Dave.

"It looks as though Carter killed Bancroft to be certain he'd never testify. I examined the knife, of course, looking for prints. There were none, and I remember that Carter had a pair of gray gloves stuck in his coat pocket. Of course Mitchell might have gone to see Bancroft and killed him before Carter arrived. Whoever did it was known and trusted by Bancroft, because there were no evidences of a struggle."

"It's Carter," Dave opined. "Everything points to him. His prison record, the mugs he is supposed to be helping, and you saw him go into Bancroft's office. Certainly it's Carter."

Clarke frowned. "That's the trouble. Things point so squarely at him that I wonder if part of the mess isn't planted. There is one way to find out, and you're the man to do it, Dave."

"Don't I come in on this case?" Sandra asked.

Bob Clarke grinned at her.

"Not yet, Sandy. This is clearly Dave's job, because it requires a man. Here is the idea. I'll put some makeup on your face, Dave. In the morning you go to one of Carter's employment offices and ask for a job. You won't look either prosperous or too smart. If they haven't shut down the racket temporarily, you'll be given work at once. Take it, go wherever they send you, and watch things.

"Phone me at exactly seven-thirty at night. If I don't hear from you, I'll assume you are in trouble. Through you, we may be able to build up a strong case, find the identities of other victims who are willing to testify in court and, with luck, unveil the unholy mind that directs the racket. It's a dangerous assignment and I'll handle it myself if you wish, Dave."

"Try and keep me from it," Dave scoffed. "I'll find some old clothes right now."

Bob Clarke sat down on the davenport beside Sandra.

"I don't want you to think I'm deliberately keeping you out of this, Sandy," he told her. "There just isn't anything for you to do yet. I know you hate crime as much as I do, and want to work with me against it."

Sandra smiled.

"Just don't forget that, Bob. My father, like yours, was murdered by criminals. I don't want to sit back and let you and Dave take all the risks. Haven't you found any clues yet?"

"None. One or two that I hoped would develop went flat. Our only chance now lies with Dave and with one other man—a thug I'd enjoy slapping down. His name is Tyko, but I don't know what rat hole he occupies and there's a good possibility that he's run out anyway, because he knows the Crimson Mask will be after him.

"Dave is right about Carter. Everything points directly at him. Yet I'm not satisfied. Mitchell owns the factory where an attempt was made to murder me, and where young Hooper almost met his death. Then there is Cullen, Mitchell's business consultant. I don't like him. He looks sly, and anything but trustworthy. He may be directing the whole thing from behind the scenes.

"Now you'd better run along. It's late, and we may need every ounce of energy we possess before this case is broken. I'll be in the drug store all day tomorrow. If anything develops, you will have to handle it."

Clarke's mind was hardly on his work the following day. He was out of contact with Dave and, worried about him. And if Bob Clarke could have watched Dave, those worries would have grown.

DAVE ENTERED one of the Atlas Employment office chains early the next morning. He was fifth in a line of about twenty when the doors finally opened. Half an hour later Dave was shown into the private, quarters of the manager. He proved to be a dark-featured, rat-eyed individual. He looked Dave up and down suspiciously.

"You able to do office work?" he demanded.

Dave gulped "Gosh, no. I ain't been to school since I was seven. But anything else—even a pick and shovel. I'll do it. I got to have a job, Mister."

"There is a new dam being built, not far out of the city. I can get you a laborer's job there at twenty-five dollars a week—five days. It's hard work, but you look strong. The job will last about two years. There is only one hitch."

Dave's eyes glowed.

"Two years! Gee, Mister, I'll do anything you say."

"Before I can give you the assignment," the manager went on, "you must pay the agency a fee. Fifty dollars. Can you raise it?"

Dave acted staggered at the sum required.

"But don't them fees usually come out of the pay, Mister? I can borrow the dough, but all the other places always took a little out of my pay until their fees were cleared up."

"We don't do business that way. If you can borrow the money, do so, and come back here as quickly as possible. A crew is going to start for the dam in two hours. There are loan companies who will lend you the cash if your friends won't come through. Use me as a reference if you wish."

Dave left, hung around a park for an hour and a half, and then returned. He paid his fee, got a written guarantee that if he lost his job through no fault of his, the agency would provide another job without charge. Then he joined a group of eight men, climbed into a big truck and they rolled out of the city.

Before noon Dave was swinging a pick and clearing out a deep excavation where huge supports for this big project would be placed. Above him the cement wall of the partially finished dam loomed like a giant, frozen waterfall. He was given twenty minutes for lunch and then went back to work.

At four o'clock Dave discovered the loophole in that five-day-work week. He was expected to labor until six o'clock—and after, if necessary. Bosses, rough men with bulging muscles, supervised the job.

No man was allowed to rest for even a minute. There were no water buckets and by mid-afternoon the combination of a hot sun and hard work made Dave feel like a man stranded in the middle of a desert.

He thought it was about time to protest the driving by the bosses. Four men had already thrown down their picks and walked off the job. All of them were sure the agency would refund their fifty-dollar fee. Dave knew better, but in order to get the wheels rolling he leaned on his pick until a straw boss came barging over.

"I'm near dead from work," Dave parried the order to get busy. "It ain't human to drive men like you been doing."

"Then why don't you quit?" the straw boss snapped. "We can get all the muscle men we want around here."

"And give up the fifty bucks I paid the agency?" Dave asked with a grin. "No, sir. Me, I'm too smart. I'll work all right, but tonight I'll see the manager of that employment agency and tell him a few things."

"You don't leave the premises," the straw boss growled. "All laborers live in the barracks and eat in the canteen. It costs eight bucks for board, and ten for a bed. Try to leave and you'll get your face smashed to jelly. Now pick up that pick and start digging."

DAVE OBEYED, and whistled softly in surprise. He was certainly learning things. Twenty-five dollars a week, but out of it came eighteen dollars for room and board. That left a net profit of seven dollars for the hardest work imaginable. No wonder the men were walking off the job.

Dave's legs would hardly hold him up when he staggered over to the elevator which would whisk him to the top of the dam. The straw boss rode up with him and he favored Dave with a broad smile. He dug into his pocket and offered Dave a cigarette. As he reached for it, the straw boss seized his wrist and turned his hand over.

"Blisters, huh? Who said you were tough enough for this kind of work, pal? What did you do before?"

Dave thought fast.

"Nothing. I was out of work so long, my hands got soft. Don't worry. I'm not squawking about blisters."

Dave didn't get the cigarette and he wondered if that had been just a neat little trap to be worked on anyone suspected of being a spy. It put him in a difficult spot. These men would resort to violence on the slightest suspicion. The racket was too big to be risked with kid-glove manners. Dave decided he had better call Bob Clarke as quickly, as possible.

But at the top of the dam he was herded into line with a score of other men and they were marched, like convicts, to the long, low-roofed mess hall. There he discovered that the appetite developed from the hard outdoor work left him the moment he saw the food that was slung in front of him. Another day, and the few pieces of meat in the stew would be able to navigate of their own accord.

Out of the corner of his eye he saw the straw boss regarding him intently. Dave picked up a tin spoon and gulped as much of the food as he could stand. Then he stretched his arms, got up, and started for the door. He was stopped by two guards posted there.

"I'm going after cigarettes," he explained. "I saw a little store just down the road. Okay?"

He was allowed to pass, and sauntered down the rutted dirt road. He found, when he entered the store, that it was operated by the construction company, and that cigarettes were thirty-five cents a pack. Dave protested, but finally paid it.

Then he asked if he could use the phone. No one seemed to care particularly and he closed the door of the booth tightly. The phone was a direct line to a small town just outside of the metropolis, and it had no dial system. Dave cupped one hand over the mouthpiece and gave Clarke's private number as low as he could.

"I'm at the Sheridan Construction job—the big dam. This is the real thing. Stiff fee, man-killing work and the rottenest food I've ever tasted. They're driving the men away. Plenty that came down with me quit already. There are thugs posted all around the place and they, look as though they'd like to get rough."

"Take it easy," Bob Clarke advised. "Keep your eyes open. Get the names of every foreman who drives you. Register the appearance of those gangsters so you can pick their mugs out of the rogue's gallery. Shine up to someone you can trust—someone who will be a good witness. Call me back tomorrow."

"Right," Dave answered. "But you'd better have a two-inch steak ready for me when I get back. I think I could chew the handle off my pick right now. Don't worry about me. Everything is—"

Dave was suddenly aware that the phone booth door was ajar, and that two sneering men stood just outside. He gulped and hung up. One of the men had a gun pointed at him.

As he emerged, his arms were quickly seized and he was hurried out of the store. A car was waiting in the road. Dave struggled, demanding an explanation. He got it in the form of a pistol butt across the head. Dave wilted, half conscious and completely unable to defend himself.

He was thrown into the car, hurled to the floor and a pair of heavy feet held him down there. When the car stopped, he was hauled out and propelled toward the door of a shack. Dave had not seen this particular building before and he reasoned that it must be located behind the fringe of forest that hemmed in the dam site.

Inside, he was shoved into a chair. A man, sprawled out in a hammock on a rickety rear porch, growled a curse and came in. He stepped up to Dave, struck him a hard blow across the mouth and then laughed.

"Well, sucker, who did you call on that phone? Maybe you're a copper, huh? Stand up while I frisk you."

There was nothing in Dave's pockets. He had made certain of that. The burly man put the flat of his hand against Dave's chest and gave him a hard shove. One of the other thugs promptly stuck out his foot. Dave tripped and fell heavily. The burly man bent over him and Dave's heart skipped a few beats. This must be Tyko, the man whom Bob Clarke had described. Tyko, the killer! Dave wondered what was in store for him.

"He ain't no cop," Tyko grumbled. "I know every flatfoot they'd send out on a job like this. Know what? I got a hunch this bozo works for the Crimson Mask. How about it—sucker?"

He kicked Dave in the ribs. Dave groaned, but he made no reply. The next ten minutes were a nightmare. Dave was tossed around like a punching bag, from one thug to another. Every few seconds Tyko would demand an answer.

Finally Dave collapsed. All the punching and kicking would not hurt him now. Merciful unconsciousness gripped him.

Tyko gave a final kick at his helpless victim and then strode out of the place. He took the car and returned in fifteen minutes.

"I just called the big boy. Know what? This guy is working for the Crimson Mask, and the boss says he must have called him on the phone. If that happened, the Crimson Mask will be out here tonight. He'll come to save this dirty spy. He's smart, that bird. He got away from us nice and proper at the foundry, but this time he won't get clear."

CHAPTER VIII

THE CLOSING TRAP

CLARKE, IN his rooms above the drug store, heard Dave's faint cry of surprise, and heard the phone connection broken immediately afterward. Dave had been in the middle of a sentence, and would only have stopped talking if he saw the approach of danger. Bob turned to Sandra who realized that something was wrong.

"Get the car out," he said. "I'm going to lock up the store. Dave is in a jam. Hurry!"

Bob Clarke drove like a fiend toward the construction job. He had taken time to apply a simple disguise, and his crimson mask reposed in the hidden pocket of his coat. There were two heavy automatics holstered on his hips. Bob Clarke once more was the Crimson Mask—and a man assailed by doubts and fears. Dave was his best friend, one of his few confidants. Nothing must happen to him.

"Bob," Sandra offered, "do you think this is just a trick to get you up here? Are you sure it was Dave who called?"

"Positive. They couldn't get that phone number out of him with hot irons. I think he was suspected and watched. They probably heard him talking about the work. Dave must have seen them, and hung up as a signal that he was trapped. This is going to be dangerous. You wanted excitement, Sandy. I think you'll get it."

"I did a little work on my own today," Sandra confessed. "I was going to tell you just before Dave called. I checked on Mitchell first. He's a shrewd man, Bob. Some of his business ethics are sharp. Last night he didn't reach his home for almost two hours after he left Warrick's house. He must have dropped his friend Cullen somewhere along the line, because he returned alone."

"Hmm." Bob Clarke bent over the wheel and tried to squeeze another mile out of the car's speed. "He said he had a big business deal with Cullen and was going to discuss it. What about Carter?"

"He's an odd one," Sandra admitted. "Before he was sent to prison for misuse of clients' funds, he was an out-and-out crook with no scruples at all. Then he served that one year, got out and he seems to be a changed man. He furnishes jobs for a lot of ex-cons, personally goes before the parole board—to plead for men he thinks deserve a break.

Like that tough-looking chauffeur, for instance. He got him out and darned if he hasn't reformed the man. Frenchy would cut a man's throat if Carter ordered him to do so."

Bob turned a corner on two wheels, straightened out, and leaned on the gas pedal again.

"If Frenchy would do that, then you can bet the other convicts he got out will do the same. Carter has a completely organized band of murderers, thieves, and all-around crooks at his beck and call. Maybe he doesn't realize this, but it certainly looks suspicious... Hang on! We're leaving the highway, and it looks like rough weather ahead."

As signs of the construction work began to appear, Clarke eased up on the gas and looked for a place to park. He found one beneath the shelter of a group of firs. The car was completely concealed there.

"Stay with the car," he told Sandra. "And don't pout. Someone has to have things ready for a quick escape. There is a gun in the side pocket of the car. Keep it ready in case someone shows up. If I don't come back in one hour, drive to the nearest phone and call Warrick. Tell him to arrange for a detail of troopers to be rushed here. And wish me luck, Sandy. I'll need it, if this is a trap."

AS HE disappeared into the darkness, Sandra examined the .32 automatic with which he had provided her. She definitely did not like the look of things. If this camp just ahead was a place where men were watched by armed guards, then some of those gunmen should be patrolling the lane leading up to it. The Crimson Mask, alone against no telling how many thugs, was in a dangerous position.

Sandra made up her mind quickly. She opened the door of the car, got out and closed it again softly. Then she crept away into the darkness, following the Mask's trail. As she neared the camp and saw the lights, in several cabins, she turned to the left and cut an arc to approach from the north side.

She found that the forest growth had been almost entirely cleaned out in this direction, and she made excellent time. Then she saw a thick bush about five hundred feet from a cabin that stood well apart from the rest of the camp. There were no lights in the cabin, but once Sandra was sure she saw a man slink up to the door.

She crouched behind the bush and looked for the Crimson Mask. He seemed to be hidden in the darkness, but he would start his search for Dave soon.

Then Sandra shivered as a feeling of weakness swept over her. Two men were forcing another out of the darkened cabin. They led him to a tree and quickly strapped him to the trunk. Sandra could not identify the man, but she knew it must be Dave. They were going to use him as bait.

Half a dozen others slipped out of the shack and disappeared in the darkness, probably taking up positions from which they could open fire on the Crimson Mask. She must warn him, reach him before he stepped into the death-trap.

Sandra started back, intending to call out a warning before the Mask should expose himself. Then she opened her eyes wide. The Mask was directly opposite her—across the clearing. He stood silhouetted against the starlit sky for a second.

Three of the killers had gone in that same direction. Unless their attention was diverted, the Mask was hemmed in on all sides. Calling out a warning would only put the gunmen on the alert. There was only one way to give the Mask a chance for his life.

Sandra did not hesitate a moment. She suddenly broke out of the woods and began running madly toward the middle of the clearing. She knew that the hidden killers might open fire on her at any moment. Sandra had never been quite as close to death before, but the discovered that there was no fear for herself in her heart—only for the Crimson Mask.

Someone yelled a command. From all sides men came barging toward her. There were ten of them, all flourishing guns. Sandra almost shouted in relief, for now the Mask had a clear passage to safety.

Two of the men seized her. A flashlight was turned on, and Sandra blinked in its ray. Tyko, cursing furiously, grabbed her wrist and twisted it until she cried out in pain.

"What are you doin' here? Who are you?"

"I—I came to see my—my husband," Sandra stammered, as her mind clicked swiftly. "He—he phoned me that he was in trouble, so I—I came up to take him home. He said the—the work was too hard."

Tyko flung her into the arms of two waiting thugs.

"We been a bunch of saps," he raged. "That dumb cluck only called his wife—or so she says. Take her' over' to him. See if he recognizes her."

SANDRA WAS dragged to the tree against which Dave was lashed. Dave's mouth was gagged, his limbs painfully tied, but nothing stopped his ears. He had heard Sandra, knew exactly what she had done, and quickly prepared to follow the alibi she had prepared. The gag was removed.

"Elaine," Dave managed through swollen lips, "you shouldn't have come up here."

Sandra yanked herself free of the restraining grasp of the gunmen and fled to Dave. She was a born actress and the tears that welled from her eyes seemed genuine. So did her voice as she implored the men to free her husband. But Sandra also managed to whisper encouragement to Dave.

"He's out there—somewhere. There is still hope."

Dave was cut loose and with Sandra at his side, they were escorted into the shack. Tyko put his foot on a chair, supported his chin in one hand and looked at them quizzically. Plainly he had fallen for Sandra's line and could not quite figure out what to do about the two prisoners.

Finally he growled orders that they were to be closely watched. Then he swaggered out. Sandra kept up her pretense, and Dave carried the game along. But there were no signs of mercy in the faces of the thugs; only that same puzzled look that had been on Tyko's evil visage.

Tyko returned after several minutes. He carried a length of rope slung over one shoulder.

"Now listen, you two," he said roughly. "We had enough trouble, see? We're takin' both of you back to town, but just in case you decide to get sassy, we're tyin' you both up. Turn around—snap into it before I change my mind."

Dave shivered. He could not protest or offer any resistance without spoiling the whole set-up which Sandra had put over, but Dave did not trust these men. Even though their prisoners seemed wholly innocent of any connection with the Mask, Tyko was not apt to let them go.

Dave submitted meekly to the tying up and it was done firmly. Then he and Sandra were forced to precede the group of gangsters along a path which led them to the top of the dam. Dave's eyes grew round in fear. Were they intending to push them off the edge?

They kept Sandra away from him and when he tried to speak to her, Tyko cuffed him across the mouth. They were placed, side by side, on the very brink of the half-finished dam. Then two of the men brought long ropes. These were tied under Dave's armpits and Sandra was treated in the same manner.

"We can't risk takin' you down the road," Tyko explained, with a smirk. "So we let you down to the bottom of the dam, see? Then we come down, cut you loose and put you in a car. Just take it easy. There ain't nothin' to be scared of."

BOTH OF them were eased off the edge. As they disappeared into the gigantic maw of the dam, Sandra turned her head toward Dave.

"Have we got a chance, do you think?" she asked coolly.

"I don't know, Sandy. That was a brave thing you did—springing the trap before the Mask walked into it. I know you're not afraid, so I'll tell you the truth. I doubt that Tyko will let us go."

In a short time their feet touched the bottom of the deepest part of the excavation. Before the descent began, their legs had been tied and both of them dropped limply, unable to maintain their balance. Dave wormed his way close to Sandra.

"So long as the Mask is out there, I'm keeping my hopes up," he told her. "I can't figure out what they intend doing. I know they wouldn't have shoved us off the dam because it would be hard to account for bodies or even for blood. The gang working on this job aren't too dumb to recognize evidence like that. If they kill us, they've got to find some way to hide... Sandy, did you hear something like a big motor?"

"Yes. It seems to be on top of the dam. What does it mean, Dave?"

Dave turned himself over until he was flat on his back. He knew what that sound meant, but he did not try to explain. Sandra would find out quickly and horribly enough. Then he saw death coming—slowly, but as certainly as the next day would dawn.

A giant apparatus was sending a huge bucket of cement over the edge of the dam. It would follow steel lines until it was suspended just over their heads. Then the bottom would open and tons of cement would pour down on them. When it hardened, they would be forever entombed and not a trace of their murder would be left. Sandra saw it coming and shuddered. Then she deliberately closed her eyes. She forced all her thoughts on Bob Clarke who, as the Crimson Mask, would carry on the work. And he would avenge their deaths. At least he was free and that was much more important than the fact that she and Dave were doomed.

The huge bucket was descending the line now, approaching closer and closer. Small particles of cement, adhering to the outside of it, were shaken loose and dropped like rain all around them. In Dave's eyes the bottom of the bucket became as large as the universe.

It was no more than twenty feet above them now. Dave saw the wire control on the bottom slowly grow taut. The lever which held the cement in place was being withdrawn. The bucket was stayed in its descent now, but it hovered above them, ready to drop its load. The bottom was beginning to open. Dave prayed, for Sandra's sake, that the end would come quickly.

CHAPTER IX

FLAMING GUNS

HIDDEN IN the darkness, the Crimson Mask saw two things simultaneously—Dave Small being lashed to a tree, and Sandra running wildly into the open. Then he heard hoarse grunts from close by.

Two men arose and rushed to intercept her. Others emerged from all directions. The Mask dropped flat.

Sandra had been right—this was a trap. And she had practically sacrificed her own life to save his.

The Mask's jaws tightened. He did not retreat. Tyko appeared soon, and the Mask watched Tyko and his men take their prisoners to the shack. Then, as he prepared to crawl forward and attack the whole outfit, he saw Tyko emerge and walk rapidly away. The Mask followed him.

Tyko went to the small company store, used a key to open the door, and headed straight for the phone booth. The Mask slipped through the door as quietly as a ghost. The darkness shielded his movements as he headed toward the phone booth.

He reached the side of it and flattened himself against the wall until his ear was pressed to the thin wood of the booth. Tyko had a booming voice, and even when he tried to talk softly it was still loud enough to penetrate the booth.

"Yeah, it was a phony," he said disgustedly. "The sap musta called his wife and she came right up. Sure we got her. Say, I don't go much for knockin' off dames. Yeah—yeah I'll do it, but the boys are gonna get nasty if there ain't an extra cut. Sure, I can get rid of them so nobody'll ever find the bodies. There's a big hole dug at the bottom of the dam and ready to be filled in. I'll drop 'em there and pour cement over 'em. It's a pipe."

Tyko listened to instructions a moment longer, then hung up. When he emerged from the booth, he walked directly out of the store, locking the door after him. He did not notice the slightly darker object near the floor.

The Mask stepped into the booth, got the operator and ordered her to check the call. Tyko had made a bad mistake here. The phone was connected with a small exchange out of the city and there were no dials.

He had apparently called the metropolitan area, for the Mask had heard fifteen cents deposited in the coin slots. It required only a moment for the check to be made.

"I'm an officer," he told the operator. "Inspector Byrne of the Metropolitan Police. You're sure about that? The number called is listed as being in the residence of Lawrence Carter. Thank you."

The Mask had no time to consider evidence now. Once Dave and Sandra were released, he could go into that phase of the case.

There was little time to lose. The Mask opened the store door with one of his keys and rushed straight toward the huge machinery used in building a dam. He saw the cement bucket on the ground near a control booth. A man had just finished hastily donning overalls, and was hurrying toward the booth.

The Mask waited for an opportune moment, then leaped. One arm encircled the man's neck. The other hand was clapped across his mouth. The Mask held him like that until the man grew limp. Then he let go, turned him around and administered a quick knockout blow.

He lowered the operator to the ground, removed his overalls and blue shirt and drew these on over his own clothes. Then he studied the man's features.

A FLAT make-up kit came from one of the Mask's pockets. He applied various creams and waxes to his face until they resembled those of the man he had knocked out. The disguise was none too good, for there was little light by which to see himself in the mirror. Yet it would pass, for that same lack of light would prevent anyone from getting a close look at him.

This rapid change required no more than five minutes. Then the Mask raced toward the control shed and examined the machinery until he knew just how it operated. He walked to the bucket, wrapped one of his guns in a piece of cloth and gently placed it on the bottom. He found a keen-edged ax and put that in the bucket also, taking care to wrap it well.

Someone was coming his way. The Mask retreated to the control shed. Tyko stepped into the small shack.

"Got to drop a special load right into the excavation," Tyko said. "Maybe it'll be set by morning and we can start building on it. I'll give the signals, so just watch me."

The Mask nodded, bent over the controls, and started the motor. He sent the bucket toward the huge cement mixer, but instead of allowing it to take on a load of cement he dumped the cement on the ground. Tyko and his men were too far away to notice.

He lifted the bucket then, sent it swaying and riding its steel line toward the edge of the dam. At Tyko's signal he manipulated the heavy object into the right position. Then he lowered it. Tyko kept highballing with his arm until it was in place. He signaled for the load to be dropped. The Mask seized the control wire and yanked it.

Then he drew his gun, crept forward until he was fairly, close to the group of men trying to peer over the edge of the dam, trying to penetrate the darkness to see just, how well their victims had been encased in cement. The Mask raised his gun and fired one shot. One man dropped over into a recess at the side of the dam's edge, a recess that was filled with water. He dropped to the bottom like a lead plummet.

The group of thugs at the edge of the dam whirled around. Tyko had a portable searchlight with him. He turned its ray in the direction of the shot. Gasps and strained curses were mixed as the ray brought into view a man who wore a crimson mask over his eyes.

The gunman fired back, but the Crimson Mask jumped for shelter. He pressed the trigger twice, and two more of the thugs curled up. The others scattered—all except Tyko. His mentality seemed a little greater than those of his men.

Tyko reasoned now that the two apparently doomed prisoners at the bottom of the dam were aides of the Crimson Mask, and Tyko was intent on killing them. He turned the spotlight over the edge. Below he could see Dave holding in his still tied hands the ax which the Mask had sent down, and sawing energetically at the ropes which bound Sandra.

Tyko growled a curse, rushed over to a supply shed and came back with another ax—a huge one easily capable of snapping the cable which held the quarter-ton bucket just over the two people who were trying to escape. The gunmen were still shooting at the spot where they had last seen the Mask, but he had left that place seconds before. The Mask realized just what Tyko meant to do.

One of the thugs came from under cover, intent on helping Tyko. The Mask's gun blazed, and the crook doubled up without a sound. He pitched to the ground. Then the Mask was racing straight ahead toward Tyko.

THE GORILLA-LIKE gang leader saw him coming, and prepared to meet the attack. He braced himself, held a gun ready, and as the Mask drew nearer he raised it for a quick shot. As he fired, the Mask dodged agilely aside, and before Tyko could use the gun again, the Mask was upon him. Tyko, much heavier and apparently stronger, gave a bleat of satisfaction. His arms wrapped around the Mask and squeezed.

Then Tyko thought something like an air-hammer was pounding at his midsection. He wheezed, loosened his grip and staggered back. The Mask followed up the attack swiftly. He could not waste a second, for Tyko's men would respond the moment they believed it safe enough to venture from under cover.

Tyko crouched, gave a wild yell, and charged. He stopped as though an invisible brick wall barred his path. The Mask's right fist snapped out, collided with Tyko's chin and sent him back on his heels. Tyko had dropped his gun, but he saw it now, only a few feet away, and he dived for it.

The Mask reached the spot first and kicked out. The gun went over the edge, straight into the pool, where the first gunman the Mask had shot had fallen, and whose half-clenched dead hand now stuck up above the shallow water. Tyko, half mad with rage, made an ineffectual grab for the Mask's legs. He was on the top of the dam and the sudden movement sent him sliding over the edge. His cries of rage turned into yells of terror.

Intent now on saving the man who had tried so earnestly to kill him, the Mask moved fast. But even the Mask's quick action was too late. Tyko's fingers clawed at the cement, but nothing could stop him. His wild yell grew fainter and fainter as he plummeted down to oblivion.

The Mask heard a shot, felt a bullet howl past his head, and whirled to attack Tyko's thugs. But they had little heart for the battle, now that their leader was gone. They scampered away and soon the Mask heard cars racing crazily down the rutted lane.

He peered over the edge of the dam. Dave and Sandra were free, and out of the way of the huge bucket. The Mask cupped his hands to his mouth and shouted directions. Then he hurried to the spot where Sandra had left the car. Fifteen minutes later he stopped and Dave and Sandra got in.

"Sandy," he said softly, as he hurried back to town, "I saw what you did, saving my life that way. I won't forget it in a hurry. Now do you think that if I asked you to stay with the car, you'd obey this time? When I promise you that Dave and I are hardly apt to get into trouble?"

Sandra smiled at him.

"Of course, Bob. It was just that I had a hunch about the trap. It was—rather awful, wasn't it? And then that man came flying over the edge of the dam, and—"

"It was Tyko," the Mask said. "I tried to save him because he alone knew the identity of the man behind this gang… Drive to Larry Carter's house and park just around the corner."

"Carter!" Dave exclaimed. "Then he is the boss. Are you sure, Bob?"

"I will be in a few moments," the Mask answered.

Sandra stopped at the designated spot. The Mask and Dave disappeared into a neighboring yard, and finally reached the rear of Carter's house. The Mask used his keys again and they stepped into the kitchen. Moving like cats on the prowl, both men made their way upstairs.

The house seemed to be empty but still they took no chances. A small flashlight illuminated their path to a bedroom. The Mask opened a closet door, appropriated a brush from the dresser and found several pieces of paper. Dave held them while the Mask brushed off several suits of clothing. He turned down the trouser cuffs and removed the dust lodged there also.

"I don't know what you're up to," Dave whispered, "but it certainly looks like Carter is our man. Don't you think we ought to grab him before he runs out?"

The Mask nodded as he carefully folded the dust in the several papers. He led the way out of the room and they spent ten minutes searching the house. If Carter was there, he certainly had a good hiding place.

As they exited through the back door, Dave saw the big garage at the rear. The second floor was lighted up.

"Easy now," the Mask warned. "Carter's chauffeur must live there, and Frenchy is no fool. Head for the lilac bush. It will shield us from the garage."

CHAPTER X

THE FINAL GESTURE

SANDRA WAS waiting impatiently, and heaved a sigh of relief when the Mask and Dave reappeared at the car.

At the Mask's orders she drove straight to Warrick's house. It was after midnight, but when the Mask was working on a case, Warrick kept late hours so that he would be handy in case his services were needed.

The Mask and Dave went in alone.

"The first lieutenant of the racket is dead," the Mask reported. "The gang of strong-arm hoodlums is broken up. Now is the time to act. Have the police raid every one of the Atlas Employment offices. There will be records to show how many victims paid the big fees. Have those people contacted. Their stories will convict the agency managers and the real king-pin of the racket. I'll be home if anything breaks. Another few hours will show up our man. Also see if you can check up on the contractor who is handling the Sheridan Dam project."

Without removing his disguise, the Mask hurried into the laboratory behind his store. While Dave and Sandra watched, he carefully examined the dust taken from several suits of clothing in Carter's home.

Then a small red light, concealed under the lab bench, began winking. That signaled that Warrick was calling Bob Clarke on the private wire.

The Mask rushed upstairs. Warrick was excited.

"Just had a call from Carter. He confessed over the phone, said he was about to commit suicide, and I distinctly heard a shot. Shall I meet you at his house?"

"Yes, in a hurry," the Mask said. He turned to Dave and Sandra. "Now comes one of the times when I must disappoint you. The case is about to be broken. It's impossible for you to be there because we can't have it known that you work with the Crimson Mask. Carter just indicated to Mr. Warrick that he is—or was—the leader of the racket, for Mr. Warrick thinks he blew his brains out."

"But Bob," Sandra cried, "if Carter confessed and is dead, why couldn't we go along?"

The Mask turned his head as he started down the stairs. He grinned at her.

"Because Carter, despite all you suspect, isn't the man," he said. "I'll tell you all about it later."

Warrick was on Carter's front porch when the Mask reached the house. There was a gun in Warrick's hand and Mitchell, who owned the Flanders Foundry, stood against the wall with his hands in the air.

"I caught him rushing out of the house," Warrick explained. "I think he knows something, and besides, Mitchell happens to be the silent owner of the construction company operating at the Sheridan Dam."

"Where is your side-kick Cullen?" the Mask demanded.

Mitchell found his voice.

"In-inside. Carter is—is dead. We came to accuse him, but he—he shot himself. Cullen says he won't leave until the police arrive. I'm afraid I—"

"What's going on here?" a voice came out of the darkness.

Frenchy Flavin, Carter chauffeur, stepped up on the porch with a gun held ready. The Mask made a half turn. Both his hands came down and wrested the weapon out of Frenchy's grasp. He stuffed it into his pocket.

"The fewer guns around, the better I'll feel. Frenchy, your employer has killed himself and confessed that he was the leader of this racket. What do you know about it?"

"The boss?" Frenchy gasped. "He—he's dead? But no—no! Listen to me. That guy wasn't crooked. I been workin' for him two years, and I know he was on the level. Somebody knocked him off."

"We'll go inside," the Mask said, as he took command of the situation. "I want nothing touched. Lead the way, Mr. Warrick."

AS THE procession filed into the spacious living room, Cullen, who was half hidden by the shadows in the room, turned around quickly and made a grab for a gun in his pocket. The Mask's weapon covered him. Cullen looked a little sheepish. He had removed a picture from the wall and apparently he had been trying to open a small wall safe hidden behind it.

"So that's how you wait for the police," Mitchell cried bitterly. "You didn't try to stop me when I got scared. You wanted to be left here alone."

The Mask disarmed Cullen, lined everyone against the wall, and then walked over to a big desk. Carter sat behind it. The phone was off the hook, dangling over the edge of the table. A gun lay on the floor just below Carter's outstretched arm. Carter lay with his head resting against his other arm. There was a bullet hole through his right temple and blood had smeared a number of papers on the desk.

Frenchy Flavin stepped forward, paying no attention to Warrick's commands. He bowed his head slightly.

"I never thought he'd do that," he said softly. "I'm goin' to miss that guy. He kept me straight for two years."

THE MASK knelt beside Carter and examined the dangling arm. He straightened up.

"Then you certainly showed Carter no gratitude, Frenchy. Stop acting. You killed him! The night Bancroft was murdered, Carter dismissed you and the car—told you he was going to have it out with Bancroft. You are the only man who could have possibly known he was going there. You beat him there, knifed Bancroft, and Carter arrived in time to see you.

"You snatched him—held him a prisoner in your quarters above the garage. You planted evidence against him whenever you had the chance. Carter was sincere. He actually thought he was helping you, and you, in turn, played a good part. You planted your own men in the various employment offices."

Frenchy's eyes were bulging out of his head.

"You—you're wrong. I had nothin' to do with this. Carter was my pal."

"Until he saw you murder Bancroft." The Mask's voice was brittle. "You gave yourself away a couple of times, Frenchy. When you supervised the attempted murder of the Crimson Mask at Mitchell's foundry, you spoke to me and used the very best English. Certainly you didn't sound like Frenchy Flavin. But you admitted being assigned to library work in prison. You learned how to speak well there. You educated yourself thoroughly.

"Tyko, your first lieutenant, was your cellmate for three years. Carter didn't get him out. Tyko was released after his term was up. Most of Tyko's hoods were also your prison playmates. Some of them Carter succeeded in freeing through your influence. Carter grew accustomed to taking your advice in matters like that because he trusted you. In return you held him prisoner.

"When the police raided his offices, you knew the game was about up. You made him phone Warrick, make a false confession, and then you murdered him. His wrists still show indentations from the ropes you tied around them."

Frenchy backed away slowly. Suddenly he spun around, dived across the floor and seized the gun just below Carter's dead hand. It blazed almost in unison with the Mask's weapon. Half mad with rage, Frenchy tried to fire again. He looked at his hand. It held no gun. Blood flowed from his shattered fingers.

The Mask's bullet had found its mark and Frenchy had hardly been aware that he was hit.

The Crimson Mask threw his own weapon onto a chair, leaped across the room and grabbed Frenchy. He forced the man against the wall, and then Warrick pressed his gun just over the crook's heart. The Mask clapped one hand to his shoulder and when it came away, there was blood on it.

"Nicked me," he told Warrick. "Nothing serious… To get on with the story—Mitchell seemed to be the most logical suspect. His factory and his construction firm were used in the racket. Of course other factories were also involved, but Mitchell's more than the rest because Frenchy had so many men planted there.

"Cullen, you also believed Mitchell was responsible. You were trying to find evidence in this room, perhaps to destroy it—or use it for your own profit. When all of you were at Mr. Warrick's home, I left you, remember? I went to your homes and examined your clothing. The leader of these crooks was in the brass foundry when I flung a piece of aluminum into a crucible of molten brass. The fumes that were emitted settled on everyone's clothing.

"Neither of you were dressed as the racket leader had been, so I reasoned you must have found time to change your clothes. Yet, I discovered no traces of the fine white flakes on any of your suits. I made a mistake there by not going far enough. I failed to examine Frenchy's clothes.

"But I did that tonight, and on a suit that matches the one worn by the racket leader I found plenty of evidence. Not that it is needed now, because Frenchy has practically admitted being the brains behind the mob."

Mitchell came forward.

"I—I really don't know how to thank you. It seems a little odd to be so grateful to a man who wears a crimson mask over his eyes like—like a bandit. If there is something I could do; financially—"

The Mask shook his head.

"I do not work for rewards, Mr. Mitchell. If you feel you must do something, see that Joe Hooper's mother is provided for. His death put us onto this vile racket. Because of him we have succeeded in breaking it wide open and saving unsuspecting victims a lot of money. Best of all, we have put Frenchy and his mob out of business... Mitchell, phone Police Headquarters. Warrick, keep your gun on Frenchy. If he moves, let him have it."

"But I say—" Mitchell began.

He turned around. The front door was slowly closing. The Crimson Mask was gone. Mitchell sighed as he picked up the phone in the hall and began dialing Headquarters.

"If we had a police force of crimson-masked men there wouldn't be such a thing as crime," he said slowly. Then he smiled. "Although the Crimson Mask seems to be an entire police force himself."

IV

SIGN OF THE
CRIMSON MASK

CHAPTER I

ESCAPE BY THREE

THE PRISON tailor shop buzzed—with machinery, not conversation. The guards, trained to sense trouble, kept moving around the big room. They carried clubs, which indicated something might be expected to happen.

"Dusty" Gluba, a squat, perpetually scowling convict, was busy piling up bundles of repaired uniforms. A guard passed close by him, but Gluba worked on industriously. He took a swift look over one shoulder, then he slid a flat package from beneath the piles of uniforms and thrust it under his jacket. It was done so fast that only the keenest observer would have noticed.

Gluba moved away. A few moments later a rangy, sallow-faced man approached that same bundle and transferred it to another bench. During the process another of those flat packages went under the rangy man's jacket, also. Then a third convict—one who bore a faint resemblance to a baboon—threw the bundle onto a truck, bent over it for a second and got himself the last of those flat packages.

It was all accomplished with the stealth and speed to which convicts became accustomed. None of the guards had the slightest idea that, right under their noses, a prison break was in the making.

Gluba's ratty little eyes flashed a signal to the other two men. He picked up a large oil can and approached a machine. The other two closed in behind him. Suddenly the oil can was caught up in the machinery, ripped open, and black oil sprayed out all over the three prisoners. They blubbered, wiped their faces and then all three looked at their prison uniforms. They were drenched.

A guard signaled them to the door.

"Okay, you guys," he grumbled. "Get to the showers, and then put on fresh uniforms. Next time watch those oil cans."

A barred door slid back and the three men passed through it. They shuffled along the corridor, saying nothing. The quartermaster department issued three fresh uniforms, and the trio marched to the showers.

They passed by a section of the old prison which was in the process of being rebuilt. Convict labor was not sufficiently adept at plastering and bricklaying, so outside help had been called in. Three masons, in white overalls and gray jumpers, stood on a scaffolding and plied their

The other guard was
desperately trying to
stop the killers.

trowels. The prisoners passed directly below and Gluba, in the lead, gave a barely perceptible gesture with his thumb.

They entered the shower room, closed the door, and quickly made sure they were the only occupants of the room.

"It's workin' like a charm," Gluba said, without moving his lips. "We take the showers, see, on account of all this oil. Then we put on the uniforms."

"Hey, Gluba," the rangy convict asked, "are you sure them clothes made outa paper will get us by the guards?"

Gluba made a motion as if to slap the rangy man across the mouth.

"Mossy," he said, "you ain't never gonna be a success in life because you ain't willin' to take chances. Of course them paper uniforms will pass. I ain't been a tailor half my life—that is, all the time I spent in prisons—for nothing. When we put 'em on, we look just like them three masons workin' on that wall. They quit exactly at four, which gives us ten minutes. So get busy. I'll give you the details under the shower."

VIDLO WAS the name of the third crook—the one who looked so much like a baboon. He was a vicious, snarling type, but ready to do anything if it would get him out of prison.

"All I ask is a chance to wring some screw's neck," he grumbled. "Them guys been on my heels ever since I got in this joint. You gonna give me a chance to tackle a couple of 'em, Gluba?"

"You'll probably get a break," Gluba answered, as he rubbed the bar of soap into his hair. "Now get this. Them three masons are walling up Tier Five. Once the wall is built, they're gonna rip the whole tier out and build a new wing to the prison. Only they gotta build that wall first so none of us birds can fly the cage. The wall is plenty high right now. We just heave the masons over that wall and nobody'll see 'em until we're fifty miles from here. Okay—all set now? Remember that truck in the yard near the gate. Handle things smooth there, or it'll be a dead giveaway. Now get dressed, and we'll surprise a party of masons."

They donned their prison uniforms, and over them they slipped the paper clothing which Gluba had manufactured on the sly. When they were dressed, their clothing was a replica of that worn by the three masons who worked on the scaffold just outside the shower room. By some clever coloring it even seemed as though part of the white overalls and the jumpers were smeared with dry plaster. They donned long, peaked white caps.

Gluba stepped back into the showers and unscrewed the white enamaled handle of one shower. He wrapped his fingers around this.

"Get one of 'em, boys. It'll work just like brass knucks."

In a moment the three men filed out of the shower room. Gluba signaled, and all three climbed the ladders set up against the brick wall which now almost reached the roof of the corridor. The masons, getting ready to quit for the day, were wholly unprepared for anything like this.

Gluba, Mossy and Vidlo were confirmed criminals, given to violence in any form. With those shower handles in their fists they made short work of the three masons and quickly dumped the limp forms over the wall. Unless someone entered the old tier through a single door which led to the prison yard, the masons would never be found until they recovered consciousness and set up a squawk.

At one minute past four the three convicts were walking briskly along the corridor which led to the main yard and the big gate. Ahead of them were other men, similarly dressed, but in real mason's clothing.

About fourteen masons and plasterers were engaged in refurbishing the old prison. They marched across the yard while the wall guards watched them. RAs were held at a ready angle until the white uniforms of the workers were in plain evidence. The guards relaxed their vigil then.

A small, plaster-smeared truck was parked near the main gate. Its tailboard was down. Gluba reached it first, slid a hand beneath the tailboard and jerked a Thirty-eight automatic loose. It had been held to the underpart of the tailboard with strips of adhesive. The gun went under his jacket in a flash. Vidlo and Mossy followed his example.

"Fourteen going out!" the yard guard called.

The gate lock opened. Here was the really ticklish part of the job. Each outside employee would be carefully scrutinized by the two guards who maintained that gate lock. After everyone had filed through the first gate, it would close. To get out beyond the walls of the prison, it was then necessary to pass through another gate.

The masons and plasterers lined up. They'd been through this a score of times before. As each man was passed, the main gate opened and he went out.

When there were only two men ahead of the convict trio, Gluba jerked his head in a signal. Three guns appeared and covered the pair of guards. Gluba spoke in a low voice.

"Be smart screws or dead ones—I don't give a damn which! Signal the tower to open the gates."

ONE GUARD had already raised his hand in the signal, because he had passed the two remaining real workers. The gate was swinging open. Then Vidlo, the baboon, could no longer restrain his natural impulse to kill. He had a gun in his hand—the authority over life and death. He shoved the gun against one guard's stomach and calmly pulled the trigger twice. The guard folded up.

Gluba let out a yell. Followed by Vidlo and Mossy, he streaked through the gate.

A wall guard opened fire, but a withering hail of lead from the automatics in the hands of the escaping prisoners drove him into the blockhouse on the wall. Before he could swing a machine-gun into action, all three convicts were rushing toward a big sedan with its curtains pulled down. They piled into the tonneau.

The driver, whose face was well covered, stepped on the gas. The rattle of the machine-gun smashed the rear window of the sedan, but didn't stop it.

An escape siren began to wail. Fast, powerfully-engined prison cars were quickly rolled across the yard, and the gate lock opened to let them through. The wall guard pointed in the direction taken by the sedan, and all the prison cars swerved to take up the chase.

From the wall towers the guards were able to watch the fleeing car and at no time did it stop. Once or twice it weaved crazily, and almost turned over when it took to the shoulders of the highway. At that moment the driver jammed on his brakes, but only for an instant. Then the car raced on again. The prison cars, in swift pursuit, flashed along with sirens screeching.

After they vanished in the distance the three escaped convicts took a quick look from a clump of bushes that concealed them. Gluba grinned and began stripping off the heavy paper uniform which he had manufactured.

"We made it!" he gloated. "Jumpin' into these bushes was a smart gag. The car never stopped and the guards think we're still in it. They couldn't have seen us jump."

The rangy thug known as "Mossy," glanced at the trail of dust left by the speeding cars. He made a derisive sound between his teeth.

"There they go, the suckers," he said, grinning. "Boy—gettin' in and outa that bus was a smart trick! The driver'll travel as far as he can, abandon the crate and run for it. The guards will split up and cover that section, thinkin' we're hidin' some place around there. And all the while we just sneak back a little to another bus waitin' for us."

"I shoulda plugged that other screw," Vidlo, the baboon, declared venomously. "Do I hate them rats!"

Gluba seized him by the arm and glared at him.

"You half-witted gorilla!" he growled. "You bumped that guy, sure, and it means the chair if we're caught now. You were the mug who opened up with your roscoe when we were robbin' the bank, too—which drew us thirty years apiece instead of maybe ten, which we'da got for plain attempted robbery. It's lucky the guy in the bank didn't croak, or we'd have left prison long ago—in baskets. No more killin', understand? Not unless we get in a tight spot."

"Or meet them bozos who ratted on us, huh, Gluba?" Mossy asked, with a grimace. "Remember how all six of 'em got on the witness stand and fingered us? They got somethin' comin' to 'em, ain't they?"

"Yeah," Gluba agreed. "Sure they have. We warned 'em, and they didn't pay no attention… But first we gotta get away from here. I know just where the car is parked. Let's go!"

GAYLORD BARTON, one of the six directors of the Security Trust Company, was in smoking jacket and slippers. He puffed on a cigar and read the evening papers, especially all details about the daring and clever escape of three men he knew. Barton's wife had read the accounts, also, and she was vainly trying to get her attention on the woman's page of the newspaper.

"Gay," she said in a strained voice, "those men are free. They swore they'd get even with you. I—I wish you'd be careful."

Barton removed the cigar from his mouth and chuckled.

"You merely read the headlines, my dear. Those three convicts are surrounded in a forest ten miles from the prison. They can't get through the ring of guards thrown around them. By morning they'll either be dead or back in prison. Too bad about the guard—he died at the prison hospital shortly after the break. That means an end to your worries, because when those men are caught, they'll be executed."

Mrs. Barton folded the newspaper, then rolled it tightly and began slapping the arm of her chair with it. The doorbell rang, and she jumped up, nervously. Barton arose, too.

"Calm yourself, my dear," he said soothingly. "I'll go see who it is."

Barton opened the front door. His eyes grew wide, his jaw hung slackly. A man in a prison uniform stood before him. There was an automatic in his fist. Before Barton could say a word, the gun bucked. Four times the killer sent slugs ripping through Barton's chest.

"We keep our promises, wise guy!" he snarled. "Like this!"

Mrs. Barton ran into the hallway. She saw her husband drop to the floor and saw the convict standing in the doorway. His long, peaked cap was pulled well down. Her eyes automatically read the numbers sewed on his jacket. Then she fainted…

Thirty-five minutes later Martin Dunn, art connoisseur and bank director, who had also been a director of the Security Trust Company, lay sprawled across the front porch of his home while blood oozed from four wounds in his chest. A slinking figure, in a convict's uniform, vanished into the darkness around Dunn's estate.

In the house, a pallid-faced servant had witnessed the killing, and his lips were soundlessly repeating the number he had seen sewed to the murderer's uniform. Then he tore himself away from the window and called the police in a voice so strained that he could hardly make himself understood.

CHAPTER II

THE CRIMSON MASK MOVES IN

FAR DOWNTOWN in the great city, where the population lived in walk-ups with cold water and dark, smelly halls, was a drug store. Located on a corner of this squalid section, it struck a pleasant note amidst all this drabness of poverty.

The store was neat and bright. In each window was one of those old-fashioned crystal bottles containing colored water, long cherished in old-time pharmacies. The store was just as old-fashioned as those age-old trade-marks of the drug profession. On the door was lettered:

ROBERT CLARKE, PH. G.

Bob Clarke was a stand-by in the neighborhood. The kids called him the "Lemon-drop Man" because the only candy he kept in the store was contained in a huge, wide-mouthed jar, and it was free for the asking. Adults knew Bob Clarke, a good-looking young man of twenty-eight or nine, as "Doc," and when their funds were at a low ebb and there was need for medicines, they could get them here without feeling under deep obligations to the druggist.

Nor did they find it necessary to resort to subterfuge in order to get credit. Bob Clarke had been fooled few times in his career. Of course, there were accounts which he systematically entered and then destroyed a week later. They were listed under the names of people who were virtually destitute. They always came in later on to make a small payment on account, but Bob Clarke never could locate their bills, and refused to accept any money until he did.

In his store, Clarke sold nothing but medicines and doctors' equipment. There were no counters of candy, or percolators, or womens' hosiery. No glittering soda fountain. All the bustle that goes with a modern drug store was missing there. The place was never crowded, but Bob Clarke did a good business just the same-some of it in a line that those who knew him best, as they thought, and saw him every day, would never have guessed.

In fact, Clarke's drug store was his avocation rather than his real life business, more or less a screen to cover the activities of his vocation, for which the store was a headquarters. In a back room where he compounded his prescriptions, were all the drugs and apparatus necessary for a first-class old-fashioned drug business. But further back—behind a door that looked like wood, but was really steel—was another laboratory, his real one.

This one contained everything necessary for tracking down crime scientifically. For such was Bob Clarke's mission in life, and such the reason for his having two identities.

Years before, his father, a police sergeant, had been shot in the back by cowardly gangsters. Bob had watched him die, and had observed a peculiar phenomenon just as death struck. His father's face had become suffused with blood until it seemed as though he wore a crimson mask over his eyes.

Bob Clarke had never forgotten that. It had been in his mind as he had walked slowly away from the hospital, vowing in his childish heart that he would dedicate his life to bringing to justice all such criminals as those gangsters who had cost his father his life.

He would take his father's place in the everlasting war against crime. Not as an accredited police officer, because in that case he would be compelled to adhere to all the laws and red tape. And, young as he was, that was not Bob Clarke's purpose. And with that purpose firmly set, he had set about fitting himself for his lifework methodically.

IN THAT, he had been aided by Theodore Warrick, police commissioner then; retired now. Warrick had been a lifelong friend of Bob's father, and he it had been who had stood beside the boy at his dying father's bedside, and had sworn to do all in his power to avenge the death of Sergeant Clarke.

With what little money that had been left to young Clarke, the boy had gone through college, and had emerged with a degree in pharmacy, so that his personal needs would be cared for. But it had been ex-Commissioner Warrick's money that had helped Bob to fit himself for his lifework until he had become the lone wolf avenger of crime he was now.

No stone had been left unturned to fit himself to cope with criminals only too well known to take advantage of all modern science has to offer in their nefarious pursuits. As a foundation, after finishing college, young Clarke had studied criminology in all its forms and variations. He had delved for long hours into the scientific detection of crooks. He knew how to disguise himself, if need be, and had learned to imitate voices.

At last, when he had believed his education complete, he had donned a crimson velvet mask which resembled the strange coloring of his father's face as he had died, thus dedicating his life to the memory of the man who had given his own life in running down criminals.

And gangland had come to know the Crimson Mask—and to fear him.

Two others beside ex-Commissioner Warrick abetted Bob Clarke in his crusade against crime. Those three alone knew that young Clarke was the Crimson Mask. Warrick had become the Crimson Mask's contact with the world that needed his services. Besides him, there was Dave Small who worked as assistant pharmacist, and who had been Clarke's only intimate friend in college. Ostensibly Dave's job was to take care of the store when Bob Clarke was busy in his role of the Crimson Mask, but there were plenty of times when Dave proved himself an invaluable ally in Clarke's work on some criminal case.

Finally there was Sandra Gray, fair-haired and lovely. Quick-witted, too, and a match for most criminals. Bob Clarke loved Sandra, though he never told her so, and rarely gave a brief glimpse into his heart that would let her know of his affection for her. His life was in such constant danger that he would never have consented for her to share it, even though she frequently shared the risks of the Crimson Mask voluntarily.

At ten in the evening, almost closing time, Bob Clarke was busy in his laboratory, behind the steel door. Dave Small, short, pudgy, and apple-cheeked, lounged over the counter, reading an evening paper. The story of the prison break interested him most.

He heard a newsboy go by the door, yelling something about murder. Dave's ears perked up. He ran to the door and called the newsboy back.

He flipped a dime high into the air and the newsboy grinned, caught it and flipped it back.

"You don't pay for my stock, Dave," the boy said seriously. "Any time you or Doc want a paper—it's free. That's the way you sold my Mother medicine last winter. Doc says he couldn't find the bill, and he wouldn't take Ma's word for it that she owed him five dollars and sixty cents. He said he was sure it was just more like sixty cents without the five bucks. Every time she asks him he just laughs and says he'll look for the bill some day."

Dave took the newspaper. "Thanks, kid," he said, grinning. "You're okay."

DAVE SMALL strolled back into the store and he whistled softly as he read the first releases of two murders committed by the escaped convicts about whom he had just been reading. He went to the steel door and tapped on it in a signal. Bob came out.

"Didn't take those hoodlums long to start gunning," Dave said. "Gaylord Barton and Martin Dunn were murdered early tonight. Witnesses saw the killer each time, and identified him pretty well. Just like a hit-and-run car, in fact. Read the numbers on his uniform. Seems like Gluba pulled the Barton kill, and Mossy gunned out Dunn."

Doc Clarke frowned and took the newspaper.

"I thought the prison guards and state troopers had those three men trapped," he said, "Looks like they were good and wrong, eh, Dave? Gluba, Vidlo and Mossy aren't exactly gentlemen. They murdered a prison guard on their way out, so now it makes no difference how many others they murder, because they can be burned only once. I wonder—"

Doc's eyes glowed suddenly. Then he shrugged.

"No, there's not much sense to it. This is a matter for the police—a routine job of running down those men. The Crimson Mask couldn't do any more than that."

Dave looked a little disappointed. "Yeah, I suppose not. Rounding up three killers like those is a matter for a lot of cops with big guns. I just thought—well, that we'd have a little action. After all, filling aspirin bottles doesn't make the heart beat any too fast."

Bob Clarke walked out into the store. As he passed behind the counter, a small, hidden red bulb glowed briefly. Bob pursed his lips, turned and hurried to his quarters above the store. There, by means of a direct wire, he was soon in communication with ex-Police Commissioner Theodore Warrick. The red bulb in the store had signaled that Warrick was trying to contact him.

"Did you read about the prison break?" Warrick asked at once. "I thought you might have. Good! That saves a lot of talk. Look, Bob, there's the very devil to pay. Perhaps you don't recall the case so I'll outline it for you.

"Three years ago the board of directors of the Security Trust Company had a meeting early in the morning. As soon as the doors of the bank opened for business, three gunmen walked in. They thought only a few clerks or so would be around. They quickly took the cashier and his assistant prisoners, and forced the cashier to open the safe the moment the time lock was off. However—in a back room—this board of directors at their early meeting saw it all, phoned the police, and those three hoods had to shoot their way out. Luckily no one was killed, though one employee was badly wounded."

"Go on," Bob Clarke said. "What are you getting at, Mr. Warrick?"

"Just this. The directors all had excellent pictures of the gunmen in their minds. The others, including the cashier, had been too excited to get a good look at the crooks. Anyway, the directors picked out Gluba, Vidlo and Mossy as the culprits. Then the hunt was on. Meanwhile the directors received threats by mail and over the phone, threatening that if they identified the three crooks, they'd lose their lives. The directors scoffed at the threats and did their duty. Those three men were sent to prison for long terms."

"So now that they are out, they're taking that postponed revenge," Bob mused. "Barton and Dunn were two of the six bank directors. And the others must be in danger. What you need is a strong guard around each one."

"I know. I've thought it all out, Bob, but here is the rub. The four remaining men on whom this mob will pick are friends of mine. Close friends. They've come to me with a request that I solicit your services. They offered a fat fee, but I told them you accepted no payment for your work. How about it? Will you either hunt for those killers, or protect my friends?"

"When you ask it that way," Bob replied, "how could I refuse? All right—I'll get to work at once. Meanwhile, don't forget a strong guard around those threatened men. Those killers are still at large."

Clark hung up, leaned back, and ran his fingers through his hair. Dave came in and propped himself on the edge of a table.

"It's not like ferreting out a criminal whose identity isn't known," Clarke said to him thoughtfully. "There won't be clues or leads to follow. It's simply a matter of either tracking that trio of killers down or trapping them somehow. Either will be difficult. They'll have holed up somewhere, and if you can't find them, how can you set an effective trap and lure them into it... Lock up the store, Dave, then get the car out. We're going up to that prison and see just how this business all began."

CHAPTER III

A GROAN IN
THE DARK

NEAR ONE in the morning, Warden Blane drove into his garage behind his private dwelling, outside the prison walls. He shut off the lights, got out of the car—and stopped cold.

"Sorry if I startled you," a pleasant voice said. "I'm not an escaped convict, Warden. Turn around and see."

Blane turned. He saw a tall, well-built man in a dark suit. A crimson mask was over his eyes. Blane relaxed, and mopped his face with a handkerchief.

"The Crimson Mask, eh?" he said. "Case big enough to interest you, isn't it? I just returned from town. Don't tell me those killers have murdered anyone else?"

"Not yet," the Crimson Mask replied. "They'll try though. Everyone concerned seems to be concentrating only on the actual roundup of those killers. I intend to start the trail from the beginning… They had outside help, of course?"

The warden sniffed disgustedly.

"How else would a car be waiting at the gates, and guns hidden under the tailboard of a truck inside the walls," he said shortly. "We know where those guns were now, though at the time none of the guards who saw those men stop for an instant at that truck's tailboard thought anything of it. Of course those damned killers had outside help! But what I'd like to know is how they paid for it. Mugs who would handle a job of that kind don't work for nothing—not even for friendship. That old business about 'honor among thieves' is pure malarky.

"Somehow those convicts got uniforms resembling those worn by masons working inside the prison. They put three masons out of the picture, took their place, and on the way to the gates picked up guns. We found the adhesive that had held the guns beneath their tailboard of the mason contractor's truck. The contractor has been absolved of all blame. Someone must have pinned those weapons there before the truck rolled into the prison.

"The escaped convicts shot a gate guard, jumped into a sedan which was provided with a driver, and tore north along the highway. My men were after them less than two minutes after they got clear. The getaway car was found, the whole area surrounded and we were positive we had them. But we slipped somewhere. I can't reason out how they got away from the cordon I threw around the entire section."

"Your cordons have worked before, Warden," the Crimson Mask said. "Perhaps this time you were led on a wild-goose chase. Perhaps your three escaped killers weren't in the car for long. Have you thought of that?"

"Where could they have gone?" the warden countered. "They were seen getting into the car—they were not seen getting out. The car never stopped—"

"But they could have jumped from the moving car—into bushes to cushion their fall," the Crimson Mask insisted. "In fact I discovered one place where the getaway car swerved off the road myself. Tires left deep imprints. Near that spot I also found footprints and broken bushes. After they jumped, all that your men followed, Warden, was a car and a driver who had orders to ditch the bus and get away himself. While you used every man available to form a cordon, your killers merely hide themselves to another getaway car and drove off... But let's get down to facts leading up to the break. Can you tell me who was the last visitor to see each man?"

"Their last visitor came to see all of them-their only visitor for a long time. He happened to be the attorney who defended them. A shyster named Olden. He spent twenty minutes with Gluba, the most intelligent member of the trio, just two days ago. Of course messages may have been slipped into the prison, and Olden might be entirely innocent."

The Crimson Mask smiled coldly.

"When a lawyer like Olden travels twenty miles just to visit three men he apparently only knew as clients, and who are hardly likely to survive their prison terms, you can bank on it that Olden saw the yellow end of the rainbow—yellow for gold. A thing like this, as of course you know, Warden, can't be effectively handled through smuggled messages. Too many chances of leaks. Now—did any new prisoners come in lately? Any with whom any of those three men would be in close contact?"

The warden shrugged. "We had to put a new man into Gluba's cell. A chap named Ronney. Young fellow who helped himself to the cash lying around a bank for which he worked."

THE CRIMSON MASK made a mental note of this.

"Thanks, Warden," he said. "I may be no luckier than an ordinary officer, but I'll do my best. Thanks also for trusting me."

Warden Blane shook hands with the Crimson Mask. "To be frank," he said dryly, "I rather expected you. Warrick called me, you see. If there is anything else—"

Suddenly Warden Blane realized that he was entirely alone. The Crimson Mask had slipped away as quietly, as a shadow. When Blane went outside the garage, he saw no signs of the crimson-masked crime fighter.

Dave Small picked up the Crimson Mask a few moments later and drove, without speaking, to a side road about a third of a mile away from the prison. He shoved a big flashlight into his pocket and got out of the car. The Crimson Mask followed.

"As you told me to do"—Dave threw a light on the dirt lane—"I looked for a likely spot to park a car. There was one here this afternoon. See the tracks of the rear tires? When the driver started away, he must have thrown the clutch in too fast, and slewed those wheels around. If that driver had been in prison for a time, say—well, in three years he could get a little rusty in his driving. Also I know no car was at this spot even as early as noon, because there's a farmhouse just up the road, and the farmer told me he came through here with a load of hay. If a car had been parked here, he wouldn't have been able to get through."

The Crimson Mask picked a wisp of hay from a bush.

"You also found traces of the hay load and did some deducting, didn't you?" he observed. "Dave, you're coming along nicely. But sometimes the clues that mean anything are not the most prominent ones, my boy. But we will say this—a car was left here for those three killers-convicts. We're positive now that they had plenty of outside help. Suppose we follow this lane and see where it comes out. I don't believe they'd have turned around farther up the lane, because if they wanted to head for the highway, the car would have been facing that way."

In a few moments the Crimson Mask had determined that the killers had simply followed the lane until it turned into a macadam road which ran east of the city where the recent murders had been committed. The Crimson Mask frowned.

"That's odd," he muttered. "Why didn't they travel straight back to town while the roads were clear, and everyone thought they were penned up in the woods ten miles away? Dave, they stopped somewhere along here. But why?"

"To change clothes," Dave offered brightly, and then his face fell. "No—couldn't be that. Those witnesses to the murders said the cons still wore their uniforms. Maybe they just took a roundabout way to town."

"No, Dave. Three convict killers, in prison garb, wouldn't want to risk traveling a mile more than necessary. Unless they had a hideout all set somewhere around this neighborhood, they would have headed in the opposite direction taken by the guards when they were lured off. That's the only answer—but finding their hideaway will be tougher than the steaks you get at that greasy diner near the store... Stop at the next place that has a phone. I've got an idea."

"Dusty" Gluba

The mask of crimson had been removed, but anyone other than Dave who might have been expecting to see Bob Clarke's face would have been startled, because the features were not the regular, good-looking ones of Doc Clarke. His brown hair had become a glistening black. His skin was darker and his cheeks bulged a bit more than Bob Clarke's. His eyebrows were shaped differently, too. But such things were easy for Clarke. This disguise was readily removable, and yet effective.

THE CRIMSON MASK, in this simple disguise, entered a small drug store and phoned ex-Commissioner Warrick.

"The trail is old and the scent cold," he said, "but it seems our friends lammed due east from the pen. Have any of the threatened men—by the vaguest chance—any property in the vicinity of Lakespur?"

"Yes," Warrick promptly answered. "Turner owns a summer place right on the lake. I've been there. It's a big place with a wide chimney with a ship set into the bricks. Incidentally, Turner is not to be trusted too far. He has been mixed up in a few shady financial deals."

"Thanks. Things quiet so far?"

"We're considerably worried about Turner," Warrick advised. "When the police arrived to guard him, he wasn't home, and he hasn't been heard from since ten o'clock. He made a phone call from his house then."

The Crimson Mask hung up, made a few casual inquiries of the druggist, and determined exactly where Turner's summer home was located. He got back into the car and directed Dave in that direction.

"We may run into a few difficulties," he said. "Turner—one of the bank directors—is missing. The mugs may have him, or he may even be working with them. Gluba's smart enough to have engineered that jail break right through Turner, or some other threatened big-shot. It's just possible those lugs are daring enough to take over the house of one of their intended victims—or it might be so arranged for them. Turn left at the next crossroads, then park the car—out of sight."

Dave followed orders. They started walking then until they topped a knoll and could look down over the shimmering surface of the huge lake. The region was deserted now, for it was long after the season. Not a single one of the houses along the shore showed any lights or other signs of occupancy.

"Better strip your gun for action," the Crimson Mask whispered. "See that big place to the right? With that metal ship set into the chimney for an ornament? That's Turner's place. Those killers might have come here when they escaped, and might have returned here after they killed Barton and Dunn. Who'd ever think to look for them in a house owned by one of the men they plainly intended to kill?"

"Maybe this Turner did make a deal, as you say," suggested Dave. "You know—talked them out of murdering him, and offered them a haven here—with a lot of money to boot, maybe."

"It's possible," the Crimson Mask answered. "We'll soon know. Skirt the house wide, get well behind it near the lake. Find a nice big rock and pitch it through any window. Then duck, and make certain you aren't silhouetted against the lake. That clear?"

Dave Small nodded and moved away. The Crimson Mask crept forward, putting on the velvet domino as he progressed. He dropped behind a bush, studied the house intently and saw that it would not be hard to climb the porch pillars to a sloping roof over which a window could easily be reached. That window was open an inch or two.

Then Small went into action. He must have chosen a big rock because it made a devil's own din. The Crimson Mask sprinted forward, depending on the fact that if anyone was in the place, they would rush out and toward the lake to find out what had caused the racket.

He went up the porch pillar with all the ease of a trained athlete, scrambled across the roof and raised the window high. He stepped in, closed the window again, and lit a match. He was in a bedroom, but it had not been used in weeks, for there was a layer of dust over everything.

THEN HE heard a muffled moan. Somewhere in this house a man was in agony.

Gun in hand, the Crimson Mask prowled the upper floor, led on by those repeated moans. As yet he had heard no sound of anyone running toward the rear of the house in answer to the racket which Dave Small had created.

Then, in one of the smaller bedrooms, he discovered a man lying in the middle of the floor, huddled in a ball and kept that way by ropes. It was an artistic job of tying a man up, and the gag was a wide strip of adhesive.

Still wary that this might be a trap, the Crimson Mask approached cautiously. He flung open a closet door. No one was hidden inside. Then he knelt beside the wide-eyed victim and gently removed the adhesive.

"Who else is in this house?" he asked.

"No—no one," came the reply, muttered through dry, swollen lips. "They—they left. Who—are you? That mask—"

"I'm the Crimson Mask," the bound man was told. "In a moment I'll have you free, but meanwhile you might start talking. Were Gluba, Vidlo and Mossy here?"

"Were they!" the man answered wryly. "And I'll talk—plenty! At least tell you all I know. I—well, I'll admit I became panicky when I learned those three hoodlums had escaped from prison and were bent on vengeance. I... Thanks for getting that rope from around my neck. Nearly strangled me. Maybe that's what they wanted to do... As I was saying, I decided the city wasn't such a healthy spot with those three loose, so I came up here to the lake, thinking I'd be safe until those three could be picked up again. I opened the front door—and ran straight into those killers!"

The Crimson Mask helped Turner to his feet and led him over to the bed. Turner sat down on it and began massaging his swollen ankles where the ropes had burned against the flesh. The Crimson Mask eyed him closely. Turner could be trying to alibi himself by allowing Gluba to tie him up.

"You're sure it was those three men who escaped from prison?" the Crimson Mask asked.

"I should know them, shouldn't I? I pointed them out in court. I saw them rob our bank three years ago. Could I forget them under those circumstances? No—I'm right about their identities. They taunted me, then one of them struck me when I accused him of killing Barton and Dunn. Then they gagged me, tied me up, and threw me into a corner.

"They played cards for about an hour, then finally they checked their guns—automatics—got three submachine-guns out of a closet and checked them also. Then Gluba kicked me in the ribs and said they'd be back as soon as they knocked off an armored car."

The Crimson Mask glanced at his wrist-watch.

"Armored car?" he repeated. "At this hour of the night?"

Turner nodded. "There is one all right. The Security Trust sends one out before dawn with a payroll for the night shift at the Glenport Aviation Company. I ought to know that, also. I voted that the firm be given credit because they are at work on defense projects, and the money is shipped from the bank of which I am a director. The truck follows the state highway due north from the city."

"Wait here," the Crimson Mask said.

He hurried downstairs, but doubt assailed him with force. Turner was one of the logical revenge victims of the escaped murder trio. Why, then, hadn't they killed him? Or were they saving that as a little postscript to the robbery of the armored truck? Perhaps they intended to keep Turner alive temporarily, as a hostage.

There were many angles from which to consider Turner's innocence, but they all conflicted with the manner of the first two murders. Barton and Dunn had been shot down before they had had a chance to say a word.

CHAPTER IV

CARELESSNESS BY INTENTION?

D **AVE SMALL** was waiting outside, worried stiff at the Crimson
Mask's delay. The man in the velvet mask led Small behind a clump
of bushes.

"Turner, one of the bank directors, is inside," he explained. "The
killer-trio had him tied up. They're getting themselves a little stake by
cracking an armored car. Turner knows the route the car will follow, so
we'll have to take him along with us. And that means he must not by
any chance, now or in the future, know you to be Dave Small."

The Crimson Mask took a flat, compact kit of make-up materials
from his pocket and went to work on Dave. In the minutes he had
changed the apple-cheeked, fair-haired assistant pharmacist into a dark,
swarthy type. Turning on the ray of a small flashlight, the Crimson Mask
studied his work intently. Then he pursed his lips and whistled softly.

"Dave, if you'd stick out your chin, raise your hand and look mad,
you'd be the image of Mussolini."

"Heaven forbid!" Dave groaned. "Say, if they had Turner, why didn't
they knock him off?"

"That is what I hope to find out—from Gluba and his pals. Let's get
started, Dave. Make sure your gun is stripped for action. I've an idea we
may need its help."

When Turner saw Dave Small, he stared at him blankly, but not for
long. It seemed that he could not keep his eyes off that crimson-masked
man.

"So you really are the Crimson Mask," he marveled. "I didn't think
you'd come in on this business. I asked Ted Warrick for your help, but
he wouldn't promise. That's when I became panicky and fled town. What
are we going to do now?"

The Crimson Mask's lips parted in a cold smile.

"Try to stop an armored car stickup—without stopping some of that
gang's lead. You point out the route, and we'll head toward town."

Turner wet his lips and gulped. It was clear that he did not like this
business, but with Dave Small racing the car at top speed, Turner had

little choice in the matter. He glumly indicated the route over which the armored car would travel.

"None of those three men mentioned just how they happened to select your summer home as a hideout, did they?" the Crimson Mask queried.

"No—no, not a word,"Turner said quickly. "Just coincidence, I guess. I didn't own the place at the time when they were sent to prison, and I don't see how they could have learned that I had purchased it when they were behind bars. Their coming to my place could not possibly have had anything to do with me—though undoubtedly they meant to search me out and kill me."

The Crimson Mask said nothing. He leaned forward and watched the road, swept by the brilliant headlights of the car. They were about five miles from the city limits and if the thugs had struck, there should be action soon. He had to stop that holdup, because if Gluba and his friends laid their hands on a substantial amount of cash, they would become as hard to catch as wraiths.

And only a moment later, they all saw the finish of a bold crime. Rounding a corner, they spotted a car pulled well off the highway. An armored truck was maneuvering to get around a vast crater in the road. One of the uniformed car guards lay on the shoulder, ominously still.

The other guard was struggling into a sitting position, and as the armored car pulled away, he began shooting. The men in the oncoming car could hear his slugs ricochet off the steel sides of the truck.

"Don't try to stop them!" the Crimson Mask warned Small. "They'll run us down if you do."

The armored car, swerving crazily, missed the sedan by a matter of inches, then roared away into the darkness. The Crimson Mask jumped out and ran over to the guard who was making a brave attempt to reload his gun.

"I'm the Crimson Mask," he said hastily. "We'll take you and your friend to a hospital."

"My friend," the guard mumbled, "is dead. I can take it—bullet through my hip, I think. If you are really the Crimson Mask—go get those rats! It was Gluba and the other two escaped cons! They blew a big hole in the road. The driver didn't see the crater in time and the front wheels went down. We had to get out and try and push the truck back on the road. That's when those rats started shooting. Bill got his in the first blast. Get them! Please get them! And give me a crack at their rotten hides!"

Dave Small

"Sorry," the Crimson Mask said. "The State comes first in taking cracks at those three. We'll send help here as quickly as possible."

The Crimson Mask raised his hand and signaled. Dave Small quickly turned the car, and stepped on the gas pedal hard the instant the Crimson Mask leaped in. The powerful engine hummed, and the sedan seemed to grow wings. The heavy armored truck would not get far unless it turned off, and the Crimson Mask had been watching for side roads on their way to the scene of the stick-up. There had been none, for at least two miles.

In a few minutes they picked up the tail-lights of the armored truck. Small switched off his own lights and eased up on the gas. All three men were tense. They knew exactly what they were up against. Three killers armed with submachine-guns, and as desperate as cornered rats. Another life—a score of lives—meant nothing to them.

"Slower," the Crimson Mask warned. "They'll think we went back to the city to spread the alarm—which means they've a hideout to go to, and not far from here… Turner, this isn't the way back to your home at the lake, is it?"

"No—no, we're heading right into rural territory," Turner replied. "I—I'm not up on this sort of thing. Haven't even got a gun—wouldn't know how to use one if I had a dozen. I'd be more in the way than any help to you, when the shooting starts. You won't mind if I remain in the car?"

"Suit yourself," the Crimson Mask retorted. "Dave, they've made a left turn! Take it easy."

When they reached the side road, they found it to be no more than a narrow lane, dark and rutted. Small turned into it. They could not see the tail-lights of the armored truck any longer, and the going became rough and bumpy. Finally their car topped a knoll, Dave Small tramped on the brake hard, and swung off the lane into a field. In a small valley just ahead, they could see a white farmhouse and a big red barn. The interior of the barn was swathed in light from the armored truck.

The Crimson Mask jumped out.

"Dave, you come with me," he ordered. "Turner, get behind the wheel. If those mugs try to roll away, drive this car right into the middle of the lane and leave it there. That truck is too heavy to guide across the fields."

TURNER SWALLOWED with some difficulty, but climbed out of the back seat and slid behind the wheel. He called softly to the Crimson Mask and leaned toward the door. His forearm hit the horn button and it raised a terrific din. The Crimson Mask cursed.

"That does it!" he shouted. "Come on, Dave! Keep your gun handy!"

They raced toward the barn. For a second, the headlights of the truck were still on and they could see two men, with submachine-guns cradled in their arms, peering into the night. Then the lights went out and they heard the big barn doors creak shut.

"Say," Dave panted, "you don't think Turner did that on purpose, do you?"

"I don't know, but I intend to find out," the Crimson Mask growled. "Listen—those men in that barn don't know how many of us there are, and they'll hardly try a dash for the house. We've got them penned in the barn, but all they have to do is get into that armored car and roll out. We couldn't stop them, unless Turner does his job. I... Stop, Dave! Look here. That stump has been blasted out. Which means there must be dynamite around the farm. Probably in a small shed somewhere. We'll part company and look for it. Whistle if you find it."

Three or four minutes later the Crimson Mask heard Dave Small's whistle and sped in that direction. Small had located the shack where the explosive was kept, and was already prying open the lid of a box labeled "Dynamite." He removed several sticks of the explosive, then found fuses and caps. He began attaching them.

"How will we get close enough to throw the stuff?" he asked. "Don't forget, those birds have machine-guns."

"Back toward the house is a tractor with a scoop shovel attached," the Crimson Mask said. "The farmer must have been doing a lot of land clearing and filling. Grab an armful of dynamite and let's go!"

Each carrying a dozen sticks, they raced across the rough land. So far not a shot had been fired. Apparently Gluba and his friends were waiting until they had a good target.

The tractor the Crimson Mask had spied was a modern job with a huge scoop shovel hooked up to its front. The Mask started the motor, operated the controls, and brought the shovel down until it formed an effective shield. Then, with Small at his side, he trundled the heavy machine straight toward the barn. Dave split a fuse, fumbled in his pocket and got out a pack of matches.

"I used to be pretty good as a pitcher," he said, and grinned. "Maybe I can fan those mugs, huh?"

As the tractor came closer, a terrific barrage of gunfire poured from the barn. Bullets pelted against the scoop shovel shield. The Crimson Mask and his companion crouched as low as possible, but a hundred yards from the barn, the Crimson Mask nudged Small. His assistant got ready. Thirty yards more, and the bullets sounded like hail.

DAVE SCRAPED a match, touched it to the short fuse, and for a second stood erect, exposing himself to the gunfire. His hand went back, then forward. The stick of dynamite hurtled straight toward the barn. It fell a little short, but the explosion rocked even the heavy tractor and a sheet of flame flashed amidst the dirt and stones.

Small grumbled something about his arm not being as good as it used to be. He split another fuse, touched flame to it, and took a second chance against the guns. This stick fell about three feet from the side of the barn. The Mask braked the tractor. The dynamite went off with a terrific roar, and the whole north side of the barn seemed to lift into the air for a second, then it settled back to earth as debris.

The angry roar of the armored car motor announced the fact that Gluba or one of his fellow killers had suddenly recalled that an armored car is pretty good insurance against attack. The car came through the now-splintered door of the barn, crashing its way to freedom. Dave Small hurled a stick of dynamite in its path, but the car was gaining speed rapidly. It passed directly over the sputtering fuse and was fifty yards away when the stuff let go.

The Crimson Mask stood erect, to see what Turner would do about all this. He could barely make out the shape of the car in which they had left the bank director, and it was moving. Turner was carrying out his part of the scheme.

Leaping from the tractor, the Crimson Mask and Dave began running. They heard a disheartening crash of metal against metal. Several quick shots were fired and when they reached the lane, their car was tilted on its side, half supported by a thick bush. Turner lay about ten feet away from it, sprawled out, and unconscious. The Crimson Mask knelt beside him, raised his head and then looked up at Dave.

"He's just out from a blow on the head. He must have been in the car when the truck hit it—hadn't had time to get away."

Turner opened his eyes a couple of minutes later. He gave a violent shudder and made a weak attempt to pull himself free. Then he saw the crimson mask on the features of the man who held him and he relaxed.

"Guess I'm just a bungler," he groaned. "It wasn't enough to warn them by accidentally leaning on the horn button. I had to drive the car too far off the lane. They hit the rear end and just swept me and the car aside. I had no time to get out—last thing I knew I was flying through space."

"Yeah," Dave Small grunted, "you're pretty good at almost catching guys." He nodded toward the Crimson Mask. "Say, the car is banged up, but she'll run if we can tip her back on all four wheels."

It required only a few moments to accomplish this, for the car, braced by the bush, was only a bit off balance. Turner climbed sheepishly into the rear seat. The Crimson Mask joined him.

"Don't feel too badly about this," he said quietly. "It probably wasn't all your fault. By the way—who knows about that armored truck taking cash to the airplane factory at this hour of the morning?"

"Not many," Turner admitted. "Just the actual bank employees needed to make up the cash, and the armored car company, of course. You don't think there was a leak?"

"I know it," the Crimson Mask said. "Men don't case a job—plan it, I mean—while they're in prison. Not one like this… Well—Gluba and his friends got clear, and with plenty of cash, too. We'll have to step to catch them now. Head for town, Dave."

CHAPTER V

MURDER STRIKES AGAIN

A T THE nearest available phone, the Crimson Mask reported the stick-up and the escape of the crooks to the State Police. A passing motorist had taken the surviving guard to a hospital, he learned, and already a cordon was shutting off all roads. With the Crimson Mask's warning of the escape from him, further precautions were taken, with airports watched and busses stopped. Gluba and his mates would have a difficult time evading this blockade.

The Crimson Mask also called ex-Commissioner Warrick and had him waken the other three men who were marked for death. They were all to meet at the Security Trust Company's board room.

Leaving Dave Small with the car, the Crimson Mask accompanied Turner into the bank. The others arrived soon, and the startled watchman let them all in.

As they sat around a conference table, the Crimson Mask took careful note of them. One director, a man named Smythe, was a prim little fellow with nose glasses and a strawberry mark directly between his eyes. The only member of the group who devoted all his time to banking, he looked stern and cold. Another, Hodges, was a tall, gangly type who looked more like a prosperous farmer than a banker. His main interests lay in fostering aviation and racing planes. Judson was an obese, bald-headed man with small eyes that seemed to be set in rolls of fat. He bore little resemblance to the usual appearance of a philanthropist—which he was.

All were impeccably dressed. Turner sat down, and the Crimson Mask informed these men as to what had just happened.

"Therefore," he concluded, "it seems pretty plain that Gluba, Vidlo, and Mossy had some inside knowledge about this armored car. I suggest a thorough checkup of any employees who made up the payroll."

"We were fools ever to send a cent to that aviation company at any such ungodly hour," Judson growled. "I've been against it for months. Hodges and I. But what could we do with four others against us? I hope this proves you gentlemen were wrong. That was our money—not the bank's. The bank was merely acting as our agent. Thank heavens the payment was insured."

"Now see here," Smythe put in primly, "this hold-up has nothing whatsoever to do with the finances of the Glenport Aviation Company. You're not accusing them of stealing it, are you? The bank, by a majority of its directors, has agreed to carry the Glenport Company because it is engaged in defense work for the Government. You and Hodges fought the idea, but we others prevailed and it still goes."

"Gentlemen"—the Crimson Mask held up his hand for attention—"this is not a time for arguing business matters. All of you are under a constant threat of sudden death. Gluba and his two killer accomplices are loose. There is no telling when they may strike. You are all under police guard—inconvenient as that may be sometimes. I hope you keep on cooperating in that respect.

"I have called you together now, in order that I might issue this warning -and to find out if you knew of anyone who might have sold out to Gluba about the armored car. If you get any inkling of that, please get in touch with ex-Commissioner Warrick. That's all."

Hodges and Smythe stamped out of the room, protesting in no uncertain terms about being routed out of bed to listen to a lecture. Turner practically collapsed on one of the benches in the bank proper, while Judson took his time in the director's room, carefully clipping the end of a cigar and lighting it slowly.

Warrick, who had come along with the men he had collected at the suggestion of his protégé, and the Crimson Mask left the bank just behind Hodges and Smythe. Hodges went directly to his car, parked across the street. Smythe's sedan was pulled into the alley beside the bank.

SUDDENLY TWO quick, distinct shots shattered the early morning calm. The Crimson Mask turned and raced back toward the bank. Hodges was inside his car, peering out of the rolled-down window.

Turner and Judson came rushing out of the bank.

The Crimson Mask raced into the alley where Smythe had parked his car. Smythe was there, draped half in and half out of the car. The strawberry mark between his eyes had grown twice as big—and much redder. He was dead when the Crimson Mask reached him.

Gun in hand, the Crimson Mask searched the alley, without catching sight of anyone. He returned to where the corpse lay and slowly pivoted in a complete circle. Then he approached a wooden fence, stood on tiptoe and finally drew a knife from his pocket. Working carefully, he pried a bullet out of the soft wood. He balanced this in his palm, then handed it over to Warrick.

"There were two shots, as you must have heard," he said. "The first one must have killed Smythe and the second went over his head after he'd dropped. Take this slug and have the police ballistic experts check it with the slugs that killed Smythe, Barton and Dunn. Then compare it with the bullet which killed the prison guard and which we know was fired from a gun in the hands of Gluba or one of his boys."

Warrick nodded and stowed the bullet away.

"I'll let you know as soon as possible," he promised. "Several radio cars arrived while you've been searching, and I sent them out to bottle up the streets. We may land Gluba yet."

The Crimson Mask nodded briefly, and returned to the car in which he had driven here. Small drove away and crossed town, turned left and headed for the poorer section where Bob Clarke's drug store was situated.

They put the car in a private garage, and removed the make-up from their faces. Half an hour later they straddled stools in a diner just around the corner from Bob's store.

"Opening early this morning, eh, Doc?" the white-aproned counterman asked. "What'll it be—the usual?"

Bob Clarke grinned and nodded.

"That's right—with a steak to top it off. I'm as hungry as though I'd been up all night."

Dave Small chuckled, and after the counterman went away, he spoke softly.

"How did Gluba ever get up the nerve to come so close to the bank and polish off Smythe? Or maybe he just doesn't care a doggone any more—figuring he'll just gun out those men and take his when it happens to come."

"Gluba is nervy enough to do that," Clarke said in a low voice. "But, Dave, the shot that missed Smythe came from somewhere inside the bank building. I'm sure of it, because the bullet was lodged in the fence on a downward slant—indicating that it had been fired from some distance above the target. Remember, Turner was inside the bank. So was Judson. The others were all on the street. Turner already has loaded himself down with suspicion.

"Hodges, I can't figure out. He used to be quite a philanthropist. On the surface, anyway. I have an idea it paid off in most instances. Once he donated a large sum, and raised the rest by subscription, to build a library. It was rumored at the time that the company which sold the land, at an excessive figure, was really owned by Hodges.

"Then again, we may be barking up the wrong tree. Gluba could have hidden away in the building and got clear after he fired. Yet—how could Gluba know those men would be at the bank at this strange hour? How could he have got in? At any rate, we'll finish breakfast and then round up Sandy. I think I'll need her in this mess. Too many angles for us to follow alone, and the store must be kept open. If gangland ever gets a hint that the Crimson Mask and Bob Clarke are one and the same, there's liable to be a nice little bomb heaved into our bedroom some night."

SANDRA GRAY arrived shortly after nine o'clock. She used a rear entrance to the store, and Small sent her upstairs to where Bob Clarke waited. Sandra held out both hands to him.

"I've been wondering just how long it would be before I was called in," she said, her tone a little accusing. "Don't lie to me, Bob Clarke! When a case like the one concerned with Gluba and the murders of those bank directors crops up, you're not idle."

Clarke grinned. "I'm afraid you won't be either," he said dryly. "It lines up to this, Sandy. There's a shyster lawyer in town named Olden. He defended Gluba and his boys at their trial—specializes in such rats. Olden visited Gluba a short time before the break—the only time he'd been there since Gluba was sent up three years ago. It coincides too closely with the escape to get by with me.

"I want Olden followed every minute. He may be in contact with those escaped cons, and there's a chance of landing them through him. It's not easy nor a safe assignment, Sandy. Olden is darned clever, and he may expect to be trailed. That's why I'm putting you on the job. He will hardly be suspicious of a pretty girl."

"I'll tell you how many olives he takes in his Martinis," Sandra promised, smiling. "And many thanks for the compliment, darling. I've followed the stories in the newspapers. Catch this killer Gluba and his two friends—and there's your case."

"We hope," Clarke said. "It seems almost too easy, the way you say it. Now, listen! I'm leaving Dave in charge of the store for the day, because I've got to become a slinking, sniveling crook just out of prison. By the way—a woman who drives a man to stealing money so she'll be well supplied with clothes. What do you think she'd be most apt to buy?"

"Perfume?" Sandra suggested. "Jewelry—perhaps a fur jacket?"

"Swell," Bob said. "A fur jacket is just the thing. Suppose you call in to Dave about once an hour. Never allow more than two hours to go by without reporting. You'll pick up Olden's trail at his office in the Randall Building."

CHAPTER VI

THE EMPTY CAB

J UST AS soon as Sandra had departed, Bob Clarke entered his laboratory and closed the steel door. He sat down before a mirror and radically changed his features until he became a droopy-eyed, wan-looking individual. He put on a cheap suit of clothes, and the gun that went into a shoulder holster left no bulge.

He called Dave Small on a private line and told of the arrangements with Sandra. Then he left the store by a back exit which led him through several courtyards and finally to a block some distance from the store.

He stopped in a pawnshop and invested a fair sum in a fur jacket. With this over his arm he sought out a taxi and had himself driven to a modest part of the city. He dismissed the cab, walked three blocks, then turned into the sidewalk which led to a small cottage. He rang the bell.

A woman of about thirty-five answered the door. Perhaps she was even a great deal younger, for the amount of rouge and paint she used made any judge of her age nothing more than a guess.

"You Mrs. Ronney?" the Crimson Mask asked in a hoarse whisper. "Mrs. James Ronney? Yeah—I thought you was. Ronney told me what you looked like. Me, I been livin' in the same hotel, y'understand what I mean? Checked out yesterday. Ronney says for me to look you up."

"Oh," Mrs. Ronney said doubtfully. "Come in. The less my nosey neighbors find out, the better I'll like it. You'd think I was serving time instead of Jimmy. He's okay, isn't he?"

"Sure—takin' it in a walk. Now have a look at this coat. Y'see, I need dough bad. Before I went up, I sort of found this coat. A pal put it away for me and it's my only stake. It's worth four hundred, but Jimmy says if I treat you right, you'd maybe be interested. Now Jimmy is a pal, see? You can have the coat for a hundred bucks."

Mrs. Ronney took the coat and her eyes lighted up avariciously. The coat actually was worth over two hundred.

"Make it fifty," she offered.

"Seventy-five," the Mask countered. "Lady, I'd have to serve five years for the job if I was caught. But you don't have to worry—the coat ain't hot. Only on your back, get it, see?"

She smiled. "All right—because you're a friend of Jimmy. Wait here. There's a drink on the sideboard if you want it."

The Crimson Mask poured himself a drink, smelled of the stuff and then emptied it out of a convenient window. Mrs. Ronney returned in a few moments with a roll of bills in her hand. She seemed to enjoy flaunting all this cash in the face of an ex-convict. The Crimson Mask took the bills she offered, bobbed his head and started for the door.

Mrs. Ronney followed him. "If you run across any more bargains like this, I might be interested," she assured him.

The Crimson Mask bobbed his head again and hurried away. He reached the next corner and retired to the doorway of an empty store. He took out the bills and riffled them through his fingers. They were brand new.

He frowned. Mrs. Ronney, the wife of the defaulter who had been Gluba's most recent cellmate, certainly had plenty of cash on hand. Was it loot from the proceeds of her husband's bank defalcations? New bills like this? The Crimson Mask doubted it, but he intended to find out.

He stepped out of the doorway and then moved back in again—quickly. A car was just pulling up in front of Mrs. Ronney's home. A man got out, and the Crimson Mask recognized him at once as Olden, the shyster lawyer. Down the street, at a safe distance, was a taxi. Sandy would be in that, following her orders to trail Olden.

THE CRIMSON MASK would have given a great deal to have listened in on the conversation between Olden and Mrs. Ronney, but in broad daylight he hesitated to approach the house. If she spotted him, his whole neat little plan would be ruined. The Crimson Mask had a rather good idea as to just how Mrs. Ronney had obtained that cash. Someone—probably Gluba or the man representing him—had paid her off in hard cash for her husband's aid in negotiating the escape from prison. If Ronney were going to prison anyway—well, why not cash in on all the possible profits?

With a grin the Crimson Mask decided to pass Sandra's cab. A look at her, beautiful as she was, would be a relief after looking at Mrs. Ronney and her beauty-parlor elaborateness.

He assumed a slouching walk, in character with his disguise, and approached the cab. As he neared it, his eyes narrowed. The driver was slumped behind the wheel, apparently half asleep—but there was no one in the tonneau! The Crimson Mask drew in a quick, hard breath.

He was certain that this cab had been following Olden. Of course it was Sandra's! He had watched the cab pull up to the curb, but had not seen anyone leave it. Where was Sandy?

The Crimson Mask stepped up to the cab and reached for the door handle. The driver eyed him fishily.

"Scram, bum," he growled. "Can't you see I got a fare?"

"Where?" the Crimson Mask asked, and peered inside, looking for something that might have been left as a clue.

The driver turned his head, then jerked all the way around. He shoved his cap to one side and scratched his head.

"Well, for the lovamike!" he gasped. "I had a dame in there—not five minutes ago! Hey—the meter's tickin'. I been gypped! I gotta find a cop."

"Never mind the cop," the Crimson Mask said. "I'll pay the fare and more. Take me to the corner of White and Carmody Streets... Yeah, sure I got dough."

He flashed a few bills, got into the cab and spent the time during the ride in searching behind the seat cushion, on the floor and in the small compartment under the rear window. If Sandra had been a passenger in this cab, she certainly had left it quickly—and inexplicably.

Of course it might have been of her own volition. Perhaps she had seen something even more interesting than Attorney Olden. Yet the Crimson Mask was badly worried.

He returned to the drug store by the same route over which he had left. Once in the privacy of his quarters above the store he hastily stripped off the disguise, then went down to the store. Dave Small was busy making up a tonic and pouring it from a graduate into a bottle.

"How'd it come out?" he asked.

"I don't know," Bob Clarke replied. "Mrs. Ronney had plenty of dough. I got part of it. Has Sandy called?"

Small shook his head. "Not yet. Should have called fifteen minutes ago, at that." He set the bottle down carefully. "You don't think anything's happened to her, do you?"

"Olden paid Mrs. Ronney a visit, Dave," Clarke said thoughtfully. "Sandy should have been trailing him. She was—I thought—but the driver of the taxi she used thought she was still in the cab and she wasn't. It's possible that Gluba spotted her, figured she was on Olden's trail and forced her, at gun-point, while that dumb driver of hers was half asleep, to leave the cab and get into another car. We'll give her another half hour—then I'm going to look for Gluba! I'm going to find him, too! If

I have to take Attorney Olden apart—and that convict Ronney at the prison, too… Okay—you'll find me here in the lab, if you need me."

HE CLOSED the steel door on his private laboratory, picked up a telephone which led directly to ex-Police Commissioner Warrick's home and contacted him at once. Warrick had news.

"You were right," he said, as soon as he heard Bob Clarke's voice. "The bullets that killed Barton, Dunn, and Smythe came from the same gun. And that gun was also used to murder the prison guard! That certainly plants all the blame on Gluba, doesn't it?"

"No," Clarke said, and instantly added: "About the money stolen from the bank. Do you know whether or not it was listed? The numbers, I mean?"

"Only in part," Warrick said. "By sheer accident the armored car crew was ordered to drop the payroll at the Glenport Aviation Company and then go on to a small town bank about fifty miles north of the city. A special consignment of cash was set aside for them. The money in that consignment was all new, and I'm told the numbers of the bills were in series. I could find out definitely and call you back."

"Do," Clarke said. "It may prove a definite lead. No luck at all in the cordon thrown around the bank?"

"Gluba slipped right through their fingers!" Warrick groaned. "I'd always estimated that crook's brain power as about nil, but he seems to have educated himself in prison—plenty! Call you back in ten minutes."

Bob Clarke hung up, leaned back in his chair and forced all his worry about Sandra to the back of his brain. He wasn't certain that she was in trouble, and even if that turned out to be true, then his only solution would be to locate Gluba quickly. Everything he concentrated on now was meant to trap that wily killer.

He knew now that the same gun—in the hands of Gluba or his fellow crooks—had killed all the victims in this case. It tied the four murders closely to the escaped convict's shirttail. Yet, neither the Crimson Mask nor the police were any nearer to locating Gluba, and putting an end to his depredations!

Clarke's memory flashed back to the episode at Turner's lakeside home. Turner, supposedly an intended victim of Gluba, had not been killed. Then Turner had been involved in two very strange "accidents." Of course he may not have meant it, but he had warned Gluba that someone was dangerously close, by honking the horn of the Crimson Mask's car. Then he had overshot the lane and had failed to stop the flight of Gluba and his men in the armored car. That he had been knocked about a bit in the process could be all in the game.

"Turner deserves to be suspected," Clarke told himself decidedly. "Somebody has been doing some swell tipping-off to Gluba. As, for instance, that Smythe would be at that meeting so early this morning—and Gluba was put wise as to the location of Turner's lake shore home as a good hideout—and probably the same person told Gluba about the route of the armored car.

"Jimmy Ronney, a ratty little defaulter, was Gluba's cellmate. Unquestionably he had something to do with the escape, but he couldn't have had anything to do with the stick-up, nor with the murder of Smythe.

"Mrs. Ronney had plenty of money, too—probably provided by Attorney Olden. Just why? Gluba? Gluba himself wouldn't dare contact her even if he'd had money before that armored car hold-up.

"Then there is Hodges—who could have fired the shot which killed Smythe. Yet if either Turner or Hodges—or both—are involved, what do they hope to get out of it all? Proceeds from robberies which Gluba will stage? Hardly. Because Gluba won't take their orders. Now that he is free, and most certainly he wouldn't turn over any loot to them—even if it were big enough for such big shots to take chances on. Nope—there must be something else far greater behind all this."

The little red light indicated that Warrick was on the wire. Bob Clarke broke off his reverie, and listened carefully to what the ex-commissioner had to say.

"There were fives, tens and twenties of brand new bills in the loot," was what he told Bob Clarke. "I have the numbers of them all. Ready to write them down? Here goes...."

CHAPTER VII

WHERE IS SANDRA?

B **OB CLARKE** had a rather long list before him when Warrick had finished. He opened a drawer in his desk and took out the several bills which Mrs. Ronney had given him. He compared the serial numbers with the list, then gasped in amazement. Mrs. Ronney had been paid off in loot from the armored car stick-up!

But how—and why? Gluba was free. Crooks like Gluba paid for favors only before they received them, and once Gluba was out of prison, he would hardly have given a single thought to whoever might have helped him.

If Mrs. Ronney held out on threat of talking, why should Gluba care? Her statements would only place her husband in a worse predicament than he was in now-and involve her as well. There was absolutely no reason why Gluba should have given her money.

Half an hour more passed, and still no word from Sandy. Obviously, she was unable to phone, which could only mean she was a prisoner, or at least being forcibly detained. Clarke paced the floor, trying to figure put just what to do. It would be dark soon.

He hurried out to the drug store, waited until Dave Small finished selling cough medicine to an old man, then called his assistant into the back room.

"Sandra must have been taken," he said. "She's smart, though—she won't say a word. Which may save her life because Gluba, or whoever has her, won't get rid of her until her connection with this killer business is known. That's a rather forlorn hope, I know, but it's all we have. Dave"—Bob Clarke's lips tightened grimly—"if anything happens to her, Gluba and his men won't go back to prison and the electric chair! There won't be enough left of them to get the straps around. Well, we've *got* to go on now, harder than before. You get over to Turner's house. Keep well under cover. Find out which side of the house is covered by the patrolman on guard duty. Then watch the other sides. If Turner goes out, trail him. Call me the moment you get a chance. Turner is mixed up with this somehow—I'm almost convinced of it! I'll stick with the store for awhile and close up early… On your way—and no slips, Dave."

As evening approached, however, Bob Clarke could not concentrate on his work in the drug store. All he could see in his mind's eye was Sandra. She was probably in one of the most dangerous situations of her life, and he was stymied. There wasn't a thing he could do, because he had no leads!

Olden perhaps? No, he could have no knowledge of what happened to Sandra, because she had been trailing him, and the taxi driver hadn't even known she was not in his car. Turner, then? There was a chance, and Bob Clarke was determined to find out as swiftly as he had ever done anything in his life.

At eight-fifteen Dave Small called in.

"Turner just slipped out through the cellar and then the backyard. I followed him. He's over at the home of Judson, one of those bank directors. I just looked in the window and both of them are talking at a great clip."

"Stay with Turner," Clarke ordered. "I'll be there as soon as I can. Keep your eyes peeled for Gluba, too. That baby seems to know everything that goes on."

CLARKE EXTINGUISHED the lights in the store, bolted the front door, then retired to his laboratory. There he donned the simple disguise he had worn before, changed to a dark suit, and slipped two automatics into his pockets. He left the building by his usual route, reached the garage where his car was kept, and drove straight to the vicinity of Judson's house.

The Crimson Mask approached the place on foot, moving cautiously. The house was well lighted up. Then he noticed that the front door was wide open. Quickly donning the crimson velvet domino, he whipped out a gun and raced up the path. He saw a dark figure sprawled out on the grass. The light streaming from the open door glittered on brass buttons.

The Crimson Mask only paused long enough to see that the policeman was not dead, but liable to be if help did not come quickly. There was a knife wound in his chest. Sprinting up the steps then the Crimson Mask raced into the house—and checked his rush suddenly. Death had been here first. Turner sat in one of Judson's comfortable chairs. His head hung down against his chest. There was a bullet hole through the back of his head.

Dave Small should be somewhere about, but there were no signs of him. Swiftly the Crimson Mask phoned Police Headquarters, then searched the house rapidly. In an upstairs room he ran upon a scene of utter confusion. Furniture had been overturned. One straight-backed chair lay in splinters. Part of the expensive rug had been badly burned. An automatic cigarette lighter lay beside the charred rug.

The whine of a radio car siren brought the Crimson Mask downstairs. In this particular disguise, with or without his mask, he was known to most policemen. Yet, they might want to ask questions, delay him, and he had no time to waste. He heard a groan as he rushed out, and stopped beside the wounded officer who lay on the lawn.

"Help is coming," he encouraged the bluecoat, and asked quickly: "Who killed Turner?"

The patrolman gazed at the crimson mask which covered the Crimson Mask's eyes and knew he was a friend.

"Don't know," he choked out weakly. "Judson—I was supposed to guard him. Gluba came—took Judson. Gluba—Vidlo—Mossy came before I saw... Was tripped and someone used—knife before I knew what happened... Don't know—who stabbed me."

"Are you sure about Gluba and his pals?" snapped the Crimson Mask.

"Positive—no mistake—"

The Crimson Mask sped to where his car was parked as the radio cars drew up. When he reached it, he saw a dark form silhouetted behind the wheel. He whipped the crimson domino off his face and kept on going, muscles and nerves tensed for trouble. This might be Gluba or one of his men, waiting for the Crimson Mask.

But a familiar voice greeted the Crimson Mask before he reached the car. It was Dave Small.

"There's the devil to pay!" Small snapped instantly. "Turner is dead—looks dead, anyhow. Judson's been snatched. Gluba, Vidlo and Mossy did it. They slipped into Judson's house somehow. They're going to kill Judson! They've practically kicked his face in already. I followed them to Judson's yacht, moored, in the river. I sneaked a boat, muffled the oars, and rowed out as close as I could. I saw them take Judson on board. And do you know how they did that little job? By tying a rope around his neck and hoisting him over the rail! You can see from that just what Judson can expect. Got plenty of nerve, those cons, haven't they? First taking over the home of one man they meant to kill—now the yacht of another!"

"Drive me to the river," the Crimson Mask ordered. "Sandra may also be on board that yacht. Step on it, Dave! We must get there before they murder Judson—or weigh anchor and sail away!"

SMALL WHEELED the car around corners at a terrific clip. He hit a cross artery, leaned on the horn button and parted traffic in the mad dash to the riverfront. There he braked, pulled onto a pier, and pointed to a trim yacht at anchor in midstream. Her single funnel was emitting smoke. Gluba was not planning to remain here long.

"Where is the boat you borrowed, Dave?" the Crimson Mask said hurriedly, as he leaped from the car. "And Dave—stay here. Give me one hour. If I don't come back, or if that yacht sails, notify Mr. Warrick and have the marine police and coast guard patrols close in. But Sandra *may* be on board, so there must be no promiscuous shooting."

The Crimson Mask slipped over to the spot where Small had moored the rowboat. He found the oars still padded with pieces of burlap, and with these effectively muting the sound of the oars, he rowed out toward the yacht. He doubted that there would be any crew on board. Gluba had probably got rid of them, and also probably knew enough seamanship to handle as small a craft as this one himself. The Crimson Mask recalled that Gluba's police record had started when he had begun looting waterfront warehouses when he was a boy. He had been raised near the river.

The anchor chain offered the best means of getting aboard. The Crimson Mask tied his dory to the chain, hoping the darkness would conceal it. Then he swarmed up that chain until he was crouched just below the deck. He drew a gun, snapped off the safety, and took a quick look over the rail.

The deck was clear. He slithered onto it, darted for the shelter of a companion-hatch and dropped flat behind it.

A hoarse bellow of agony came from somewhere deep within the confines of the ship.

The Crimson Mask crawled around the hatch, peered into the companionway ladder, then slid down it noiselessly.

He prowled the corridor, his gun ready for instant action. He passed by several closed cabin doors, following the sound of voices which seemed to come from the last cabin.

Suddenly he heard a yelp of alarm. A gun banged and the bullet whistled above his head.

He whirled. Mossy, the rangy convict, had come out of one of the cabins behind the Crimson Mask and had opened fire.

The Crimson Mask's gun bucked twice. Mossy made a grab at his shoulder, thrust his gun into his coat pocket and darted back into the cabin from which he had emerged.

The Crimson Mask broke out in a cold sweat. He was in a bad predicament now. Mossy had left the door open, probably intending for the Crimson Mask to barge in. Mossy was wounded, yes, but not badly, and he would be set to open fire the moment his mates drove the Crimson Mask into range.

The man in the blood-hued domino hesitated only a second before he dived for the nearest door and plunged into a darkened cabin. He heard Gluba shouting to Mossy—orders which spelled the end of the Crimson Mask. Mossy answered with a string of curses that proved his wounds did not handicap him entirely.

"We'll rub out Judson first, and it'll be a pleasure!" Gluba called back in a loud voice. "Keep that damn Crimson Mask penned up so's we'll have time to do it slow!"

Making quite sure that there were no communicating doors with other cabins, the Crimson Mask racked his brain, trying to figure out just how he could save Judson and round up the three killers at the same time.

He heard Judson give another scream of pain, and that settled it for the Crimson Mask. With a weapon in each hand, he slipped into the corridor, keeping his eyes on the forward cabin in which Gluba and Vidlo were slowly murdering Judson. He kept his ears open for the slightest sound from the aft cabin where Mossy was holed up.

Judson yelled again, and the Crimson Mask knew then that if he waited much longer, he would only have a corpse to rescue. So far he had heard no reference to Sandra being a prisoner, nor had he heard her voice, and hope welled that she was not here after all.

He gave a surging forward drive, both guns poised for quick shooting. The cabin in which Judson was screaming was dark. The Crimson Mask leaped inside it. He heard Judson floundering around on the floor and instantly his mind clicked. This was a trap!

He whirled. But the cabin door was already being slammed, and an instant later came the click of a key.

The Crimson Mask's guns pumped bullets through the panels of the door, but only drew a derisive howl from Gluba.

"Stay there and keep Judson company!" Gluba yelled gleefully. "The cowardly rat won't be so scared on the road to hell if you're with him!"

CHAPTER VIII

FIGHT FOR LIFE

THE CRIMSON MASK found a light switch and turned it on. Judson was on the floor, efficiently tied up. With fiendish cleverness, Gluba had fastened a sharp pointed knife so that its blade sliced into Judson's chest every time he breathed. That was what had made him scream in pain, and act as a lure to inveigle the Crimson Mask into this cabin.

The Crimson Mask removed the knife and then, without pausing to cut Judson free, attacked the door. It looked flimsy, but turned out to be solid and strong. He could not batter it down with his shoulder, so picked up a chair and attacked the panels with this. Under a savage battering they cracked, but still stopped an attempt to get out.

Then the Crimson Mask heard a muffled explosion. It seemed to come from deep in the hold. Two minutes later thick, black smoke came billowing down the corridor and swept beneath the door. The Crimson Mask coughed, and quickly turned his attention to Judson.

"They've fired the ship," he said, "and we're locked in this cabin. Keep your head, Judson. Panic will only insure Gluba's plans to finish us."

"Don't worry," Judson growled. "I'll keep my head all right. That cursed knife kept slicing into me until I nearly went mad. Gluba is a fiend, Crimson Mask. So are those two mugs with him—especially Vidlo, who is nothing more than an animal!"

Judson mopped blood from his chest and waited for the Crimson Mask to offer a suggestion. It was getting difficult to see in the cabin, even with the lights on, for the smoke was black and thick.

"They must have punctured the fuel tanks and set fire to the oil," the Crimson Mask snapped hurriedly. "The whole ship is liable to blow up at any moment. Stand back while I try to shatter the lock!"

He pumped four slugs through the lock mechanism and the door flew open. Choking black smoke billowed in, sending them retreating for a few more gasps of air. Then the Crimson Mask waved his arm in a signal for Judson to follow him, and Judson stayed close to his heels. The Crimson Mask made his way along the corridor by sense of touch alone, until he reached the companionway ladder. Cool air should have been filtering down it, but there was none. He went up the ladder and found that the hatch door had been closed and was probably battened down.

"Why don't you keep on going?" Judson called nervously.

"Can't! They closed the hatch on us. Bullets won't smash the strip of steel that holds it in place either. We can't go up—so we'll go down. You know this craft, Judson. See if you can find the engine room."

Judson led the way. Both men were coughing badly, and Judson reeled unsteadily. The agony he had endured was beginning to tell. The Crimson Mask supported him as they passed through a bulkhead door and finally reached the engine room. There a sheet of flame met them. The floor was covered with oil that blazed furiously.

"Can't—stay here!" Judson managed to say between racking coughs. "She'll blow up in a minute!"

"Find the galley!" the Crimson Mask yelled "The galley, Judson!"

Judson leaned against the wall, and then his knees buckled. The Crimson Mask bent, picked Judson up and slung him over one shoulder. Judson was not unconscious, and he was able to give the location of the galley.

HERE THERE was a little fresh air, sweeping down from the big ventilators. The Crimson Mask put Judson down, climbed up on the electric stove and stuck his head and shoulders into the air ventilator which projected above the deck. He tried to squirm his way up it, but the metal sides were too slippery.

He jumped down and rummaged through the galley. In a few moments he had a rope and a piece of sturdy pipe, about half an inch round. Judson was practically unconscious now, and perhaps three minutes had passed since they left the engine room. The gasses from the burning oil would soon fill the ship, then would come an explosion to rip her wide open from stem to stern.

There was little hope that any help would arrive from shore. It was a dark night and the smoke arising from the funnel and the air vents would hardly be noticed. Flames might eventually break through, but when that happened, the Crimson Mask and Judson would be dead.

The Crimson Mask raced back toward the engine room and stopped when he came to the engineer's quarters. Inside he found a big hammer. Working furiously, he bent the piece of pipe until it formed a crude hook. Then he returned to the galley, climbed up on the range once more and hurled the pipe through the ventilating funnel. It fell back. He groaned and tried once more. This time it landed out on deck. He seized the rope which was attached to the hooked pipe and slowly pulled it. And this time the hooked end caught on the edge of the funnel's mouth!

The Crimson Mask dropped back to the floor, dragged Judson over and quickly tied the rope around him. Then he grabbed the rope and slowly pulled himself up until he emerged from the funnel and fell, panting on the deck.

Cool, fresh air quickly revived him, however. He scrambled to his feet and hauled Judson oat of the death-trap.

Hoisting the unconscious philanthropist to his shoulder, he staggered along the deck. At the stern, he looked overside, and saw the dory which Dave Small had borrowed, still tied to the anchor. He took a firm grip on Judson, thrust a leg over the rail, and jumped.

He hit the water and went down—deep—because Judson's weight was added to his own. Fighting desperately, he reached the surface just at the moment he was sure his lungs would crack. He swam to the dory, let go of Judson for a second, then grabbed the man's wrist just as he started to sink.

Not so badly encumbered now, the Crimson Mask crawled into the dory and dragged Judson after him. He cut loose, seized the oars and with his rapidly waning strength began rowing away from the yacht.

Judson stirred and groaned. The Crimson Mask shipped oars for a moment and raised the bank director into a sitting position.

"Are you positive there were no other prisoners aboard?" he demanded.

"I didn't see anyone," Judson answered weakly. "Gluba and the others stayed with me all the time. Is Turner aboard? Is it he you're thinking of—or perhaps Hodges?"

"Turner is dead," the Crimson Mask said. "I'm not thinking of Hodges either. Let it go. I explored the ship pretty thoroughly. It wasn't so big that anyone could be hidden there. I—"

A TERRIFIC explosion drowned his voice. A sheet of flame arose from the surface of the water and seemed to engulf the yacht. Judson groaned dismally as he saw his ship split in half. Within ten minutes there was only a burning pool of oil left.

The Crimson Mask rowed to shore, helped Judson out, and they dropped to the pier in exhaustion.

"I had a small fortune tied up in that ship," Judson said bitterly. "Listen, Crimson Mask, I'm not like the others who were and are threatened by Gluba. I won't take it lying down any longer! If I don't get them first, they'll finish me. There are only two of us left now. Hodges and myself. I'm not up on ways to track down killers like Gluba. I'll need help. Find them, Crimson Mask, and I'll pay anything you want!

"There is just one thing I ask—let me be in on the kill! You saw how they tortured me. You know that they intended for you and me to be roasted alive in that ship. Those men don't deserve to go back to prison— not even if it is only to wait for an execution day. They'll break out again—I know it! So help me, if I get the chance, *I'll* kill them! I don't care what the consequences are either."

"I don't blame you, Mr. Judson," the Crimson Mask said soberly. "If we stay on the defensive, we'll end up like a lot of small nations in Europe. Gluba has help—plenty of it, apparently. More than likely he also has a hideout that will be hard to find. We must first plug any leak that tips him off and provides him with bullets and guns. Then we must pin him into a trap. I have my own ideas. Probably you have some, too. If you should find anything significant, get in touch with ex-Commissioner Warrick and I'll come at once. Meanwhile, it might be best if you stayed under cover. Gluba may not be so careful if he thinks both of us are dead."

Judson nodded. "I'll go back home. If the police are there, I'll stay out of their way until I can slip inside, get some clothes and then go to a hotel. You have my promise—when, or if I locate Gluba, I'll contact you." He stuck out his hand. "Thanks for what you did, though words are weak. If you hadn't showed up, I'd be at the bottom of the river right now."

The Crimson Mask watched Judson vanish in the night. Then Dave Small came out of the gloom, pale with worry.

"You haven't got Sandy!" he exclaimed. "Doc—she wasn't aboard that ship?"

The Crimson Mask shook his head. "I searched it. She wasn't there. Did you see any signs of Gluba and his men leaving the ship?"

"None. But it's so dark out there they could have slipped ashore without me seeing them. Judson wasn't murdered then? That was Judson who came ashore with you, wasn't it?"

"Yes. They were subjecting him to a pretty stiff course of torture when I arrived. They had the yacht set to burn or blow up, and certainly that was meant for Judson—not for me. They couldn't have known I was coming. It rather eliminates Judson as a suspect—so far anyhow. If Judson had helped them escape, why should they torture and try to murder him? "Yet"—the Crimson Mask frowned—"why should they do that anyway, even if Judson didn't help them and they were just seeking revenge? They, didn't torture the others. Turner is dead—shot through the back of the head. Upstairs, in Judson's house, I found evidence that someone had apparently been trying to destroy the house. The rug was burned and the furniture smashed."

DAVE SMALL grabbed his friend's arm.

"Wait a minute!" he put in excitedly. "Isn't it possible that someone was being held a prisoner *there?* Sandy, for instance? Perhaps she burned her ropes loose and set the rug on fire that way?"

"I thought of that." The Crimson Mask nodded. "In fact a cigarette lighter had been used to set the fire. If it was Sandy she'll be waiting for us at home and be ready to blow this case wide open. If she isn't—then we're just as much in the dark as before. I think we'll pay Attorney Olden a visit, if Sandy doesn't show up. Where's the car?"

The Crimson Mask removed his domino and wrung water out of his clothes as Dave Small sent the car rolling back to the drug store. Their hopes were blasted—for Sandy wasn't there.

The Crimson Mask's eyes became cold and hard. He changed clothes and put on a fresh disguise, consulting a newspaper photograph constantly as he built up the features of the man depicted. Small gave a grunt of astonishment, but asked no questions.

"Dave," Bob Clarke said, "the first thing to do is to find where Sandra is, now that we're certain she couldn't have been in Judson's house. We've got to force the hands of our crooked friends. I'm sure that far more lies behind this prison break, and the murders that followed it than we can see now. Gluba and his boys have vanished. Olden was their attorney, and I don't think his nose is exactly clean in this business. We'll concentrate on him first."

CHAPTER IX

SHADOW IN THE NIGHT

ONLY TWENTY minutes later Dave Small and the Crimson Mask were inside the big building where the criminal lawyer maintained offices. It was long after business hours, and the building was empty.

Olden's office door was, of course, locked. The Crimson Mask used a key on it—a thin, blanked-out key, which was coated with a preparation that took impressions of the lock perfectly. He withdrew the key, studied the shape of the lock pictured on it and then, with the small pair of clippers he cut out the proper design.

Now he had a thin, yet strong key which matched the lock, and in two seconds the door opened. They stepped inside, turned on the lights—and both men cried out in surprise.

The office was torn apart. Whoever had been here certainly knew how to search thoroughly. Chair cushions were slit open, rugs torn up, desk drawers pulled out and their contents spilled on the floor. The big safe in a corner stood with its door yawning wide, and the various papers and books it had contained were strewn all around.

"Wasn't Gluba a cracksman?" Small asked pointedly.

The Crimson Mask nodded. "One of the best, in his day. Perfectly capable of opening that box. It's old, and sensitive fingers can detect the drop of each tumbler. I wonder where Olden is?"

Small shrugged. "Perhaps stretched out on a morgue slab by now. Gluba and his boys wouldn't hesitate to rub him out, even if he was their attorney."

The Crimson Mask sat down at the desk and with a gloved hand, picked up the phone. He dialed ex-Police Commissioner Warrick's home.

"Judson just called—told me you'd saved his life," Warrick said. "He's on the war path—says the only way he can save his own life is by getting Gluba, and it seems he's right about that. Hodges has locked himself in the bedroom of his home, demanded that a squad of police be posted outside, and he just sits and shivers."

"Have you heard from Olden, Gluba's lawyer?" the Crimson Mask queried.

"Saw him just a short time ago. He's been at Police Headquarters for hours. Says he means to stay there until Gluba and the others are brought in. Insists that he must personally see that they get a square deal. He's been there so long I'm wondering whether he isn't either trying to establish a foolproof alibi for himself, or hiding out in the safest place he knows."

"Wait for fifteen minutes," the Crimson Mask said. "Then get in touch with some officer you can trust. Have him relay word to Olden that his office has been burglarized, and that he must get over there at on. That's no lie either. Somebody certainly went to town on it."

The Crimson Mask hung up and faced Dave Small.

"I'm going to pull a stunt that may make us or break us," he said grimly. "We have to take chances when Sandra is in trouble. I haven't shown the worry that's kept mounting in me, Dave. My sole hope is that whoever snatched her means to find out her connection in the case before he disposes of her. Sandra is smart enough to realize that, and by keeping quiet she has a chance of holding on to life. I want you to stay out front with the car—after you drop me off near Police Headquarters."

DRIVEN THERE, the Crimson Mask took up an advantageous position across the street from Headquarters. His mask was tucked away and he attracted no attention. In a few moments Olden came out. The lawyer looked like a turtle with its head drawn down in its shell, except that in Olden's case he used the turned-up collar of his coat.

Obviously the man was deathly afraid of something. He looked up and down the street carefully, half raised his hand to signal a cab, and thought better of it. Instead he turned north, kept close to the building line and every dozen steps looked over his shoulder. Some sixth sense warned him that he was being trailed, but Olden saw no signs of the man who dogged every step he took. The Crimson Mask had long ago become expert at shadowing.

Olden was heading in a direction away from his office. Finally he wheeled suddenly and turned into the entrance to one of the big railroad terminals. He walked directly up to a series of lock boxes, used to check parcels, opened one of them and stepped close to it. Apparently, he thrust something inside, for when he turned away he was stowing the key into a vest pocket and was obviously more at ease.

He took a taxi then, proceeded directly to his offices, and let himself in. The Crimson Mask, meanwhile, stopped beside that same block of lock boxes, dropped a dime into the one next to Olden's and merely removed the key. He took another cab and reached Olden's office two minutes behind the attorney.

Olden was cursing because of the destruction of his office furniture when he heard a soft step behind him. He turned quickly and reached for his hip pocket. A gun jabbed his ribs and he raised both hands high. His face was ashen, his lips trembled, and for a moment he couldn't even talk.

"I—I'll play ball," he managed finally. "I—I'll do anything you say. Anyway I didn't get in this because I wanted to. Gluba forced it on me. Don't shoot. I'll give you what you want."

"Quiet," the man with the gun growled. "Lift your hands, shyster, while I see what's in your pockets."

"Certainly," Olden quavered. "You'll be disappointed though. I—I haven't got the papers on me."

The gunman took a weapon from Olden's pants pocket, then continued the search. Olden held his breath as the check locker key was critically examined by his captor.

"That—that's just a key to my safe deposit box at the bank," he stammered.

The key was dropped back into his vest pocket and Olden suppressed a long sigh of relief. Then the man with the gun backed away a few steps.

"Olden," he said caustically, "you're a blackmailer. You'd sell out your friends and clients for a dime. Now I'm issuing an ultimatum. You'll get those papers into my hands! You'll likewise find out where Gluba and his rats are holed up. Call me when you've done that—and if I don't hear from you by dawn, you'll be the star performer at an inquest. This is the last warning I'll give you. Gluba first—then those papers, understand?"

"Yes—yes," Olden gasped. "I—I'm afraid of Gluba anyhow. I—I think I know how to find out where he is."

The man with the gun pushed Olden into a chair and backed out of the office. Olden did not move for five minutes after he left. Then he reached for the phone, but his hands shook so badly that he gave up the idea until his nerves had steadied themselves. When he did get his wits back—aided by a long drink from a bottle of whiskey—he grabbed the phone and made several calls. Olden was desperate, caught between two fires, and selecting the one salvation for his puny little life...

A PATROLMAN, on duty in one of the best sections of the city, peered into the darkness around an estate. He thought he had observed a dark shadow flitting through the gloom. Then he shrugged. Anyone moving that fast would make a lot of noise.

What he'd seen must have been the shadow of some branch. He walked on, whistling softly.

There was no one about when that same dark shadow returned. This time it resolved into a man who carried a woman in his arms. But he moved just as quietly despite his added burden. At the edge of the estate he gave a long, low whistle. Car headlights flashed around the corner and Dave Small pulled up in the sedan.

"Bob," he said softly, "is she all right?"

The Crimson Mask nodded and laid Sandra gently down on the back seat.

"She's been drugged," he muttered. "Heavily too, but we can handle this if we get her to the store in time. Step on it."

For another hour both men worked over Sandra until finally her eyes opened. She gave an involuntary start of fear, then a wan smile touched her lips when she saw Bob Clarke looking down at her.

"I wasn't much help, was I?" she asked weakly.

He patted her hand.

"More than you know, Sandy," he assured her. "Suppose I guess what happened to you. If I'm right, just nod your head. Don't try to talk. You spotted Olden and trailed him. He headed toward the northeast part of the city. You were in a taxi right behind him. Then your cab stopped for a red light and another car pulled up alongside you.

"The man in it pointed a gun at you, signaled that you were to transfer from the cab into his car and you did—because he must have looked as though he'd shoot. He took you to an elaborate house and asked you questions about why you were trailing Olden. When you hedged, he drugged you because he had no time to continue his questioning then."

Sandra nodded in full agreement. Bob Clarke, with a knowledge of medicine as complete as that of any practitioner, felt of Sandra's pulse, took her temperature and was satisfied that there would be no ill effects. Sandra, still well filled with the drug, slipped back into a quiet sleep.

Clarke motioned to Dave Small and they tiptoed out of the room.

"She's all right," Clarke said. "Now we'll pull our final trick. Sandy could convict the man we want, but then her connection with the Crimson Mask would become public knowledge. So we'll let our man convict himself. The stage is set, Dave. We'll raise the curtain in a few moments. Go downstairs to the lab and take one of those submachine-guns from the arsenal. Then come back here while I fix your face up a little."

Small returned in a few minutes to find Bob Clarke at the phone, directly wired to ex-Commissioner Theodore Warrick's home. Clarke hung up.

"Mr. Warrick just called," he said. "Judson has found out where Gluba, Vidlo and Mossy are hidden. He's waiting for me, Dave. We'll land those killers this time. Now here are your instructions. Follow them carefully. A single hitch may spoil the whole thing."

CHAPTER X

THE CRIMSON MASK'S TRICK

WHEN A car pulled up, Judson was walking up and down the front porch of his home. He ducked low and drew a gun. Then he saw a man get out of the car and approach the house. The man wore a crimson mask over his face. Judson arose.

"I wasn't sure who it might be," he apologized, as he put the gun away. "Perhaps Gluba knows that I've discovered his hideout. He is hidden in a house well out in the country. An isolated place—the summer home of a man I know." He laughed a little wryly as the Crimson Mask asked a quick question. "How did I discover all this? Mossy's the answer. Cash goes a long way with crooks."

"Good," the masked man said. "Then let's get started."

Judson held back, and his eyes narrowed suspiciously.

"Wait a minute," he said. "You've got a mask on your face, and what I can see of the features below it resembles the Crimson Mask as I've seen him. But the rest of your body doesn't agree. You're shorter, heavier—"

The crimson-masked man chuckled. "Very observant, Mr. Judson. I did change my physical appearance a bit. I can reassure you however.

We were in a bad predicament on a ship not long ago. We fought through smoke and flame to reach the galley, and I hauled you up to the ventilator. Only the two of us knows that, so—"

Judson nodded. "I'm satisfied. But you can't blame me for being cautious. Listen—should we notify the police first? Do you think the two of us can handle those three killers?"

"Why not?" The Crimson Mask shrugged. "I've got a tommy gun in the car."

The Crimson Mask wheeled the sedan out of the city, following Judson's orders as to direction. Judson kept turning around nervously.

"I could swear we are being followed," he said. "Yet I can't see anything."

"Your nerves are on edge," the masked man told him soothingly. "Who'd want to trail us? Our enemies are Gluba and his men, and we're looking for them, not they for us. Relax. You'll need your wits in a short time."

The masked man finally parked the car on a dark, lonesome road. They got out and the masked man cradled a submachine-gun in his arms. Directly ahead, surrounded by a dozen tall elms, was a two-story house. Lights glowed on the lower floor and all shades were carefully drawn. Judson drew his pistol and spun the cylinder.

"Maybe we should have called on the police," he said nervously. "You're sure this isn't more than we can handle?"

His companion grunted something, crouched and studied the house. He drew a flashlight from his pocket, pointed it straight up into the sky and turned it on for about ten seconds. Then he motioned Judson forward.

Crawling on all fours, gradually they drew closer and closer to the house. Suddenly a siren whined. The roar of several powerful motors approached and five heavily-loaded police cars pulled up. Men, well armed, sprang out and quickly circled the house.

Judson gaped.

"How did they know Gluba was here?" he asked.

The masked man shook his head, then shrugged.

"Don't know. Be careful now. Gluba is bound to fight. He's doomed anyway, and if I know his type, he'd rather go out shooting than be strapped in the chair."

THE CRIMSON MASK crept away. Less than a minute later Judson's jaw dropped a notch. The Crimson Mask was already close to the house, but he was swinging from one tree to another. Judson couldn't figure out how he had reached that vicinity so fast. A uniformed police lieutenant and four patrolmen came up beside Judson.

"Keep your head down," the lieutenant ordered. "We're closing in."

The small force moved forward. From all directions a similar advance was being made. Gluba and his two fellow convicts were unaware that their liberty was about ended. Then two quick shots rang out. Instantly all lights in the house were darkened. Two patrolmen, close to the rear of the place, started a wild dash for the porch.

A machine-gun cut loose. One patrolman stumbled and fell. The other dropped beside him and pulled his wounded mate back to safety. Bullets whanged all around them.

Judson, well behind the cordon of police, kept looking up. He saw the Crimson Mask reach a tree that towered directly above the house. The man in the mask clung to its branches and slowly uncoiled a length of rope which was strung around his waist.

He crawled further out on the branch until he was about three feet above the sloping roof of the house. Then he let himself down carefully until he was sprawled on the shingles. Working as quietly as possible, he crawled up the side of the roof to the chimney.

Tying one end of the rope around it, he let the other end fall over the eaves and slid down again, using the rope to slow his descent. He swung off the edge, lowered himself until he hung just outside a window, and in a moment he had this open.

From below Gluba and his men were firing furiously, shouting their challenge to the police. The Crimson Mask slipped into a room on the second floor, drew both his guns then moved toward the door. He maneuvered along the hallway. Gluba, firing through a shattered window on the first floor, barked an order.

"Vidlo, take the other tommy gun! Beat it to the second floor. Them cops ain't shootin' back! They're pullin' a trick. If you see anybody—blast away!"

Vidlo picked up a gun and bounded up the steps. He headed for the front of the house. Suddenly he raised the submachine-gun and his finger squeezed trigger.

The Crimson Mask, standing boldly in the center of the hall, made no demand for Vidlo's surrender. The baboonlike killer gave his victims no break and deserved none himself. The machine-gun's slugs banged into the floor at the Crimson Mask's feet. But Vidlo himself reeled back, hit the banister and smashed it. He plummeted to the first floor and crashed into a limp heap. The Crimson Mask's guns had fired first.

Mossy, handicapped by a bullet through one shoulder, swung around to meet the attack from behind. He saw the Crimson Mask and the two still-smoking automatics in his fists. Mossy dropped his gun and raised his good arm.

Suddenly Mossy lunged forward in a surprise attack. The Crimson Mask stepped aside agilely. One gun slashed down and Mossy caught the muzzle along the back of his neck. He kept on going, but he was out on his feet. He hit the wall and slid down to the floor.

Gluba, eyes flashing in fear and hate, came barging out of the living room with a submachine-gun raised. He saw Vidlo on the floor, spotted Mossy sprawled out, and yapped a string of curses. Then a gun came hurtling out of the darkness. It hit Gluba on the forehead.

HE WAS rugged enough to shake off the stunning effects, but before he could get his rifle into action, the Crimson Mask was upon him. Seizing the barrel of the rifle, the Crimson Mask pushed it straight up and rammed a hard right into Gluba's stomach. The killer wheezed in pain, let go of the rifle and used his fists. He got in two powerful jabs, and once Gluba thought he had won the fight when the Crimson Mask staggered back a few steps.

Gluba charged, with a yell of triumphant rage. The man he thought was about finished met that lunge with fists that punched as methodically as pistons. Gluba was hurled back against the wall. He tried to duck a left, and shoved his face straight into the path of a knockout right punch. Gluba's knees buckled and he toppled forward—into the Crimson Mask's outstretched arms.

The masked man dragged Gluba to the front door, threw it wide, and called out a warning.

"Don't shoot! I've got Gluba and his men!"

The police swarmed forward. Judson, running slightly ahead of them, suddenly lifted the submachine-gun he had picked up from where the Crimson Mask had laid it down. The gun blazed. Gluba, half conscious, was startled out of his semi-coma. He saw Judson and tried to squirm around behind the Crimson Mask.

"He'll kill me!" he yelled. "Judson will kill us all! Get him! Get that gun!"

Judson looked around. The police were hemming him in. He yanked the trigger of the gun again. Then he screeched in frustration, for none of the police fell under that withering hail of fire. He threw the gun down, reached under his coat and pulled a heavy pistol free. But even as he raised it, the Crimson Mask let go of Gluba, and the convict killer promptly fell to the ground, groveling there and yelling for mercy.

The Crimson Mask charged straight at Judson. The banker pulled his trigger twice, but his target weaved cleverly and both bullets missed their mark. Then the Crimson Mask was upon him.

For a brief moment, Judson did his best to fight back, but he was no match for this crimson-masked crime fighter. His gun was torn from his grasp, fists pounded his face, and sent him reeling back into the arms of the police.

Judson covered his face and cowered away.

"I—I lost my head," he stammered. "Seeing Gluba made me go crazy. That man meant to murder me—just as he murdered my friends…"

"Gluba did not kill Barton or Dunn," the Crimson Mask said quietly. "You did. You engineered the escape from prison. You used a crook named Ronney as your contact man with Gluba. He got word to Gluba and planned it all. You provided the means for an escape—the guns fastened beneath the tail-board of that truck. You saw that two cars were waiting, one to lure the guards in another direction while Gluba took the second car and met you by appointment—at Turner's lakeside home.

"You took Gluba's prison uniform and Vidlo's gun-which had killed a guard. You then murdered Barton and Dunn. The numbers on the convict uniform pinned all the blame on Gluba, but you were wise enough to use the jacket of another convict when you killed Dunn. That would make it seem the whole gang was intent on carrying out their threats of three years ago."

JUDSON LOOKED puzzled. "I killed them?" he protested. "Why should I murder my best friends?"

"Because they—along with Smythe, Turner, Hodges and yourself— were the real owners of the Glenport Aviation Company. Months ago, before the crisis in world affairs developed to the pitch where it is now, the business wasn't a good investment for the bank, so you gentlemen bought it out personally. Now, with the Government ready to provide millions for its expansion, you realized just how great the potential profits would be. You wanted them all for yourself, so it became necessary to get rid of the others. It would then have been an easy matter to transfer title to yourself without arousing any suspicion. Just another of those philanthropic gestures for which you are noted.

"On the surface everyone believed that the bank owned that factory, but when we held a meeting at the bank just before Smythe was killed, you slipped and stated that it was the private investment of you and the others which had been stolen—not the bank's money. I wondered about that and checked up.

"Hodges is the only intended victim left, but you would have reached him in due time and then, before suspicion was aroused against you, you would have 'discovered' Gluba and his men. You would have been the infuriated friend of their victims, and been hardly blamed if you aided in shooting the convicts down. You wanted them to die. Everything was arranged for that from the beginning.

"You had recalled Gluba's threats to get even. You approached Ronney, so he could contact Gluba. Gluba believed you wanted to get him out to help swing a big job—the holdup of an armored truck from your own bank. That was just a stall. However, you couldn't resist the idea of letting them get you some cash, so you revealed all details of the truck's route.

"Meanwhile Turner showed up at his lakeside home. He accused Gluba and his boys of killing Barton and Dunn. Gluba instantly realized what had happened. He came to have a showdown with you—after the stickup. You tricked him and his men, probably by drugging them. You held them prisoners in your own home.

"Then you killed Smythe by shooting from a window in the bank. Only you or Turner could have done that, because you were the only ones inside when Smythe was killed. Turner may have suspected you. At any rate he went to your house and you murdered him—again using the gun which had killed the prison guard.

"But Gluba and his men are tough birds. They tipped over a cigarette lighter, set fire to the rug and burned their ropes away. They came downstairs just after you killed Turner, and they knifed the patrolman on guard at the front of the house to make their get-away. I saw him after that happened and wondered why, if Gluba had shot Turner, he should bother to use a knife on the patrolman. Anyway Gluba got you, and he took you to that ship from which I rescued you."

"Don't believe him!" Judson muttered, darting wild glances at the police. "Didn't I find Gluba for you? Would I turn him over if he could convict me of murder?"

"You found out where Gluba was hiding when Attorney Olden phoned you, Judson," the Crimson Mask accused flatly. "You'll probably never know why he did that. You were forced into working with me and the police. All you really wanted now was a chance to shoot Gluba down. That's why you fired warning shots to arouse Gluba, so he'd fight. That's why the machine-gun you picked up held blanks.

"Mrs. Ronney knew about your plans and she blackmailed you—even got Olden into the affair. She gave Olden a confession which involved you, and Olden proceeded to pull some fancy blackmail. You paid Mrs.

Ronney off in money which Gluba had stolen from the armored truck. Mrs. Ronney's confession is in the hands of the police right now. So is she—and Olden."

GLUBA WAS adding his voice to Judson's condemnation. A police car rolled up, and Judson was hustled inside. The police lieutenant looked around for the Crimson Mask, but he was gone.

Dave Small, behind the wheel of the Crimson Mask's car, drove back to the city. He wore a crimson domino just like that of the real Crimson Mask. Small grinned.

"Judson almost tumbled," he said. "I guess we don't look much alike so far as our shapes go, Bob."

The Crimson Mask laughed. "It worked though. I followed you out here, Dave, warned the police who were ready for action, then got into the house while you slipped away. Judson must have been surprised when he saw me swinging through the trees. Olden, too—when he approached that check room box.

"I disguised myself as Judson, visited Olden and searched him. I substituted another check room key for the one I found in Olden's pocket. I turned that over to the police. They got the confession, got Mrs. Ronney, and picked up Olden.

"It had to be Judson or Hodges, but I wasn't sure which. That's why I risked everything on visiting Olden disguised as Judson. When he showed fear, I knew Judson was our man. So I slipped into his house and found Sandra—well hidden in a sub-cellar... Step on the gas, Dave. Maybe she'll be awake when we get back."

V

THE CRIMSON MASK'S SCORPION TRAIL

CHAPTER I

SIGNS OF MURDER

THE SIDEWALK under the marquee of the Stellar Guild Theater was brightly lighted and jammed with people. Policemen on special duty struggled good-naturedly to hold onlookers back, while sleek limousines disgorged ermined women and silk-hatted men before the box office. Half the city seemed to have turned out for the fall opening of the Stellar Guild's newest play, "Stars Over Egypt."

As a trim, gray-haired man briskly threaded his way through the crowd toward an alley beside the theater, a policeman sprang to intercept him, then fell back, saluting smartly.

"Excuse me, Mr. Warrick," he apologized. "I thought it was another of them Stage Door Johnnies after a date with Greta Blake."

Theodore Warrick returned the salute, smiling faintly. Although long since retired as police commissioner, he was still greeted by salutes of sincere respect and liking from men who had worked under him. Now his smile broadened.

"I am a Stage Door Johnny this time, Cassidy," he chuckled, "but not with flowers for Miss Blake. Richard Arken, her leading man, asked me to see him in his dressing room before the first curtain."

"Yes, sir," Cassidy said. "I'll get you right in."

MOMENTS LATER, Warrick was outside a tiny dressing room shaking hands with Richard Arken. Although past middle age, the leading man of "Stars Over Egypt" retained a youthfulness of face and carriage that kept him a great favorite with audiences. He was already dressed for the stage in a costume of ancient Egypt that enhanced his rugged physique. But under the dark make-up lurked unmistakable signs of tension that did not escape Warrick's sharp eyes.

233

The actor glanced nervously up and down the empty corridor before drawing his visitor inside and indicating a chair. He seated himself before the make-up table, puffing heavily on a cigarette for a moment.

"Good of you to come," Arken began finally with nervous abruptness. "I was afraid you wouldn't pay any attention to my note. But I had to send for you." His face was grim as he added: "We're up against a menace we can't fight by ourselves any longer."

"You know, of course," Warrick reminded him, "that I'm no longer connected with the police, have no official capacity."

"Yes," Arken said. "Yes, I know. But you're the only man in the world who can help now. Not you, yourself, but another—someone only you know how to contact."

"You mean the Crimson Mask?" Warrick asked quietly.

"Yes, the Crimson Mask," Arken said vehemently. "You remember Val Lawrence? He and I founded the Stellar Theater Guild. Val always had the leading role, while I always played second lead—until this season."

The sight that greeted the Crimson Mask's eyes was of torture.

"I remember," Warrick said sympathetically. "He was accidentally killed a week ago, wasn't he? Something about being stung by a scorpion out at your summer rehearsal farm."

"It wasn't an accident," Arken contradicted in a hoarse whisper. "He was murdered! That live scorpion was one of the props in our play and always kept in a locked cage. Someone let it loose in Val's dressing room and then used a hypodermic to pump Lawrence full of concentrated venom. It was cold-blooded murder, I tell you!"

"But the police—"

"The village constable out there accepted what we told him," Arken broke in. "We didn't want any bad publicity to spoil our opening, for one thing, and we were afraid of the killer. But we knew it was murder. You see, Val was a Scorpio."

"A Scorpio?" Warrick frowned. "I don't understand—"

He was interrupted by a sharp knock on the dressing room door.

"Onstage," came the voice of a callboy; "One minute to first curtain!"

"Hang it!" Arken frowned at his watch. "I've got to go right away. Look, I've arranged for an orchestra seat for you, Mr. Warrick. Won't you see the play and then come back here afterward? I must tell you the whole story. For unless the Crimson Mask helps, every member of the Stellar Guild is slated for an equally horrible death!"

"I'll be here," Warrick promised grimly. "And I think I can safely assure you of the Crimson Mask's aid—if what you say is true."

"Thank you," Arken said fervently. Then he snatched a heavy costume bracelet from a jewel case on the dressing table and ran out, leaving the jewel case gaping open. Warrick closed it absently and went out, frowning, to find his seat.

As the curtains parted for the opening scene of "Stars Over Egypt," Warrick gradually lost his frown and became absorbed in the play. The Stellar Guild merited its reputation as America's finest theater group. The beautiful Greta Blake was superb, and Arken's acting was no less flawless.

Clint Delante's supporting role was well handled and the balance of the cast, although not members of the Stellar Guild, had been selected for their outstanding ability. Even the play itself, dealing with astrology in ancient Egypt, was above average.

Tragedy struck so unexpectedly in the first scene that its coming froze everyone in that vast theater into shocked paralysis for a moment.

Warrick had been lounging back comfortably in his seat, enjoying himself. On the stage, Richard Arken had turned away from Greta Blake and was facing the audience, arms outflung, as he delivered a brilliant monologue. Warrick saw death come, as a glinting sliver of light that whistled over the heads of the audience from somewhere back in the darkened auditorium. It flashed into the glow of the footlights and became a speeding arrow that struck Richard Arken full in the throat!

The gruesome snick, as the point tore in, and the grating impact against Arken's vertebrae were clearly audible in the sudden, grim silence. Arken staggered forward, clawing at the long protruding shaft, his face contorted with agony. Then a bright crimson flood gushed out between his fingers, and he fell at the very edge of the footlight trough, dead.

WARRICK WAS the first person to move. As the first sighing gasp of horror burst from the assemblage, he leaped to his feet and shouted for the doors to be closed and guarded. He knew there would be a number of police among the audience who would spring to emergency posts until more police aid arrived. Then he whirled and raced for the stage amidst a bedlam of cries and shouts.

On the stage was a milling crowd that had raced from the wings, some to kneel beside Arken's body, others to hover over Greta Blake, who had mercifully fainted. A slender, bald-headed man in shirt-sleeves raced onto the stage, wringing his hands and shouting for the curtain to be drawn.

The ponderous inner drapes began to swing majestically out of the wings, and fresh cries of terror rose from the audience. Warrick stopped in mid-stride, staring. The curtains swung together, hiding the tragedy on the stage but revealing a fresh terror.

A huge square of white had been painted on the purple curtain and against that white hung an immense double circle, divided into twelve equal arcs. Inside each arc was a painted symbol. Warrick recognized the device instantly as a zodiac, a chart of the heavens familiar not only to students of astrology but to astronomers, surveyors, and meteorologists as well.

The entire chart was painted in dead black with the exception of two signs. These two were painted in vivid crimson. Gazing at them, Warrick understood now what Arken had meant in saying that Val Lawrence had been a Scorpio.

Warrick knew enough about astrology to know that the date of a person's birth determines his own particular sign of the zodiac, that according to astrology a person's life is governed by his birth sign. Arken had said that Val Lawrence was a Scorpio—and the sign of Scorpio, a coiled scorpion, was one of the two blood-red symbols on the curtain!

The other symbol marked in crimson was the sign of Sagittarius. The ex-police commissioner felt certain that Richard Arken had been born under the sign of Sagittarius—the symbol of the archer with his bow and arrow. It was equally obvious that the murderer had painted the huge zodiac with its two bloody signs to advertise his gruesome handiwork.

But why? Was Arken murdered to prevent his revealing a clue to the earlier death of Val Lawrence? Or was there, as Arken had hinted, a plot afoot to murder all the members of the Stellar Theater Guild?

These thoughts sped through Theodore Warrick's mind as he vaulted to the stage and hurried behind the curtains that spoke of death. There was no ready answer to the questions, however. Of only one thing was he certain. Here was a task that would call on all the ability of that enemy of crime—the Crimson Mask!

Grimly, Warrick pushed through the shuddering group around Richard Arken's body and quickly identified himself.

"You'd all better stay in sight on the stage until the police arrive," he ordered crisply. "Has someone phoned them?"

"I did," the bald-headed man said tremulously. "I'm Arthur Simmons, stage director for the Stellar Guild."

A DISTANT wail of police sirens backed up his statement. Warrick glanced down to where the stout and dark-complexioned Clint Delante knelt beside the body in silent grief. Just then a broad-shouldered man with a shock of wavy blond hair burst through the curtains.

"This is terrible—awful!" he cried, rushing up to the group. "I saw the whole thing. Poor Dick!"

"Who are you?" Warrick asked, remembering that this man had been racing down the middle aisle when he first reached the stage.

"Mason," the blond man panted. "Jerry Mason. I'm a member of Stellar Guild. A business manager and agent for the actors. That arrow came right over my head from somewhere behind me. I couldn't see anyone and people jammed around so that I couldn't get loose to come up here until just now."

A detail of police, headed by Detective-lieutenant Kane rushed onto the stage. Warrick gave them the details of what had occurred in a concise report.

"The killer must still be in the audience," he concluded, "and whatever weapon he used to hurl that arrow won't be easy to hide."

"That's great!" the lieutenant snapped disgustedly. "Except that somebody started a panic and at least a hundred people pushed their way out before the doors could be blocked. You can bet the killer was among 'em." He eyed the ex-police commissioner curiously. "How come you're here, Mr. Warrick? Is the Crimson Mask on the job?"

"Not yet," Warrick answered grimly, heading toward the wings. "But he will be as soon as I find a telephone!"

CHAPTER II

THE CRIMSON
MASK TAKES OVER

O **N THE** dimly lit corner, the old-fashioned drug store showed the only light in the neighborhood, though it was only nine-thirty in the evening. But in that stronghold of respectable poverty, people had no money to squander on unnecessary lights so they went to bed early, as decent people should. They slept calmly, knowing that if illness should strike unexpectedly, the light at the drug store would be a friendly beacon of ready help.

There was little of the modern drug store behind those cheery windows—no confusion of gorgeously colored counter cards, no displays of candies, perfumes, alarm clocks or the thousand-and-one knickknacks that, in most stores, have crowded drugs back to some remote corner. This was simply a drug store, with only ethical pharmaceuticals lining its spotlessly clean shelves.

The one exception was the huge jar of lemon drops prominently displayed. But that was not for sale. It was a free and unstinted gift to wistful kids who had never had any money of their own to spend for candy, kids who otherwise might be tempted into petty thievery to satisfy a natural craving for sweets.

Behind the store was a neat prescription room, and few persons knew or cared that the certificate on the wall read "Robert Clarke, Ph.G." To the grown folks, the pleasant-faced young druggist was always "Doc" or "Bob." And to the kids he was the "Lemon Drop Man."

Why he stayed in that penniless neighborhood, or how he could afford an assistant like jovial, pink-cheeked Dave Small, was a mystery. But the fact that he was there was a great blessing for those who lived in the district.

Beyond the prescription room, however, was a white-tiled laboratory that outsiders never saw. In it, Bob Clarke made chemical and bacteriological analysis for physicians, but there were instruments there that would have made any doctor open his eyes wide.

For neither blood-counts nor bacterial analysis require comparison microscopes with special stages to hold fingerprints or cartridges. Nor

THE CRIMSON MASK'S SCORPION TRAIL 239

do they involve moulage materials, calibrators, fingerprint equipment or slide projectors. Those things are the tools of modern scientific crime detection, and if the underworld ever so much as suspected their presence behind that little prescription room, one of crime's greatest stumbling-blocks might be "eliminated."

For Bob Clarke, the idolized druggist, was also the Crimson Mask, most feared of all crime avengers!

His identity concealed by clever make-up or a mask of crimson silk, his activities unhampered by the red tape of police routine or legal restrictions, he repeatedly solved mysteries and smashed crime rings that baffled the police.

The creation of the Crimson Mask was neither an accident nor a casual hobby. Years before, Bob Clarke's father, a sergeant of police, had been shot from behind by cowardly thugs. As the officer lay dead, his own blood formed a crimson mask across his face. Bob Clarke had stood there above the body and sworn to dedicate his life to the eradication of crime.

Theodore Warrick was also present at the end of the brave officer's life. He had seconded, planned and financed the preparation for that career. And so, from the mask of blood on a dead man's face, the Crimson Mask was born.

Besides Theodore Warrick, only two others knew the true identity of the Crimson Mask. One was chubby, loyal Dave Small, who ran the store while the Mask prowled at large and who frequently gave valuable aid to his friend's work.

The other inside member of the crime-fighting group was a girl— slender, blond, beautiful Sandra Gray. Like Bob Clarke, she was fighting crime to avenge a murdered father, and her courage and ability had already proven her an irreplaceable aid.

IF SANDY, as they affectionately called her, guessed that behind the Crimson Mask's admiration for her lay a deeper, stronger emotion, she gave no sign. For she, like the Crimson Mask, knew that as long as humanity looked to them for defense against vicious crime, there could be no time for love in their lives.

When the tiny light winked beneath the drug store counter, signaling a new appeal to the Crimson Mask through his sole contact, Theodore Warrick, their own lives became secondary to that call. Bob Clarke, trim in his crisp white jacket, was thinking of these things as he helped Dave Small unpack cases of the vitamin capsules they were forever giving away to poverty-stricken mothers. The sudden glow of the signal light was like an echo to his thoughts.

"Action, Bob," said Dave tensely. "I wonder what it'll be this time."

"The same as always," Bob Clarke answered grimly, as he headed toward the private phone concealed in the rear of the store. "Someone thinks he has concocted a sure-fire scheme for beating the law. The details may vary from one case to another, but that's the basis of almost all crime."

He went through the rear door, whose flimsy-looking wood panels concealed a backing of the strongest steel armor, and took up his private phone. Then, for several minutes he listened in silence while Warrick's voice succinctly detailed the tragic events at the Stellar Guild Theater and all he knew of what preceded them.

"This case has some new touches," Bob Clarke commented finally, when Warrick was finished describing the murder. "I'm particularly interested in the flaunting of that astrological angle by means of the zodiac and the murder methods. It sounds to me like either a challenge to the police or, more likely, a hidden threat to other prospective victims. I'll be over there within half an hour. Suppose you meet your old gray-haired friend, Bert West, at that coffee shop next to the theater about ten o'clock."

"I get it," Warrick said. "I'll be there with all the information I can pick up that might prove usable…"

At exactly two minutes to ten, an elderly man whose graying hair framed a gaunt, lined face, entered the restaurant and approached the table where Warrick sat alone. He extended his hand, smiling at the surprise in the ex-police commissioner's eyes.

"Great heavens!" Warrick gasped. "You look at least sixty-five years old. Even your hands are those of an old man's."

"I'll be sixty-four m'next birthday," the Crimson Mask quavered, smiling. "Seriously, I picked this disguise because a man of my apparent age isn't as noticeable poking around where he doesn't belong. Well, what are the developments now?"

"Not much," Warrick admitted. "The audience was so full of society people that the police had to sift through the net pretty fast. Caught a couple of known petty crooks but that's all. No sign of the killer or the bow he used."

"Is there still a police guard at the theater?" the Crimson Mask asked.

WARRICK SHOOK his head. There didn't seem to be much point in leaving one. A cursory checkup of the place didn't show anything that seemed even remotely to connect up with the crime. After all, the killer seemed to be a part of the audience and sifting that crowd was about all the police had any reason to do. Frankly, I discouraged anything but locking the place up for the night—insofar as I could. I had an idea you'd want a free hand to prowl there later."

"Good," the gray-haired man approved. "I'll look it over, presently. You said the arrow didn't pass completely through Arken's neck, didn't you? In that case, I'd rule out a bow as the weapon. A long bow will drive an arrow through a three-inch plank, let alone a man's neck. And you didn't hear the twang of a bowstring, either. Probably the arrow was shot from a spring gun hidden in a walking slick or furled umbrella. Did you get anything on the Stellar Guild itself?"

Warrick waited for the Crimson Mask's order of coffee and doughnuts to be brought before answering.

"Yes," he said then. "Arken and Lawrence started the theater, with Greta Blake, Delante, Mason and Simmons joining in to put it over. The Stellar Theater Guild is a stock company with equal shares and equal profits to all. If a member dies or retires, his stock is divided among the survivors. But all the members had money of their own to begin with and Stellar has made money ever since. They own their theater here and a farm in the mountains near Wendtville, Pennsylvania, where they spend summers in rehearsal. Stellar is considered the most successful theater guild in the country."

"Not much excuse for murder there," the Crimson Mask mused. "Any sign of personal friction among the members?"

"Not friction, exactly. But they all acted reserved and furtive. I'd guess they know something they aren't revealing about the murders. By the way, I wired the Wendtville constable for details on Lawrence's death, in case you want them."

"Fine." The Crimson Mask finished his coffee and rose. "I'll drop over in the morning to see what you learn. Now I'm going to look over the scene of the crime for myself."

For a few minutes, the Crimson Mask strolled up and down the street with apparent aimlessness. Actually, his sharp eyes were scanning every passerby. If the killer or his allies happened to be watching Warrick, they might make a shrewd guess as to the identity of his "old" friend.

Then, certain that he was unobserved, the Crimson Mask slipped into the dark alley beside the theater and made his way to the stage door. A master key from a ring he always carried let him in. He closed the door softly behind him and froze. From the darkness had come a faint whisper of sound.

FOR FIVE minutes the Crimson Mask stood motionless, hand on his gun, listening intently. When the sound was not repeated, he decided his ears must have picked up the scurry of mice. He relaxed and snapped on his pencil flash.

Ahead lay two short flights of steps, one leading down to the dressing rooms, the other up to the stage. The Crimson Mask chose the stage for his first investigation. There were reasons for this. Why, he asked himself, was the inner curtain drawn instead of the main one, when the tragedy, had occurred? Possibly it was the murderer's own idea to have the zodiac appear as a means of producing further horror.

Could it be that the stagehand did it purposely, or, perhaps, in his excitement he pressed the wrong lever? Also, the zodiac sign must have been painted on only recently, for it would certainly have been noticed before. Whatever the truth of the matter was, the killer had certainly created the desired effect.

Threading his way past a litter of scenery, lights and prop furniture, Bob made his way into the wings, where the switch panel was located.

He flashed his light over the switch panel beside the stage, quickly locating the two curtain-control switches. One switch was marked "Main Drop," the other "2nd Drop." Closing either switch started a motor which, winding one of the control ropes overhead onto a revolving drum, drew the proper curtain in or out.

By all rights, the "Main Drop" switch should bring out the new curtain, but when the Crimson Mask tested the control, it was the inner curtain that began to move. And when he pressed the inner curtain control switch the main drop appeared. He whistled softly. Somehow, the curtain controls had been reversed.

A glance at the back of the switch panel showed the wiring intact. His flash moved on and picked out an iron ladder leading to a narrow catwalk above the stage for the use of electricians and scene-shifters. Beside this ran the actual control ropes that pulled the big curtains. Without hesitation, the Crimson Mask went up the ladder. A moment later, kneeling on the narrow platform, thirty feet above mid-stage, he was gazing narrow-eyed at the killer's ingenious handiwork.

The rope that should pull the main curtain had been cut and spliced onto the drum for the inner one. The inner curtain had, in turn, been similarly spliced to the new drum. In order to operate the main curtain at the opening of the play, the killer or his accomplice had deliberately closed the "2nd" switch.

Later, after the murder, any one of the stagehands answering the call to bring down the curtain had instinctively closed the "Main" switch, thus unwittingly bringing the inner curtain into view. It was cleverly arranged, but one thing was obvious. The killer, or his accomplice, must have had complete access to all parts of the stage.

THE CRIMSON MASK turned, and his beam, spraying along the catwalk beyond where he knelt, fell across a man's feet planted solidly on the platform. The unseen lurker grunted as the light revealed his presence. There was a swift flurry of movement. The Crimson Mask, on his knees and with his gun tucked into its holster, tried to scramble back. But he was too late. Something whistled through the darkness and smashed against his head with stunning force. The pencil light dropped from his fingers. He felt himself toppling forward helplessly, toward the bare stage thirty feet below!

One hand, clawing desperately, caught at the edge of the catwalk. His attacker leaped forward and stamped on the clutching fingers, kicking them loose.

The Crimson Mask fell across the control ropes, felt the crude splices break under his weight. Desperately he clutched at one of the severed ropes. Then he was hurtling downward, into pitch darkness!

CHAPTER III

MYSTERIOUS BOTTLE

GRIMLY, THE CRIMSON MASK knew a split second interval of complete hopelessness. Then a terrific jerk nearly tore his arm from its socket and the direction, but not the speed, of his plunge changed. Unconsciously, he had wrapped the broken control rope around his hand as he fell and reaching the end of that rope had changed his straight fall into a pendulum-like swing toward the wings.

But this was by no means a way of escape, for his swing at the end of the rope would smash his body against the wall with a force no less devastating. The Crimson Mask's brain whipped through a realization of his predicament and hit upon a faint hope of escape, all in the space of a heartbeat.

With a sudden jerk of his dangling legs, he changed the direction of his plunge, let go the rope, and hurled straight out into inky blackness. He was pinning everything on his fleeting memory of how that stage wing was arranged. He could never survive a head-long plunge against the wall at that speed.

There was an instant of sickening uncertainty. Then the Crimson Mask's outstretched hands touched velvety fabric, and the next moment his plunging body was burrowing deep in the folds of the huge curtain. His desperate gamble had worked! He had missed the stage wall by inches!

Clutching at the curtain to slow his descent, the Crimson Mask slid down to the stage. For a moment, his overtaxed nerves and muscles nearly precipitated him to the floor. Then the sound of clattering footsteps on the iron ladder across the stage snapped him out of his reverie. His mysterious attacker, disappointed at not hearing the Crimson Mask's body smash to the stage, was attempting flight.

The Crimson Mask sped across the stage like a furtive phantom and launched himself at the dark shadow darting away from the foot of the ladder. A whirlwind of smashing blows met his attack. The Crimson Mask drilled in grimly, fighting to get a knockout blow at his assailant. He caught a handful of rough fabric and something clattered to the floor under his feet. Setting himself, the Crimson Mask put all his strength into one devastating blow.

But disaster struck then. His foot came down on the invisible object on the floor. It rolled under his weight, throwing him off balance. His fist glanced off his opponent's shoulder instead of landing a direct blow. And before he could recover his balance, a vicious kick sent him sprawling. Until now, the Crimson Mask had not drawn his gun because he hoped to overpower the mysterious assailant and make him talk. Now he reached for his gun, anticipating a vicious attack.

The dark figure leaped forward, a sharp beam of light suddenly lancing out from a flashlight in his hands. The light limned the Crimson Mask in its glare and showed him just clearing the gun from his coat. The sight brought a sharp gasp from the attacker. Abruptly the light clicked out, the dark shape whirled away and a moment later the outside door slammed. Apparently the Crimson Mask's disguise as an old man had made him appear helpless and unarmed. The sight of a ready gun had given his attacker an abrupt change of heart.

The Crimson Mask rose painfully and reholstered his gun. He knew pursuit was useless and he was curious over the queer object that had upset him. He found his flash undamaged, thanks to its special construction, and snapped on the light.

The object dropped by his assailant was a glass bottle, long and round like a pickle jar. The Crimson Mask picked it up in his handkerchief, so as to preserve any possible fingerprints, and studied it narrowly. Although empty, it smelled faintly of acid and the inside was acid-etched part-way up one side. Blown into the neck was the numeral "7" and a queer mark.

THE CRIMSON MASK tucked it away, frowning. In his laboratory, it might tell a great deal, but for the moment it was only another part of the unsolved mystery.

He still wanted to examine the dressing rooms. Since it seemed unlikely that other enemies lurked in the darkened theater, he went down boldly and switched on the overhead lights. Name cards on the doors showed that Arken's dressing room faced Greta Blake's at the front of the corridor. That of Arken drew his interest first.

He stepped inside and snapped on the light.

Chaos met his eye. Every drawer and box in the room had been emptied with cosmetics, jewelry, costumes and personal effects strewn carelessly on the floor. The Crimson Mask's eyes narrowed. This was not the result of a police investigation. More likely, the mysterious prowler was responsible. But what had he been looking for? And did he find it? The Crimson Mask reflected grimly that the answers to those two questions might be the answer to the whole mystery. He knelt then and began a methodical examination of every item in the heap on the floor.

His search was rapid but thorough. When he finished, only two items held his attention. One was a three-line newspaper clipping mentioning the suicide of a man named John L. Jones. It had been stuck in the lid of Arken's costume jewel box. The other item was a hand-drawn, personal astrological horoscope for Richard Arken on the stationery of Jerry Mason, actors' agent.

The Crimson Mask put these two items into his pocket and quickly went through the other dressing rooms without finding anything of further interest.

He left the theater then, locking the alley door behind him, and hailed a cab. On sudden impulse, he gave the address of Mason's office. His original plan of rushing the mysterious bottle to his laboratory for study could wait. The connection between the horoscope on Mason's stationery and the astrological murders seemed to be more important at the moment.

Mason's office address turned out to be his apartment on the fourth floor of a swanky apartment house on the outside of the city. The Crimson Mask strode through the empty lobby, rode the automatic elevator to the fourth floor and paused before Mason's door while he adjusted the mask of crimson silk that was his trademark.

Then he rapped sharply. There was no sound from inside.

He rapped again louder, and thumbed the buzzer. When he was sure the apartment was empty, he brought out the master keys and let himself in, locking the door behind him. His hand flash showed a large living room, in one corner of which sat a modernistic desk and file cabinet.

Before examining the desk, the Crimson Mask located a window opening onto the fire-escape and unlocked it for quick flight, should Mason come home unexpectedly. Then he went to work. The cabinet revealed nothing of importance, but the contents of a fat brown envelope in a desk drawer made his eyes widen.

Jerry Mason handled several stage stars besides the Stellar Guild members. But what made the Crimson Mask's lips purse in a soundless whistle was the evidence that Mason had every one of these stars insured for amounts ranging from ten to fifty thousand dollars each.

The deaths of Arken and Lawrence alone would pay him a hundred thousand in cash. That he needed that cash was evidenced by carbons of letters to the insurance companies, each asking for an extension of time in which to pay up premiums on other actors. Jerry Mason needed cash, but it was not proof that he was involved in the murders. Still, it was a lead worth extensive plumbing.

The Crimson Mask returned the policies and papers to the desk drawer and rummaged further. In another drawer he found a pile of astrological books and copies of horoscopes bearing the names of his clients. The Crimson Mask was grimly thoughtful as he closed that drawer. Definitely, Mason would bear closer investigation.

ABRUPTLY THEN, his eyes caught the gleam of a slip of paper tucked into a corner of the desk blotter. He centered his flash on the slip and stared in amazement at the typed, unsigned note it bore.

"Mason," it read, "you've seen Val Lawrence and Richard Arken pay for their treachery. Your turn will come soon. Are you ready to die?"

The Crimson Mask straightened from his reading. And as he did so something hard and unyielding jammed into his back. He had been so absorbed in his sensational discoveries that he had been blind and deaf to his surroundings. Now he saw that the window he had unlocked was wide open.

"Stand still, pal," a harsh voice growled, close to his ear. "One move and your backbone'll come flying right out through your belt buckle." A hand lifted the Crimson Mask's gun from its special pocket, returned there and found the mysterious bottle inside his coat. There was a sharp intake of breath at this discovery. The crimson-masked figure stood tensely, cursing his own carelessness, alert for any sign of relaxed vigilance on the part of his captor. He was in a bad spot, for the crimson mask across his eyes branded him irrevocably as the man marked for death by everyone in the underworld.

Suddenly the flashlight was jerked from his hand and turned fun on his face. From behind came a gloating chuckle.

"Well, well! So the terrible Crimson Mask is caught at last, like a kid with his hand in the jam jar. Boy, will I collect plenty dough from certain people when I hand over your corpse. You know what you're gonna get, don't you?"

"I know what you *think* I'll get," the Crimson Mask drawled coolly. "But getting rid of me has been tried by experts, and you don't act like an expert."

Though every nerve quivered at the anticipation of burning lead, the druggist detective deliberately turned and studied the shadowy bulk of his captor. He saw at once that this was a bigger, heavier man than the one who had attacked him at the theater.

A snarl of rage burst from the other.

"You almost took a slug for that crack, wise guy," his captor threatened. "You'd take one right here and now, too, if this dump was soundproofed. But I got a better idea, Mask. Climb out and down that fire-escape, slow and quiet. You and me are gonna take a little ride out in the country where it's nice and private and no coppers around to butt in. After all, I might as well do this up right, huh? It ain't every day I get a chance to bump the Crimson Mask. Get going!"

The Crimson Mask could do nothing but obey. The menacing gun never wavered. Any move he made either to attack or escape would bring quick, certain death. The Crimson Mask was too fearsome a captive to be permitted the slightest chance of a break. Helpless, he climbed slowly down the fire-escape and let himself be prodded to a big sedan that waited in the shadows.

"Get under the wheel, chump," the other ordered. "You're driving to your own funeral. And get your mitts away from that pocket!"

A vicious jab of the gun emphasized the sharp command. The Crimson Mask stopped his furtive fumbling with the edge of his coat. But he had accomplished his purpose. His left hand now clasped a tiny vial that had been placed in a secret pocket of his coat just a few hours before.

THE VIAL was one of Dave Small's ideas—simply a few drops of oil in which floated a sliver of silvery metal about the size of a match head.

As he climbed into the sedan and slid under the wheel, he contrived to loosen the cork and toss the vial into the rear seat, unnoticed. Then, with the gun jabbing viciously into his side, he brought the car out onto the street and started driving toward the open country.

From the corner of his eye he studied his captor's face. He had never seen the brutal, battered countenance before, but he would never forget it now. Then he realized that unless his luck held, that cruel face might be the last thing he saw in this world.

"Say," the thug snarled abruptly. "What's burning? I smell something."

The Crimson Mask made no answer but a glint came into his eyes and little muscles suddenly ridged the line of his jaw. Surreptitiously, his elbow pushed the window crank beside him, rolling the window down an inch, sending a draft of air circulating to the back seat. He tensed for split-second action.

"If you're tryin' something—" the big thug snarled, half-raising the gun in his hand. "I don't like that satisfied look on your—Hey! The car's on fire!" But the windshield had already shown the Crimson Mask a reflection of leaping orange flame from the back seat. It was the moment for which he had been waiting. The tiny vial he had opened and tossed back there had contained only a sliver of metallic sodium, but that sliver in contact with the air had generated a little spot of intense heat.

The blast of air from his opened window onto that spot had caused the back seat cushions to burst into roaring flame.

The uncanny appearance of the blaze occupied the burly thug's whole attention on the back seat for an instant. In that instant, the Crimson Mask went into action.

CHAPTER IV

THE MYSTERIOUS JONES

H IS RIGHT hand chopped down on the thug's gun wrist, driving the weapon to one side. At the same time, his left fist arced up and cracked solidly against the massive, brutal jaw. It was a blow that would have felled an ordinary man, but the Crimson Mask's opponent shook it off with a bellow of rage. The gun roared once, sending a slug into the back of the seat.

The big man was hampered by trying to line his gun on the Crimson Mask across his own body. The masked man blocked a vicious blow and felt gristle collapse as his answering punch smashed into the thug's already battered nose.

At that strained, tense moment, the car, which was still rolling unguided down the dark street, responded to the pressure of struggling bodies against the wheel and shot off at an abrupt angle. Climbing the curb, it bumped over sodded lawn and stopped with a roaring crash against the bole of a tree.

The Crimson Mask, who by now had managed to get hold of his own gun that was in his enemy's pocket, was thrown against the dash with stunning force. The impact burst the opposite door open and the big man tumbled out, leaving part of his coat and the captured gun in the Crimson Mask's hand.

But the same impact hurled the flaming back cushions against the front seat. Instantly, a sheet of flame and a shower of burning fragments of the fabric swept over the masked man, momentarily blinding him. From outside suddenly came two sharp explosions and slugs whipped past his face. But the leaping flames or the jolt of the accident spoiled the thug's aim.

The Crimson Mask shot once, blindly, in the direction of the sounds and then launched himself in a leap that carried him out through the open door and clear of the flames.

He struck the ground and rolled over, blinking his eyes clear of smoke and glare, and coming up with his gun ready for action. Then he grunted in anger. His captor was gone and with him, the mysterious bottle. For the second time in an hour, the Crimson Mask had escaped with his life but lost his attacker.

A moment later he heard the reason for the big thug's unexpected flight, when the shrill blast of a police whistle reached his ear. Apparently a patrolman close by had heard the crash and the shots, and was racing to investigate.

Already lights were springing up in surrounding houses. For the moment, at least, the Crimson Mask had no desire to waste time or tip his hand by submitting to a police investigation. The thug's idea of sudden flight seemed wise. But first he had an important job to do.

The front seat of the sedan was already consumed in flames, but the Crimson Mask jerked off his singed coat, wrapped it around his head and plunged back into the holocaust. Though the flames seared his wrists and hands, he caught the steering wheel and put every ounce of his superb strength into a twisting jerk.

The light steel of the rim and spokes bent without breaking, but the thick plastic of the wheel itself shattered into long splinters. The Crimson

Mask hastily gathered these splinters, tucked them into his pocket and fled into the darkness as the policeman came pounding across the pavement toward the wreck...

SANDRA AND Dave were waiting anxiously in the Crimson Mask's quarters above the drug store when he arrived. Although dead tired, he paused only long enough to have his blistered wrists coated with salve and to change into fresh clothing. While Sandra applied the unguent, he quickly sketched the details of what had occurred.

"You'll go to bed and get some rest now, won't you?" Sandra pleaded when he had finished.

Bob Clarke, the Crimson Mask, shook his head, smiling.

"Not quite yet, Sandy." He produced the splinters of steering wheel he had salvaged. "Somewhere on these scraps I hope to find a clear fingerprint or two of my burly chum, although my prints may have smeared them when I drove. I want to try to identify that thug as quickly as possible, for he may be a lead to the mystery behind the murders."

They watched in silence while Bob Clarke's deft fingers dusted the fragments, photographed them for permanent record and then sat down to analyze his findings. Thorough knowledge of the Henry fingerprint system enabled him quickly to translate the loops and whorls and arches he found into a simple classification formula.

When he had eliminated his own prints and those too smudged to be usable, he had two clear impressions left that could only be those of his huge attacker. With the index of these before him, he turned to his private phone.

"I hate to disturb Warrick at this hour," he said, "but tonight's developments indicate more murders unless we smash the plot quickly. In that case, every second counts."

He turned to the phone, apologized to Warrick and gave a concise report of the evening's events.

"Now I need your help," he continued. "I wish you'd get in touch with the police and find out all they know about the burned car, and whom it belonged to, if possible. Then read them the fingerprint classification I'm going to give you and see if it's on file. Also, get any dope you can on a suicide named John L. Jones. Now get pencil and paper and I'll give you the fingerprint index... Ready? L over L, nine over twelve..."

After finishing, he cradled the phone. Within ten minutes Warrick called back.

"You got something," he said excitedly. "The car belongs to Delante, who reported it stolen yesterday. Those prints belong to a thug named

Sandra Gray

Beef Slattery who did time for beating up merchants in a protection racket. But get this! Until a month ago, Slattery was employed as bodyguard and chauffeur by Greta Blake!"

"Whew!" Clarke whistled. "That *does* introduce some new angles. I think I'll visit some Stellar members in the morning before I see you."

"Say," Warrick interrupted, "I just thought of something. Where did you say you found that Jones suicide clipping in Arken's dressing room?"

"Why, lying in the top of the case where he kept the jewelry that went with those Egyptian costumes he wore on the stage."

"Bob, I just remembered that when Arken ran out to go on the stage, he left that case open and I closed it. There wasn't a sign of a newspaper clipping in there then."

BOB CLARKE frowned puzzledly. "Then someone planted it there after you left," he said. "For what reason? Did they mean it to be found by the police after Arken's murder, or was it intended for him by someone who didn't know he wouldn't be back to read it? By the way, did you get any dope on John L. Jones?"

"The Records Room was closed for the night," Warrick answered. "I'll get you the information first thing in the morning."

Bob Clarke hung up and recounted his new information to the others.

"Got some work for us, then?" Dave Small asked eagerly.

"Your job will come later, Dave," said Clarke. "But I have a job for you, Sandy. Greta Blake, like most stars, is hungry for publicity. If a young lady writer named Sandra Gray asked permission to write a magazine article on the home life of a star, she'd practically get the run of Greta Blake's home for a few days. I'm sure she'd forgive us the deception, afterward."

"You'll know all there is to know about Greta Blake," Sandy promised. "From where she throws her used nail polish bottles, to what she talks about when she mumbles in her sleep."

"Good." Bob Clarke smiled. "And speaking of sleep, we had better get some ourselves. Let's break this up."

Early the next morning, a well built, middle-aged man who wore glasses and carried a cane, hammered on the locked stage door of the Stellar Guild Theater. It was the Crimson Mask in a new disguise, fresh and alert despite less than three hours of sleep. A fake phone call had already told him that Arthur Simmons, a Stellar Guild member and its stage director, was at the theater. After a short wait, the door opened and Simmons, looking haggard and jittery, appeared.

"My name is Dawson," the Crimson Mask prevaricated. "May I come in and talk to you for a moment—about last night?"

Simmons hesitated and then jerked his head for "Mr. Dawson" to enter. He closed the door, turned, and his eyes suddenly bulged. His visitor was holding out one hand, and draped across his spread fingers was a mask of crimson silk, the trademark known to everyone in the city.

"The Crimson Mask!" Simmons whispered. "I heard you were investigating Dick Arken's murder. What can I do to help get the dirty rat who did it?"

"Give me straight answers," the Crimson Mask answered grimly. "Who, besides yourself, had access to the theater at any time of the day or night without arousing suspicion?"

"Any Stellar Guild member," Simmons answered promptly. "Don't forget, we're all equal owners of the theater and everything in it. This, of course, is my office during the season, but the rest are always poking around, experimenting with lights and scenery and effects. Why?"

"Mr. Dawson" explained how the control ropes had been crossed to bring out the zodiac on the inner curtain and how he had very nearly been thrown to his death while investigating. Simmons grinned lopsidedly.

"So *you're* the one." He jerked a thumb up toward the catwalk, now littered with tools and coiled rope. "I've been putting in new control ropes and cussing whoever busted the others all morning."

The Crimson Mask's eyebrows lifted.

"Do you always make your own repairs?" he asked.

Simmons made a sour face.

"It's the stage carpenter's job. But after what happened last night, I told him not to come back until I called him. He went on a binge and I couldn't locate him this morning. So, more to keep from thinking about what happened than anything else, I decided to do the job myself."

"Will they try to keep the show going?" the Crimson Mask asked.

"I don't know." Simmons shrugged helplessly. "Val and Dick were the only ones groomed to play the lead. Clint Delante couldn't take over without weeks of rehearsal."

"Tell me," the Crimson Mask said with studied casualness. "What made Jones kill himself?"

It was a shot in the dark but it hit home. Simmons stiffened and his eyes flickered.

"How did you find out about Johnny Jones?" he cried hoarsely.

CHAPTER V

MURDER FOR VENGEANCE

YOU'D BETTER tell me the whole story," the Crimson Mask said a little later.

"You're right," Simmons said. "Reputations don't mean much to a corpse. This Johnny Jones was a neurotic who came from somewhere upstate last spring to set the world afire with his plays. Thought he was a second Eugene O'Neil. Val and Dick were in town, but the rest of us had gone to the rehearsal farm. We didn't know anything about what happened until it was all over.

"Anyhow, Jones tried to sell us a play based on astrology. Val and Dick read it to please him, but it was rotten. And besides, we were already scripting "Stars Over Egypt," which has an astrological theme. When they told Jones that, he blew his top and hysterically started accusing them of stealing his idea. He made so much noise that they booted him out and forgot him.

"Some crank is always accusing a playwright of piracy, but Jones was really off base. He rushed home and killed himself, leaving notes blaming the Stellar Guild. Luckily, we kept the notes from the newspaper boys or they'd have crucified us. That's why we've kept it quiet. Stage reputations are shaky."

"Then," the Crimson Mask said quietly, "you received the death threats?"

Simmons gave him a startled look and then nodded.

"You're either a good guesser or way ahead of me," he admitted. "Yes, we got death threats. Here. I kept mine."

"Mr. Dawson" concealed his elation behind a poker face as he unfolded the proffered note. It was typewritten on plain paper, without an address or signature. It read:

> Johnny Jones is dead. How does it feel to know you murdered him, as surely as if you'd stabbed him in the back? He'd be alive today if he had received kind treatment, instead of the careless brutality that shocked his oversensitive nature.
>
> But, of course, you didn't know that Jones wasn't his real name. You didn't know he was too proud and ambitious to hunt success through pull. So he told no one that he was my brother—the brother of one of your own Guild members. I didn't know what was happening until too late to save him, until there was nothing left but vengeance. And he will have that.
>
> Lawrence and Arken will pay for what they did. Johnny thought you stole his astrology plot, thought even the stars had betrayed him. But the stars hadn't failed him. They are going to avenge his death—soon!

The Crimson Mask's brain was spinning over the fantastic development. He tucked the note away in his own pocket.

"You haven't any idea who wrote this?" he asked.

"None," Simmons denied. "They came to all of us through the mail in plain envelopes. All I know is that I never had a screwball brother, or any brother. The devil of it is, we all came together just a few years ago, so none of us really knows any of the others' background. Anyone of us could have sent the letters."

"Didn't you do anything about the notes?"

"Oh, we talked about them but decided it was another crank gag. Besides, we were scared of bad publicity over Jones' suicide. So, even when Lawrence died, we kept stalling, telling ourselves it was only coincidence. Then Dick got his warning yesterday and sent for you."

THE CRIMSON MASK controlled his emotions. So Richard Arken had been warned that he was to die. What had become of that warning note, then? And who was the vengeful killer? It might be Delante, Mason, Simmons himself, or even Greta Blake. There was nothing in the note to indicate whether the writer was a man or woman. But the sudden flood of unexpected information had opened limitless vistas of new possibilities to the Crimson Mask.

"Keep this little talk to yourself for now," he told Simmons. "I may ask you for more information later."

At the door he turned and asked, casually: "Who does your astrological horoscopes?"

"Jerry Mason," answered Simmons promptly. "He's the only one of us who can handle the mathematics necessary to cast an accurate horoscope. He does work for most of the stage and screen stars as a sort of hobby."

Half an hour later, the Crimson Mask sat at ease in Theodore Warrick's library, recounting the amazing information he had obtained. The report had come in from the constable at Wendtville with no new information on Lawrence's death. Before starting his recital, Bob Clarke had quickly sketched a picture of the mysterious bottle, and learned that Warrick had never seen one like it and could offer no suggestion as to its use or importance.

"That solves it," Warrick exclaimed when Clarke had finished. "The police report I got this morning confirms all you learned about Jones, even to the fact that they have never located his family. I'll have the police check on the family background of each member of the Stellar Guild and we'll have the killer. It all ties in with the typical grudge-killing pattern I've seen so often. We know Jones was mentally unbalanced and that trait probably ran through the whole family."

"I wish I could think that would settle it." Bob Clarke frowned. "But there are too many loose ends. The missing death threat note, the planted suicide clipping, the mysterious bottle and Beef Slattery. None of those tie in. I'm sure there's more to the murders than mere revenge. There's a money pattern in there somewhere."

"How about Mason?" asked Warrick. "You found that he was broke and could recoup through insurance on his clients. His lateness in getting on the stage last night could have meant that he shot the fatal arrow and stopped to hide the weapon."

"Maybe," the druggist detective mused. "Have the police look into everyone's past, anyhow. Meanwhile, I'm going to visit a dark horse. Clint Delante is as much a part of this as any member, yet he has never once appeared as suspect. I'd like to see what might be hiding under that quiet surface."

DELANTE'S APARTMENT was on the second floor of a walk-up flat. As the Crimson Mask approached, his eyes narrowed at the sight of a sedan parked in front, with its motor idling. A rat-faced man sat watchfully at the wheel, slitted eyes studying each passerby along the street.

The Crimson Mask felt the impact of that calculating stare as he turned boldly into the building. Still disguised as a substantial middle-aged man, the Crimson Mask calmly entered the foyer, selected a key from his master ring and let himself in as though he lived there. As he turned to climb the front stairs, he sent a quick glance back toward the parked car. The rat-faced man was leaning over to peer through the glass of the door, one hand hovering above the horn button as if to signal.

The Crimson Mask plodded up the stairs to the fourth floor, taking care to show himself plainly at each landing window as he passed. The rat-faced man below relaxed.

Instantly the Crimson Mask raced silently down the fourth floor hall. He darted down the back stairway and a moment later was quietly applying his ear to the door of Delante's apartment. The rumble of conversation from within became audible speech that made the Crimson Mask's eyes turn flinty and his fingers close over his gun.

"For the last time, punk," a cold voice was snarling, "do you talk, or do I have to persuade you some more?"

A low moan was the answer. Then a weak voice that could only be Delante's gasped:

"Don't! Please, don't burn me any more. I tell you, I didn't murder them and I don't know who did. I don't even know what you're hunting for. Let me go!"

The Crimson Mask frowned. Was someone accusing Delante of the murders of Arken and Lawrence? A muffled crash reached his ears, coming from some inner room, and a third voice called:

"Not a single thing in his bedroom either, Carson. It looks like maybe we hit a duster on this one."

"Yeah," the first voice agreed coldly. "He's too soft to be playing dornick. Well, that leaves two others. "

"Gonna leave this guy tied up, Boss?"

"To finger us to the cops afterward?" the first man answered. "Don't be a sap, Fats. Bring me a good, thick pillow." The Crimson Mask's face was cold. A killing shot, silenced by a muffling pillow, was to be Delante's callous fate. But the Crimson Mask's hands had not been idle as he listened. He had already selected a suitable master key and slipped it quietly into the lock of the door. Now he straightened, slipped the identifying crimson mask over his eyes and drew his gun.

Then he braced himself against the door, turned the key and pushed.

CHAPTER VI

SOME NEW ANGLES

ABRUPTLY THE door whipped inward on a frozen tableau of violence. Delante's apartment was a wreck—with drawers emptied, furniture overturned and cushions slashed. The actor himself, his swarthy face puffy with purple bruises, was lashed to a chair. A ring of burned matches around his bare, blistered feet told a mute story of brutal torture.

At sight of the Crimson Mask he cried out sharply and then toppled against his bonds in a faint.

Bending over Delante was a gaunt, hard-faced man whose right hand held an automatic and his left the pillow that was to serve as makeshift silencer for the weapon. At one side crouched a fat, moon-faced thug, licking thick lips in anticipation of the brutal murder.

Both whirled at the sound of the opening door and then froze. There was something unutterably terrifying about the crimson-masked figure in the doorway, covering them with a rock-steady pistol.

"Drop it!" the Crimson Mask barked. "Now, back up against the wall and keep your hands in sight."

Desperation made the fat thug's fingers move tremblingly toward the front of his coat. Instantly the Crimson Mask's gun swung in a silent threat.

"Behave, sap!" the gaunt leader growled at his companion. "This is the Crimson Mask—and he's poison."

"Rat poison," the Crimson Mask agreed coldly. "And the worst rats I know are ones who would torture and kill a bound victim. In case you consider making a break, just remember how I feel. You"—he gestured at the fat thug—"take out your gun and drop it on the floor."

Sweat beaded the fat thug's face. Fearful lest any of his movements be misconstrued, he carefully lifted out his gun with two fingers and dropped it on the floor.

"Kick it over here," the Crimson Mask commanded. "Then untie Delante and place him on the couch." Meanwhile the gaunt Carson had flattened against the wall in apparent submission, both hands spread against the plaster at each side. But one hand was covering and pressing upon a small button set in the wall.

It was the buzzer, common to all walk-up flats, which unlocked the front door downstairs. The sound of its intermittent buzzing was barely audible in the apartment, but it would be easily heard by a man in the street outside. Carson hid a grin of triumph.

"All right," the Crimson Mask snapped, when Delante's limp figure had been made comfortable. "What were you two trying to get out of Delante?"

"I'm not talking!" Carson snarled.

"How about Beef Slattery?" the Crimson Mask asked quietly. "Are you as sure he won't talk?"

He was fishing for information and the result surprised him. Carson's eyes showed only hatred and blank amazement.

"What's the gag?" the gaunt man demanded. "I don't know anybody named Slattery."

There was no denying the genuineness of the denial. But if Beef Slattery was not working with Carson, what was his part in the mystery? And for that matter, what was Carson's?

"Listen, Mask," said Carson abruptly, "we're both after the same thing—the guy who bumped them actors. Now, I'll make you a straight proposition. You find out who the rat is and tell me before you tip the cops. I'll pay a grand in cold cash on delivery for the guy's name—two hours before the cops get it. How about it?"

The Crimson Mask concealed his amazement behind a stolid face. There was an undeniable sincerity in the gaunt thug's voice. For some unfathomable reason, Carson did want the name of the killer.

AT THAT moment, the unlatched hall door behind the Crimson Mask's back inched noiselessly open a space, and a face peered through. It was the vicious, snarling face of the thug who had been on guard in the car below. By not so much as a flicker of the eyes did either Carson or the fat hood betray the presence of their ally.

With an evil grin twisting his face, the newcomer eased the door open wider and crept toward the Crimson Mask's unprotected back. His right hand held a cocked pistol, which he slowly raised.

The masked man, at that moment, was shaking his head in bewilderment. He said, very quietly:

"I'll make you a proposition, Carson. You will notice that I have pulled back the trigger of my gun and am holding the hammer back only by the pressure of my thumb. If the thug who is creeping toward my back drops his gun and lines up beside you, I'll try not to let my thumb slip off the hammer. But if he either shoots or hits me now, I'm very much afraid a bullet will go into your heart. Is it a deal?"

A snarling curse of fury and amazement sounded behind the Crimson Mask's back. Carson's jaw dropped, and the fat hood bleated in superstitious terror.

"Drop the gat and get over by Fats, Hack!" bawled Carson hoarsely. "The guy ain't human and he ain't fooling. Hurry up before he gets sore or his thumb slips, you flatfooted ape!"

By that time, even the cynical Carson was willing to believe, as did so many thwarted crooks, that the Crimson Mask truly possessed supernatural powers. The Crimson Mask's swift action was not due to any sixth sense, but to carefully cultivated powers of observation that might seem almost miraculous to the average man.

Habit, gained during rigorous preparation for crime fighting, had made him instinctively photograph every detail of the room with his keen eyes the moment he crossed the threshold. He had seen the buzzer and, later, seen Carson's hand cover it.

He had seen cords tighten on the back of the gaunt hand as Carson pressed the concealed button and had guessed that he was signaling to the man below. After that it had been only a matter of keeping his ears alert for the soft sound of the third man's arrival. The Crimson Mask had kept quiet because he wanted this third man to walk, unsuspecting, into his trap.

"Hurry up, blast you!" Carson growled. "Do you want to get me plugged?"

"Okay," the newcomer said reluctantly.

His gun thudded to the floor at the Crimson Mask's feet and the gaunt Carson sucked in a deep breath of relief. Hack edged around their Nemesis' tense figure in sullen fury.

He was directly beside the masked figure when he suddenly exploded into action. Whirling, he butted into the Crimson Mask with a beefy shoulder and at the same time, shot a fist at the poised gun.

Although the Crimson Mask was not unprepared for such a move, the fury of the attack threw him momentarily off balance. His thumb was knocked from the hammer of his gun by the blow and the same impact discharging the automatic, sent a slug smashing into the center of the fat thug's throat.

CARSON YELLED and made a dive for his own discarded weapon. Hack, having butted the Crimson Mask aside, was lunging to retrieve his gun from the floor. Fats was out of the fight, falling forward with blood gushing from his shattered throat.

Carson had caught up his gun and was swinging around to level it at his enemy. The Crimson Mask's gun spoke first and the weapon flew from Carson's shattered hand. The gaunt man yelled with pain.

But in that instant, Hack had caught up his own gun from the floor and leaped at the Crimson Mask from a crouch, firing as he moved. The masked man dodged as he saw the muzzle lift toward him and felt the heat of the slug sear his cheek. His own weapon leaped and thundered before Hack could fire again, and the thug died in mid-leap, went crashing to the floor.

The crimson-masked figure whirled instantly to cover Carson. Then a grunt of dismay escaped him. The hall door was open and the gaunt man was gone.

Wounded and with his gun shattered by the Crimson Mask's bullet, he had fled.

The Crimson Mask raced for the hall, intent on capturing Carson to make him talk. Then he abruptly halted and lowered his gun. Pursuit was useless.

His ears caught the slam of the front door below and, an instant later, the roar of a car motor.

The Crimson Mask turned back, conscious of terrified cries from other apartments. The frightened neighbors would soon have the place overrun with police. He did not fear the police, but for the present he had no desire to waste time getting his identity established.

A hurried search of the dead thugs' clothing revealed no information. As he started for the door, his eyes fell on a bulky scrapbook carelessly tossed in one corner. He saw that it was Delante's, filled with newspaper clippings of Stellar Guild activities.

On impulse, he tucked it under his arm.

Then, with a quick glance at Delante to make sure the actor would be in no danger until the police could rush him to a hospital, he went quietly down the back stairway and out through an alley as police sirens screamed up to the front of the building.

ONCE MORE in his neighborhood pharmacy, Bob Clarke relaxed in the rear of the store. He looked at Dave Small and grinned.

"Hasn't Sandy come back yet, or contacted you?" he asked.

Dave shook his head.

"I tried to phone her at Blake's apartment but nobody answers," he said. "I was going to pretend I was her editor."

"I don't like it." Clarke frowned. "Even though she probably went somewhere with Greta Blake and couldn't call. And if we start making inquiries, we may tip someone to her connection with the Crimson Mask. But if she doesn't call by six o'clock, I'm taking up her trail."

Between bites of a meal fixed by Dave, he related the day's activities and findings.

"I'm convinced," he finished, "that Delante didn't know what the thugs were after, and I'm equally convinced Carson isn't subtle enough to have committed the two murders. No, there must be two interlocking puzzles that will click together into one pattern when we find the key piece. By the way, Dave, do you know what a dornick is, or a duster?"

"Huh?" Dave looked startled. "Not unless you mean a feather duster. Why?"

"Carson and Fats used those words today and I have a feeling they'd tell me something if I could identify them. They're slang terms peculiar to some special trade or locality, I'm sure."

HE TOOK up Delante's scrapbook and settled down for an intensive study of the clippings. Somewhere in the set-up or membership of Stellar Guild was, he felt certain, some tiny, overlooked clue that would unravel much of the mystery. He started with the most recent clippings and worked backward.

Most of them were ordinary press agent's stories. Now and then he found an item of straight news. Where an ordinary man would have given up at a hurried glance, Bob Clarke swiftly read and digested every word of every clipping. Much of his success as the ace of crime fighters was due to his ability to wring every tiny thread of possible information completely dry before abandoning it.

As the pages leafed by, Clarke's hopes dropped. Then, as he was about to give up in disgust, an unpasted clipping fluttered from between blank pages at the back of the book.

He read it with startled eyes. But his first hope that he had found the key to the mysteries was quickly dashed. Dave, drawn by his friend's first exclamation of excitement, read over his shoulder:

THE FORTUNES OF OIL

Dora Number Seven, Cloney Oil Company's newest and richest gusher, has just pumped its twelve millionth barrel of high grade crude oil, while three hundred yards away, on land leased from the Stellar Guild Theater, the second of two test wells has been abandoned as dry.

Immediately after Cloney's well came in, private drillers leased land from the farm used for summer rehearsals by Stellar Guild in an effort to tap the lame pool. This project, however, has been abandoned when no oil was reached, even at depth exceeding that of Dora Number Seven.

Geologists say Cloney Field is apparently situated directly above an oil dome whole boundaries do not reach under Stellar Guild land.

"Whew!" Dave whistled. "For a moment I thought, you had the case right in your lap, Bob."

"I still might have," Bob Clarke answered slowly. "There's something mighty fishy about all this. I just remembered that those slang words Carson's thugs used were oil field terms. To 'hit a dornick' means to be stopped by hard rock. And a 'duster' is a dry well that has never located oil. So it's certain those men were oil field hoodlums, and I'll bet that mysterious bottle has some connection with oil. Dave, suppose you get on the telephone and get the real facts on this oil business. Try some oil men or the state geologist. I'd like to get more facts before I tip my hand to the Stellar Guild members on this angle."

Just then the signal light blinked, indicating a call from Warrick. Bob Clarke lifted the private phone.

"Can you get over here right away?" Warrick asked. "There are some developments I think you'd better know about."

CHAPTER VII

WHERE IS SANDY?

B **OB CLARKE** stopped only long enough to don a new disguise suitable for any situation that might arise. Before leaving, he asked Dave to phone him the moment he heard from Sandy. It still lacked a half-hour to the six o'clock deadline he had set to hear from her.

Twenty minutes later the Crimson Mask was at the home of the ex-police commissioner.

"I'm glad I caught you in," Warrick said when he was assured of his visitor's identity by the secret handshake. "Great things are happening, I think. Better put on your mask before we get to the library."

With his crimson identification in place, the masked figure followed Warrick into the library and stopped short. A man was rising from a chair—a broad-shouldered man of indefinite age with the complexion of a blond. But the color of his hair was completely hidden by a turban of stained bandages swathing his head. He stared at the Crimson Mask in frank curiosity as Warrick introduced them.

"The Crimson Mask—Mr. Jerry Mason."

The Crimson Mask studied Mason keenly as they shook hands. It was the first time he had met his principal suspect face to face, and he found himself wondering if those blue eyes were the eyes of a vicious murderer.

"Mr. Mason's had a trying experience," Warrick explained. "Tell the Crimson Mask what you told me, will you?"

"Gladly," Mason said, as they took chairs. "I was at my desk about one o'clock this afternoon, in my apartment, when I heard a noise behind me. Before I could turn, something slammed into the back of my head and I went completely out. Three hours later I came to on the floor in a pool of blood, to find my whole place ransacked. Apparently nothing was taken, which ruled out robbery. Anyhow, I bandaged myself the best I could and hurried here. I knew Mr. Warrick had brought you in on the Stellar Guild murders and I thought this might tie in with them, in some way."

"Mind if I look at the wound?" the Crimson Mask asked. "I know a little medicine and that might be serious."

"Go ahead." Mason shrugged. "I suppose you really want to see if I'm faking, but that's all right with me."

A glance showed the Crimson Mask that Mason had suffered a vicious blow that could well have proven fatal. He dressed it from Warrick's first aid kit, advising Mason to see a doctor as soon as possible.

"By the way," he said casually. "What do you charge for those astrological horoscopes you cast?"

"Nothing." Mason smiled. "It's purely a hobby. But the way show people hound me for charts, I may have to commercialize it in self-defense. If you'd give me your birth date, Mask, I'd like to erect a chart for you."

"July Thirteenth," the Crimson Mask answered after a moment's hesitation. "I'd rather keep the year to myself."

"Okay," Mason said, grinning. "I'll give you a solar delineation, anyhow. Your ruling sign is Leo, the lion. And speaking of lions, we've got an old one caged in the theater basement eating his head off. We leased him for use in the show and his owner won't take him back."

"Is the show definitely finished?" the masked figure asked.

"Maybe not. One of the actors I handle came in to tell me this morning that he was at liberty. I made him a proposition to take the lead in 'Stars Over Egypt' if we go on. He's one man I know who can handle the part on short notice. As long as we have Greta Blake, we can usually manage. I phoned the rest of the Stellar Guild right away and they were in favor of reopening as soon as possible."

"May I speak to the Crimson Mask outside?" Warrick interposed.

AT MASON'S wave, they stepped out, closing the door.

"Could that wound be self-inflicted, Bob?" Warrick asked then.

"It could be, but inflicting it would take either real nerve or sheer desperation. Somehow, I believe that story. "

Then he described the attack on Delante earlier in the day.

"But why let Mason off with a bump on the head?" Warrick frowned. "And why torture and try to kill Delante? It isn't logical. But I have some other news. The police checked the Stellar Guild members. All of them had clear family backgrounds with no missing brothers anywhere—except Mason's. Mason blew into town twelve years ago. Prior to that, his history is a total blank. What do you think, now?"

"I think," the Crimson Mask answered grimly, "that I'd like to ask Mason some pertinent questions. Let's go back in."

He threw open the library door and stopped short. The room was empty. An open window leading onto a terrace indicated the route by which their suspect had fled.

"That does it!" Warrick cried, and ran to the telephone. "He's the guilty one, I'm sure. I'll call the police right away. He won't get far."

When he returned from phoning instructions to the police, who cooperated with him partly because of his previous record as commissioner and partly because of his connection with the Crimson Mask, Bob Clarke was pacing the floor. His face was set in a deep frown of dissatisfaction.

"I wish he hadn't done that," he declared. "For all the circumstantial evidence, I can't believe Mason is the murderer."

"He's put himself in a bad light by running away," Warrick grunted. "What were you going to tell me awhile ago?"

The Crimson Mask told of his discovery of the clipping, indicating the possibility of rich oil strikes as the motive for the crimes. When he had finished he went to the private phone connecting Warrick's home and the drug store.

"It's six o'clock," he said. "I want to see if Sandy has called and also find out what Dave has dug up about the oil deal."

"Not a word from Sandy, Bob," Dave's voice reported a moment later. "But I got the dope on your oil lead and you won't like it. The clipping was right. As soon as the Cloney well started gushing, a wildcat outfit leased a wide strip of Stellar Guild land adjoining Cloney's field and started sinking wells. They put down two wells within a thousand yards of this Dora and never hit a drop of oil."

"Any chance that someone's wrong?" Clarke asked. "Is that information authoritative, Dave?"

"The best, Bob. Straight from the State geologist. He gave me a lesson on skale formations and defractionation tests for hydro-carbon molecules that meant no oil. It seems the outfit drilling on Stellar land brought soil samples to him for the latest chemical test before they gave up and dropped the lease. He said there was definitely no oil under the surface soil."

"Okay," Clarke said, and cradled the phone. "Sorry, Mr. Warrick, but my lead seems to have petered out. Still, I hate to give it up. A battle for oil property would be the best motive for three-fourths of what's happened so far."

"Then, do you think—"

Warrick's answer was interrupted by the shrill ringing of the telephone on their regular outside line. He answered it and listened in tense silence. When he hung up, his eyes were dull.

"What is the astrological birth sign of a person born October Seventh?" he asked softly.

"Libra," the Crimson Mask answered, after a moment's thought. "The symbol of Libra is a pair of scales. Why?"

"Because Greta Blake was born October Seventh—and her body has just been found hanging from the scales of the statue of Justice at City Hall!"

"Where's Sandy!" the Crimson Mask cried, fearful for her safety. "Any traces of her?"

He knew the answer, even before Warrick gently shook his head, a pitying look in his eyes. Sandy had been with Greta Blake. The answer was obvious. Sandy had been captured by the killer when he murdered Greta Blake.

"We've got to see the body!" the Crimson Mask snapped. "There may be dust on her clothing under her fingernails that would tell me where to pick up the trail."

"The medical examiner says she was stabbed to death around noon and hanged from the scales after the offices were closed down tonight. It gets dark early now, and at the dinner hour, that section of town is nearly deserted."

TEN MINUTES later a morgue attendant was leading them to the sheeted form on the slab.

"Gruesomest thing I ever saw," he was telling them. "I discovered it right after they phoned you."

He turned back a corner of the sheet to uncover the dead woman's right shoulder. Warrick and the Crimson Mask bent forward in tense amazement. A crude picture had been drawn on the dead flesh. It appeared to be a sketch of two rough triangles side by side, their bases overlapping, and with a number of fine black dots scattered above them.

"What on earth—" Warrick gasped.

"A message," the Crimson Mask whispered, his voice filled with excitement. "It was drawn in a hurry with eyebrow pencil. Sandy did that, Ted! She was left unguarded near the body long enough to draw that. She knew I'd examine the body and find the picture. She's trying to tell me where she is."

But the interpretation of the crude pictograph was an enigma. The Crimson Mask's brain spun desperately, seeking a clue to the meaning, while fear for Sandy's safety gnawed at his heart. Her life depended on his deciphering the message. Two triangles and a cloud of dots. Triangles and dots. Dots and triangles—"

"Ted!" he clutched Warrick's arm.

"I've got it! Not triangles, but *pyramids!* Pyramids and stars! Don't you see? She means 'Stars Over Egypt.' It's her way of telling me that she'll be at the Stellar Guild Theater, I know. Probably she was afraid the killer might see the marks. If she simply wrote the name of the theater and he saw it, he'd either connect her with me or at least get rid of her the way he did Greta Blake. This way there was a chance that even if he saw it, he might not guess its meaning, or realize that Sandy had put it there."

"It might be a trap," Warrick warned. "I'll get a squad of police to rush us—"

"No! She'd be killed at the first alarm. Even if it is a trap I've got to go alone, find where she's being held and try to get her free. You stay near a phone. Have a squad ready but don't move until you get word from me."

CHAPTER VIII

DEATH FOR THE CRIMSON MASK

DESPITE THE anguish in his heart, the Crimson Mask's nerves were steady and his brain was functioning coolly as he crept down the dark alley beside the theater a short time later. Years of intensive training had given the Crimson Mask the ability to maintain cool, steady nerves through the most trying ordeal.

The stage door was too exposed and too obvious for safety. He went around to the back of the theater and found a basement window. It was locked but his special diamond glass cutter gave him quick and noiseless access to the catch. He raised the window, adjusted his mask and slid through.

He dropped to the floor in inky, silent darkness that had the feeling of a small, unoccupied room. It must, he knew, face the same corridor as the dressing rooms. A brief flash of his pencil light showed stacks of dust-covered scenery and, across the room, a closed door. When no sound reached him from the corridor, he inched the door open and slipped out.

Somewhere close by, he knew, should be a door into the larger main basement. If the killer had a hideout around the theater, it should be somewhere near that little-used cellar. A moment later he found the door and eased it open. A thicker darkness loomed before him.

A rank animal odor assailed his nostrils. Somewhere in the darkness, soft feet padded and a heavy body scraped monotonously against metal. The Crimson Mask's hair lifted as he remembered Mason's mention of the hungry lion, but a moment's listening convinced him the beast was pacing a narrow cage. He slipped inside and closed the door. The unseen lion grunted at the smell of his presence.

Only a jungle animal, dependent on its sense of smell, could have detected the Crimson Mask's presence. From the time he had entered the window until he entered this larger basement, not a whisper of sound had betrayed his ghostly progress. His rigorous training in boxing, fencing and similar strenuous activities had given him such a perfect coordination of nerves and muscles that it enabled him to move as silently as a cat.

The Crimson Mask was about to flash a light toward the cage when scraping sounds came from the far end of the basement. He barely had time to throw himself behind the shadowy bulk of a big furnace, when a light bloomed out and two figures came from behind a low partition. He caught his breath. One was the hulking Beef Slattery. The identity of his companion was completely hidden by a black hood that covered head and face and draped down over his shoulders. Beyond any doubt, the hooded figure was the astrological killer. Was it Jerry Mason? There was no way of telling.

The Crimson Mask fought down an urge to leap at the grim figures and shoot it out. Until he had found and freed Sandy, if she still lived, he dare not risk such a move. Then he drew back as the flash beam swept past his hiding place and outlined the lion's cage.

The beast blinked and snarled at the light.

"Grumpy's restless," Slattery chuckled. "Maybe he's heard about the Crimson Mask bein' a brother Leo and is sore about it, eh, Boss?"

"He's probably hungry,'" the hooded man answered, his voice obviously disguised by some mouth attachment. He'll have a *good* meal when the Crimson Mask comes to get his girl friend."

THE CRIMSON MASK stiffened at the words. So the killer knew Sandy was his assistant. The pictograph on Greta Blake's body was bait for a death trap. Was Sandy already dead, then?

"Are you sure the dame worked for him?" Slattery demanded.

"It's obvious," the hooded leader snapped. "She drew that sketch on the corpse when she thought I wasn't looking. Who else would be likely to see or understand such a message? Of course she knows him. Now get up and keep watch. He should be showing up, soon."

The Crimson Mask's lips thinned. The killer had underestimated his speed in interpreting and responding to Sandy's appeal. As the corridor door closed on the two, he snapped on his own hand flash and raced for the partition. He rounded it and stopped short with a gasp of dismay. There was nothing before him but a bin half full of coal.

For a moment his iron nerve almost failed as he threw the tight beam over the walls and floor without seeing a sign of a door. Then a stray beam struck light from a sheen of metal in the coal pile. He bent over and a moment later was pushing a tiny, hidden lever. A hidden motor purred and a section of the floor moved away, revealing a flight of steps down into a dark sub-cellar.

The Crimson Mask fairly leaped down the steps, gun in hand, his flash spearing a lance of light ahead. He was in a damp, cell-like room from which several doors led off. Sandy, bound and gagged, lay behind the third door he tried. He raced to her side and slashed her bonds.

His heart leaped as she stirred and groaned.

"Sandy! Sandy!" he muttered. "Are you all right!"

"Bob!" she cried joyously. "I knew you'd come. I'll be all right, when the blood gets back into my arms and legs. Help me sit up."

Moments later, with his arm around her for support, she was able to climb the steps that led out of her prison.

"Did you discover the killer's identity?" he asked her then.

"No," she said. "He was always concealed by that hood, even when he—he stabbed Greta Blake. Oh, it was horrible! So cold-bloodedly ruthless! And he laughed when I screamed. That man is a fiend."

"How did he capture you two?" the Crimson Mask asked, as he shut the trap and led the way across the basement.

"Greta Blake was giving me an interview when the hooded man and his sidekick walked in with guns," Sandy began. "They tied and gagged us, and brought us here hidden in the back of a car. Until you came, I thought I was going to get the same thing poor Greta got."

"We aren't in the clear yet," he said somberly. "The only way out is through that corridor outside, and if they happen to start back down here, we'll be trapped."

"Well spoken, Crimson Mask!" a sardonic voice sneered from the darkness. "You're trapped right now, in fact." A flashlight suddenly limned them in its cold glare, revealing the gaping muzzles of two pistols centered at their heads. The two had been lying in wait in the darkness, just inside the corridor door.

"It was unfortunate for you," the hooded man chuckled, "that we saw the open trap-door when we were returning. That made it easy to set our little trap here and wait for you to walk into it. Slattery, get that gun he is holding so grimly. And be careful."

THE HOODED man was no more than two feet from the Crimson Mask, the flashlight in one hand glaring in the masked man's eyes, the pistol in his other hand pointing uncompromisingly at his chest. From the opposite side, Beef Slattery's hulking figure closed in, his own gun ready for action.

Between the two and hampered by Sandy's nearness, the Crimson Mask was powerless to lift the pistol in his own hand. At the first movement, both guns would blast and Sandy would share in the hail of eager death. It was that thought, not fear for his own safety, that made the Crimson Mask submit when Beef Slattery jerked the gun from his hand.

"Now, Slattery," the hooded man said, "remove that mask from his face."

And before the Crimson Mask realized it, the mask was torn roughly from his face. But that didn't matter too much, he thought, for he was still expertly disguised and no one seeing him now could possibly identify him as Bob Clarke.

To all appearances the Crimson Mask was held in check by those who held the upper hand at the moment, but it was only apparent submission. His senses were alert for a break, no matter how slim, and he got it as Slattery snatched off his mask and stepped back. Unconsciously, the hooded man moved the light an inch toward his henchman. The movement left the Crimson Mask clearly outlined in the beam, but it brought the shadows closer to Sandy's figure. In that instant, the Crimson Mask went into action.

"Run!" he shouted, and gave Sandra Gray a shove that sent her flying out into the darkness.

At the same instant, he sprang into a headlong plunge, straight between the hooded man and Slattery. A gun flamed almost in his face and the slug whined viciously past his head. Then his arms were around the hooded figure, bearing it back as his right fist smashed for the hidden jaw.

Beef Slattery's sluggish mind was too dull for the sudden burst of lightning action. He tried to decide whether to fire at the Crimson Mask or pursue Sandra's pattering footsteps. And in that moment of indecision, the Crimson Mask had reached a position where Slattery could not shoot without hitting his leader. The big thug roared in fury and sprang after the running feet.

"Beef, you fool!" the hooded man snarled, fighting to line his gun on the Crimson Mask's body as they wrestled. "Let her go. She can't break out through the locked door. Come here and help me!"

The Crimson Mask drove the gun aside with a furious blow and fought to trip his adversary. He could hear Beef Slattery's shuffling footsteps behind him. For a moment their figures were full in the glow of the fallen flashlight. The druggist detective heard Slattery's grunt and the swish of a gun barrel through the air. He tried to swing his opponent aside, tried to duck. Then his head seemed to explode into a great ball of fire that faded into darkness...

HE AWOKE in the puddle of yellow light from a flashlight to find himself flat on the floor with hands and feet bound. Beef Slattery was bending above him, squeezing large chunks of something that dripped sticky liquid on his clothes. His nostrils caught the reek of fresh blood.

The Crimson Mask blinked to clear his eyes of the red haze that misted his vision. He tried to see around him in the darkness. Had Sandra escaped, or was she somewhere close by, dead or a prisoner? He could see no signs of her, nor could he tell from the actions of his captors whether or not she had got free. Yet if she had, they would hardly be staying to invite possible capture. His heart sank.

"That's enough," the hooded man rasped. "Take Grumpy's fresh meat outside, Beef. With that blood on him, your pal will smell like dinner to Grumpy."

They moved back, and the Crimson Mask started involuntarily at the sight of the lion's cage shoved close to the corridor door. As the two stopped by the door, Slattery reached back and turned the key in the lock on the cage gate.

"So long, Mask," the hooded man chuckled. "I hope you two have a pleasant visit. Okay, Beef."

The burly thug swung the cage door wide open and raced out after his leader. The last thing the Crimson Mask saw, as the light vanished, was the lion, snarling and slavering, padding eagerly out of his cage. Then darkness closed in.

The Crimson Mask knew he had never been closer to death. The lion, normally docile, had its jungle instincts aroused by hunger and the smell of blood. Soon it would completely forget its fear of man and charge. Already the Crimson Mask could see its shadowy form stalking a narrowing circle about his body. An attempt to move his legs brought a warning snarl from the beast.

With infinite caution, the Crimson Mask moved his bound hands until numbed fingers located a secret pocket in the front of his coat. Fearful that his movement would precipitate an attack, he drew out the tiny razor-edged knife and worked it into position to saw at his bound wrists.

The lion was growing bolder. Its snarls rose to coughing grunts as it stopped pacing and crouched low to the floor. The Crimson Mask sawed desperately, sweat beading his forehead, as he saw the beast's tail lift in stiff jerks. It was, he knew, the signal of attack. One rope parted.

With an echoing roar, the lion charged!

CHAPTER IX

BLAZING AUTOMATICS

WHEN THE heavy body catapulted forward, the Crimson Mask put every ounce of his strength into a desperate gamble. As his wrists jerked free from the confining ropes, he dived sideward, out of the way of the charging beast. One raking talon tore down his arm as the lion missed its target by inches. The king of beasts roared furiously and whirled to attack again.

The Crimson Mask rolled again and came up onto his knees. His ankles were still tightly bound and there was no chance to cut the ropes. He got to his feet, hopping clumsily to maintain his balance on numbed legs, as the lion whirled. His hands fumbled at his waist and whipped off his belt.

As the lion crouched to charge again, the Crimson Mask spun the slender belt into the beast's face and cracked it like a whip. It was a feeble weapon against three hundred pounds of enraged jungle beast, but he was gambling on the strength of habit. He knew that lions are trained to retreat before a cracking whip and he was hoping to arouse that familiar terror to offset the lion's lust to kill.

He cracked the belt again and deliberately walked toward the lion. Slowly the beast inched back, snarling horribly, but retreating. Confidence flowed into the Crimson Mask's veins as he forced the raging creature toward its cage.

Suddenly a door slammed open upstairs and hard feet hammered down the steps to the corridor. It could not be the police, he knew, for this was only one person. The new sound, however, broke the lion's resistance. With a last snarl, it slunk into its cage. The Crimson Mask slammed and locked the iron gate.

With the sound of grating bolts, the corridor door inched open and a hand fumbled for the light switch. In the sudden glare from bulbs overhead, the white, frightened face of Arthur Simmons peered cautiously in.

"Good gravy!" he gasped, his jaw dropping at sight of the bloody, disheveled, unmasked figure of the Crimson Mask. "Who are you?

What—what's going on here? I heard the lion roaring from clear outside. How did you get here?"

The Crimson Mask hesitated. His present disguise was totally different from the one he had worn to interview Simmons that morning. He decided to keep his identity—as that of the Crimson Mask, not Bob Clarke—secret a bit longer from Simmons.

"I don't know how I got here," he growled. "I was walking down the alley when something cracked me on the head. I woke up in here with the lion clawing me, and I had sense enough to drive him off by snapping my belt like a trainer's whip."

Simmons eyes nickered nervously around the gloomy basement.

"We better get out of here," he whispered. "You'd better see a doctor about those gashes on your shoulder. Shall I call a cab for you?"

"There's a doctor's office just down the street," the injured man said. "These cuts aren't as bad as they look."

Tortured by fears for Sandra, the Crimson Mask almost ran ahead of Simmons. The thought of her once more a prisoner of the two killers—or worse, a victim—was maddening. He had to find out at once, somehow...

THEY REACHED the stage door now. No light had been turned on up here and the foyer was in heavy shadows. Abruptly one of those shadows moved away from the wall and became the silhouette of a gaunt man whose right arm hung in a sling, but whose left hand held a blued automatic rock-steady. It was the murderous Carson.

"Okay, rat," he snarled at Simmons. "Not even a busted wing is going to keep me from feeding you the slugs you deserve. How about one in the belly for a starter?"

Simmons squealed in terror and tried to flatten himself closer to the wall. Carson's slitted eyes held a maniacal gleam, and his thin lips twisted with the lust to kill. His finger whitened against the trigger.

The Crimson Mask was unarmed and still stiff from being so tightly bound. But as the automatic roared its thunder, he hurled himself aside and forward. His outstretched arms caught Carson's legs and jerked. The automatic boomed again and a slug tore the floor close to the Crimson Mask's body. But Carson was already plunging down, and before he could fire again, the Crimson Mask closed his grip over the gun-hand and twisted.

A shot seared his arm as the gaunt man fought wildly to press the gun into his opponent's body. But the Crimson Mask had squirmed to a better position. Now his right fist shot up and cracked against Carson's jaw, hard. The gaunt man abruptly stiffened and the gun slid from his grasp. The dread Nemesis of crime struck again, to make sure his opponent would stay out of the fight for a long time.

Then he scooped up Carson's gun and climbed to his feet.

He had been wondering, during the brief but bitter struggle, why Simmons had made no sound or taken no part in it. Now he saw the reason. The stage director was crumpled on the floor against the wall, his bald head in a pool of dark blood.

The Crimson Mask bent and made a hasty examination. A slug had creased Simmons skull above one ear, opening a nasty gash that bled profusely but doing no serious damage. The man was out cold from the shock. There were no other wounds on his body, though a gash in the wall showed where another slug had missed by inches.

As he finished his examination, feet pounded in the alley outside. Quickly he dug into a cleverly concealed pocket and donned a crimson mask he always kept there for emergencies such as this. Then the stage door burst open and Warrick raced in, his face a picture of dread at what he expected to see. Behind him crowded a squad of police holding tommy-guns in readiness for action.

"Mask!" Warrick bawled in relief as the disheveled figure confronted him. "Are you all right? We heard shots as we drove up and, then they stopped. I was afraid you—Say, you're wounded!"

"Did you get a call?" the Crimson Mask demanded tensely, ignoring his friend's anxiety. "Did—"

"Yes." Warrick smiled at the other's quick breath of relief. "Your—er—plan went through. The call came in from the party you sent on ahead. But that shoulder of yours looks bad, Mask. "

"Just a scratch." The Crimson Mask grinned, examining the marks of the lion's claws on his shoulder. "Most of this blood on me was squeezed out of chunks of raw meat, so I'd be more appetizing. But Simmons, here, could stand a little first aid."

"Who's this onion?" one of the police growled, nudging Carson's sprawled figure with his toe.

"Handcuff and handle him with care," the Crimson Mask advised grimly. "His name is Carson and he's as deadly as a rattlesnake. He was the one who attacked Mason and tried to murder Delante."

"Is he the killer of those show people?" a policeman asked.

THE CRIMSON MASK shook his head. "He was hunting for the killer, himself," he said.

"He needn't hunt any farther," Warrick said quietly. "We caught Mason and this Beef Slattery together in a car, not over a block from the theater, just half an hour ago. Slattery shot it out with the police and got away for the time being, but Mason gave up without a murmur."

The Crimson Mask's face showed frank astonishment.

"Did Mason confess?" he asked.

"Not yet," Warrick grunted. "But the police will break him down. He claimed Slattery had kidnapped him right after he ran away from my place and was taking him somewhere to kill him. What spoiled that story was the fact that Mason had his own gun, fully loaded, in his coat pocket."

"Were there any rope marks on Mason's wrists?" the Crimson Mask asked in sudden excitement.

"No, but he explained that glibly enough. He said Slattery held him with padded handcuffs that didn't leave marks. It was obviously a lie. While Slattery was battling the police, a couple of wild bullets went through the car. He was evidently scared and thought up a quick story to save his neck when he surrendered."

He leaned close to the Crimson Mask and added, in a whisper:

"I sent Sandra home. She had a narrow escape after you let her get out. The doors and windows here were all locked so she couldn't get out of the theater without making a lot of noise. Finally she heard them capture you and got really scared, so she smashed out a window and jumped. Slattery nearly caught her before she got to the street."

The Crimson Mask's eyes were suddenly glittering and a tight smile touched his lips.

"Mr. Warrick, have Simmons fixed up and bring him back here. Get Mason and Delante here, too, and hold them all until I return. I believe when I check on a few points I'll have the whole case solved. Have Carson, here, kept in a cell where I can question him, if necessary, a little later."

"He's on his way there right now," Warrick promised. "Is there anything I can do to help you?"

"Not for the moment—Wait! There is something you can do easier than I can, because of your authority. Telephone the Pennsylvania State geologist. Impress on him that this is police business and have him phone me right away, here at the theater. I'm afraid if I call him, he might not want to talk. It's late, I know, but try to locate him."

"I'll locate him," Warrick said grimly, "if I have to call out the National Guard."

A HALF hour later, as the Crimson Mask came out of the theater basement with a grim smile on his lips, the telephone in the theater office began to ring. He answered it and quickly identified himself.

"I'm Swanson, the Pennsylvania State geologist," an irritated voice said. "What the devil's the idea of routing me out of bed at this hour of the night? I already answered a lot of fool questions for someone from there earlier this evening."

"This won't take but a minute," the Crimson Mask soothed, "and it will aid the police in apprehending a murderer. The first question, and I want a strictly off-the-record answer, is: What kind of outfit is the Cloney Oil Company?"

"Don't quote me," Swanson said, "but they're the dirtiest, crookedest operators in the country."

"The second question," the Crimson Mask said. "Do crooked oil companies ever pretend to dig deep wells and deliberately keep from striking oil, simply to fool the owner of a piece of land?"

"Do they? That's an old lease-war trick that plenty of them have pulled. As a matter of fact, Pete Cloney himself nearly went to jail a few years back for trying that. Say, if he's up to those tricks again, the State wants to know about it."

"You'll have full information and evidence within a few hours," the crimson masked man promised. "Now for the third question." He gave a concise description of the mysterious bottle and then asked: "Is that a piece of oil field equipment, do you know?"

"It certainly is!" Swanson sounded surprised. "You've described an acid test bottle perfectly. That's the old-fashioned way of testing whether or not wells were going down straight as they should."

"What? You mean that wells sometimes curve during digging?"

"Sure, especially holes drilled with a rotary rig. The bit hits a stone or gets worn a little more on one side and starts drilling off to that side. On a well that goes down three or four miles into the ground, it doesn't take much bending to end up clear under someone else's property. That's why all of the drillers take frequent tests."

"How do they make those tests?" the Crimson Mask asked, excited.

"Today they use complicated electrical equipment. But small companies still use the acid bottle test. They take a bottle like the one you described, fill it partly full of acid and lower it into the well. After it stands awhile, the acid etches a mark around the inside of the bottle. Naturally, if the well is straight, the acid line is straight. But if the well bends, the bottle lies partially on its side and the acid line is etched up higher on that side. Old time drillers can look at an acid mark and tell almost to the foot where the bottom of their well actually lies. Anything else I can tell you?"

"No, thanks," the Crimson Mask said fervently. "You've told me plenty. You'll get details on this within a day or two."

He cradled the phone and leaned back while his mind dovetailed together the astonishing information he had just received. His keen, analytical mind, trained to sort and catalogue disconnected facts, was rapidly building a complete picture of the motive behind the fiendish crimes. It was astoundingly simple, once the pattern became clear.

The bottle he had possessed for such a short time had borne a cryptic symbol and the number seven. Undoubtedly that was the identifying mark of the well it had been used to test. And beyond any doubt, that well was the Cloney Oil Company's new Dora Number Seven. Furthermore, the acid line had been far off from the normal level, indicating that Dora Number Seven had been dug at an acute angle.

THE ANSWER was obvious. Cloney's new well was actually pumping oil from a pool, not under Cloney property but under the land owned by the Stellar Guild. But if that fact became known, Cloney would have to pay Stellar for every barrel of oil that had been pumped by Dora Number Seven.

So, to conceal the theft, a henchman of Cloney's had obviously leased the adjoining Stellar land and sunk fake wells to discourage other drillers from accidentally tapping the rich resources far below. It would not be difficult to falsify the tests so that everyone would believe Stellar's land was not worth drilling into.

For who would suspect an apparently honest and independent driller of deliberately avoiding a strike with his own well?

Meanwhile, Cloney went on growing rich on stolen oil.

But what part did the theft play in the murders? The Crimson Mask felt that he could answer that question with a fair degree of accuracy. Someone had discovered the theft, someone who hoped, by the murders, to gain complete possession of the Stellar Guild's land and its hidden wealth.

Who that someone was remained to be proven. The Crimson Mask had a fairly sound idea who it was by this time, but before he confronted Mason, Delante and Simmons with his findings, he needed additional evidence.

He left the theater office, snapping off the light, and returned to the basement, a smile of satisfaction on his lips.

CHAPTER X

TRAPPED RAT

THE STELLAR GUILD office at the theater looked like the receiving room of a hospital. Simmons sat behind his big desk, hands supporting a head that was swathed in thick bandages. Beside the desk sat the sullen Mason, wearing gloves. He looked like Simmons' twin with a similar turban of gauze around his own head. Both men showed evidence of severe headaches by wincing at every sharp sound.

Delante, looking pale and pain-racked, sat close by with bandaged feet propped out before him on a chair. A thick cane lay across his lap.

Warrick stood off to one side, talking in a low voice with a uniformed policeman who had brought Mason from jail. From time to time, both men frowned at their watches as the period of waiting grew more tense.

"Why doesn't he hurry?" Delante grumbled, examining his watch for the tenth time. "I had no business getting out of bed, anyhow, with my feet in this horrible condition."

"*Your* condition!" Simmons barked. "How about me? Here I've nearly had my head blown off and you whine about sore feet."

"Shut up, both of you!" Mason snapped. "Isn't there enough noise?"

"You!" Delante cried, inching away. "I know all about what you've been doing. Where they're going to take you, a little thing like a headache won't matter—murderer!"

Mason started up, his eyes glittering with an insane light.

"Blast you!" he screamed wildly. "You're trying to pin those murders on me to save your own filthy hide. Well, you won't burn me for them!"

His gloved hand darted to his pocket and came out with a blunt, small-caliber automatic. He leaped to his feet, covering the startled group with the weapon.

"Say!" the policeman bawled in amazement. "He didn't have that gat when I brought him in."

"Never mind," Mason said hoarsely, backing toward the door. "I've got it now and I won't hesitate to use it. I didn't murder anyone but I will, before I'll sit still and let you send me to the electric chair. I'm leaving, and the first man who sticks his head out this door inside of five minutes get a bullet in it! Sit still, all of you!"

"Mason, you fool!" Warrick said angrily. "You can't get away with this. You'll be caught eventually, and this will only make things tougher for you."

"Stay there and shut up!" Mason growled, and backed from sight.

"I'll get him!" the police guard shouted, tugging at his gun as he raced toward the now empty doorway. The office was a sudden tumult of excitement.

Suddenly, the plunging officer stopped short. From outside, in the vast empty auditorium of the theater came the sudden pound of heavy feet, shouts, a scuffle. Two shots blasted thunderously, followed by the thud of a falling body. Before anyone could move from the sudden paralysis of surprise, a man appeared in the doorway.

SUDDENLY THERE was a sharp gasp of indrawn breaths. The man in the doorway wore a crimson mask and carried a pistol.

"Mask!" Warrick cried. "Did you—Is he—"

"He won't run away again," the Crimson Mask answered grimly.

"Thank goodness the murder carnival is over," Simmons sighed. "Have you figured what it was all about yet?"

"Most of it," the masked figure said. "Chiefly it was a plot to ruin the Stellar Guild in order to buy your farm. There's a fortune in oil under it."

"Oil!" Simmons cried. "But test wells showed—"

"They were fake wells," the Crimson Mask corrected, and repeated the geologist's information. "Cloney field is dry. They're stealing Stellar's oil through a well that slants over into your pool underground. To prevent its discovery, they paid drillers to fake wells so your farm would be pronounced worthless. They've stolen millions of barrels and might never have been caught except for a double-cross by one of their own thugs.

"This man, Carson, wanted to grab that oil himself. He stole a test bottle, evidence of the theft, and tried to buy Stellar's farm. But Stellar didn't want to sell. In desperation, Carson finally tried to sell his secret to Val Lawrence for half the profits. Lawrence wanted to take it up with the whole Stellar group together so he called a meeting for the following week, when everyone would be present. That delay was fatal."

"What do you mean?" Delante demanded.

"Carson's story was overheard by another member who couldn't see splitting a fortune a half-dozen ways. He plotted to kill Lawrence and Carson, break up the Stellar Guild and grab the whole thing for himself. The recent Jones suicide gave him a weird idea for a perfect murder chain, with the police busy hunting for a killer who never lived-the mythical vengeful brother. The murderer sent the threatening notes and killed Lawrence, but Carson had disappeared. He was hiding from Cloney—the boss of that oil company—about that time, which saved his life.

"But Carson, not knowing someone else shared his secret, thought Lawrence had simply died at an unfortunate time. So he came out of hiding and repeated his proposition to Arken. This time, the killer was waiting. He attacked Carson, got the test bottle, but Carson escaped. Now Carson knew he had an enemy and set out to find him by attacking each member, hunting for the missing bottle. He complicated this mystery badly by attacking Mason and Delante and Simmons before I knew where he fitted in."

"What made Arken call for me?" Warrick asked.

"My guess is that it was about the oil," the Crimson Mask went on. "And he was killed before he could take that up with you."

"Did Mason kill him?" Delante asked.

"No. Probably Slattery, the killer's accomplice. The arrow was shot by a spring inside a hollow mop stick, from an old projection booth up under the balcony. Slattery and the killer murdered Greta Blake later to make sure that Stellar wouldn't go on with a new leading man."

"Wait a minute," Delante said. "It was Mason himself who brought in that new leading man. If he was the killer—"

HE BROKE off as another policeman suddenly appeared in the doorway, caught the Crimson Mask's eye and nodded vigorously. Then he disappeared. The Crimson Mask turned back, his eyes suddenly cold.

"Mason wasn't the killer," he said quietly. "The real killer was—Arthur Simmons, your stage director!"

"Wha-a-at?" Simmons bounded up, red-faced and raging, "I—you— Why, you yourself shot Mason when he tried to—"

"Correction," the Crimson Mask interrupted, and his pistol was suddenly pointing straight at Simmons. "I did not shoot Mason! Nor did anyone else." He raised his voice. "Right, Mason?"

"Right, Mask," Jerry Mason affirmed, coming through the door.

"He pulled a gun on us!" Simmons howled.

"A gun you gave him behind that desk, Simmons, when you were urging him to make a break," the Crimson Mask accused. "You wanted him killed, didn't you, so your scheme would be complete."

"You can't prove it!" Simmons shrieked.

"It's already proven," the Crimson Mask contradicted. "The police made Mason wear gloves tonight. Now he knows why. So only one man's fingerprints would be on that gun. I've been telling my story to you here, waiting for the signal I just got—the fingerprint expert's own report that the only prints on that gun were yours.

"Also, Simmons, I found the typewriter down in that sub-basement that wrote the threatening notes. Your prints were on those keys, too. The moment I realized you were one of the persons who could have operated those curtain controls to make the zodiac appear, I suspected you. Any innocent stagehand would have closed Number One switch and the wrong curtain would have come out at the beginning. For another thing—"

With an incoherent yell of fury, Simmons drove the Crimson Mask aside and plunged for the door. Strangely, the Crimson Mask made no effort to use his gun. It was Jerry Mason who knocked Simmons half across the room and followed it up with a hurricane of furious blows. When Warrick and the Crimson Mask finally pulled them apart, Simmons was a beaten, whining wreck.

"You earned that right," the Crimson Mask told Mason. "He knew about your blank past and plotted to place the full blame on you. It was his plan to have you either shot by the police resisting arrest, or to kill you himself and plant you as a suicide with a confession note by your body. Slattery dropped that first gun into your pocket before he fled the police tonight, hoping you'd be panicky enough to fight them and get killed. Simmons slipped you this gun and talked you into making a break tonight for the same purpose."

"I was so scared I didn't help my own case any," Mason confessed ruefully. "I knew someone was framing me and I could see the net tighten, but I couldn't wiggle out any way I turned. That's why I fled tonight, when I overheard you and Mr. Warrick discussing me. But I ran right into Slattery's arms, then.

"He was hiding outside and heard you give me your birthdate, so even that acted against me. And insuring my clients, the way almost all agents do, only gave me an apparent motive. When you grabbed me outside just now, Mask, and told me the score, I nearly cried for joy."

THE CRIMSON MASK nodded.

"It was a tight frame," he admitted. "Shall I tell about your blank past, or will you?"

"I'll tell," Mason said. "I got into trouble, years ago, and went to prison for awhile. That's why, when I came here, I changed my name and hid my past. But I've gone straight ever since, so help me."

"He has," Warrick seconded. "Mask, what I don't understand is why Simmons threw you to the lion tonight and then made an effort to rescue you, just after you escaped by yourself. That seems crazy."

"It did to me, too, until you told me about that other prisoner, the girl." He purposely avoided revealing Sandra's name in order not to connect her with him. "About her being chased when she got away. Then I got it. Simmons knew she would bring the police and he'd be caught with my body practically on his doorstep and no time to cover his tracks. He probably had all sorts of evidence lying around at the moment. So he conceived the idea of hiding his hood and running back to save me in order to establish his innocence. But he overplayed his hand by claiming he heard the lion's roar from outside.

"I tested, later, and found the sound didn't carry into the alley at all. Then he wasn't insistent enough about who I was for a really innocent man. When Carson appeared, I thought for a moment he was there to get me, until I realized I was in a disguise he'd never seen. Then I saw that he was talking to Simmons and had discovered for himself that Simmons was his doublecrosser. I already knew that neither Delante nor Mason could be the hooded man, because in the fight downstairs I stepped on his toes and banged his head. Neither one of you two could have taken that in your present condition without a groan."

"Say," Mason asked excitedly, "is that true about a fortune in oil? Can we get anything out of Cloney?"

"No doubt about it," the Crimson Mask assured him. "Their well stands as indisputable proof of the theft, and the State has a record of every barrel they've pumped. You'll collect plenty. And by deepening those fake wells, you should have a nice additional flow of direct oil. I think your worries are pretty well over, in more ways than one. So, if you will excuse me, I'll go about my business. Frankly, I need a good night's sleep."

When the Crimson Mask had gone, Warrick smiled at the group.

"But as far as crooks and murderers are concerned," he said meaningly, "the Crimson Mask never sleeps."